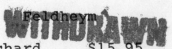

Books by Richard Hoyt

THE DRAGON PORTFOLIO

RICHARD HOYT

TOR

A TOM DOHERTY ASSOCIATES BOOK

THE DRAGON PORTFOLIO

Copyright © 1986 by Richard Hoyt

First printing: November 1986

A TOR Book

Published by Tom Doherty Associates, Inc.
49 West 24 Street
New York, N.Y. 10010

ISBN: 0-312-93168-9

Library of Congress Catalog Card Number: 86-50323

Printed in the United States

0 9 8 7 6 5 4 3 2 1

—for Jeff Grigsby

Cui bono?
—Who profits from this?

Ceremony's Eve, Beijing . . .

1

DENG Shaoqi woke up refreshed, and surprised himself by thinking of a pun in English. Deng's nephew—the physicist son of the more famous Deng Xiaoping—had married an American girl and so Shaoqi's English was getting better. His native Mandarin was a language filled with puns, and Cantonese was even worse. Inasmuch as his Chinese surname, Deng, was pronounced "dung" in English, he wondered if Sing Sing Boyd might not be amused as well as flattered.

Three hours, he'd slept. Deng thought this nap, the daily *xiu-xi*, was one of the loveliest if more inefficient traditions of the Chinese civilization. There was nothing better on a hot day than a big bowl of noodles followed by *xiu-xi*. He hoped his country would always retain some form of this calming nap, but that was a question to be answered after he was dead.

He checked his watch. There was time to take a small walk in the garden before the driver came to take him to the ceremony.

Deng put on a blue Mao jacket and a cap and took an old man's stroll through the willows. The air was hothouse warm and humid, and the sky was overcast; it would be raining in a few minutes. He looked at the lilies and at the gold and yellow carp moving lazily through the water, hardly moving their translucent fins. If Deng Shaoqi was no longer a vigorous walker, he was yet alert enough to hike the twisting paths of memory. He sat on a flat stone that was his accustomed resting place, and watched the fish; one of them in this pond, a large orange carp with black spots, was a beauty.

Beyond the wall, the exhaust of a laboring truck made a terrible racket on Beijing's Bright Mountain Street. Deng shook his head, then smiled. While Chinese trucks fell apart, the Japanese, flattened by American bombers in 1945, were now exporting trucks over the world. South Korea—laid desolate by war in 1952—was introducing a small truck in the American market. For Deng, the popping and banging of the truck were celebratory fireworks, an appropriate beginning for this special afternoon of his long and eventful life. Although he had never risen to the prominence of Deng Xiaoping, Deng Shaoqi had fought the good fight as well.

The wall around his compound on Bright Mountain Street didn't do much to block out the smell of Beijing. Chinese cities had a certain sweet-sour odor about them, a smell somewhere between hot sesame oil and day-old piss. Deng remembered the fishy smell of the tidal mud and marine air at Tsingtao where he used to go on holiday. He used to take long walks at Tsingtao, alone with the warming sun and the breeze coming off the South China Sea that whipped the clumps of grass growing on the dunes, and sent sand scurrying across the road.

In Deng's opinion the beer made at Tsingtao was unmatched by the Europeans. He remembered having to smile artificially when a West German businessman served him Bavarian pilsener with photographers taking pictures. The German beer was good, but it wasn't Tsingtao—every time

Deng drank Tsingtao he thought of those long walks in the wind.

Deng had always tried to live modestly, but party connections meant perks, and being Deng Xiaoping's brother wasn't bad. Here he was, officially a candy man, and Deng Shaoqi had a house in the city, and a house in Jade Spring Mountain. Jade Spring Mountain was quiet, and comfortable—luxurious by Chinese standards—and off-limits to foreigners, so there were no open-mouthed tourists cruising the streets. On the weekends, he sometimes went to Tianjin, which was about seventy miles south of Beijing.

He recalled his trip with Deng Xiaoping to the United States in 1980. Their hosts had taken him for a drive in a posh suburb in Silicon Valley south of San Francisco. The wealth was incredible. He had actually watched a garage door open to receive a car. This was at a private residence! And what's more, Deng was convinced that it wasn't a propaganda stunt planned for their benefit. Their hosts told them that in this neighborhood almost all garage doors were equipped to be opened by the driver, who had a kind of electrical transmitter in his car. Deng could hardly believe it! Yet he had also read stories about divorce rates in America, about an epidemic of killer VD among American queers, and about how American women didn't want to be women anymore.

Like his Uncle Chen Li, Deng felt that the strength of the family was one of China's best resources. A family meant something in China. A man had responsibilities. Deng wondered if a house might not only be as comfortable as the people inside were comfortable with themselves and their lives. Such freedom as the Americans espoused had its costs.

One, then another drop hit the still water in an open space on the pond. Deng felt a drop on his cheek. He looked at his watch. Time for his pills and a cup of tea before the car came. He rose slowly from the flat stone, his knees making a slight popping sound. Outside the wall a scooter, slowing down, went *pop, pop, pop, pop,* each *pop* softer than the one before.

He felt another drop on his cheek, then another, and a drop on his nose, and knew he should have brought his umbrella. Then it came, raining hard, lashing at Beijing with a vengeance. Deng, who was immediately drenched, hurried his pace as best he could. Once he had accepted his fate, the water wasn't so bad and he grinned as he walked. His physician would be horrified, but Deng knew he would dry out.

Deng got to the porch and began stripping off his wet clothes before he went inside to change. Most Chinese would willingly put up with a civilized bowl of noodles before *xiu-xi,* and a change of clothes if they got caught in a rainstorm. But as attractive as this was as a minimal goal, communism unrelieved by incentive couldn't deliver even that.

Dry, clothed, and sipping his tea, Deng Shaoqi waited. He saw the gates being opened. A black limousine entered, red flags flying on the front bumpers.

Deng Shaoqi pitied the poor Russians. Limited by paranoia, excited by notions of grandeur, they were also profoundly stupid, in Deng's opinion, perhaps congenitally so. Deng found most Westerners to be a half step behind the Chinese in intelligence, but the Russians were truly pathetic and so genuinely dangerous. For years the Russians had remained in the comforting womb of the abstract, promising utopia, while Europe was reborn, and the Americans pushed ahead, and Asia blossomed.

The Russians remained steadfastly poor. No food? The weather, Moscow said. Drought? A hard winter. No heat or space to live? All the comrades were working on this problem. Nothing worked? Shirkers and drunks. All this so the comrades in charge could maintain the big lie about the mounting threat from Western Europe and America. The Russians were so pathetic. They blamed everything except their own obstinacy and an economic system that flat-out didn't work and never would work.

The Russians were too stupid and stubborn to recognize the simplest truth of life. Give a man a choice between an egg roll and a bamboo rod across the backside and he'll take the egg roll every time. The Soviets had turned their entire country into a labor camp rather than admit that fact.

Deng wondered if he might be able to import some American gumdrops one day.

The driver held an umbrella for Deng Shaoqi and gave the old man an arm to help him settle into the back seat. The driver shut the door and got in the car; he turned the windshield wipers on and—*click-click, click-click, click-click*—drove slowly down the driveway. Deng Xiaoping would be at the ceremonies as well; Deng Shaoqi looked forward to spending a convivial afternoon with his little brother.

Ireland,
six months earlier . . .

2

IT was at Dun Laoghaire, just south of Dublin, that Lucien Salvant woke on the morning of his fortieth birthday— his mouth sour from a long night of Guinness—and found himself impaled on the cusp of life. The sheets smelled musty and the room was cold. He knew he had to do something. He had to take a chance. He got up slowly, turning his head carefully so as not to joggle things; quick movements apparently compressed his brain, and made him wince. Salvant washed his teeth twice, but the night-fur clung stubbornly. He looked at his off-color tongue in the mirror. He took four aspirin. He wondered if he would be able to buy an *International Herald Tribune* before breakfast; his best bet was the train stop by the ferry terminal.

The streets were shrouded with a wet mist when Salvant went to get the paper. Eyes narrowed against the pain, he walked like a waiter with a full tray, heel rolling to toe so as to prevent the sloshing of his brains. The windows of the dining room were fogged when he got back to the small hotel. He sat down with a cup of weak coffee and considered the sweating glass. In the kitchen, his eggs and bangers—popping and snapping in the grease—echoed like muskets joined in battle.

Owing to his uncertain heritage, Salvant's friends liked to speculate on the origins of his physical appearance, concluding that he was American Unknown, a mongrel. He was no Cajun because his eyes were blue; however, his hair was curly enough that all he had to do was bunch it up in the morning with the palm of his hand and it was ready to go. The possibility of a little belly was clearly there, but he would never be thick or fat. Neither was he an athlete; he had known this early on and so pumped books in high school while his friends grunted away at building their lats and delts to impress the girls who poked out in the right places. Salvant said the only muscle it made any sense to worry about was his bell clapper, and his was apparently average in size.

He had been born alone and remained alone, living with a series of women of honorable imagination who eventually realized that he wanted nothing to do with children. He had no experience or confidence in the institution that nurtured others; he was unwilling to chance doing unto another human what had been done to him: he had been left alone at birth.

Excluding the Dun Laoghaire hangover, Salvant's habits on his sabbatical were the same every morning. He sipped strong coffee—the caffeine jump-started his bowels—and began with the book review, then went to that day's personality profile, maybe a feature on the Nigerian economy, a story about the latest Common Market quarrel, and so on, until he had read the entire paper. He always wanted to write the editors and thank them for the pleasure, but never did. He had composed hundreds of such thank-yous in his head but never mailed them.

Salvant's favorite reading in the *International Herald Tribune* was the classifieds. A lawyer in Tripoli had a comforting, if optimistic, ad to anybody thrown in jail by the Libyans. There was a hotel for sale on Guernsey. Salvant liked to consider the prices of apartments in Abu Dhabi or villas on the Costa del Sol. He even read the ads for international secretaries on Tuesday—girl Friday wanted by a mysterious mogul; executive secretary desired by an executive who travels. Were these women really secretaries? he wondered. Where did those people get all that money? Just look at the Rolls-Royce ads. Amazing! Making its first appearance in that morning's edition was an advertisement from a company in Hong Kong that found private islands for people—in the strictest confidence.

Salvant saved the personals for his second cup of coffee. The personals were wonderful. He wondered which ones were sent by the KGB and which by the CIA or MI6; which from cocaine smugglers and which from isolated agents of the international financial underworld. He thought of putting his own ad in the personals, sort of a paladin, a knightly champion. Yes, an attendant of Charlemagne! Salvant laughed out loud, ouch! then sucked in his breath between clenched teeth, damn! Both the laughing and the sucking zapped his forehead.

The cook thought he had said something, and peered from around the door to the kitchen. "Coming up."

Academic life wasn't what it was cracked up to be. Quantrell College had a fine reputation; the campus was gorgeous and the tuition expensive; the students were the sons and daughters of the wealthy, but Salvant couldn't face returning to the classroom. He remembered those earnest faces—they were really only interested in sex and smoking dope—pencils at the ready, wanting everything, a, b, c; one, two, three. Salvant's imagination went every which way, and when he tumbled onto something new, he liked to follow it like a jazzman. This was infuriating to those who had been taught that the world could be divided into neat little boxes and everything had its place—hence the invention of closets and outlines. To appease this portion of his constituency, Salvant had hyped himself on caffeine each morning, and plunged doggedly down the path demanded by the syllabus. By the time he finished each day, the beaverlike chewing of his thumbnail had reduced the lip of his plastic foam cup to shreds.

Eventually he had gotten sick of everything: Poe, Jack London, John Dos Passos; whatever it was those guys at Yale were saying this year; Modern Language Association conventions; the lot of it. The conventions were possibly the worst, forcing Salvant to stand around drinking coffee, thumbnail gnawing at foam cups, with absurdly serious professors dressed in tweedy jackets and out-of-date neckties. The longer the beard and the tweedier the jacket, the more insufferable they became.

On top of that there was faculty politics. God! After teaching at both the University of Wisconsin and Quantrell, Salvant had come to believe that the lower the stakes, the higher the passion. Life was one never-ending reworking of the curriculum, inching ever closer to perfection—a condition academics apparently thought possible—only to see everything fall apart. Another never-ending issue was faculty review: should professors be required to publish in scholarly journals? This subject brought forth flushed, crimson faces, high blood pressure, and hysteria, along with much bluffing and not a little secret praying. Then there was the practice of giving inflated grades to suck up to students in general; everybody condemned this unconscionable behavior that was the only alternative to listening to the little bastards complain.

Salvant thought both students and professors were deluded.

After breakfast, Salvant opened the door, turned his shoulder to the wind, and set forth to the ferry terminal. He had just eight more months of his sabbatical to find something; then it was back to Quantrell. He'd have to put in another six years on the rack of academia to qualify for another sabbatical. So what if he was tenured, and could retire and be employed at the same time? He couldn't do it.

Salvant joined a line for his ticket, then walked up the

stairs and into a long, narrow room that had large windows overlooking the next ferry berth. He swung his valise to the floor and flopped cross-legged next to it. The room was beginning to fill.

He considered his problem. He thought about department meetings, academic-speak, tepid spaghetti in the faculty dining room, grading papers. What he really wanted to do was sit around and read all day and maybe try writing a novel of his own. Salvant considered his copy of the *International Herald Tribune*. He looked at the personals again. Fuck tenure! He took out his notebook and jotted:

Trustworthy, educated New Orleans man, 40, no family ties, seeks adventure, unusual employment, short or long-term, anywhere. Confidence assured. L. Salvant, P.O. Box 1257, Seville, Spain.

The doors at the end of the room were opened and the crowd pressed forward, the travelers eager to be among the first aboard and thus first in line where the duty-free whiskey was sold. Salvant lingered, thinking about the ad. Suddenly he tore it out of the notebook, folded it, and started licking stamps. He jumped up and ran back to the mailbox by the ticket window, thrust the envelope inside, and rushed back— fourth to last passenger to board.

He found himself a place to sit and watched Dun Laoghaire recede in the distance. Dublin had been fun, especially the pubs, but Salvant had grown tired of the wind and the rain. He was eager to get back to Spain. Spain was warmer and cheaper, and the Spanish girls were lovely.

Later, when the lines had receded, Salvant went down to join the stragglers in the whiskey line. All the whiskies touted in magazine ads were gone, so Salvant bought himself a liter of the cheapest scotch available. A bargain was a bargain, but Salvant couldn't help laughing at himself. He knew that when he got to London, he'd kick back on his bed and have himself a drink and think it was wonderful even if it tasted like cow pee. The bottle had an impressive-looking label, and that was fun.

What a kick it had been to send the ad in to the *International Herald*. He was so excited he forgot about his headache. Lucien Salvant opened the paper again and reread the notice by the Hong Kong company:

Tired of noise and hubbub? Private islands, isolated estates found in Southeast Asia. Strictest confidence. Satisfaction guaranteed. References. South China Land Corporation, P.O. Box 1236-B, Hong Kong.

3

BY the test of magazine models and television actresses, Ella Nidech was no longer young at thirty-eight. However, unlike them, Nidech had considered mortality and so—in the eyes of men with adult imaginations—she was a sensuous woman. She had alert green eyes, jet-black hair, pale skin, and an intelligent face. She was long-legged, but with a butt that was perhaps overly impressive. When Nidech encased her caboose in a good pair of slacks, men's heads swiveled like gyroscopes. She had modest boobs but was satisfied they wouldn't get tangled in her knees when she was fifty-five. Any man who wanted more than a civilized mouthful was an oinker as far as she was concerned.

Nidech was divorced, having stupidly married a jerk when she was twenty-five, an unbalanced union that had lasted four years. She was the holder of a Ph.D. in international affairs from Johns Hopkins University. And finally, she was a Company rep, the CIA's Hong Kong station chief.

Under the pseudonym of Flora Lewis, Nidech was established as the executive vice-president of research and development of the Bee-Vee Toy Corporation. These duties were actually performed by a man using a different title. Her family and friends truly believed her to be a Hong Kong toy executive, and every year she dutifully, if somewhat coarsely, sent boxes of plastic weapons to her nieces and nephews and the children of her friends. She felt these awful gifts were demanded of her by her cover.

Bee-Vee, named for the founders, two British traders named Mr. Butler and Mr. Vickers, made plastic models of assault rifles and machine pistols that it marketed as toys on the American market. The executive vice-president of marketing had wonderful charts on the walls depicting youthful tastes in plastic machine guns and rocket launchers. For example, when Israel periodically went to war, sales boomed in Uzi and Mini-Uzi submachine guns, and Galil assault rifles—especially in Jewish neighborhoods in New York, Miami, and Los Angeles. Toy M16s had been popular in the Vietnam War, and when the Rambo movies became the rage, Bee-Vee gave its workers a bonus; the pretend Rambos didn't know the model of M16 they were firing wasn't issued until 1982.

Bee-Vee marketed all kinds of toy weapons: pistols with clips that popped into the side, drum-fed assault rifles, modern versions of the Gatling. Larger models of these toys, cast in metal and billed as "replicas," were sold through advertisements in *Soldier of Fortune, Gung-Ho, Mercenary,* and other magazines. Other than having a plugged barrel or missing firing mechanisms, these "replicas" were in fact the real McCoys, manufactured by Bee-Vee in Hong Kong's New Territories and sold to rebels in Afghanistan, and to others whose causes were sanctioned by the American State Department. The replica business was highly profitable because there was no need to retool the dies from the real weapons.

The market for French small arms improved remarkably after the success of the Exocet by the Argentines during the

Falkland Islands war, although there was no logical link between a surface-to-surface missile and assault rifles or submachine guns. Nevertheless, due to the number of political opponents requiring assassination in the Third World, Bee-Vee was moved to market a French sniper rifle, the 7.5mm FR F1, when the American 7.62mm M21 was just as good and used a readily available NATO cartridge. The French and the Belgians were enthusiastic participants on the international arms market, and so their weapons were frequently copied by Bee-Vee; the Belgian 7.62mm NATO Fusil Automatique Léger was very popular. After the Falklands, Belgian manufacturers, in an effort to cash in on the Exocet celebrity missile, made sure their sales reps were French speakers. Outside of the Soviet bloc countries, Bee-Vee was the world's largest manufacturer of Soviet AK-47s—so that mischief in wretched countries could be blamed on the Russians.

The toys were stamped "Made in Hong Kong." The replicas and real weapons were allegedly manufactured in the country that made the originals. This was a standard business procedure in Hong Kong, which had for years served as the covert outlet for Chinese imitations of European brand-name products.

Ella Nidech's office was located on the twenty-second floor of a rose-colored forty-six-story high-rise on Des Voeux Road Central on Hong Kong island. This splendid building had fuchsia-tinted reflecting windows, and mauve trim around the ground-floor windows. Owing to the color, Nidech thought it looked rather like an erect penis and once wrote to a woman friend in the United States how she had to spend hard days in an air-conditioned hard-on.

Nidech's office, which contained equipment for communicating with Langley, was periodically checked by Company technicians, and at least two of her subordinates were on duty twenty-four hours a day.

The fateful call, relayed from the American embassy in

Hong Kong, came in the first week of March. The twenty-four-year-old who took the call was a recent graduate of Princeton University, and had come by the Hong Kong plum through connections. A clerk, he was given the title of intelligence analyst to help him with his ego. He was secretly in love with Nidech. He found women his own age squeaky-voiced and shallow, girls still. Nidech had a warmth about her that triggered masturbatory fantasies. He listened, then said, "One moment," and put the embassy caller on hold. "Ella, we have a caller who insists on talking to somebody from the Company. Very important, he says."

"I'll take it," Nidech said.

On the phone, a man said, "Am I speaking to someone from the Central Intelligence Agency?"

Nidech said, "I'm sorry, but we don't have intelligence people here, but I can take a message and forward it to their nearest representative. Your confidence is assured."

"I represent an unusual broker. We have Chinese secrets for sale at a fifteen percent commission. These are fresh from the councils of Beijing and from key Chinese military units. We are wondering if the United States government is interested?"

"Where can our people get in touch with you, Mr. . . . ?"

"If the American government is interested, we can arrange a preliminary meeting at which time I can show sample goods. These are first-rate secrets, guaranteed genuine. I wish to meet with one American representative only, discreetly of course."

He hung up. Ella Nidech, still holding the receiver, blinked once, twice.

4

THE President had been privately convinced that he needed a delicate man by what happened to François Mitterand when French agents were caught sinking a Greenpeace vessel in New Zealand. Mitterand had tried everything: omission, half truths, outright lies. Nothing worked. In the end he'd had to sack good friends, hardworking men who had had little to do with the New Zealand fiasco.

Mitterand had appeared at a summit of European, American, and Japanese leaders looking haggard, his eyes over huge bags. Unfortunately, a reporter for *Newsweek* magazine overheard a sympathetic Margaret Thatcher, obviously worried about his health, recommend hot whiskey with a touch of honey in it. *Le Monde* published a cartoon of Mitterand being mothered by Maggie Thatcher. Poor François had never been so humiliated.

The way the President saw it, John Kennedy could have used a delicate man to damn it kill Fidel Castro once the decision had been made. Instead, the Company had cast enthusiastic Cubans and Italians in Keystone Kops schemes.

Richard Nixon got flushed down the toilet because an asshole with an indelicate touch was chosen to tape the doors during the Watergate burglary. A sloppy tape job, that's all it boiled down to. The guard saw the tape and phoned the cops and that was it for Richard Nixon. And Jimmy Carter could have used a delicate man capable of decisive action when the Ayatollah grabbed the American embassy in Tehran.

Mitterand's problem was only the topper, to the President's way of thinking. The real need of a delicate man lay in the history of screw-ups that had plagued the Company since it had taken over from the old OSS. The coup de grâce to the bad old days was applied by Richard Helms in his appearances before the Senate Intelligence Oversight Committee in 1977. For some inexplicable reason—never completely understood by the infuriated people in Langley—the former DCI told the Senate everything, just puked up the whole mess with reporters for the *Times* and the *Post* poised like Queequeg, pencils at the ready.

In spite of all the righteousness and breastbeating that followed, life went on. And the Company, facing perfectly awful morale among the troops, still had a secret war to fight. It was either that or let the Soviets do whatever the hell they pleased. All bullshit aside—and all manner of noble intentions notwithstanding—that just happened to be the problem.

There were congressmen who denied the existence of a need to do anything other than collect intelligence, but that also was voter puckey and everybody knew it. The senators to whom DCIs nominally reported knew there was a need to shoot a prick every now and then. As long as the violence fell upon foreign nationals in foreign lands, the senators were prepared to accept, with an agreed-upon genial ignorance, a certain amount of tit-for-tat. They did insist that those involved in the administration of Old Testament justice be responsible and few in number.

It fell upon Peter Neely, the director of the Central Intelligence Agency, and his deputy, Ara Schott, to nominate a delicate man for personal approval by the President. It was disingenuous for a Company man to refer to anything by its real name; although Schott coined the usage, Neely almost immediately referred to this as delicate work, and the candidate as the delicate man.

The question came down to who was the most skilled and trustworthy agent for the delicate job of applying an appropriate tit when a tat went beyond the pale or when excrement was clearly headed for the fan?

Although Neely and Schott both knew who they would choose in the end, they covered their butts by drawing up separate rosters of candidates, which they then discussed and dutifully trimmed to short lists.

The standards were complicated and exacting. For example, an individual so positioned to do personal chores for the President must be free of greed, the single most important reason for the Soviet Union's recent spectacular success in gaining access to American and NATO secrets in recent years. This was true from the Falcon and the Snowman to allegations against members of the Walker family. Brits spying for the Russians were sometimes motivated by politics, but more and more they were victims of the debilitating "American disease," as it was called by intelligence officers in MI5, British counterintelligence. KGB officers were simply buying British and American secrets. It was known that Moscow Central referred to its shoppers for secrets—operating under cover of Tass correspondents and Soviet foreign service comrades—as "housewives." The term "stealing" secrets was considered amusing in NATO headquarters after the rash of German sellouts uncovered in 1985.

The Company's counterintelligence people and the FBI had begun a renewed effort to detect hints of "methane," the tell-tale smell of an individual who was rancid with greed, his desire smelling like swamp gas or flatulence—the odor of dung.

Methane was so gripping on some imaginations that there was a documented case of an individual who had sold submarine communication secrets to the Soviet Union—endangering the lives and fortunes of 240 million of his fellow countrymen—for a lousy $10,000, not enough to buy a Honda with an FM radio.

Neely and Schott agreed in advance to strike from their respective lists any agent who had ever felt compelled to buy a BMW automobile or Gucci shoes. Looking for the slightest hint of methane, they went so far as to make a list of purchases deemed symptomatic of incipient desire, and therefore of a potential sellout. Bewildered candidates, who were not told why, were required to submit lists of things owned, rented, or leased, and then had to take a polygraph examination on the truthfulness of their answers. Schott was especially tough. He argued that ownership of a Sony VCR disqualified an agent for delicate work, and struck one man from his list because he wore silk underwear. Neely argued the case for Sonys and Hondas, both of which he owned.

In the end, they chose James Burlane.

Burlane was a tall man with unkempt blond hair, a long face, and an equally long and slightly twisted nose, who was given to unpressed cottons and utilitarian hats he could mash into his hip pocket. Burlane was forty-four and had to use reading glasses. He was a half to a full step slower than younger delicate-man candidates. Individually, there were agents who were better linguists than Burlane, and who could shoot straighter, and who had larger bladders; poor Burlane couldn't make it past two hours, a condition that had once nearly done him in on the Trans-Siberian Express. Furthermore, he suffered the handicap of originally being a farm boy from a place called Umatilla, Oregon, a fact the grinning President challenged, asking was that possible. This was rather like MI6 giving a killer's license to a chap from Manchester. Neely and Schott normally considered a degree from an Ivy League university to be a proper minimum.

There were two variables in which Burlane was so outstanding—the second was possibly unique—that his selection was obvious.

First, James Burlane was a man who got things done. He liked to be turned loose to do a job, which he got done any way possible. He urged Neely and Schott to read Alfred T. Mahan's *The Influence of Sea Power Upon History*. Mahan had observed that British imperial admirals let their captains make decisions in the confusion of battle; French admirals insisted on controlling everything from the flagship and so watched their warships slide under, French captains watching through telescopes for instructions to return British fire. Did the French agents in New Zealand, so far from Paris, get rattled when they had to think for themselves? he asked.

Second, Burlane had a natural immunity, if not an allergic reaction, to methane. This was a curious personality tic. He was the only Company representative who did not know, nor did he apparently care, what his salary was. Four years before the decision to pick a delicate man, he and Ara Schott had established a system whereby Burlane signed his paychecks before Schott filled in the amount. Schott dealt with the Merrill Lynch man who handled Burlane's money. Burlane signed blank checks so Schott could pay his bills. Burlane signed blank tax forms and turned them over to the woman who did his taxes.

Burlane's investment portfolio was a concern to Schott, not Burlane. Burlane never asked how much money he had. He had access to cash if he wanted; all he had to do was sign his name. In Burlane's opinion a person's intelligence was best determined by dividing the sum of books read by the number of items conspicuously consumed. Burlane had enough money to eat, drink, and have a comfortable place to sleep. He drank local beer with friends, dark Jamaican rum and tonic on occasions where people wore ties, and smoked a joint with a girl friend now and then. He drove a bilious-yellow, eight-year-old Toyota Corolla hatchback. He owned enough clothes to fill his traveling valise. That was it.

What is more—and this also was Burlane's idea—he was given a monthly lie detector examination over such things as the nature of recent purchases or any loans or other indebtedness incurred. Every month the polygraph operator ended the examination with this question:

"Are you now or have you ever used your employment in the Central Intelligence Agency for your personal benefit or gain?"

Burlane always looked the examiner square in the eye and said, "Absolutely not."

The needles ran as straight as a bagman to the bank—with nary a hitch or hesitation.

Another thing that impressed Schott—if not Neely—was Burlane's attitude toward the Company. Schott understood the psychological dynamics of working in the secret world. Company employees were no less changed by their work than were cops or newspaper reporters. It was the Company's duty to be paranoid, so those given to paranoia were encouraged, promoted, and listened to.

The necessity of this paranoia was the snare of the secret world. The result, as inevitable as Mr. Murphy's law, Burlane maintained, was a series of foolish if not preposterous schemes the Company had come up with over the years, beauts like the plot to send Fidel Castro a wet suit with poisonous fungus impregnated in the rubber.

Not wanting to screw up their chances for more power, otherwise sane men committed themselves to outrageous, preposterous operations. Schott said John Kennedy could have used an irreverent delicate man when the Bay of Pigs adventure was conceived. Burlane had the capacity to remain calm while everybody around him was engulfed in the familiar manure of Things Gone Wrong.

Burlane told Neely and Schott that they lived in a pretend world. If he saw the flip side of everything, the cynical and the ironic, then that was because he was a realist. That was the human condition. He laughed, yes, but at the unfolding of inexorable truths. The rest of them with their solemn faces—the Neelys and Schotts of the world—were kidding both themselves and the public. They were naïve at best, and demented at worst.

James Burlane was also a veteran of the Big Muddy, or mud, as the Company reps normally called it. This was officially VHD, short for Very Hazardous Duty. By any name, VHD meant a rep could get killed. Burlane had the seeming ability to slog unscathed through the most terrifying mud imaginable.

It was decided that responsibility for Burlane's delicate missions would be shared by Neely and Schott, who would serve as case officer. Schott was to Burlane what Ungar was to Madison. Schott was the firstborn, tidy, a left-brainer; Burlane was loose, randy, youngest, a right-brainer—said to be the model for Nicholas Orr's fictional spook, Humper Staab, although Humper would never have worn one brown sock and one black sock to be interviewed by the President of the United States, which is what Burlane did.

After meeting Burlane, the President assented to his assignment as the Company's delicate man. Burlane later claimed that all the President had wanted to talk about was the Chicago Cubs, and what it was like for Burlane to grow up in a place called Umatilla. Burlane had told him how fun it was to use a frozen cow pie as a pretend discus. Then Burlane said he was just kidding, really: he and the President had had a sober discussion about social contracts and the ethical responsibilities of delicate work. He said the President had invoked the names of Thomas Hobbes, John Locke, and Niccolo Machiavelli. Burlane left it to Neely and Schott to decide which version of the interview was correct.

With the President's approval, Ara Schott systematically expunged all mention of Burlane from the Company records. Schott started a rumor that the man who was James Burlane had succumbed to dysentery while on a mission in Mozambique, and began drawing Burlane's pay from a classified fund where all receipts were bogus for reasons of national security.

Since Burlane had rarely been identified even before his alleged disappearance, physical descriptions varied wildly. There were those who claimed that James Burlane, the imaginary, favored superspy, was a myth, an invention of the disgruntled. A Company anthropologist whose job it was to analyze tribal governments in Africa held that James Burlane was a communal invention of the Langley work force, a deity needed to solace people who had been screwed so many times they assumed it was the norm. These mythical tricksters were found in all cultures, the anthropologist said, from the Central African Republic to the Central Intelligence Agency.

Although Burlane did in fact hump as many women as attracted him and were agreeable to the pleasures of the bed, he didn't stab people. Rather, he "stitched" them. Or he "ran a zipper." A listener of National Public Radio wrote to John Ciardi (Burlane himself? Schott later wondered) asking if Ciardi knew the origins of the terms, which the listener alleged were current CIA argot. The amused Ciardi addressed an inquiry to Peter Neely.

Ciardi received the following reply:

Dear Mr. Ciardi,

We are very pleased to help National Public Radio and other cultural and civic-minded organizations. Our archivists have traced the origins of "stitching" and "laying a zipper." We regret to say they were coined by a callous agent who does not exist and never did exist. The identification of said agent is therefore impossible. The terms refer to a perfect row of bullets by an assassin. Requiring cold-blooded, measured shooting ability, "stitching," or "laying a zipper," is the *ne plus ultra* of assassin's skills. This same unknown person also coined the terms "boring" or "laying a Holland." This is when a marksman lays a steady hail of bullets on one spot—boring, or laying a (Holland) tunnel—as in "He bored the Rooskie's forehead with twenty." This is said to be a spectacle of disintegrating flesh.

Cordially,

Randolph Barnes, Assistant to Peter Neely

The man who never existed was James Burlane, who, giggling, slapping his thighs, had ghostwritten Barnes's reply. Of course, Barnes didn't exist either. Writing with his left hand, Burlane/Barnes scrawled, "Tell Bob Edwards to keep up the good work, and I like Scott Simon, too, and you, and good old Red Barber down there in Florida. A civilized crew." When Burlane wrote with his left hand, it came out looking like it had been written by a big, eager kid.

It was upon this man, then, the ambling grinner from Umatilla, Oregon, officially deceased, that the nation came to depend in delicate situations.

5

SHE could have called for a car and driver, but Susan Wu missed being able to walk unrecognized through city streets as she had been able to do in Singapore when she was a girl. She slipped on some old jeans and a bulky sweater. She curled her long black hair into a bun and hid it under a floppy-brimmed hat. She put on some good Italian sunglasses and hiked down to the Admiralty stop of the colony's sleek subway system, the MTR. Although Susan was barely five-two, and weighed but ninety-seven pounds, the mirage of film rendered her voluptuous by Chinese standards—thus qualifying her for Sing Sing Boyd movies.

What made her a star—besides her role in *Chan Rides Low*—were her independent eyes. They always riveted the camera in movie playbills. Although she liked men, in fact wanted one of her own, she was capable of mocking them, a fact that both annoyed and charmed her male fans. In jeans, sweat shirt, and floppy hat, she was another Chinese girl—perhaps a bit more sloppy than most. She was obviously a looker yet did nothing to show it off, in fact never taking off her sunglasses.

Susan got a seat, for which she was thankful; that gave her a chance to reread the article she had clipped from the *South China Morning Post* about the *sam ku* Wong Tsei-Ling, who lived in Kowloon.

Sam ku, literally "third aunt" in Cantonese, meant Tsei-Ling could communicate with ghosts; she had *yin* eyes, which meant that she could sometimes see the residents of the spirit world. The article had to do with Wong Tsei-Ling's storied past as a geomancer, a scholar of the Kiangsi school of *fung shui*. Kiangsi school geomancers believed that different land forms incorporate the spirit of various animals. Hills, for example, were dragons; it was foolish to build a house on a dragon's tail.

Only a geomancer, a scholar of the immutable rules of *ch'i, li, so,* and *ying*—that is, breath, laws, mathematical principles, and the physical world—could attest as to whether a proposed structure had good *fung shui* or bad *fung shui*. No Chinese would build a skyscraper with bad *fung shui,* much less work in it.

According to the article, these particular Hong Kong moneymen had wanted the best geomancer available, so with some fanfare they had chosen the most famous, Wong Tsei-Ling. Followed by Hong Kong television cameras, Wong Tsei-Ling had visited the proposed site—an expensive plot of Hong Kong real estate—and studied the architect's sketches. She consulted her compass, considered all the factors, and concluded that as the proposal stood, the siting was impossible; it would be haunted by spirits. However, she said, the architect could prevent this by making the windows hexagonal *Bhat Gwa* mirrors—this could be done with reflecting glass—or by making the windows round. Either shape would scare the spirits away.

If she used her gift for profit, her *fung shui* would turn bad, but Tsei-Ling agreed to accept twenty Hong Kong dollars for her advice. The British architect was nevertheless forced to choose. He chose to make his rectangular windows round; the result being a skyscraper the Chinese began calling the Building of a Thousand Assholes. The architect said it was the Building of a Thousand and One Assholes.

A photograph of Wong Tsei-Ling accompanied the text. Susan Wu couldn't help but think Wong was one of the homeliest women she had ever seen. Susan's sister had been a plain girl, and Susan knew it had been a burden.

Susan Wu wanted to have a talk with her dead sister and get some things off her mind.

Wong Tsei-Ling lived in a tiny room off an alley running into Shantung Street in the Mong Kok district of the Kowloon peninsula. The room was painted pale blue. There were blisters of paint on the ceiling, and water stains ran down from the corners of the single barred window. Outside, drying clothes hung on bamboo rods that extended from window to window across the alley. The *sam ku*'s room reeked of fish and garlic. There was a blackened wok and an aluminum teapot on the floor beside a gas burner. Besides the wok and burner, the room contained an ancient, decrepit Chinese sea trunk, and a mildewed pad upon which the woman with the *yin* eyes slept and received her guests.

Wong Tsei-Ling invited Susan Wu to squat on the pad, then went next door to get some water for the teapot. When she got back she put the water on to heat and squatted on the pad with her guest and the conversation began in Cantonese.

"How can I help you?" the *sam ku* asked.

"I would like to know if you could contact my sister?"

"What is her name?"

"Wu Wing-Ling."

"And she was born?"

Susan Wu unfolded a piece of paper. "At two minutes before midnight, October 21, 1955, in Singapore."

"And your name is?"

"Wu Mei-Ling. I was born seventeen minutes after six in the morning, February 21, 1957, in Singapore."

"I'll need to know the circumstances of your sister's death."

"I . . ." Susan Wu stared at her hands. "She died about three-thirty in the afternoon, July 6, 1982. She and both my parents were killed in an automobile accident three miles south of Batu Pahat on the southern tip of the Malay Peninsula."

Tsei-Ling said, "Tell me everything now. I need to know everything."

"My father was a drama professor at the University of Singapore. The family was on their way to visit my uncle's family in Kuala Lumpur. My uncle was a comptroller at the University of Malaysia. I was to have gone on the trip, but I didn't want to. I was allowed to stay home after a terrible fight and only because I had to study at the library."

"I see," Wong Tsei-Ling said. "There must have been bad *fung shui* for an accident like that."

"We—that is my sister and I—we fought terribly."

"You were younger, spoiled, she thought, and better-looking. Is that not correct?"

"Yes. She was to marry first, my father said, then me."

"She was unmarried when she died, I take it."

Susan Wu cleared her throat. "Yes," she said as the *sam ku* got up to make their tea. "I never felt right getting married with her dead like that. She would have married first. But . . ." Susan accepted the tea and took a sip. "I've been afraid to contact her. She'll be furious with me. She was so jealous, it was hateful. I'm twenty-nine years old, and there comes a time when a woman thinks about things like children."

"And what is it you do for a living?"

Susan was momentarily embarrassed. "I'm an actress."

"Susan Wu. I knew that." Tsei-Ling grinned. "In Sing Sing Boyd's kung fu movies. I saw you in *Wong's Savage Revenge* last week. Do you think a *sam ku* doesn't watch the telly?" She grinned and gestured with her hand. "My friends down the hall have a big Sony. By the way, I really liked you in *Ho Strikes Back*." Tsei-Ling got up and went to the trunk. She came back with a tin can and some fake bills with a large green HELL printed on one side. She put the bills in the can and lit them; the women contemplated the burning paper. Tsei-Ling waited for the ashes to finish burning, then gestured for her guest to continue.

"I want to find out how she is and whether I have her permission to marry if I find a man I like."

"Don't be afraid to interrupt if you have a question to ask. That's why you're here. I suspect she may have put bad *fung shui* on you." Wong Tsei-Ling took a sip of tea. "I'll see if I can find her. If I do, she'll take over my body and speak through my lips. I won't be able to remember anything when I'm finished."

The *sam ku* smacked her thin lips, and closed her eyes in concentration. As she settled into the world of Stephen King and Edgar Allen Poe, she pursed her mouth and made odd sucking sounds; small explosive noises rose from her throat. She traveled fast. She was a lightning rod.

This business went on for ten long minutes while her unsurprised guest waited.

Finally she opened her eyes and glared at Susan. "So. I'm dead, and you're a movie star. I'm dead because I did what I was told. You have everything and I don't have anything, and it's your fault. I hate you." The *sam ku* stopped, making sputtering sounds. "I curse you." The smacking and sucking and burbling rose in intensity and passion. "Why did you wait for four years before seeking me out?"

Susan Wu hesitated. "I . . . was afraid."

"I want a husband." Tsei-Ling began flubbering her lips lazily, the sound resembling an outboard motor idling at the dock. Spittle flew. Susan Wu leaned to one side.

The flubbering stopped. The *sam ku* leaned forward, staring at Susan Wu but not seeing her. "This husband will be a wealthy *gweilo*. A millionaire."

"A *gweilo*?" A *gweilo*, literally "ghost" in Cantonese, was the Hong Kong term for a white man.

"I've been cursed to marry a *gweilo* because you use a European name. There aren't any *gweilos* here. Since you're to blame in the first place, you can find me one from the living. And he'd better be a good one. Why should you have everything just because you're good-looking? I might have been an actress too, but never had a chance."

Susan Wu was dumbfounded. It was possible for a *sam ku* to marry a living man to a dead woman or a living woman to a dead man. That was done all the time in Hong Kong. But where would she find a *taipan* to go along with something like that?

"If you don't find me what I want, you'll never have a love that will last. Never. That is my curse, sister. You may have children, but they'll never know their father. Be an actress if you want, be Susan Wu on the movie marquee, but be alone as I am."

"And if I find you a husband?"

"Then you're released from bad *fung shui* and can marry whenever and whoever you please. I'm going now. I'm tired of talking to you." Wong Tsei-Ling's *sam ku* trance suddenly disappeared and her face returned to normal. "What happened?"

"You found her and she put a curse on me. I'm to find her a *gweilo* husband, a millionaire, or never have a love that will last."

"A *gweilo*?" Tsei-Ling was astonished.

"She can only marry a *gweilo*, she says, because I use a *gweilo* first name. She's been cursed. I have to find a *taipan* who'll marry her. Where?" Susan spread her hands in frustration.

Wong Tsei-Ling put a sympathetic hand on Susan Wu's shoulder. "She's a spiteful one, your sister. But you must do what she says or forget ever having a man of your own. If you do find what she wants, I'd like to perform the marriage ceremony, Mei-Ling. I just love weddings." She poured them each another cup of tea.

*   *   *

After the distraught actress had gone, Wong Tsei-Ling put some rice on to boil. She opened her sea trunk and considered her collection of Chinese movie fan magazines and romantic novels.

Susan was a beautiful woman, it was true, but it was at times like this that Tsei-Ling felt grateful for having been born plain. In Tsei-Ling's experience in communicating with the other world, beautiful women were almost always plagued by spiteful spirits. The more good-looking and talented the women, the worse their curse seemed to be. Looking back, Tsei-Ling couldn't remember a deviation from that general rule. Dead sisters and mothers were especially tough on beauties.

When Tsei-Ling was younger—before she had discovered her powers as a *sam ku*—she had wanted to get married and have a family. This was the dream of all Chinese girls. But even in a world of arranged marriages, there was no market for an ugly thing like Wong Tsei-Ling.

With the rice steaming contentedly, Tsei-Ling squatted on her pad and pulled a newspaper clipping out of an envelope and read it slowly, smiling. If she really did marry the dead sister of the movie actress Susan Wu to a live European millionaire, the newspaper reporters would come again and they would take her picture. After the wedding, she would be interviewed on television. It would be like the time she'd saved the Building of a Thousand Assholes from bad *fung shui*.

6

THE man from Umatilla studied Ella Nidech's report while Ara Schott waited, trying to anticipate Burlane's reaction. "Have you ever seen fourteen little pigs attack a sow's dozen tits?" Burlane asked.

"I . . ." Schott looked uncertain.

"The little bastards just go nuts, squealing and struggling and pawing and burrowing. Cracks you up to watch 'em. The little twisters go *wee! wee! wee!* All this to avoid hind tit."

"Which leads to what advice, Jimmy?"

"We just may have ourselves some methane here. I think we should find out what the drummer has to sell," Burlane said.

"So does Neely."

"So what's the problem?"

"Ella Nidech."

"Something's wrong with Ella Nidech?"

"Nothing's wrong with Ella. It's Neely.'

"What are you talking about? What's wrong with Neely?"

"Neely wants you to take it over, Jimmy. Hong Kong

32

reverts to China in eleven years, and Neely's got the jitters about the place. He thinks it's delicate.''

"I see.''

"Everybody's got the jitters. Neely told me to send you, says he wants a money player on account of the President's interest. The President's friends don't want us to fuck up our relations with China because of that enormous market over there. The European market is diddly squat compared to one billion Chinese. This is delicate business, and he wants you to go.''

"All Nidech has to do is listen to the drummer make his pitch. She'll have a matchbook recorder. What's to go wrong?''

"Nothing, but we'll have to give Neely a good reason she should do it.''

"Okay,'' Burlane said. "The drummer got in contact with Nidech, didn't he? What if he knows she's our Hong Kong station chief? Someone in the business of selling state secrets just might know that, wouldn't he? Ordinarily a station chief would take the pitch. If I do the talking, I either have to be her local subordinate or someone from the outside, most likely her superior, and most likely from Washington.''

"There's that, I guess.''

"If we don't send our senior Hong Kong agent, the sellers might think we're careless and so not very smart, a reason to bump up the asking. If I go, they'll think we're too interested; the price will go up, guaranteed. We're shopping in Hong Kong here, not K-Mart. It's duty-free, yes, but we've got to be careful. We've got to bargain a little and check the merchandise carefully.''

"Yes, we do.''

"Tell Peter Neely that if we're stupid or too eager, it'll cost us bucks. Monies, as you people say, right out of Neely's budget. We'll give him a choice between sexism and greed, and see what happens.''

*   *   *

One of the first things to go was television, which for several years had been Cactus Jack Bonner's only entertainment. Cactus Jack was a sports fan, and he loved the Oilers. There were those who said it was his desire to see the Oilers kick the manure out of the Dallas Cowboys someday that kept Jack going after he had become bedridden. Shortly after they canned Bum Phillips, whom Cactus Jack loved because of Phillips's crew cut and big old Texas-ass boots, Jack's mind took a turn for the worse.

One day the nurse at Alamo Dreams turned on the set for a Houston-Atlanta game, and Jack didn't know what was going on. He appreciated the leggy cheerleaders for reasons he didn't understand, and found himself staring at their crotches. What wits he had left fled at the sight of the uniformed behemoths crashing into one another; he began making small sounds that didn't stop until the nurse—realizing the trouble—turned off the set. Thereafter Jack was afraid to watch football. He didn't know what they were doing to one another. The tapes of *Bonanza* and *Rawhide* that Jack liked to watch soon had the same effect. Pretty soon he couldn't tell Rowdy from Little Joe.

Then these strangers kept coming in and staring at him. In his periods of lucidity—these disappeared slowly, day by day—he recognized Clint and Flub as his two sons, but the moments when his mind worked rarely coincided with their visits. When he was clear, he wondered where the hell they were and why they didn't put him out of his misery?

In his lucid state of mind, Jack Bonner knew he must be a sight. He had no teeth and his jaw seemed to be disappearing. His useless legs had begun to curl up so that he rested on his side mostly, more and more coming to resemble some enormous fetus. He was fed through one tube and drained through two more. Whenever his kidneys started acting up, the solemn-faced physicians—who kept up to date by reading the slick ads in the *Journal of the American Medical*

Association—ordered the nurses to pump him full of expensive antibiotics; the curative powers of these expensive drugs were highly touted by the companies that manufactured them.

Thus infections that would have brought a merciful end to Cactus Jack's misery were held in check. Jack's heart, which had always been devoid of fat, pumping flawlessly through his vigorous seventies, had become a curse.

Cactus Jack Bonner's hormones had ruled his body as he began his eighties. Jack had been a ladies' man in his youth, an unregenerate cocksman, and he seemed determined not to give up on basic pleasures. He always swore his dick would be the last to go, even after his brain, and he was right about that. His dick had started running his life at puberty—before he had any brains at all, really—and continued to do so long after he was rational. He would lie there remembering the women of his youth, a center pole of desire forming a Big Top under the bed sheets.

Jack clung tenaciously to the memories of the young Chinese women furnished him by his old friends Chiang Kai-shek and General Lee Tzu Ying. Chiang and Lee were first-rate Chinamen as far as Jack was concerned, Chinks who knew how to do business. At the urging of Cactus Jack and his friends, Ike and Henry Luce had seen to it Chiang and Lee got what they wanted: the isolation of Red China, and American tax dollars for their personal bank accounts. In return, Bonner and the other members of the China lobby were well taken care of.

When Jack lay recalling the small, skilled hands and wonderful mouths of the young women who slipped into his bedroom on his visits to Taipei, his nurses had to be agile to avoid his gropes. The memories revisited him still, floating by in the eternal, confusing mélange of dreams. He had forgotten precisely how lovely it felt when they caressed his balls, how they had warmed him to his core. He only knew, dimly, that they had made him feel good. This was, without him knowing it, Cactus Jack's way of telling them he loved them for giving him such sweet memories.

Long before he lost the ability to enjoy the Oilers or a John Wayne movie, Cactus Jack came to hate the nurses who jabbed him with needles and changed his diapers. Under the guise of healers, they prolonged misery. How they could live with themselves was beyond him. This was not to mention his asshole sons, Flub and Clint. Cactus Jack Bonner envied his old friends Chiang and Lee. They had been allowed to die when their time came.

As it was, he knew, he was being kept alive so some physician could make a few extra bucks. Before his mind went completely, Jack used to dream of shoving fistfuls of scalpels and stethoscopes up doctorly rear ends.

Although the public was largely unaware that Cactus Jack Bonner was lingering on in Alamo Dreams, the financial world got excited periodically with rumors that this or that disease or fever had set in, that Jack was at last on the brink. This excitement was prompted by the fact that until Jack's death—and in view of his incapacitation—the Bonner fortune was really run by a group of Jack's aging cronies, who were reluctant to give up the fun of investing all that money.

T. Boone Pickens was said to have his eye on Bonner Oil, which was publicly owned but was in fact controlled by Jack Bonner as majority shareholder. When Jack died, speculation went, then Pickens would move. On top of that, Jack owned resort hotels, whiskey distilleries, soft drink bottlers, a cigarette company, and a chain of movie theaters. In addition, the estate included hundreds of millions of dollars in securities. This money was literally being wasted in the view of money people—an unconscionable state of affairs to those who would be pleased to spend a little of it.

The question to which there was no definitive answer, only speculation, was whether Flub and Clint Bonner were as smart and tough as old Cactus Jack. For all their loud talk of doing the Texas high poke, the truth was Jack's old-crony lawyers weren't about to give up the estate's money until Bonner was completely dead. As long as Jack maintained body temperature, control of the money was theirs. Flub and Clint, in their late thirties, were as yet untested in competition with genuinely big players.

7

THERE was much clearing of throats and shuffling of papers and checking of wristwatches around the table, so James Burlane knew they wanted him to do something *verboten*. In such a situation, Burlane knew, a collective decision had been made after lengthy discussions, conducted with agreed-upon euphemisms and codes, aimed at giving each participant an out in case anything went wrong. In obscurity lay refuge from blame. The ritual now involved getting the delicate man to do what they had concluded had to be done.

Peter Neely opened by introducing Arthur Demott, the attorney general, and Lewis Farnum, the secretary of the treasury. Ara Schott, Neely's deputy, was there as he was at all important meetings.

Neely got quickly to the heart of the matter. "I take it you've been reading about Blowfish in the *Times* and the *Post*."

Ahh, now Burlane knew. Blowfish was Gene Holt. He

38

said, "Pretty lurid charges. Holt's got imagination, you have to give him that."

Ara Schott said, "Drugs, extortion, cons and scams of every imaginable description, and more recently two kidnappings in the United States and one in West Germany. Enough of the charges are probably true."

"But nobody can prove it."

"We can prove some of them, no problem."

"You can't find him."

DeMott said, "We find him, then he's gone. We always go in like boy scouts and file for extradition. Well, hell, that does a lot of good. Dan Rather almost snickers when he reads the item. The President and the people on the Hill are asking what we're doing over here, playing with ourselves?"

Burlane saw the muscles working in the attorney general's jaw. The one thing bureaucrats couldn't stand was to be laughed at. They could take criticism from the media. They could handle pressure from the Hill. They had accepted tongue-lashings by presidents. In all these cases they defended themselves as best they could, accepting defeat as a hazard of duty. In all these, however, they were taken seriously, as though they had good sense, and mattered. "It's the Doonesbury cartoons isn't it? Be honest," Burlane said.

"Day after day after goddam day, the bastard. The one Sunday was the last straw," DeMott said. His face grew even tighter.

"That's why we're meeting here today, isn't it? To get Garry Trudeau off your backs." Burlane burst into loud, guffawing laughter.

"Jimmy!" Schott said.

Neely forced a smile. "Gene Holt's got money enough to oil the locals in any Third World country he chooses, Mr. Burlane. He's got his own jet."

Burlane looked at the attorney general, who wanted to speak.

DeMott said, "We haven't been able to find him for three

years now. We've tried everything and then some, believe me.''

"We try. Do we ever try." Secretary Farnum sighed. His T-men were impotent against the bastard Holt. "We just don't think we're going to get him into court.''

"So what is it you want me to do, short of doing violence to a cartoonist?''

Peter Neely said, "We're bored with being portrayed as the Marx brothers, Mr. Burlane. Enough is enough. The President says he never wants to see another Doonesbury cartoon with Blowfish in it. Ever. I told him he never will, even if that involves delicate work.''

There followed a silent moment of understanding. This was standard operational procedure, a bonding of their fortunes. They were scared little piggies, their pink butts lined up neatly in a row. They had assured the President something would be done about Gene Holt, but this always carried with it the unspoken agreement that the President would be protected from blame. In the history of the American presidency only once—in the case of Richard Nixon—had this system broken down.

Burlane noted that Neely had resorted to Holt's code name, Blowfish, when he got down to the nitty-gritty. "Oh, then you want me to kill Gene Holt?" he said casually. This was like talking about cocks and cunts in the Court of St. James.

The men around the table paled at the unmentionable four-letter word.

James Burlane did not always agree to assassination requests. When he did, he always insisted on the bald truth. The silence of the four men was assent and they all knew it, but silence could not be taped; go ahead, lawyers, argue silence.

Burlane regarded the scene: Dante rendered by Norman Rockwell. Since killing Gene Holt really only put Burlane's butt on the line—not theirs—he felt entitled to have a little fun. These were not kings or potentates; Schott excluded, they were men who sought power for reasons of ego, and thus in his opinion disqualified themselves from consideration. He scorned them, not Schott, but certainly Neely, Farnum, DeMott, and the President.

The indelicate delicate man from Umatilla, Oregon, grinned—an avenging angel—and said, "We'll call this one The Trudeau Hit, Ara. Sure, I'll kill the motherfucker . . ." Burlane looked at Schott and winked. "But I'm going to want a nice piece of change for overtime."

Marijuana smoke drifted out of Gene Holt's pug nose and was swept away by the air conditioning. The rotor of the air conditioner was out of alignment, so there was a disconcerting *ting, ting, ting* amid the reassuring *hummmm.* Holt adjusted his Japanese binoculars and broke wind, smiling at the momentary relief from the torment of his bowels. "I'll tell you the truth, Roddy. I'm sick and tired of having to live in one fucked place after the next. Nothing but heat and mosquitoes and bribe, bribe, bribe, one damned beaner after another with his hand out. Enough is enough."

"Mmmmm." Roderick Brixton paused thoughtfully, then turned another page of the loose-leaf folder. "It took chutzpah to put an ad in the *Herald Tribune.*"

"If Marlon Brando can do it and Raymond Burr can do it, I don't see what's keeping me."

"However, it was wise of you to check everything out."

"Oh, you have to in something like this. Rupert McIntyre says the same thing as Vesco, Roddy. Exactly the same. The South China Land Corporation can do exactly what it claims. Pak Tze Fan can take care of everything: finding the property, negotiating the price, haggling over bribes. Asia's where the action is, Roddy. Everybody says so. Why would we want to keep living in places like this? Can you give me one good reason why?"

"A well-organized and clearly written report, professional

work. It ought to be, with McIntyre's background and connections." Brixton turned a page. "And his price."

"McIntyre says Pak's the 'Mountain Lord' of a Chinese
tong society, a solid man to do business with. Safe. Vesco
would've made the move himself except he's such a pussy."

"The Society of the Red Lotus. Very colorful."

"What do they pay cops anyway? McIntyre deserves a
little moonlighting." Holt took another hit on his bong. He
held his breath, still talking: "I like all this extra stuff he put
in, but I guess I paid for it. You'll note there that while
McIntyre says Hong Kong has a reputation for being a safe
city and the police are highly regarded, everybody knows
they're infiltrated top to bottom by members of secret triad
societies. In fact, Pak has contacts in the overseas Chinese
communities throughout Southeast Asia."

"That's why he's safe."

"That's why he's safe, and that's how he finds the property. An unusual real estate agent."

"He deals drugs on the West Coast," Brixton said, still
reading the report.

"Of course he deals drugs; drugs and real estate's where
the money is."

"They say this . . . what's his name . . . here it is."
Brixton read from the report: "Kwok Lai Kwon, the
muscleman of this society, has more than forty-four confirmed kills, and is known among kung fu aficionados as the
'Fragrance of the Red Lotus.' "

"The odor of death. Isn't that wonderful?"

"McIntyre says Red Lotus is one of several Asian dealers
who buy their heroin from an alleged organization of poppy
growers formed and secretly run by an unknown Mr. X.
Uh-oh, listen to this: 'The Red Lotus has recently begun to
expand its West Coast markets'—ahh, where is it—'preci-
pitating a renewal of tong wars in Seattle, San Francisco, and
Los Angeles, and leading to rumors of a pending confronta-
tion with Mr. X.' Does this mess us up, Mr. Holt?"

"I don't see why. We'll be seeing him on another matter entirely. Read me the next part, Roddy."

"It says that Pak has recently purchased his own private island, Fong Wai Chau, as the base for the Red Lotus operations . . ."

"See what I mean? He's no virgin."

". . . 'Any raid on Fong Wai Chau would necessarily involve police boats or helicopters, and since Pak obviously has key connections in the Hong Kong police, the odds of a successful law enforcement operation are considered negligible. Although the island is subject to Hong Kong laws, it is for all practical purposes sovereign.' "

"I'll have to send Vesco a case of something for the McIntyre tip. Say, he photocopied an Interpol summary on me, did you see that? A guy like McIntyre throws in a little extra there, hell, there's a guy you can do business with."

"Red hair that's as 'kinky as an Ibo bride's,' " Brixton quoted from the report, then burst out laughing.

"A little flair there. Read me the whole bit, Roddy. It's fun to be immortal."

Roderick Brixton read from the photocopied entry:

" 'Gene Holt is a short man with a muscular, athletic body, and red hair one source said is "as kinky as an Ibo bride's." He has a long upper lip, a bob of a nose, and laugh lines have taken over his face. All this makes it difficult for him to lead a normal life outside of hiding. Holt himself has attributed the lines to his amusement at The Parade—by which he means fools who think somebody is going to do them a favor. Plastic surgeons have reportedly despaired of changing his countenance in all but minor ways.

" 'Holt has lived in a series of hideaways in the Third World where government officials and military officers are bribable, and the comings and goings of Learjets and yachts are as much a part of life as monsoons, dictators, and sweltering heat.' "

Holt laughed derisively. "If I wrote them a note, you

know, tormented them with my signature, do you suppose
Interpol would put an entry in Bob Vesco's dossier that he
can't play cribbage for shit? We could have it mailed from
Manhattan. Roddy, I see in today's summary where the
gentleman from Cartagena has not met his obligation.''

"He has not, I'm afraid.''

"See what I mean about operating down here? Now, that
guy ought to know none of us can do business unless people
pay their bills. It's not just losing the cocaine, Roddy, it's
not just that. The man has no sense of ethics, you understand, no idea of proper behavior among civilized people.''
Holt shook his head in sadness and dismay. "The South
Americans are too lunatic to be dependable business partners.
I think that's the Catholic foolishness, Roddy. That's the
problem with the man from Cartagena; I'm certain of it.
Worshiping virgins makes people lose perspective.''

"It must be terrible,'' Brixton said.

"The women are either whores or virgins, nothing in between. The beaners worship the señoritas, then turn them
into brood mares. That's an inversion of human nature. If the
women ever get pissed off down here, it'll be like South
Africa. In Asia, people know what women are for.''

"I think the men are probably safe as long as they've got
the church, Mr. Holt.''

"There are just too damned many players in the cocaine
game. They can take the stuff in on sailboats. They can fly it
over the Gulf. And pot? Hell, a smart beaner can truck it
across the American border in semis. And it's dangerous!
You get macho assholes hijacking sailboats and wasting one
another, not to mention United States marshals, which is
very rotten PR, Roddy. Very rotten. You get guys from *60
Minutes* down firing questions like God's lawyers.''

"It jars the Americans from their lethargy.''

"Well, hell, yes, it does. It pisses 'em off! It's stupid and
totally unnecessary. There's just no way to exert any discipline in a situation like this. You spend all that money for

bribes and you just never know when they're going to screw you over. Never. Fuck you, gringo! That's their attitude.''

"It does get tiresome, I agree. Shall I offer a contract on the man from Cartagena, Mr. Holt?''

"He doesn't leave me any choice. Now, you take Asia, Roddy. We'll be dealing with Malays, and Malaysians, Indonesians, Filipinos, Japanese, Koreans, Chinese, the Thais. Those people are serious about bribes. They know what the deal is. You pay a man money and he gives you a service; he doesn't go for your kidneys. If you don't bargain hard, he'll walk off with your shorts, but that's another matter. A Chinaman'll deliver every time.'' Holt bunched his face and relieved himself of gas. "Do these people have to put beans in everything? Whew!''

"I'll try another chef, sir. When I saw Vesco's man Sammy in Bermuda last week, he said he knows of a wonderful Belgian who's single and likes adventure. He's wonderful with sauces, Sammy says; if we don't take him, Vesco will.''

"Vesco wants him?'' Holt looked momentarily interested. He would have loved to have stolen Vesco's prospective chef just to razz his fellow fugitive. But Holt had learned never to be too optimistic in Latin America. He sagged. "We've tried that, Roddy. No matter how good the chef, he still has to have something to work with. We call attention to ourselves if we have too much stuff shipped in. When the chef orders a chicken and the chicken looks like a roadrunner, then you know it ain't gonna taste like a capon. Skin and gristle. They don't have truffles and asparagus at the market in these places. They have beans and rice. What would the Belgian cook? Skinny chicken Barranquilla. Bony fish à la Managua. Think if we lived in Asia, Roddy. The Chinese are everywhere. We could eat Chinese food. Succulent duck. Wonderful roast pork.''

"That would be nice, sir! Asia does sound nice.''

"God, it's been years since I've gotten to sneak into a casino. Read the part about Macao."

" 'The Society of the Red Lotus is especially powerful in the Portuguese colony of Macao, where Pak Tze Fan has been seen openly consorting with international fugitives in the gambling casinos.' "

"See? I might even be able to have a little fun once in a while. These societies are sort of like a Masonic lodge, with kung fu, secret signs, and blood oaths. We can take vacations in Bali, maybe, or Penang." Holt's face twisted. He sucked in his breath, waiting for a pain in his bowels to recede. He said, "You know, Roddy, Chinese food never does this to me. Never. I can eat as much as I want and I don't gas up like this."

"This could be an expensive proposition, Mr. Holt. Are we to draw on our reserves in the Caymans?"

Gene Holt looked surprised. "Draw on our reserves? Don't be silly, Roddy. Who wants to spend his own money? Somebody else will pick up the tab. It's always more fun that way."

Brixton grinned. "We'll take all the extras, eh, Mr. Holt?"

"I'll figure out a way. All a person has to do is read a newspaper every day. That's where we found the ad for the South China Land Corporation. That's where we'll find the money for our island."

8

THE message from Hong Kong arrived two weeks after Lucien Salvant got back to Seville: *Does no ties mean you are single, an orphan, what? When and where were you born? Why did you place the ad? Can you be specific? Hong Kong man.* There was a Hong Kong cable address and a post office box for Salvant's reply.

Dear Hong Kong man: I am an orphan. I am divorced, and I have no children. My adopted parents are dead. I have no brothers or sisters. I was born on January 28, 1946, in New Orleans, Louisiana. I am an associate professor of English, Quantrell College, New Orleans, on a sabbatical leave which ends September 1. I am sick of faculty meetings, grading papers, and trying to understand whatever it is the Yale critics are saying.

While the imaginative vagabonds were in Ibiza scoping bare breasts on the beach or in Morocco smoking hashish, Lucien Salvant stayed in Seville. It was pleasant in Seville, and cheap; the tourists were on the Costa del Sol. Also, nothing beat the *calamares*—fried squid—and *tinto*, a red table wine that sold for fifty cents a liter. Salvant was in Seville because of Miguel de Cervantes and Ernest Hemingway.

Seville was home of La Feria, a high-spirited, drunkenly wholesome affair, said to be the largest celebration in Europe. Since La Feria did not attempt to challenge Rio's orgy of the erotic and bizarre, Salvant had never heard of it until he arrived in town. La Feria was a distinctly Spanish affair. It was a celebration of things Spanish: music and dancing, splendid horsemen, and lovely women. In Seville, it seemed, every night was a cause for celebration. The city's bars bulged at night—doors open, singers and drinkers and talkers spilling onto the sidewalks.

Salvant thought a green-eyed Spanish girl dancing the *Sevillana* was especially wonderful. He admired the sexy flash of thigh when she sent her skirts sailing. He was an appreciative voyeur when she teased the room with smoldering looks over her bare shoulder, arrogant and proud—at once erotic, grand, dramatic, and out of reach, *amigo*. Salvant knew Gloria Steinem would not have approved, but he couldn't help himself. He thought the Spanish dancers were fabulous.

There was a reckoning for this excess. On Sunday, the many Holy Virgins for whom Seville's streets were named exacted their terms. This was the rhythm of joy and pain in Seville.

From the day he arrived, Salvant set out on foot each day to learn about Seville: the splendor of its avenues; the life of its bars and back streets; its monuments to various virgins and saints; the charm of its bridges; and the taste of its coffee. When a cop with a whistle and white gloves tried to calm a honking snarl of Spanish drivers, the city belonged to Cervantes; at the *plaza de toros* on a Saturday afternoon, it was Hemingway.

In the evening, Salvant considered his adventures each day over a pipe of hashish on the roof of the largely empty building where he lived. The wind was warm. Clothes on lines strung across to the next building flapped as soft as leaves.

Loco martes was the first thing Lucien Salvant thought of when he returned from his month-long foray in Ireland; the thought was not so much prompted by the lure of cheap booze as it was by a vague hope of spending a warming night with a companionable female. *Loco martes*—that is, Crazy Tuesday—at La Casa Quixote was a tradition for transients of the American community in Seville. Every Tuesday, La Casa's clientele could drink all they wanted from eight o'clock to midnight for three hundred pesetas—about two U.S. dollars. The ensuing drunkenness was conducted in the familiar mother English.

Salvant had been in Seville for four months, so was considered a veteran, but after his Ireland trip there was a large sprinkling of new faces among the regulars. One of these was a flashy Latin with curly brown hair and broad shoulders, a stylish dresser with a grin that stayed in place, enjoying life. He was trim and athletic, a talker. "Frank Quetglas. You're Lucien Salvant, I bet. I thought everybody here was under twenty-five, but one of the *jevas* at the bar said wait until Salvant gets back from Ireland. 'He's degenerating before your very eyes,' she said."

Salvant looked at the gathering of college girls by the bar and sighed. "They have those marvelous bodies—so wonderful to look at—those butts!"

"I've sworn off *singar* for a while," Quetglas said. "It can be done." He looked rueful.

"Sex? Sworn off?"

"See the one over there? *La jevita* there in the Calvin Kleins?"

"How could I miss?"

"*La lleve* Thursday night in a park a couple of blocks over. She got all *caliente* and wanted to, so I thought, what the hell. I did it to her dog style in the rain and people came by and saw us. I was so embarrassed. I was disgusted with myself. I've sworn off for a while.''

"Glad I didn't happen by.''

"Shall we have ourselves another?'' Quetglas led the way to the bar. "In Miami, the bartender'd giggle. Can you believe how the Spanish drink rum and Coke?''

"It's wonderful.''

"Dos Cuba Libres,'' Quetglas said to the bartender. "Say, what are you doing here, Lou? The good places are Ibiza, where everybody's *basilando* with one another, *mucha concha,* or the Moroccan mountains where you can eat, sleep, and smoke hash for twenty bucks a week.''

"I'm an English professor on sabbatical. When I got to Spain and had my first drink poured by a Spanish bartender, I knew I'd found my place.'' Salvant watched in admiration as the bartender poured a slender glass half full of rum and topped it off with Coke. "I've even learned to like these. On September first I'm like Cinderella. I'll have to go back to Quantrell College to explain to my students one more time— God, how many times now—that the word 'hopefully' is an adverb, and what it is adverbs do.'' He held his glass to Quetglas for a toast. "May you pork the brunette on clean sheets! By the way, what the hell kind of name is Quetglas anyway, and what is it you do for a living?''

Quetglas laughed. "I'm a Cuban, a Miami Cuban. I figure, hey, I speak English, I learned Spanish from my folks but can't write it worth a damn. I made it all the way through college without taking a Spanish course. That's why I'm here: to polish my Spanish so I can peddle bananas, chocolate, and coffee. I want to get into the importing business.''

"I can't imagine why you'd want to brush up your Spanish with these kids.'' Salvant gestured at the students swilling rum and Coke. "What did you study in college?''

"Physical education at first; I wanted to be a gymnast. I pumped iron and everything. You should have seen me, arms pumped up like stupid-looking balloons.'' Quetglas flexed his biceps and laughed. "Then drama, because I'd heard about the cast parties. Man, all that *tremendo bayu*. You wouldn't believe it. But now, man, now I want to be a businessman. I want to make some *dinero*. Some bucks. Know what I mean, man?"

Thus it was, across the river from la Torre del Oro—the Tower of Gold—the repository of the conquistador's New World treasure, and well into the trees of la Avenida de la Virgen Fatima, that Lucien Salvant fell in with the simpatico Frank Quetglas.

9

IN the first week of April, Lucien Salvant and Frank Quetglas went on a hashish-buying expedition to a town northeast of Seville. They left Seville in an aged bus that crossed the Rio Guadalquivir and followed the river north. They rode through several small towns. As they rode, they reviewed the responses from Salvant's message in the *International Herald*.

Quetglas, looking over Salvant's shoulder, said, "That's the one, man; there's something about it, Hong Kong and everything. Better than being a personal secretary to some dude in London. The London guy'll be wanting you to spank him or play with his *pinga*."

"I like Hong Kong too."

Quetglas had a beguiling, nonstop grin. He was an enthusiast, and Salvant liked him. He wore a red bandanna and three gold chains around his neck. He said, "This'll be good stuff, man! Good stuff, I swear on my mother."

Salvant didn't have much faith in Quetglas, who was much given to hyperbole and futile swearing about how Fidel

Castro had driven his family from Cuba. After a twenty-minute ride, during which Quetglas gave Salvant a monologue about how it was that Cuban women had the biggest butts on the planet, the bus pulled to a stop at yet another town, and they got out in the hot sun. They walked up a cobbled street that was deserted. The shops were closed. The people were inside taking a siesta. Salvant heard sparrows flutter and twitter, nothing else.

"I think we go this way," Quetglas said. He didn't seem sure.

"Are you certain?" Salvant felt a twinge of anxiety. Quetglas was lighthearted, unpredictable. Were all Cubans this crazy, Salvant wondered out loud—the women with unrivaled butts, the men merry gigolos like Quetglas.

"I'm pretty sure," Quetglas said. "You should see my sister's *poto,* man. *Que bonita fayo!* It's sweet. It really is. It's a Cuban butt, yes, but not giant, man. Just right. Trim." Quetglas held an imaginary *poto* in both hands. It made no difference that he was talking about his sister's derrière; he could just as well have been describing the fender of a new Ford.

They walked in the heat. The streets all looked the same and there was nobody to be found anywhere.

"A guy's *hermana* is something special, you know, Lucien. I'm a Catholic and we Catholics worry about our sisters and stuff. Probably the priests do it to us, all the time talking about the Virgin."

"You don't know where the hell you are, do you, Frank?" Salvant was hot, and mopped the sweat on his forehead with the back of his arm. He didn't want to have to sit in the heat until everybody was finished sleeping.

"No problem," Quetglas said. "We walk up here a ways and there's a square. All these streets eventually end up at the same square. The guy takes a little nap, then spends his time in a bar there. When they open up again, he'll be there. How else is he going to find buyers?"

Suddenly an old Austin mini with scarred silver paint pulled alongside.

"It's him, our man," Quetglas said. *"Qué suerte!"*

Salvant followed Quetglas into the back seat and they settled in, knees up to their chests, but then the Austin wouldn't start. Unfolding awkwardly, they got out to help push, then leaped in again. The driver and his friend took them through a series of cobbled streets.

After ten or twelve blocks, the mini stopped in yet another narrow street, and they were led into a small room. Beans were cooking in the kitchen. There was a card table in the middle of the room and the driver asked them to take a seat. Quetglas sat at the head of the table, under a huge crucifix.

A woman in her eighties, dressed in widow's black, helped Salvant and Quetglas with their chairs. The driver rolled four huge black eggs onto the table. They must have weighed a kilo each. They had a swirled, marbled appearance. It took Salvant a moment to realize they were incredible balls of hashish wrapped in cellophane. He had never seen anything like it. The driver also sat two half-eggs of hash on the table.

Quetglas was excited. "They look like dinosaur eggs, don't they, Lou? Great big eggs."

The widow picked up half an egg and sniffed it. *"Bueno, bueno,"* she said.

Quetglas said, "A smuggler'd have to have a pretty big asshole to handle one of those. Can you imagine that, Lucien?"

Salvant didn't care if he spent a few extra pesetas, but Quetglas was intent on saving every last peseta possible. Quetglas was from Miami and knew how this was done. He was in charge. "Don't mention money, man. Let me do the talking," he said.

Salvant was pleased to do that, since the only things he could do in Spanish were order food and ask directions. "Go for it, Frank."

"I know how these things are done. We Cubans love all this talk. We're famous for it."

The old woman put half an egg of hashish underneath Salvant's nose and babbled happily. *"Bueno, bueno,"* she said. She waited for Salvant's reaction.

Salvant took the egg and weighed it in his hand. The egg was heavy and cool. He liked the way it felt. He inhaled its aroma deeply and with much sincerity. He lingered over the odor, narrowed his eyes, considered it carefully. "Ummmmm! *Bueno!"* Salvant said solemnly.

Quetglas didn't want Salvant to act enthusiastic. He said, "Be cool, man. It's okay to smell, but don't say anything. You could cost us money."

The old woman smelled her half-egg as though it were a bowl of strawberries.

Quetglas rubbed his half-egg against his thigh, then smelled it, looking very serious.

"What the hell are you doing?" Salvant said.

"We gotta find some way to bring them down," Quetglas said. He looked unhappy and said something to the men in Spanish. "I told them we wanted the black stuff." He looked miffed. "This isn't the black stuff."

"They could be balls of henna for all I know," Salvant said.

"I told them I wanted the black stuff," Quetglas said. "That's why we rode all the way out here. This isn't black."

Salvant smelled the hash and waited. At last Quetglas and the Spaniards made a deal, and the driver cut the hash with a knife. He weighed it on a balance scale.

"I got us ten pesetas off on each gram," Quetglas said. He'd gotten a bargain. His pride was intact. He was excited.

"That'd be about seven cents a gram. Helluva deal!" Salvant said. He shook his head.

Quetglas, still beaming, started to walk out the door.

"Aren't you going to pay them?" Salvant said.

"Oh." Quetglas was embarrassed. He'd been so excited about his seven-cents-a-gram savings that he'd forgotten to pay, and what was worse, everybody knew it. He unbuckled his trousers and fumbled with some blue swimming trunks underneath. His money was on an inside pocket of his trunks. The pocket was twisted, and Quetglas couldn't get at the money. He fumbled frantically. It looked as if he were digging at his genitals, and everybody laughed, including the little old lady. She especially thought the good-looking, excitable Quetglas was hilarious.

"Having fun, Frank?" Salvant asked. "Just where did you hide that money anyway?"

"It's here. It's here in a little pocket, but the damned thing's twisted." Quetglas grinned foolishly. He had an ability to laugh at himself that was charming. "The pocket. The pocket's twisted." He fumbled at his crotch, and they all laughed louder, him included.

He finally got the money and paid for the hash. Everybody was happy. They'd gotten a deal. The young men had made a sale and could buy some gas for their mini. The old woman would get some salt pork for her beans.

"Buen dia," she said. She spoke Spanish in the quick Andalusian manner.

The mini refused to start again. Quetglas and Salvant pushed as before. The two young men drove them to the bus stop where they could catch a ride back to Seville. The Americans had met some young women the night before. Quetglas was confident. "We're gonna get laid, man. We'll get high and get laid, wait and see." There was a communist poster on the whitewashed wall across the street from the bus stop. He read the poster and said, *"Que comemierdas!* What shit-eaters!"

"What does it say?" Salvant asked.

"It's the communists. Change with us, they say." Quetglas shook his head. *"Idiotas!"* he said. "People like buying things and selling things. Doing a little dealing. It's in their blood. *Comemierdas.*"

"One of your basic urges, like coveting your neighbor's ass or his wife," Salvant said.

"That's it exactly! It's biblical."

When Lucien Salvant got back to Seville, there was another message waiting from his mysterious Hong Kong correspondent:

Are you prepared to live in Hong Kong? Good life, few responsibilities. Extremely high pay. Long-term contract.

Salvant grinned. This was spooky stuff. Fun. He wanted to travel in Morocco before he returned to the purgatory that awaited in New Orleans. He answered:

Yes, so far, but need details. Moving in two days. Contact c/o American Express office, Tangier. Salvant.

Two hours before he was to take the bus to Algeciras where he would get to see the backside of Gibraltar—which to his imagination was as mysterious and fun as the dark side of the moon—Lucien Salvant received another message:

You will be contacted in Morocco by my representative, Stanley Ho.

10

EAST is East and Ella Nidech, leggy in her designer jeans, hooded Radcliffe College sweat shirt, and wearing Nike running shoes, was definitely of Rudyard Kipling's West. For all their alleged progress in the treatment of women, nobody ever accused the Japanese or Chinese or Moslems of being ready to have a woman represent them in something like the China buy. Nidech was the first customer into the White Stag pub when it opened at eleven-thirty. This was as she and the drummer had agreed upon. An old man in loose blue trousers and dirty T-shirt was sweeping the litter from the previous night's closing. Nidech took a seat in a booth facing the street and lifted her feet to accommodate the passing broom.

Nidech had been a female supernerd for four years at Radcliffe and then had gone to Johns Hopkins to study international relations because she'd wanted to be a spy; her mother blamed the obsession on Ella's watching *Get Smart*. She thought she had to have straight A's all the way to her doctorate, and would have made it had she not run afoul of statistics.

After all that work, after she had finally landed the Hong Kong job, everybody said if anything really good came along, she should not get her heart set on following it through. She relieved an itch under her bra strap and slipped the safety off the Walther PPK in her handbag. She retrieved a tiny recorder from the handbag and fastened it to the bottom of the table with a turn of her wrist.

The old man with the broom had left the front doors open in order that the bar might be aired by the sweet and sour odors of the Wanchai, a sex district gone to seed—a combination of carbon monoxide, mildew, sweat, semen, urine, and garlic. Nidech's skin was already sticky, and the day had hardly begun.

A near biblical darkness descended, the first *splat, splat* signaling the coming downpour that lashed into the peeling facades of strip joints and come-on parlors. Then a Chinese man in an immaculately tailored three-piece suit stepped inside and folded his black umbrella. He carried a neat little briefcase, and might well have stepped in from Wall Street. He strode directly to Nidech and extended his hand. "Miss Flora Lewis, I take it. I am Stanley Ho."

Nidech nodded. "Pleased to meet you, Mr. Ho."

Ho sat and put the briefcase on the seat beside Nidech. "Would you like coffee?"

"Yes."

Ho said something to the sweeper in Cantonese and the sweeper disappeared to the back of the pub. "I'm a businessman, Miss Lewis. I don't ordinarily talk to people in your line of work. I followed your instructions to the letter in coming here. I appreciate your patience in explaining how that is done. It was very interesting."

"If you followed them to the letter, we'll be fine. Everything we do has a reason. Thank you for your cooperation."

"Before I begin, my employer asks your assurance of confidentiality. This is, ah, a delicate matter."

"My firm understands completely and sticks by its word. We do require the identity of your employer."

"He is Sing Sing Boyd."

"Sing Sing Boyd?" Nidech seemed momentarily surprised.

"Of the kung fu movies, yes."

Sing Sing Boyd! Ella Nidech let that digest. The kung fu men had Chinese secrets to sell? "Well, tell me what Mr. Boyd has in mind, Mr. Ho."

"As you probably know, Mr. Boyd does more than make kung fu movies. He's quite a wealthy man, actually. He seems to be interested in everything. He owns his own fleet of fishing boats. He has a fashion line he markets in the United States. He owns companies that make imitation brand-name television sets and tape decks. I'm a . . ." Stanley Ho paused, as though searching for the proper word.

"You're a salesman," Nidech said.

Ho smiled. "Thank you. Yes, that's exactly it. As you may know, in 1997 the British lease will expire and Hong Kong colony will revert to the Chinese. The agreement is that the Guandong province of south China will be a special administrative unit where capitalism will be allowed to flourish with only a modest amount of socialist intervention. The truth is that Hong Kong's a thriving, productive city and the Chinese want to keep it that way. Mr. Boyd naturally wants to protect his interests come 1997."

"I see. Of course he does." Nidech waited while a young man delivered their coffee.

When the young man had left, Ho listened to the rain for a moment, then continued. "As you know, several years ago there was a change of economic policy in China. A faction loyal to Deng Xiaoping was successful in introducing a number of measures aimed at reinvigorating the economy. The Chinese leadership reintroduced competition and returned to the market—with limits, of course. Unfortunately Beijing doesn't have any recent experience in capitalism. In 1949 the business community fled, some to Taiwan with the Kuomintang and the rest here to Hong Kong.''

"Beijing shouldn't have any trouble. They say you never forget how to ride a bicycle.''

Ho smiled. "I assure you, Beijing wishes it were that easy. The truth is that the Chinese have wasted all those years since 1949 on an economic system that never had a chance of working in the first place. It was embarrassing, but they didn't want China to remain impoverished forever. Boyd has done his best to help Beijing out—functioning rather like one of your American business consultants. In the process, he made friends in unusual positions in Beijing. Incidentally, after China began experimenting with free enterprise, senior officials warmed quickly to the charms of the capitalist way.''

"I'll bet they did.''

"The Politburo decreed that to get rich is to be a patriot. The comrades themselves want desperately to be patriots, Ms. Lewis, but none of them have any investment capital. Economic equality has always been a joke in the Soviet Union, of course, but China has been different. The Chinese leadership needs start-up money like everybody else. The Chinese banks don't have the money. Nobody has it. There are those officials who do, however, have access to classified military and government documents. If your government spends a fortune to steal these documents, they ought to be worth something on the market.''

Stanley Ho opened the briefcase and gave Ella Nidech a stapled document. "Would you like to look at this? This was given to Mr. Boyd by one of his acquaintances in Beijing. Take your time, I'll order us some more coffee. Would you like breakfast? I can have some brought over from next door. How about a good British breakfast with bacon and broiled tomatoes? They have British breakfasts here. Bangers if you like. Would that be tasty?''

"More coffee'd be fine,'' Nidech said. She began looking

through the document. It was in dense technical Mandarin and contained what she recognized as maps and designations of Chinese units deployed on the frontier with Russia. "And all this says?"

"It gives details of units, weapons, and training. These are quality secrets. Do you think your firm might be interested?"

"If they're accurate, possibly."

"Mr. Boyd has several well-placed sources. There is a cost, as I said, and it may be substantial depending on the material. As I said, officials in Beijing are very anxious to earn start-up capital."

"And the cost . . ."

". . . will depend on the seller's assessment of how difficult it would be for you to steal them yourself. Mr. Boyd would receive a fifteen percent commission for his services as middleman, plus a small favor—as a gesture that your company is a serious, responsible business partner."

Nidech, listening, took a sip of coffee.

Ho continued, "Mr. Boyd has figured out a way to wash three-point-nine trillion Hong Kong dollars into U.S. dollars—that's a half-billion U.S.—and bring them back into Hong Kong through a third party. Hong Kong does not tax corporate income earned outside the colony. It will cost the American taxpayers nothing if the IRS cooperates, and Mr. Boyd will make a substantial sum."

"I'm sure my company would insist on a closer examination of the document before it can commit itself to any kind of continuing arrangement."

"Certainly. Take it! As I said, it is a sample. Your own satellite photographs should verify some of it. Take your time. If your firm agrees to help Mr. Boyd launder his money, then Mr. Boyd will help you out by acting as middleman between you and his friends in China. These gentlemen will then have enough capital to manufacture pop-up toasters and baseball bats for export to the United States." Ho grinned wryly.

"Plus Sing Sing Boyd gets to avoid paying the British colonial government taxes on half a billion dollars."

"Everybody profits. Do you think we may be able to do business, Miss Lewis?"

"I have no idea. I'm not the one who decides."

Ho said, "Certainly. I understand completely. Let us know when you decide, and we can negotiate the necessary arrangements for doing business." He gave her a business card that said he was a Hong Kong tax consultant. "It has been a pleasure meeting you."

Nidech and Ho slid out of the booth at the same time, only as Nidech scooted, she retrieved the Company's recorder from under the table and slipped it into her handbag. She shook hands with Stanley Ho and they left the White Stag in opposite directions.

Ella Nidech took the far side of the street, the sunny side. Her interview with Stanley Ho was going to be the start of something fabulous, she knew, and it was hers. Sing Sing Boyd was peddling secrets for Chinese officials. She decided she'd have to see one of his half-baked kung fu movies. She strode across the street, thinking, hot damn!

The roar of a motorcycle . . .

From behind Ella Nidech, from nowhere . . .

. . . . the yank of her arm . . . her handbag gone . . .

"Motherfucker!" she screamed at the biker's back. This was delivered in equal parts of surprise, rage, and shock that she'd been so stupid. Christ, had she ever screwed up.

The biker straightened suddenly; Nidech saw neat spots of red walk up his white T-shirt. The corpse dropped Nidech's handbag; the cycle veered and headed for the other side of the street where it crashed into the side of a parked delivery van.

Nidech sprinted for the cycle. A bullet zinged by her foot.

She dived, rolling.

The killer was going for her!

She was up, cutting left. Another bullet. Shit!

She cut right, left, then right again as bullets whined to the right and left of her. She grabbed the handbag and dived at the same time, protecting her face with her shoulder.

She got on her feet sprinting again, cutting left, then right, bullets zinging and whining. As she rounded the corner to safety, a hail of bullets splattered against the edge of the building.

She was alive. She felt a fabulous rush. She jumped into her Honda, started the engine, and mashed it into low gear. She was awash with sweat. She laid smoke like Shirley Muldowney, laughing, hands trembling, riding an adrenaline high, knowing why it was that men went to war. She kept an eye on the rearview mirror. She turned on the radio, punched up a rock and roll station, and turned the volume up to ear-splitting. She geared the Honda in and out of turns like Richie Ginther or Phil Hill. She was alive! Yes!

But who the hell was the biker?

An ordinary thief, no doubt. A Hong Kong purse snatcher.

And who had tried to kill her?

Those were small-caliber shots that came in a nutty hail. The killer had laid the slugs up the biker's back as if he were working a sewing machine.

Dysentery in Mozambique! She knew immediately what had happened. She might have known Neely wouldn't trust her alone with the China buy. Without telling her, James Burlane had ridden shotgun. A baby-sitter! She'd been baby-sat, and then Burlane had seen her hand the bacon to a snatch artist. Every intelligent woman in the world knew it was stupid to carry her handbag on the street side. Snatch and roar was a universal M.O. for urban thieves.

Nidech felt humiliated that one of her colleagues had seen her screw up like that. Then the bastard had casually stitched the biker and made her dance like a greenhorn at a dude ranch. Ella Nidech was furious. She'd damned near pissed her pants while that asshole had looped slugs at her feet. She resolved by God to do something about it! Some people dammit just had to have their asses kicked into the twentieth century. She couldn't very well send a letter to *Ms.* magazine, but there was someone she could write to and get a little action. Indeed there was.

11

THE Company technical people accepted the alleged secrets from the Hong Kong drummer with much merriment. Documents of this kind almost inevitably turned out to be bogus, forged by third parties, or transparent horseshit. The lab examiners had no way of knowing where the document had come from and assumed from the beginning that it was yet another crude attempt at disinformation.

The drummer's sample turned out to be genuine. Even the crankiest paranoids were forced to concur; no application of telling chemical or examination by microscope suggested otherwise. Everything was correct: the age and kind of paper, the ink, eccentricities of language. The units and their disposition were exactly correct; they matched satellite photographs. Those professionals responsible for estimating such things as the numbers and kinds of planes, tanks, trucks, and armored personnel carriers scrambled to see how their figures matched up. This was followed by cheers and champagne in some offices, and a shaking of heads in others.

Chinese bureaucrats selling state secrets to raise venture

capital! Peter Neely, having once risen through the corporate ranks of IBM, did not seem surprised at what appeared to be a bizarre consequence of Deng Xiaoping's efforts to reintroduce private enterprise into the Chinese economy.

In spite of the fact that Ara Schott logged Sing Sing Boyd in as the Chief Thief, he still maintained the offering was bogus. Schott never assumed anything was genuine. Nobody, but nobody at the Company could match Schott for suspicion and cynicism. Even after the technical people said the paper and ink were genuine, and the language authentic, he complained that the Company was somehow being had.

Just how the Company was being had, Schott couldn't say. He'd never before been so frustrated by lack of evidence to support his paranoia. This was apparently a genuine document and they were being told they could buy more if they wanted. All they had to do was pay Sing Sing Boyd 15 percent commission. What is more, Boyd was doing it with aplomb, as though he were opening a candy store. Here, have a free jawbreaker, kid, and remember there're more where those came from. Schott was confounded by all this.

Neely asked Burlane what he thought of it.

"Pure methane." Burlane held his slightly twisted nose in his left hand. "Methane's always a good investment. It costs money to start a business, even in China. How else're these guys going to get the yuan they need? I say buy."

Neely considered the advice, saying nothing.

"If they got rich under Mao, they got tortured or thrown in prison. Now they're patriots. I don't know why you're all acting so shocked. Methane was inevitable once the Chinese started introducing free enterprise; it's human nature, Peter. Hey, one billion Chinese! This is the future. I'd get in on the action if I were you. Help these guys out and help yourself. Everybody wins."

"Seriously now, Mr. Burlane. I have to report back to the NSC."

"What's the matter with paying Sing Sing Boyd a commission for brokering Chinese secrets? They've got something to sell, and we want to buy. He sends out his drummer and gets us together. He's an agent. That's an honorable profession.''

"What if the Maoists find out?''

"We don't know who Boyd's friends are, do we? They could be members of the Politburo for all we know. I agree that it would be a delicate matter if knowledge of the arrangement got into the hands of Deng Xiaoping's political enemies. I would restrict need-to-know, that's true.''

In times of crisis Neely always allowed his mind to be changed by the last person he talked to. Since Neely always consulted Ara Schott for major decisions, this meant that Schott really ran the Company, not Neely. Neither of them was bothered by this arrangement. Owing to his lack of political friends, Schott knew he didn't have a chance at Neely's job. Neely himself sometimes longed for the corporate world where he could make some real money, but Neely's wife enjoyed politics and Georgetown cocktail parties, so returning to IBM was impossible.

Ara Schott said, "This is very delicate, I think.''

"I agree, Ara.''

Thus Peter Neely asked the National Security Council to consider the delicate matter. After he finished the summary prepared for him by Schott, Neely said to the President, "We've had the document examined carefully. There seems to be no question of its bona fides. It is our tentative conclusion that Mr. Ho and Mr. Boyd could not be working directly for Beijing, but for themselves as they say. Beijing would never take the risk of losing the details of their Russian defense to the Kremlin. What if Ella Nidech had turned out to be a Soviet agent? Or one of us?''

The secretary of state, Stuart Kaplan, doodled on a pad, saying nothing.

Henry McArthur, the secretary of defense, said, "Hell yes, let's buy 'em.'' Then, just as quickly, he sensed danger.

His eyelids halted mid-blink so that he looked like Robert Mitchum. McArthur's instinct for danger had more than once saved him from his lack of intelligence. He finished blinking. His mouth closed slowly. He licked his lips. He had remembered the general who had told him that the first three rules of combat were to keep your head down, your mouth shut, and to stay the fuck out of swamps. This was what the CIA assholes called mud.

The President was an older man, jovial, who had prospered by being impervious to blame, a condition to which all presidents aspired but few attained. It was as though blame in the general sense came at him in a hail of particulars, like tracers from a demonic machine gun—a tumble of things gone wrong. But the President, television commentators said, wore an invisible shield, something out of *Flash Gordon* or *Star Trek*; a hail of blame zinged off the shield while he grinned affably and told jokes.

At the meeting of the National Security Council he listened to the details of Stanley Ho's wonderful offer, biting his lower lip, his left eye narrowed in concentration.

Secretly the members of the NSC all wanted to buy everything Boyd had to sell. They were curious and wondered what would happen. But nobody wanted to take responsibility. They all wanted the President to speak up. If he said yes and something went wrong, Dan Rather and Jack Anderson would blame him. The President would grin and joke his way through the ensuing fuss. The television people would poop out first because there was no action to tape, then the newspapers would run out of new leads, after which the story would be left to the history books, which nobody read.

Once the story was history, the administration was safe.

However, of the ruling entourage, only the President had a full invisible shield against blame and responsibility for screwing up. The reason the President's advisors sensed mud before the secretary of defense was because McArthur was a personal friend of the President and so shared much of the storied shield. The rest of them were protected to lesser degrees, and so were by instinct cautious from the start.

"Can we trust this man Boyd?" Secretary Kaplan asked.

"Judging from our limited previous dealings with him, yes," Neely said.

"Boyd's half white isn't he?" McArthur said.

Kaplan looked cooly at McArthur. He said, "What would happen if the Chinese intelligence service got its hands on one of the enterprising comrades at the photocopying machine? We need to think that through, I would imagine."

The President looked alarmed. "Didn't they . . . didn't they say they were going to . . . they promised to order their peasants to like cheese, didn't they? And they're buying our wheat for their noodles." The President fell into a thoughtful silence. He cleared his throat.

Neely said, "There are risks in a matter as delicate as this. We could be looking at muddy country, yes."

"Big mud?" The President concentrated.

"Pretty big, Mr. President. If the Maoists found out, it wouldn't be good for Deng's people."

The President said, "Mr. Neely, what is the name of our special fellow? The curious one you sent to talk to me."

"James Burlane, Mr. President."

"Yes, Jones Voorlaing. That's it. He's our, our—what's that called?"

"Our delicate man, Mr. President."

"Yes. For these situations. What does Voorlaing think?"

"Classic methane, he says." Neely, reading from his pad, quoted Burlane's opinion. The members of the council were noncommital as before. As before they watched the President for a cue.

"Methane," McArthur said. He looked eager.

Catching the spirit, the President grinned. "Voorlaing's right, isn't he? This administration believes in the free market. We . . . we have to stand by our principles." He laughed out loud.

Around the table bellies rocked with laughter. Quicker than Ed McMahon, they were.

McArthur said, "That's absolutely right, Mr. President."

"The market's a wonderful place." Stuart Kaplan smiled and folded his eyeglasses. If he was being ironic or was disgusted, the secretary of state concealed it with diplomatic tact. He stared pensively at his whitened knuckles.

The President liked the response. He said, "Sure, support a communist capitalist!" That settled the issue. "We'll let Jones Voorlaing do it."

Neely said, "Mr. President, I think James Burlane should stay in the United States until we clear up some of the details with respect to the American connection of Stanley Ho's proposition. Later on, Mr. Burlane can join our station chief in Hong Kong."

"And who is that?" the President asked.

Neely stopped breathing. He'd always referred to Ella Nidech by her current code. Neely hated this affirmative action bullshit. If it weren't for the watchful eye of Senator Rollo Hinkley, he'd have sent Burlane straight to Hong Kong. "Nidech, Mr. President?"

"Midick?" The President looked amused. "Do I know him?"

"Ella Nidech, Mr. President."

"You call him Al, do you? Capable of delicate work, is he?"

"I've every confidence, Mr. President."

"It's settled then. Midick." The President shook his head, still grinning. He rose, signaling that the meeting was over. Then he stopped, his hand at his chin, and said, "Peter, can I speak to you privately, please." Waiting for the room to clear, the President said, "Do you think the Cubs will do it this year, Peter?"

Neely, who maintained the President's confidence in his performance as DCI by keeping up on the Chicago Cubs, said, "I think it depends on their pitching, Mr. President. If

Timmy Farr can round out the rotation and if their late-relievers can come through, they've got a chance. I think it was smart picking up Abell. His knuckler really hops, they say. Another Hoyt Wilhelm or Gaylord Perry.''

"He's crafty. A professional.'' The President saw that the room had cleared. He looked grave.

Which is when Neely realized the reason for the private chat. Garry Trudeau was back in the *Post* making fun of the administration for its inability to catch the phantom outrage, Gene Holt. The President didn't like being laughed at.

The President said, "I was wondering if there is any progress on the Jones Voorlaing delicate matter. The business with that Blowfish fellow, Gene Holt.''

"We're analyzing reports from South America. I think we're closing in on him, Mr. President,'' Neely lied. "He's a slippery one, always on the move.''

The President, confident because of Neely's encyclopedic knowledge of the Chicago Cubs, grinned and sang a little tune:

"Old Jonesie came out with his old rusty gun.
He swore he would shoot him if he didn't run.''

Then the President turned serious. "Jonesie'll take care of it,'' he said.

When Peter Neely got back to Langley he sent a short message to Ella Nidech in Hong Kong:

Dear Ms. Lewis. Yes to the drummer's kind offer. We prefer to negotiate each item separately, however, with the option to withdraw if the chief thief has misrepresented any of the terms or items. Hastings and I will be sending along instructions. Meanwhile, keep us current, please. Parson.

Neely thought of adding that James Burlane would be coming to assist her once the American end of the proposition was clear, but thought better of it; better for the time being to let her think the China buy was entirely hers. There was an edge to her report that he found unsettling. Although Nidech didn't mention it specifically, Neely had the feeling that something had gone wrong in Hong Kong three days earlier. Burlane had reported nothing unusual in his mission of riding shotgun on her transaction, but Neely wondered if she might not have left something out.

Four days later, the Treasury Department, which had been watching Clint and Flub Bonner for reasons of its own, reported that the inscrutable, natty drummer had visited the Texans in their Houston digs, and on the following day had taken a flight to Madrid. Such reports were routinely keyed into a computer at Langley, Virginia, so that the Company's vast network of covert operations—a thousand bats zooming in the night—might somehow be coordinated.

12

WHEN Stanley Ho was still Ho Lin-Bai, he had ridden the MTR or a tram, but now that he was on the road for Sing Sing Boyd, he rode in limousines—this one a pretentious Bentley that glided soundlessly toward the obelisks that rose, Hong Kong-like, above Houston and reflected the sky with windows tinted colors found nowhere in nature.

Ho was born in a New Territories village and learned how to sell in a luggage stall in Kowloon. He moved quickly to handbags, then cameras and ghetto blasters, followed by jade and ivory. Finally, he sold diamonds and precious jewelry. Not only did he have a mind for numbers, but from the very beginning, Ho showed a nice touch for closing deals. Later, he went to work for Sing Sing Boyd and became Stanley Ho, elegant in his three-piece suit.

This trip was special. Ho was going one on two against Clint and Flub Bonner. Ho had been in on some real deals before—one for so many Hong Kong dollars that it had sent shivers up his spine. But Clint and Flub were Texas oilmen.

He fancied they were rather like Bobby and J.R. Ewing on the telly.

Stanley Ho wished fervently that the Bonner brothers wouldn't expect him to eat cheese hors d'oeuvres. *Gweilos* inevitably brought on the cheese, a little treat. Ho's tastes didn't include cheese. He couldn't abide the yellowish goo, thought it had the taste and consistency of yellow shit. Then all that nonsense about aging it like wine. Aging that stuff? That was as bad as Filipinos sucking fermented duck eggs. Yuch!

To close a sale in Bangkok once, he'd eaten—smiling all the while—a meal that so seared his mouth and throat that he'd been forced to go to a physician for a tincture. Ho was a disciplined and experienced salesman; he did what he had to do. Ho had closed deals with Muslims who didn't like the Chinese, with crazed Filipinos, and careful, arrogant Japanese, but he knew he'd have to be extra careful with the Bonners. They were exemplary at what they were known to privately call the Texas high poke—screwing everything in their path—although their fun had so far been modified by their father's lawyers.

The Bentley turned in to a walled, guarded estate and up a leisurely road that curved through gracious gardens. Ho found himself carried past a mile or two of stables, tennis courts, and swimming pools to the grounds surrounding a wonderful antebellum mansion painted an awful mauve, and complementary bilious colors, with white trim. The house stood in splendid isolation, for which, Ho supposed, the Bonners' neighbors must be grateful.

When the car stopped, Ho opened the door to the sound of barking Irish setters. A doorman escorted him inside where he was met by a second manservant, who took him to the study where Clint and Flub Bonner awaited.

"Mr. Stanley Ho," the servant announced.

And there stood the two *gweilos* whom he recognized from photographs in magazine articles. They both had the same bony jaws, but one was short and broad, with a little belly, and the other tall and lean. The short one, wearing designer blue jeans and a tweed jacket, offered his hand and said, "Flub. You betcha!"

"Clint. Damned right!" Clint Bonner wore designer jeans and a sweater.

"You Americans!" Ho said. He had been told Americans liked to joke. Ho lacked a sense of humor as he understood the term, but he did his best. He remembered, too late, the ritual of the whiskey and wondered if he would have to drink that piss.

"How about a drink, Mr. Ho?" Flub said. "We got some good bourbon whiskey here, Tennessee sippin' whiskey."

"A special treat," Ho said.

As Flub poured the whiskey he said, "Yours is one of the more interesting propositions we've heard in some time, and that's a fact, Mr. Ho."

"Flub and me like it laid right out, hair up, so we can have a good look it, if you know what we mean. If we catch you leaving something out, we don't do business."

Stanley Ho was amused but didn't show it. On the contrary, he was a model of sincerity. For all their talk about high poking, there was a limit to what Clint and Flub could spend without the approval of Cactus Jack's lawyers. Ho took a sip of the awful whiskey and told the Bonners about Boyd's empire of the martial arts screen, and Boyd's many friends in Beijing. "One of these contacts is capable of delivering to Mr. Boyd photocopies of the fourteen bids for the Sunyang oil fields."

"The British and French consortium too? All of them?" Clint said.

"Everything. All the competitors."

"Sort of takes the worry out of things if a man had his hands on the numbers," Flub said.

"That occurred to Mr. Boyd."

"Say, you wouldn't mind telling us where our old mare is running in the race?"

Ho smiled. "Unfortunately, Bonner Oil is fifth. Behind the British and French consortium, Exxon, Texaco, and Shell Oil."

"Fifth? I'm hungry," said Clint. He poured himself a tad more whiskey. He punched a button by the intercom and said, "Rosie, can you fix us a big platter of goodies, some olives or whatever?" He suddenly remembered something. He looked at brother Flub, then at Stanley. "Some of that new cheese maybe, a little treat for our guest from Hong Kong. This is smoked Norwegian cheese, wonderful stuff."

Flub Bonner topped off Stanley's glass of whiskey.

Stanley Ho looked eager. "Oh, cheese! Cheese is delicious. It's impossible to get good cheese in Asia." He wondered if he would be able to keep it down.

"And Sing Sing's nick? What would that be?" Flub rested his hand on his belly.

"I think in Cantonese. Sometimes my English is not the best."

"How much does Boyd want?"

"I see. Yes, it does seem like there is a price for everything these days. As you may have read in your newspapers, it has been decreed in China that to get rich is patriotic. There was precedent for these instincts, but they were driven from China and suppressed until recently."

Flub said, "But you folks in Hong Kong never lost the touch."

Ho smiled. "No, we did not. Nor have they lost the touch on Taiwan. Mr. Boyd's contacts are Chinese bureaucrats who would love to become rich patriots but lack the capital to start their own businesses. They're like businessmen everywhere; they sell what they have to sell. The cost of the Sunyang bids is five hundred million dollars firm, please."

"Firm, please?" said Flub.

"On a profit of six billion or more, that's what? Fifteen

percent? Sixteen? That's based on the low estimates of the reserve, so the real cost to you could slide as low as eight or nine percent.''

Flub considered that. ''The payment would be made when?''

''When you are awarded Sunyang. Mr. Boyd has been told the Chinese are prepared to sell to the highest bidder regardless of who makes it. A decision has been made that the government needs hard currency more than unprofitable politics. If you adjust your bid to win and don't get the contract, Mr. Boyd doesn't get his money and the contact in Beijing won't get paid.''

''Well, that's all wonderful, Mr. Ho, but you gotta remember you're dealing with Clint and Flub Bonner here, not Texaco or Shell. I find it hard to believe you couldn't nick one of them for a hell of a lot more than us. What do you think, brother Clint?''

''Yes, I'd like to know the answer to that one,'' Clint said.

''There are other considerations,'' said Ho.

''There always are,'' Flub said.

''Happily, the additional considerations are at no cost to you.''

''Clint and me've yet to find a whole lot that's really free, Mr. Ho.''

''I'd be surprised,'' Clint said.

''Mr. Boyd has been reading about your father's failing health. He says please do not think him coarse if he suggests that if you add a codicil to your father's will giving a half-billion dollars to a long-lost heir—a proxy for Mr. Boyd— then Mr. Boyd can avoid paying Hong Kong taxes on his Sunyang money. Mr. Boyd has done the Americans a favor in the past and there will be no inheritance taxes.''

''Sing Sing Boyd wants a Hong Kong wash,'' Flub said. He slapped his little belly with his hand.

Clint Bonner couldn't help laughing. ''Jesus, you folks are great to do business with.''

''Mr. Boyd couldn't buy this convenience through Texaco

or Shell. This is a unique opportunity for Mr. Boyd and the
sole reason I came to you first.''

Flub glanced at Clint. "Do us a big old favor, huh, Mr.
Ho?''

"You'd have your foot solidly in the Chinese market, Mr.
Bonner. Think of that! One billion Chinese! What if they do
get their economy turned around? What then?''

"Try that cheese, Mr. Ho.'' Flub grabbed a finger of the
smoked Norwegian.

Ho took a piece and bit into it without gagging, appearing
to savor the flavor. "It's very good,'' he said, and added,
"Furthermore, Mr. Boyd has located a gentleman in Burma
who possesses extraordinary skills as a forger. All he re-
quires are recent samples of your father's handwriting, and
samples of witnesses' signatures.''

"You appear to have thought of everything, Mr. Ho, I'll
grant you that,'' Flub said. "But there remains one small
problem. Just who in hell is going to believe that Clint and
Flub Bonner would let some fuckhead walk off with five
hundred million bucks of their money?''

Clint smiled and took a deep draw on his mean little cigar.
"Ain't no way, Mr. Ho.''

Stanley Ho looked dumbstruck. "But if it was your father's wish and the case was convincingly detailed, then
surely—''

"No Texas daddy gets that kind of respect,'' Clint said.

Flub said, "A half-billion bucks? No, no, doesn't happen.
If we didn't tear this alleged heir a brand-new asshole,
folks'd know it was a Bonner high poke.''

Ho tried to act nonplussed, but it wasn't easy.

Flub said, "There may be a way, Mr. Ho, but it won't be
easy. Unfortunately my brother and I have—''

"Reputations,'' Clint cut in. "Our father was a colorful
man when he was younger.''

"Colorful is the word,'' Flub said. "We'll have to have

time to think it over. Because of our reputations, you've given us a very difficult poke indeed.''

Stanley Ho brightened. Greed, he knew, overcame all obstacles. "You should think it over. If you agree, you may contact Mr. Boyd in Hong Kong. If not, then please let us know so that we may approach Texaco or Shell. We promise to hit them for the maximum.'' Stanley Ho took another piece of cheese—a large piece—and ate it while appearing to actually enjoy it.

13

AFTER ten days of wandering through warrens of alleys and bazaars in Tangier, Lucien Salvant left a note for Stanley Ho at the American Express office. He doodled with his pencil, thinking, then wrote: *Mr. Ho. I've gone to Marrakech with stops in Larache, Rabat, and Casablanca. Expect to arrive Marrakech April 28; please see attached itinerary. Cordially, Lucien Salvant.*

That done, Salvant walked downhill to the train station and bought a ticket to Larache, the first stop of consequence.

The three-hour ride seemed twice that long because of the tiresome vista of low, rounded hills nearly devoid of vegetation, and the realization that time was running short. In September, Salvant faced the purgatory of committees and the limbo of Robert's Rules. He recalled a heated argument over a course called Interdisciplinary Bayou—a study of Louisiana swamps from bugs through economics—which had been proposed by the education department. On grounds of civility, Salvant had been forced to stifle laughter. He ground his teeth at the memory.

From the distance, Larache had a charm and a promise that Salvant couldn't resist. It was a small town of uncertain economy that stood on a hill overlooking the south shore of an inlet that led to the bed of a stream that was now dry. The tip of the promontory was guarded by the derelict remnants of a Moorish fortification. Salvant wanted to poke around the fortification. He got off the train.

He found himself a modest hotel, threw his single valise in his room, and went for a walk to the square that was the center of Larache. The air was balmy and the sun would soon be setting over the Atlantic. The square had a small garden and some benches in the center. Veiled women gathered in the garden. The men strolled around the perimeter, some of them walking hand in hand. Teen-agers and young people gathered on the broad overlook at the western end of the square. Water churned in a rocky cove below. The walkers talked and laughed softly. The sun shimmered orange above the water.

Larache was not a tourist town, and Salvant was one of the few Europeans in sight. He joined the Moroccan men for their evening walk, cutting into the crowded sidewalks and strolling, he imagined, like a veteran. He paused with the young people to contemplate the sun dipping into the Atlantic, which had taken on the appearance of a vast, calm sea of mercury.

On the second time around the square, a small Asian man waited in front of a sidewalk café where Moroccan men drank sweet mint tea and ate pumpkin soup. He caught Salvant's glance. "Mr. Lucien Salvant?"

"Mr. Stanley Ho?"

"That's me."

"I almost missed you." Ho rose to shake Salvant's hand. "I saw you get on the train. I'm finished with my soup. Shall we walk while we talk? It's a lovely evening."

"Sure," Salvant said.

Stanley Ho joined the traffic circling the town square at

Larache. "Mr. Salvant, I work for a man named Sing Sing Boyd, who is probably best known abroad for his kung fu movies. Perhaps you've seen some of them. I'm told they're shown on the American telly in the middle of the night."

"Much leaping and kicking." Salvant was amused at Ho's efforts to match the Moroccans' leisurely pace.

The sun was a fourth of the way into the maw of the Americas when Stanley Ho began his pitch. "Mr. Boyd, who is half white, by the way, has investments and business interests throughout Asia—in Hong Kong, Singapore, Taipei, Seoul, and Tokyo."

"The new Asia."

"The envy of Europe. Yes, they're doing very well on world markets. As you no doubt know, information is as necessary in the business world as it is in betting on horses. When there are Chinese among the executives or directors of Mr. Boyd's competitors, then he is properly covered. He has the eyes and ears he needs. His problem is those companies that are run by *gweilos*, not only the British *taipans*, but also Australian businessmen, and Germans, and Americans."

"And a *gweilo* is . . . ?"

"A ghost, literally. It means a white man. *Gweilos* are as clannish as we Chinese are alleged to be." Ho smiled pleasantly. "I don't intend that to be a racial statement in the usual sense. But really, don't you think most of us are most at home with others of our kind? This is mostly a matter of being comfortable." They were at the overlook, and Ho paused to enjoy the fabulous sun inching slowly into the west.

"Within limits it's harmless enough, I guess, but a little boring, don't you think?"

"I'm glad you added the latter. I agree. Considering my employer, I could hardly not."

"So there is a disconcerting gap in your . . ." Salvant searched for the right word.

"Access, I think, is close. Mr. Boyd, being biracial, is an

anomaly. Is he *gweilo* or is he Chinese? To the Asian public, he is Chinese. In private, he is Chinese when he is among Chinese, *gweilo* when he is among *gweilos*. Mr. Boyd has an epicanthic eye fold; he is marked as Asian, so that he is considered a Chinese capitalist in Hong Kong, not a European trader in the strictest sense of what the Chinese call a *taipan*. You understand his problem."

"Certainly."

"Mr. Boyd got to thinking: wouldn't it be wonderful if he had a *gweilo,* uh, I hesitate to use this word, a *gweilo* spy floating among the *taipans*—someone who could sail, perhaps, and certainly play tennis. Someone with the intelligence and presence of mind to drink whiskey and eat cheese with the European capitalists and remember the useful details. Now then, how would he go about recruiting someone to spy on his peers? He couldn't, could he? One's first loyalty is to one's own. Mr. Boyd then considered the possibility of setting up his own man. That's a pretty big problem, wouldn't you say?"

"Yes, I would say." Lucien Salvant walked as though he were in a dream; he felt and understood the moment clearly, savored it—the passing tableau of Moroccans, the warm air, and smell of salt. The sun dipped lower, losing its yellow, then its orange, turning to red, cooling to purple.

"Mr. Boyd's man wouldn't be a *taipan*, really. That suggests old wealth; the expatriate capitalists who actually run the colony. Incidentally, the original *taipans* made their wealth in the opium trade, Mr. Salvant, and there are those who still thrive on variations of it. Considering its addictive properties, the *taipans* regarded it as a commercial item of extraordinary profit. It had a wonderful curve of supply and demand. Those *taipans* trace their power to the great old trading firms of the British empire."

"Quite a problem for your Mr. Boyd."

"Yes, it is. To be welcomed into the circles of this old Hong Kong wealth, any newcomer must have quite a lot of money indeed. So Mr. Boyd began collecting lists of aging, wealthy men around the world. Perhaps there was a way to do business after all—through a judiciously placed heir. He found his man, an American; Mr. X, I'll call him.''

"No names, eh?" Salvant grinned.

"Not just yet, I'm afraid. This Mr. X was a storied chaser of women. Mr. Boyd hired a detective to see if there was any truth to rumors of his past. The detective said there was circumstantial evidence pointing to at least one bastard child, a son—by a woman from Lake Charles, Louisiana—about halfway between Houston and New Orleans. The woman was later killed in a car accident that may have been murder. The son, who would now be forty, was most likely born in the anonymity of a larger city—the closest to Lake Charles are Beaumont and Houston in Texas, Baton Rouge and New Orleans in Louisiana—but could have been born anywhere along the Gulf Coast.''

"I was born in New Orleans.''

"We know that, Mr. Salvant, which is why I'm here. The detective did come up with a list of twenty-two white male babies who were given up or abandoned by their mothers in New Orleans in late January 1948 and early February 1949. This was the critical period, depending on the length of pregnancy.

"I was born about January twenty-eighth, they think.''

"You were on the list, one of nine of the orphans our detective could not find. When my employer spotted your ad in the *International Herald*, he knew it was good *fung shui*.''

"Fung shui?"

"That means something like luck or fortune, but a lot more than that also. Not only were the heirs of Mr. X's estate willing to do business, but the Central Intelligence Agency is also indebted to Mr. Boyd so that if, say, a half-billion dollars were to be willed to Mr. X's long-lost, illegitimate son, there would be no inheritance taxes. The matter of the taxes, incidentally, has already been agreed upon.''

''A half-billion dollars?'' Salvant was incredulous. ''What on earth did Boyd do to earn that kind of money?''

Ho shrugged. ''Services rendered is accurate enough. Some of Mr. Boyd's dealings are quite complicated. Mr. Boyd would like to hire you to be the fortunate heir, Mr. Salvant.''

''What? Me?''

''Heir to a half-billion dollars which, of course, will really belong to Mr. Boyd. This would be until 1997.''

''And then?''

''Then the colony reverts to China. We don't know, really, what will happen after that. The feeling is not much will change. The Chinese assure us it won't. We'll see. You would live like a''—Stanley Ho paused—''prudent millionaire. You would move to Hong Kong. You would be given a house and a car, plus a companion who'll double as a bodyguard.''

Salvant looked startled. ''Bodyguard? For what?''

''When you're worth a half-billion dollars you're a prime target for kidnappers. There's no way we can completely avoid that problem. It exists for all wealthy people.''

''I see.'' The sun was now a sliver of purple over the Atlantic that hovered, blinking, ready to surrender to the horizon. ''You're not prepared to tell me who Mr. X is, I take it.''

Stanley Ho said, ''If I told you now, you would anticipate the gentleman's passing, wouldn't you? You might behave differently or say things you might not ordinarily say; I think that's human nature, Mr. Salvant. For this to be believable to the public, you'll have to be properly surprised. Mr. X's legitimate heirs and Mr. Boyd are anxious that no questions be asked. You'll have to trust me, and wait.''

Salvant's stomach tightened. ''Do I have to decide tonight?'' The sliver of purple disappeared into the Atlantic. In Lucien Salvant's almost perfect world, all he would have to do each day was kick back and read novels, and book reviews, and old atlases and books on geography, mushrooms, and ocean currents, or whatever, and maybe write if he felt like it. A *taipan* wouldn't have department meetings. Salvant said, "Can you imagine what it's like to wake up with a hangover on a Sunday morning and have to grade a pile of term papers in which the first word of the final paragraph is always 'hopefully'?"

Ho grinned. "I hope that means 'yes,' because I think you'll have a good time in Hong Kong, Mr. Salvant. It has its pleasures once you've become acclimated." Taking Salvant's silence as assent, Stanley Ho slowed before one of the cafés. "Shall we celebrate our bargain with a cup of mint tea? It's sweet, but good." They sat at a small wooden table.

It was dark now, but the air was still balmy. The Moroccans walked on, talking, enjoying friendship and the concluding pleasures of the day's rhythm. The following night, weather permitting, they would be back in force walking around the town circle, hand in hand, murmuring, enjoying the smell of the air.

14

THE air conditioner of Kwok Lai Kwon's Chrysler worked for exactly half an hour, then unaccountably stopped. Air conditioners in Mitsubishis and Subarus sometimes broke down too, but Kwok was in no mood to be fair or objective. He had to suffer the wretched heat on top of everything else, and this was clearly Lee Iacocca's fault, the lying bastard.

Kwok knew he shouldn't have rented an American car. He had stupidly believed all that Iacocca manure. A Chrysler! He remembered the ads he had seen on the Los Angeles leg of his trip. This thin-haired man in a gunmetal gray suit saying this car had his name on it? Iacocca? These Americans were something with their advertising. Kwok had to give them that.

The traffic was snarled up ahead, so Kwok Lai Kwon made a quick right, hurriedly, without checking it out.

There were even more people up ahead, and there were people on both sides streaming toward that crowd. These were mostly men in T-shirts that were too small for them, and tall, gaudily dressed women. Kwok pulled just short of

the blocked intersection, determined that his Asian calm
should prevail.

Kwok Lai Kwan remembered the American movie where
General Patton had bellowed at his commanders in a rage
after their tanks ran out of gas. It was the first rule of
common sense that if you claim a territorial monopoly, you'd
better have enough goods to keep everybody happy, or you'll
lose them. Thanks to the Asian poppy growers, increased
supply was not forthcoming, and here Kwok was, forced to
do the San Francisco Police Department the favor of eliminating a few Chinese-American hoods.

He killed them with his .357 magnum if they fancied
themselves cowboys, or with kung fu if they had been watching Sing Sing Boyd movies. It was Boyd, in fact, who was
rumored to be the man behind the obstinance of the poppy
growers. If that were true, Kwok wished most fervently that
Pak Tze Fan would prevail upon Boyd to change his mind. If
Kwok had to keep killing people at this pace, something was
bound to go wrong.

Kwok mopped the sweat from his forehead with the back
of his hand. There were people everywhere. The damnable
heat had fogged his brain. He couldn't find a way out. What
the hell kind of city was this?

He'd had enough. He put the hateful Chrysler into gear
and bulled his way through the people, ignoring the shouting
and people pounding on the car with their fists. He hoped they
destroyed the Chrysler. Suddenly he was free of the bodies,
but was forced to turn right.

He was in a parade of some kind, behind a flatbed truck
loaded with muscular young men in black leather costumes.
Despite the hot leather, they waved joyously at the crowds
that had gathered along each sidewalk. Kwok wondered how
they did it.

Some of these men had whips or were chained or hooded.
Others had huge silver studs around their wrists and ankles.
There was an executioner. A medieval monk brandished an
ax. Several of the young men had round patches cut out of

the seat of their trousers showing hairy, muscular buttocks. Ugh!

Kwok was disgusted and turned left, pushing through spectators, raced two blocks, grinding his teeth, pushed through more people and turned left again, only to find that the parade was apparently taking snaking U-turns through the city.

This time he was behind a group of men dressed in a variety of costumes. There were construction workers, musclemen, waiters, gorillas, businessmen in neat suits, men in tight jeans and tank tops; there were cowboys, and polo players, and men with purple mohawks. All these men, the whole bunch, had their genitals out and were joyously twirling their baggage at one another and at the crowd for everyone's enlightenment and amusement.

Kwok reminded himself to remain tranquil. He would be out of the area in a few minutes, plenty of time to draw the necessary blood. He had to remain steady for head-smashing. He wheeled left, forcing his way through people, then made a hard right and gunned it, scattering more parade-watchers.

The crowd at the next intersection parted. The far side of the street was crowded with people, so Kwok turned right.

As he did an outlandish fairy—dressed in a fluorescent yellow tutu—glided past on roller skates, waving his wand at the cheering onlookers. Then there were more roller-skating, grinning fairies, wearing tutus of various fluorescent colors: mauve, fuchsia, red, orange, purple. Some held hands as they skated. Others did little pirouettes for the benefit of the spectators, who applauded with gusto at each demonstration of roller-skating skill.

What kind of madhouse was this? The Fragrance of the Red Lotus did his best to keep calm. He was on his way to kill people, a routine assignment, and he had to wind up among these nuts; this was a city of crazy people. He reminded himself to remain in control of his emotions. He looked at his watch and his jaw hardened.

Up ahead was a float that Kwok thought was an unfolding

rose at first, with slender young men sitting on the petals. Then he realized the rose was a vagina and the young men were young women.

Kwok was awash with sweat. He smelled like a goat, he knew. His silk shirt clung to his torso. He had the windows down, but there wasn't a hint of breeze. Why had he been so cheap? Fan was paying for everything, not him. He could have rented a Japanese car. No problem. But he was in America, and so had rented a local car, like he drank the local beer. Kwok thought Coors and Henry Weinhards were good—especially Henry Weinhards, which he thought had to be one of the best-tasting beers in the world. But Kwok wished he could get his hands on Lee Iacocca. Kwok thought Iacocca could use a little lesson about pleasing customers.

Then Kwok Lai Kwon was kissed on the cheek. Sweetly. A gentle little smack.

He turned, aghast, to face a grinning, bearded fairy in a pink tutu.

"A faggot Odd Job. Support from the Orient! Oh, you nice man," the fairy said. He waved his wand gaily.

Kwok's face turned hard. What if that fairy had AIDS? He felt sick to his stomach. He rubbed his cheek on his shoulder and tromped on the accelerator, aiming Iacocca's inefficient machine at an intersection crowded with a group of sun-burned men wearing sequined jockstraps and jaunty straw hats. Swearing, they bounded to safety, their bellies rising and falling.

When Kwok was at last free, he swabbed more sweat from his forehead. He was late for the killing but as calm as possible under the circumstances. Lucky he only had to murder three or four people. He made a phoenix eye fist with his right hand:

Rock steady.

When Kwok got back, he would have to remind his apprentices to always check out local festivals and holidays when they planned a kill. And never, never plan a hit in San Francisco during Gay Pride Week.

Kwok began the inhalations preparatory to combat. In the first half hour, as now, this inhaling was slow and deep. In the moments before combat he would inhale quickly, violently—making a *sshht!* sound—and yell *"Hai!"* That sometimes, but not always, launched a spinning back-kick. This was a fierce, dramatic ritual that everybody expected of the Fragrance. Only Kwok's friends had heard it and loved to imitate it when they were drunk. The dramatic inhaling and yelling never failed to leave his opponent weak-kneed and insecure, a disadvantage that guaranteed Kwok would win.

Although the end result of Kwok's spinning back-kick was not unlike having one's brain shattered by a bullet, it was far less merciful. Kwok Lai Kwon's opponents always heard the kick that killed them.

The sea was actually fairly calm, but to Gene Holt, looking down on the dinghy far below, they might have been in a typhoon. The dinghy seemed to be bouncing dangerously close to the rusting hull of the freighter, although the man with the oars didn't seem concerned. Holt had to step into the harness, a thick strap running between his legs. If he'd have known it was going to be like this, he'd have worn a jockstrap. Christ!

A sailor, breathing garlic and speaking one of those stupid languages of the Third World, snapped him in. The swarthy-skinned crew had gathered on deck to watch. It was a break in their routine and they chatted quietly, shifting on bandy legs. They picked their noses and dug at their asses. No wonder they were plagued by hepatitis. They joked and laughed. Holt assumed he was the butt of their jokes. He did his best to look blasé, the old pro at being on the lam.

With his stout little arms and legs sticking out like popsicle sticks, he was hoisted from the deck by a crane used to unload cargo. The crane operator was caught up in the fun and swung him over the water with more energy than was necessary.

Holt, dizzy and suffering from vertigo, saw the rusting

hull coming at him as he swung in a huge circle. Shit! he thought. He held up his arms to cushion the impact and heard the crew laugh. It turned out he wasn't even close to the hull. He was allowed to swing for a while, then the crane operator began lowering him toward the awaiting dinghy. Things went okay until the bottom, where the problem was to match swinging man with rising and falling boat.

The man in the dinghy had to steady his small craft with one oar while he snagged Holt with his free hand. He shouted instructions to Holt in Chinese. Since the harness caused Holt's arms to stick out like the Tin Man's, there was little he could do to help. Then the boatman caught his foot and pulled him aboard the dinghy, ending the sport.

Gene Holt was slightly dispirited as he was rowed to the waiting sloop. He had spent all those years learning beaner talk. Was he now going to have to learn Thai or Indonesian? He supposed he'd have to, or put up with people laughing at him without him knowing about it.

The boarding of the sloop was far easier, and Holt, exhausted by tension and bullshit, went below and slept all the way to Fong Wai Chau.

Holt was impressed as he stepped onto the catwalk where the sloop had berthed. He looked up at the top of the cliff that rose high above the rocks at the base of the inlet. He said, "You said there would be a view. Indeed! Very nice, Mr. Pak."

Pak bowed slightly. "I'm pleased that you like it. You'll enjoy your stay here."

"I'll be able to do a little sailing, no reason why not. Some fishing maybe."

"Sure you will. It shouldn't take us long to find something you like. It takes connections, but there's a market out there and we'll find you something you'll be pleased with."

"This looks just wonderful."

"I assure you that you'll be entirely safe here, Mr. Holt. Fong Wai Chau is impregnable from three sides. And from

the front we have this.'' He gestured toward the cliff. ''And
these.'' He pointed to the steep hills that rose on either side of
the inlet. Then, gesturing to the villa on top, he said, ''The
island belonged to the heirs of a British *taipan*.''

''Oh, dear. You got a bargain, then.''

''The heirs were looking ahead to reversion,'' Pak said
with satisfaction.

Holt surveyed the steep hills. Wooden stairs zigzagged up
the hill on the side of the boat moorings. ''This is something
I hadn't imagined. These islands just come straight out of the
sea, don't they?''

''Some are worse than others. As it happens, this is one of
the steepest. I don't believe I've seen another quite as bad as
this. A perfect retreat.''

''Impregnable, I agree. They'll have to come at us from
below.''

''Or from the air. Exactly right,'' Pak said. ''We have
police friends in Hong Kong to warn us of any operation
involving helicopters. If they want to try, let them; we have
our places to hide. Shall we take the copter up? The stairs
will leave you exhausted. Besides that, the guards have been
complaining that some of the boards are loose.''

Holt looked at the stairs again. ''The helicopter, I think.''

Holt and Pak, guarded by the watchful eyes of Kwok Lai
Kwon, walked to the waiting helicopter. A few minutes later
the three men were rising from the concrete pad, the pilot
and Kwok in the front two seats, Holt and Pak in the rear
two.

Gene Holt, the enthusiastic immigrant, clenched his fist
and gave a jolly thumbs-up. ''Go East, young man! All
right!'' Bye-bye beaners. No more flatulence. Asia! Yes!
He'd show these scammers what a savvy round-eye could do.
Holt couldn't wait until he had his own island base. A sanctu-
ary like Fong Wai Chau. A home.

15

ARA Schott glared at James Burlane. Schott didn't think Ella Nidech's letter to Senator Rollo Hinkley was any laughing matter. Burlane was good, yes, but there were times when his tilted sense of humor got the better of him. These were the times when Schott had to bring him around, a chore Schott hated because Burlane had lately taken to blaming it on having grown up in Umatilla, Oregon. Burlane called this his Umatilla defense.

"It's true, Ara. In Umatilla, men are men and sheep sleep with their eyes open. You can never tell what we'll do around women. You just never know."

"Jesus Christ, Jimmy, you don't even know that woman. If she'd been a friend, she might understand."

"How did I know she was going to write a letter to Rollo Hinkley?" Senator Rollo Hinkley, Republican of Connecticut and chairman of the Senate Intelligence Oversight Committee, was married to a vice-president of the National Organization for Women.

"She has a point. What if one of those slugs had ricocheted in the wrong direction?"

"Believe me, Ara, it was a low angle. Besides, I saved the Company's bacon, didn't I? Laid a zipper up that mother's back." Burlane held out his hand, using his finger as the barrel of a machine pistol, and squeezed off a burst, raising the pretend muzzle as he did. He made a *vvvzzzttt!* imitation of a sewing machine with his lower lip beneath his tongue, which he vibrated on the roof of his mouth. "If it hadn't been for me, the bacon'd be gone down alleys unknown and we all know it."

"This kind of horseplay has to stop, Jimmy."

"It did her good, believe me. You should have seen her run. She looked like a wide receiver on a fly pattern, like Del Shofner maybe, or Max McGee. Did her dive stunt-man perfect, and came up sprinting and zigging and zagging and ducking." Burlane followed the imaginary Nidech's evasive tactics, squeezing off rounds in zigzag patterns, and describing his fleeing target. "Good form. Flowing hair there. Long strides. Legs of a thoroughbred. Look at those hips. Yum!" Once again Burlane fired the machine pistol, making *vvvzzzttt!* sounds with his tongue. "What a butt!" He made exaggerated kissing sounds with pursed lips.

"Goddammit, Jimmy!"

"She did an ace job in the bar, Ara. I had the booth wired. She followed her instructions to the letter. She took the pitch casually—no promises or commitments—professional all the way."

"Rollo Hinkley wants an investigation and a report delivered directly to him. I had to give Neely your report in which you cleverly admit to . . ." Words failed Schott.

"To scaring the living shit out of her. She's got to learn to be more careful, Ara. There's no congratulating yourself ever in this business."

"None of that makes any difference, Jimmy. She's calling it sexual harassment and she wants an inquiry by the long dogs.'' The long dogs were counterintelligence reps, the people who spied on the spies, and were named for long-bodied Dachshunds who were sent into dangerous holes after badgers and moles.

"What if you'd been riding shotgun and I'd walked out of there with bacon in a handbag, then didn't put the fucking strap over my shoulder? The damned recorder's hardly larger than a pencil eraser. She should have used her imagination. She's lucky I can shoot straight.''

"Come on, Jimmy . . .''

"She's got all kinds of trunk space. She was born with it.''

"Dammit, now!''

"If you had been me, you'd have done the same thing.''

Schott looked hard at Burlane. "There're more civilized ways of making a point.''

"She wants equal rights, equal rights she gets. Next time she'll be more careful. What if somebody's ass was on the line, mine or yours?''

"No. The lady wants long dogs, long dogs she gets. Hinkley's not giving us any choice, Jimmy.''

"Oh, bullshit. Now she knows what mud feels like. Listen, you can be sure next time she'll shove the bacon down the front of her jeans before she walks out of there. She'll be a better agent for it. Let me talk to Hinkley.''

Schott said, "Neely doesn't want us to be accused of old boyism on top of everything else.''

Burlane looked stunned. "Jesus Christ, Ara, can you imagine what will happen if Rollo Hinkley gets even a hint of my delicate work? You've chosen me to do everything you don't want discussed in Congress or leaked to the newspapers. I do what we all know has to be done, fuck the rules. I'm the public's private hit man, Ara.''

"Oh, Jimmy.''

"The taxpayer's torpedo. A blade for gays and straights,

Christians and Jews, little kids and old people. Umatilla to the rescue.''

"Come on now, Jimmy."

"Come on, my ass, Ara. We're looking at the truth here. I do what we all know needs to be done."

Ara Schott snapped a pencil. "Jimmy, a responsible United States senator has asked for an investigation of this matter. Under public law, we are obliged to reply. Just what in hell are we supposed to do?"

Burlane rolled his eyes. "Obliged to reply? Sure, tell the long dogs how I came to snatch Philby from Yalta or how I rode that train across the Soviet Union with Colonel Jin peering over my shoulder. How many hours do you think before Dan Rather will be telling the country all about it? Tell the long dogs and Rollo Hinkley how I took out that asshole Arab, and the Bolivian cocaine man. Death by measles in both cases, Ara. Nobody was the wiser, and the editorial writers did everything but say good riddance to whoever did it. We can tell them how I stole electronics secrets from the Japanese. Tell them all about my delicate work, Ara."

Ara Schott clenched the muscles of his jaws. "She's got us—"

"—right by the nuts. She says sing, you ask what song. I've turned you and Neely down several times. Each time I was right, a fact which you later admitted. I clearly saved your hides. Where else in this company of suck-butts are you going to find a delicate man with the guts to do that?"

"Two of Hinkley's staff investigators came over to Langley on Monday, Jimmy. They talked to people. There is no record that you have ever worked there. Well, they didn't believe that. They as much as accused everyone of lying to them. They represented a United States senator, they said. They were furious. They demanded answers. Then they ran over to the long dogs looking for more. The dogs are drooling. Shit!''

"I bet they are."

"On top of that, it turns out that Ella Nidech graduated at the top of her class at The Squirrelhouse, and ranks in the top two percentile of graduates in the last twenty-five years. She did a hell of a lot better than you did."

"I can write my name in the snow after one can of beer. Can she match that? I'll send her a note of apology, Ara. How about that?"

"A note of apology won't do, Jimmy. It's too late for that. She wants to do a little stitching of her own. You'd be surprised what she can do on a pistol range. I've seen her scores."

"How about flowers? Women always wilt when you send them flowers. I could send her flowers, roses, maybe, with a note, 'Please forgive me, Ms. Nidech, Jimmy.' Or I could cut off my trigger finger and send it to her, the Company van Gogh."

"As it stands now, you're going to have to stay loose here on the East Coast while we try to get things worked out. We have to keep it away from the long dogs if we can. Maybe the President will help us. Meanwhile, Ella Nidech will handle the China buy. She is under orders not to expand need beyond herself."

"You could have the President invite old Ella and me to the White House for tea in the Pink Room."

"Dammit, Jimmy!"

"What if the China buy leads to mud?"

"We'll send you."

"Regardless of Rollo Hinkley?"

"If there's mud, yes, regardless of Rollo Hinkley. Both Neely and the President want this to be handled as discreetly and with as few people as possible. You're just going to have to sit this one out for now."

"We gotta keep the dogs away, Ara."

"Stitching a zipper up that guy's back was like signing

your name, Jimmy. Why didn't you slop your load into the guy's back like everybody else? He would have come off the bike. He was wearing a T-shirt, for God's sake—she couldn't miss the neat zip!''

"I like to do clean work."

Ara Schott shook his head like a spaniel shedding water. "This is the modern world, Jimmy; if you shoot at a woman's feet, she doesn't just say, ha, ha, pretend mud. She takes it seriously. What do you think Gloria Steinem would say? Yes, grin your goofy grin. Now you see my problem. Asshole! If you think I want a bunch of women around here picketing the place, you've got another think coming, friend or no friend. That's exactly what would happen if we ignore Rollo Hinkley."

"You sound like George C. Scott when you get pissed, do you know that?'' Burlane started to say something else but closed his mouth.

"Oh, what is it?"

Burlane raised an eyebrow. "Would there be bisexual women at the demonstrations, do you think?"

"Fucking pervert."

"It's the Umatilla in me."

"That's what I mean," Schott said.

16

WHEN she had first been informed of Edward Gein's scheduled visit, Ella Nidech had felt triumphant and vindicated. A long dog! There was justice. The long dogs worked in an ultrasecret world, but on those rare occasions when they surfaced to take a sworn deposition, Company regs required confirmation by Langley. Nidech, who had the regs memorized, did as she was required, addressing an individual currently called Gretchen—although his/her gender was unknown to Nidech—who was currently in charge of the dogs.

Gretchen: Request ID confirmation re: scheduled deposition here by long dog Edward Gein. Lewis.

The reply from Langley startled her:

Lewis: Initial inquiry negative. There is no long dog Edward Gein. Stand by, please. Gretchen.

A half hour later another message arrived: *Lewis: Our initial reply based on insufficient data. The answer is positive on Edward Gein's scheduled deposition. Please cooperate. Gretchen.*

Nidech was curious. How could the dogs have had prob-

lems with "insufficient data"? Gretchen had the identities of
the dogs on Company computers. Nidech cabled back:
*Gretchen: Have you been included in the need re: E. Gein's
visit? I'm confused. Please repeat instructions, re: Edward
Gein. Lewis.*

The wait was even longer the second time.

Something was up, Nidech knew.

Finally the reply came:

*Lewis: Edward Gein is the assigned nom de guerre of a
dog selected from our ranks without our knowledge. He is
Parson's personal dog, as per Company regs. We are not
included in the need. Gretchen.*

Peter Neely! Nidech reread her messages and Gretchen's
replies. The sequence of messages was pregnant with suggestion.

First, she knew, the long dogs had been perplexed by
Nidech's request for an ID check. Gretchen had never heard
of Edward Gein. Further, Gretchen did not know the nature
of the case. In very sensitive cases—such as suspected deep
moles or in cases deemed extraordinary by the President—
Peter Neely had the authority to dip secretly into the long dog
roster for a personal rep.

Secrets were currency in the struggle for power within the
Company. The dogs especially didn't like secrets they weren't
in on. What was going on, Gretchen had wanted to know?

It was spelled out in the Company charter that the DCI had
the power to circumvent SOP only for the most unusual
cases, and then only with the approval of the President. It
was assumed within the Company that Ara Schott would
actually serve as the rep's field manager in these cases.
Schott had risen through counterintelligence and knew his
stuff. All Ara Schott had to do was call up the long dog
dossiers on his computer terminal and select his people without telling Gretchen. Schott had the authority to do that.

And proceed in secret.

Sexual harassment was hardly the same as selling out to

the Russians. Nidech was disbelieving. Surely Neely and Schott had more important things to do with their time.

Gretchen had been so pissed that she had broken Company regulations in telling Nidech about Neely's intervention. No man would break policy and risk his career to tell her about Neely. Gretchen had to be an angry woman—or women—warning Nidech that the old boys were doing everything they could to protect Burlane's precious reputation.

Nidech was disgusted that Peter Neely should use his extraordinary power to keep sexual harassment charges secret from the rest of the Company.

Well, Neely and Schott could keep Edward Gein's mission secret from the Company dogs, but they couldn't stop Gein from delivering his report to Senator Rollo Hinkley. That was one rule that superceded all others, namely: Thou shalt tell the truth to an official inquiry made by the United States senator who was elected by his or her colleagues as chairman of the Intelligence Oversight Committee. To lie to Rollo Hinkley was to court a charge of contempt of Congress.

Nidech sent one more message to whomever it was who was in charge of the long dogs.

Gretchen: If you need any shopping done in Hong Kong, send me sizes and a list. Fabulous buys on handbags, perfumes, jewelry, watches. Also copies of Paris originals done to measurements sent from U.S.A. Guaranteed lowest rates. Lewis.

That message broke Company regulations against personal messages; Nidech and Gretchen were even. Then Nidech began to fret. Would she be put on the Company's shit-list for having blown the whistle on Ara Schott's personal friend? The Company had finally given her some responsibility years after she had earned it. Had she now blown everything because her damned feelings were hurt by a joker with a machine gun?

Then she thought no. Peter Neely couldn't jerk her around right under the nose of Senator Rollo Hinkley's wife. Eleanor Huxtable-Hinkley was a vice-president of the National Organization of Woman. Nidech felt okay.

Then the questions returned, persistently.

Would all those damned men say they were right all along, that women were humorless pains-in-the-ass? That women couldn't take it? That if it hadn't been for Burlane baby-sitting her, the biker would have stolen a tape recording of a man offering to sell Chinese secrets to a fuzzy-headed broad pretending to be a spy?

Worse yet, what if there were no such person as James Burlane, Ara Schott's favored agent? If he were a Company joke as some claimed—a mythical spook—then she'd made a fool of herself. Or what if he really had died in Mozambique? They'd never trust her in the future.

There was one positive side effect to all this worrying. In the ten days she had to wait for Edward Gein's visit, Ella Nidech lost twelve pounds and was able to get into a pair of jeans she'd worn as a graduate student.

17

O<small>N</small> the day of Gein's visit, Ella Nidech awoke as usual
to the buzzing roar of Hong Kong stirring in the morning.
This was a special day: today Edward Gein would hear her
out and she would know, one way or the other, whether or
not she had made the mistake of her life.

The roar seemed to funnel its way between her apartment
building and the next so that the sound reverberated and grew
in intensity with each floor. This was the sound of Hong
Kong waking in the morning—money runners out of the
blocks, Chinese yuppies with shined shoes and double Wind-
sor knots, and white shirts, heading for the first turn.

Dreaming of what? Nidech wondered.

In one of her letters to her father in the United States,
Nidech asked him to imagine a Chinese auctioneer and a
diesel engine competing for attention in a tiled bathroom.
That was the sound of Hong Kong waking, she said. Beginning with the starting of the engines of vegetable trucks in
the New Territories, the awakening built slowly from the
calm of early-morning darkness, caught its stride at ten when

the shops opened, and stayed in high gear, echoing among the buildings, until far into the night.

Nidech first winced at all the competing and wheeling and dealing but later adjusted to it; she supposed this was like Eskimos adjusting to never being warm. She was by nature an independent woman and liked her privacy; the manic Chinese activity made her feel claustrophobic. She endured as best she could. After scrapping and competing for the Hong Kong assignment, she could hardly complain. Maybe Rome would be next.

In New York, cocktail conversation inevitably got around to violence on the subways. In Washington, white folks in the Virginia suburbs, in Georgetown, Chevy Chase, or out in Montgomery County always got around to addressing the problem of what to do about the lazy, violent blacks who were multiplying like smelt, then voting when they turned eighteen; the black folks grumbled about the whites screwing them over every way imaginable. In Hong Kong, people talked about bargains, the racetrack at Happy Valley, or the Hong Kong stock exchange, regarded locally as a form of racetrack.

Nidech liked to go shopping the same as everyone else. She had found herself a congenial Hindu tailor on the Kowloon side, and whenever she spotted a dress she liked in a fashion magazine, she showed him the picture, picked out the material, and returned the next day for the second fitting.

At first Nidech didn't mind picking up a tip here or there. It was fun going to the races, and she got a certain thrill in tearing open the Asian *Wall Street Journal* every morning to see how her stock had performed.

Nidech turned onto her stomach, listening to the hubbub on the streets, wondering if she would wind up selling real estate. She tried to imagine herself trying to convince a young couple of the benefits of a large kitchen or closet space in the hall. Maybe her sister was the smart one. Maybe Nidech should have found a good-natured, fertile hunk, and had kids and watched television like everybody else.

She went from euphoria to doubt, and back and forth. Ever since she had messed up with the handbag, she had been wondering if the intelligence business was really for her. How could she have had a lapse of judgment like that? She had walked out of the White Stag carrying the bacon as if it were on a serving tray.

Her instructions had been to arrange the meeting at the front of the bar. Burlane, no doubt, had cased the White Stag well in advance. The old man probably left the door open every morning so the place could air out, which meant that Burlane probably scoped her talk with Ho, if he didn't have his own recorder under the table somewhere.

Had Burlane used high-powered binoculars to examine the pores of her skin and the inside of her nostrils as he listened in on her conversation with Stanley Ho? That kind of invasion of her privacy made Nidech the sorest of all. She popped out of bed and went to the john. She showered and brushed her teeth, deciding she would take a taxi to the Hilton and treat herself to an expensive American breakfast. That would calm her. Then she would meet with Edward Gein and do what her conscience told her she had to do. There were times, dammit, when a woman had to stand up for what was right, and this was one of them.

Ella Nidech felt proud of herself. But by the time she got dressed and flagged a taxi—she never drove her Honda to work at Bee-Vee, that was insane—she waffled once again, beset by second thoughts.

The long dog, Edward Gein, was, appropriately, a tall, slender man. He wore a neatly pressed tropical suit that belonged in the pages of *Gentleman's Quarterly*. He had jet-black hair and deep brown eyes. His hair was fashionably cut, and his tie was neatly tied. He was a friendly man, encouraging in manner, and extended his long arm to shake her hand firmly. "I'm very, very pleased to meet you, Ms. Nidech."

"I'm pleased that the Company takes these matters seriously,'' Ella Nidech said. She couldn't tell him she knew about Peter Neely without jeopardizing her ally in the long dogs. "I'm afraid I can't add a whole lot to the letter I sent to Senator Hinkley and to the report I sent to Mr. Neely. I tried to include all the details there."

Gein retrieved a notebook from his briefcase and said, "Are we safe here?"

"It's been teched." She gestured for him to sit.

Gein hitched his trousers before he sat so there would not be undue wear on the knees. The crease in the trousers was thus kept knife sharp. Edward Gein obviously liked to look his best. He said, "First, I will tell you that this case is being handled through Neely rather than the long dog command. Peter Neely and Ara Schott are, ah, protective of James Burlane. I'm almost certain that they're concerned that my investigation of your sexual harassment charge does not lead in embarrassing directions. Once you do what they've done, and remove an agent from contact with normal Company channels, it can't be for any reason they'd want to read about in the *Times* or the *Post*. You know how those things go. No matter how honest Peter Neely tries to be with the Senate, there are practical limits to what he can tell them. Senator Rollo Hinkley is only interested in the facts of this incident and in justice. He can't ignore it." Gein paused. "If you went over his head, wrote a letter to the redoubtable Eleanor Huxtable-Hinkley, Rollo'd find himself eyeball-deep in some real bad mud. Can you handle direct language, Ms. Nidech?" Gein attended to his tie. He leaned forward and narrowed his eyes to indicate this was serious business.

"As direct as you want to use."

"I want to get this man. I want justice. Once and for all I want to get him. You're the first person who's had the backbone to put anything substantial in writing."

"Then he's still out there somewhere doing business as usual. What about the Mozambique dysentery story?"

Gein's face grew tight. "That's a rumor floated by Neely

and Schott. Oh, he's very much alive, Ms. Nidech, very much; they didn't dare lie to me on that one. I guarantee that Rollo Hinkley does not like being lied to. He won't put up with it, and both Neely and Schott know it. They lie by omission. It's my job to make sure all the questions are asked. To do that, I have to have all the facts, and have them straight. Hinkley is from Massachusetts. His voters like to see the administration embarrassed, so if I err, it is to be on the side of rigor. Senator Hinkley and I had a little chat before I caught the plane out here.'' Gein checked the cuffs of his cotton broadcloth shirt. Still looking at the cuffs, he added, ''Also, we dogs don't like the idea of these Burlane cases being taken from us.''

Nidech was startled by Gein's vehemence. Her eyes widened. ''Cases? Have there been other complaints?''

''Have there?'' Gein shook his head in wonderment; how could Nidech be so dense as to ask a question like that? ''Nobody will write anything up, though. The steely-eyed golden one, a letch? The savior of the Western World, a practical joker? A couple of times we thought we had something going, then Neely and Schott would snatch it from us at the last second.''

Ella Nidech was relieved. ''I'm not grandstanding, I assure you, Mr. Gein. It's time this man learned a lesson.''

''You're not grandstanding, believe me.''

''I was worried I was going to be regarded as some kind of crackpot feminist. Can you imagine some jerk stitching the pavement you were walking on? He fires it in a hum, I swear. He knows how to shoot. You should have seen the biker's back.''

''If he was using his machine pistol, it is one of a kind,'' Gein said. ''Custom built.''

''Custom built?''

''I told you. I'm going to nail James Burlane. I'm building a file. I'm learning a few things, too. For example, I can tell you that the Company—on Ara Schott's orders—paid a gunsmith to spend two years building and rebuilding that pistol according to Burlane's specifications. That's full time devoted to one agent's pistol. They apparently started with a Heckler and Koch P76 and went from there. Talk about the cost of B-1 bombers! He's made anonymous appearances showing off his shooting to rookies at the Squirrelhouse, did you know that?'' Gein was genuinely angered at the secrecy surrounding James Burlane. His lips whitened with rage. "Neely told me Burlane does 'special projects.' "

"And those are?"

"He didn't tell me. He told me next to nothing in fact. I find that kind of secrecy interesting, don't you? It makes a person wonder."

"Under whose control did he do these 'special projects' of his?"

Gein held up the palms of his hands. "That's not clear either. Possibly for Neely and Schott alone, or maybe for the secretary of state or for Aristotle."

Ella Nidech was interested. "Really! A private errand boy."

"But you don't have to worry. Although I'm working under Neely, my report goes directly to Rollo Hinkley. I'm still a dog, remember. Did I tell you Burlane's been grounded pending my report? Sometimes these inquiries drag on a bit." Gein gave Nidech a lopsided, sardonic grin. "A careful investigator takes his time, don't you agree, Ms. Nidech? What do you say we go to one of those dim sum places and eat pickled duck's feet or whatever? You should have been here long enough to know what's good."

Ella Nidech was pleased that Gein was a professional, and determined to do a thorough job. He wasn't the kind of man to be intimidated. She liked that. She said, "Sure, let's go eat." Nidech began gathering her things, and they dropped the topic until they were settled into a proper French restaurant, Hong Kong offering the best of foods from around the world. They ordered a drink, and while they considered the menu, Ella Nidech got to the nitty-gritty.

"Tell me, Mr. Gein, what was James Burlane's version of what happened? I assume you read that as part of your investigation. Whose idea was it anyway? And how does Mr. Perfect justify what he did to me?"

"Burlane claims Neely and Schott didn't want you to meet with Ho without protection, but worried about leaks from your shop—

"Oh, Christ!" Nidech interrupted. She was disgusted.

". . . Yes. You might as well hear the whole sorry story—or their version of it anyway. Neely and Schott agree that's how it started. By the way, I'm not privy to the case involved, so that won't be addressed in the report. Neely and Schott decided it was judicious to have Burlane ride shotgun— Squirrelhouse SOP."

"Why didn't they just tell me?"

"Burlane says, and Neely confirmed this, that they didn't want you to think Burlane was horning in on whatever it was you were working on. The only thing they told me was that you were carrying Company bacon in a matchbox recorder. They just wanted to be certain you weren't being set up by someone bent on wasting you."

Nidech slumped in her chair.

"Burlane claims the biker surprised him as much as he did you. He came out of an alley just behind Burlane's position above the street. Burlane stitched him so you could recover the bacon."

"Sure, then he zinged a couple of clips in right at my feet. What if one of them would have taken a bad bounce? Did he take that into consideration?"

Gein opened his mouth, hesitated slightly, and said, "This isn't the first complaint, like I said. That comes from Neely and Schott giving him so much freedom."

"But why? Why scare the pee out of me? What was the point of that? Did you ask him?" Nidech pleaded with her hands.

"We asked him." Gein looked uncomfortable.

"Well?"

"Ms. Nidech, I . . ." Gein clearly didn't want to answer that question.

"I would like to know the answer, Mr. Gein. I think I have that right, don't you?"

Edward Gein's face colored. He stared at the floor. "He, ah, said, ah, that you had this fabulous keister and long legs and he wanted to see you run, and he, uh . . ." Gein was red-faced. "That's the phrase he used, 'fabulous keister.' "

"Finish it, please." Nidech's face was tight.

"He said he wanted to see if your tits bounced when you ran, that's his phrase as well." Gein swallowed, then coughed. "It's jerks like Burlane who give the rest of us a bad name." He stopped, angry, then said, "That's what they get for letting him be that independent, Ms. Nidech. It goes to his head. He thinks he can get away with anything. We need to be very, very careful and get every detail and get it right."

Nidech felt encouraged. Ordinarily she was not comfortable with men who were such impeccable dressers, or with men who were BYU straight—Gein sipped a Perrier while she had a martini. Still, he was everything a dog was supposed to be: smart, dedicated, no bullshit. The long dogs were the Company's last perimeter of defense. They were the elite, the best, and if they screwed up just once, they could pull everybody down with them. They were the hardest of hard-core. The instructors at the Squirrelhouse used to scare the wits out of their students with stories of the long dogs' efficiency; just once think of working for the other side and a betoothed snout will grab you by the short hairs, they were told. She said to Gein, "I'll do everything I can to help, believe me," she said.

"I admire you for your courage, and guarantee that I'll give you as good an investigation as I can." Ed Gein retrieved his wallet from his jacket pocket and showed her a picture of a beautiful little girl. "This is my daughter, Laura. She'll be twelve on October fourth. I guarantee that I don't want her to grow up having to put up with guys like James Burlane. He's an embarrassment.''

After lunch, Gein went with her to the scene of the action, referring to it as the ''Burlane outrage.'' He took pictures of the corner of the wall where the stitching could be seen clearly. He took pictures of the marks in the street, and of the booth with the door open so Senator Rollo Hinkley—and his Senate committee, if necessary—could see where Burlane had been hiding and what he had done.

Then Nidech signed a series of sworn Q. and A. affidavits that provided Hinkley with the details of James Burlane's behavior. Nidech was impressed with Ed Gein's thoroughness, although it got a little tiresome going over each detail three or four times. Gein was a dogged investigator, going carefully, logically, from fact to fact. As far as she could see, Gein left nothing unattended. In that respect, he was more like a bulldog than a long dog. He was obviously bent on giving Senator Rollo Hinkley all the ammunition he could conceivably use.

Then Ella Nidech realized what was happening. How could she have been so dumb not to see? Gein's first loyalty was to the dogs, not Peter Neely, nor even Rollo Hinkley—certainly not to Eleanor Huxtable-Hinkley. Gein smelled a jackpot of secrets, a mother lode, in the special treatment accorded Burlane. He was determined to exact a full measure of Burlane's hide—everything from his custom-built pistol to his relationship to Neely and Schott. In the end, the dogs, coveting the power that went with knowing secrets, would know all there was to know about James Burlane; there wasn't a damned thing Neely or Schott could do about it.

Peter Neely had clearly picked the wrong dog from Gretchen's roster. When the fruit of Edward Gein's effort got back to Gretchen, as it most certainly would, the doyenne of the long-snouted dogs would drink champagne in celebration of her good fortune.

18

WHEN Lucien Salvant called in from a pay phone at the YMCA at Central Park West and Sixty-third Street to a number in the Manhattan telephone directory listed as that of the Central Intelligence Agency, his call was monitored by a woman who listened for zits—telltale key words—which she entered into a computer as he talked, her fingers hopping nimbly on the keyboard. When she entered the name "Stanley Ho," the computer responded with a colorful blinking of lights and an annoying *yeep-yoop! yeep-yoop! yeep-yoop!* She had tumbled onto a zit.

"Mr. Salvant, I'm going to put you on hold for a moment while I transfer your call," she said. She punched one button, then a second, which dialed a number in Langley, Virginia. A woman answered, and the New York woman said, "I've got a zit for you, first code, the computer says. A Dr. Lucien Salvant, who says he's a professor at Quantrell College in New Orleans. This is zit Ho, Stanley."

There was a pause on the phone while the Langley woman hit Control Z on her keyboard, punched the return key, then

114

entered Ho, Stanley into the zit bank and waited for the results. She read them quickly, then said, "Put him on, please." The Langley woman proceeded to debrief Lucien Salvant. This was called squeezing the zit, or gaining all details possible of the potential infection in the nation's security. The Langley woman was said to have a built-in antenna that detected the merest hint of psychotic nonsense, poo-poo in the lingo. If she had thought Salvant was a nutter, she'd have gone back to reading her novel and let him tell his poo-poo to a recorder.

She didn't. She encouraged him. She listened. She asked questions. She was interested in what he had to say. She asked him twice to repeat how he had come to put his ad in the *International Herald*. And while she grinned in the privacy of her office, she did not laugh out loud. She had him repeat his correspondence with the man from Hong Kong. She asked him for a physical description of Stanley Ho. Three times, she had him repeat the details of Ho's proposition. The conversation was being taped so all she had to do was concentrate on asking questions. She got everything clear, all of it: his reasons for putting the ad in the paper, his correspondence with Sing Sing Boyd, Stanley Ho's proposal in Morocco.

When she was finished, she told Salvant he would be contacted for an interview with a Company representative.

Later, when she was writing a summary of the interview for whatever Company reps would have to deal with it, she couldn't help but shake her head at Salvant's insane ad in the *International Herald Tribune*. She admired him for his madness, but also felt a little sorry for him.

When he had finished telling James Burlane the story of Stanley Ho's visit in Morocco, Lucien Salvant slumped disconsolately on the park bench and watched the pigeons waddle but never saw them. It was a lazy, warm day in Central Park, the tranquility broken only by the blare of ghetto blasters and the echoing roar that seemed to rise out of the pores of the city's streets and sidewalks. This sound was ever present, rising even through snow.

An obese pigeon with yellow eyes and bobbing head paused at their feet.

Burlane could only think Salvant had to be hitting the thrillers pretty heavy to agree to be a shill for Sing Sing Boyd. Then Salvant, an apparent eagle scout, had turned around and scurried straight to the Company. What a break for the Company!

Burlane said, "Tell me about this guy Frank Quetglas you hung around with. You didn't meet him until after your ad in the *Herald*, did you?"

"Awww!" Salvant waved his hand at Burlane. "I can't imagine he has anything to do with this Hong Kong business, if that's what you're thinking. His parents immigrated to Miami from Cuba and he likes to have a good time. I think he's up front."

"You do know you crapped in your mess kit, don't you?"

"I know that," Salvant said.

"In the end you may wish you hadn't come to us, but thank you."

"I figured it was this or grading papers. What would you do?"

"You might want to go back to the papers before this is finished. He didn't give you a clue as to how you're supposed to come by all this money?"

"He said I'd have to act surprised for it to work. He said I'd know when the time came."

"Assuming Mr. Boyd's employees are not listening in to this conversation, you may be all right. I want you to go back to New Orleans and do as you were instructed. When the time comes and you inherit the money, go to Hong Kong as required. Have a good time. We'll be in touch."

"That's all?"

"That's all for now. I don't want you trying to take any

kind of notes. No journals, please, Mr. Salvant. If I find you
have one, I'll probably steal it. No secret pictures or any of
that spook stuff. You must be patient.''

"I see.''

"Lucien, you must pay attention to Stanley Ho. Do what
he says. If some badass gets hold of you and turns mean, I
want you to protect yourself. You're a bit player and there's
nothing you know that's worth suffering over. Tell them
everything you know. Tell them about me, if necessary.
Hold nothing back.''

Salvant sighed. "Oh, boy.''

"There is a certain safety in being a bit player. Better for
them to get me than you.''

"What do we do?''

Burlane shrugged. "Not much, really. We wait. We watch.
We study. Eventually you'll be assigned a control, who'll be
rather like a basketball coach.'' He grinned. "A playing
coach.'' He stood and offered a hand to Salvant.

"That's it?''

"Box out on the boards. Don't cross your feet on defense.
Always keep moving. Don't take bad shots.'' With that
James Burlane, whistling, left Salvant sitting on the park
bench.

After Burlane got back to his hotel, he freshened up and
went down to the bar for a leisurely whiskey and a look at
the *Times*. In the financial pages he came across a story
about the phenomenal profits anticipated by the companies
bidding to develop China's Sunyang oil fields. The estimated
net over a ten-year period ranged from six to ten billion
dollars. Bonner Oil was one of fourteen competitors, despite
China's long-standing hostility to the failing Cactus Jack
Bonner.

On that problem, Flub Bonner was quoted as saying he
and his brother Clint were part of a new generation. "What's
past is past," he said.

James Burlane ordered a second Jack Daniel's. He sipped

the whiskey and reread the article. Stanley Ho had gone from Hong Kong, where he had made his pitch to Ella Nidech, to Houston, where he had talked to the Bonner brothers, to Morocco, where he had recruited Lucien Salvant. Three zits. They were related, Burlane knew.

Burlane bought some change from the bartender and walked down the street until he found a telephone booth. He slipped a quarter into the machine and dialed a downtown Manhattan number.

"Randy Goetz, please." Burlane waited for Goetz's hello, then said, "Randy, this is your man, Robin. I want to buy thirty thousand dollars' worth of common stock in Bonner Oil, please."

There was a pause on the line. "From your special account, I take it."

"Or forty, or fifty thousand. Whatever. No, what the hell. Make it a hundred K if we can scrape it up. I should have enough capital accumulated where I could borrow if need be."

"Not a good buy. I'd stay away from the Bonners if I were you." Robin never requested an investment that made any sense and obviously had access to inside information of some kind. Goetz always felt obliged to resist awful investments— even from someone with a record like Robin's. Goetz couldn't stop himself; he felt responsible for his clients' money, and always hated it when people threw their money at rainbows and rumors.

"Remember my trip to Singapore last month to install the croissant setup? On a Cathay Pacific flight to Manila I met this beautiful Filipina who had this blouse that was sort of inefficient. And . . ."

"I believe." Randy knew that Robin's alleged profession—he said he was in the baking supplies business—and his stories were bogus, but Robin apparently had fun making them up.

". . . this woman had gotten laid by Flub Bonner himself—

this was at a party in Singapore. He has the tiniest dink you can imagine, she said, smaller than her little finger. She said he has a belly like a hairy honeydew.'' Burlane's voice turned squeaky as he described the size of Flub's appendage and his honeydew belly. "And all that money, she said. But he's okay at bragging. He bragged about how Bonner Oil has tumbled onto a huge new reserve in the Caribbean.''

"And so who wins the prize this time?"

"I hadn't given that a lot of thought. Any suggestions?"

"The multiple sclerosis people got it last time out. They did okay."

"Before that it was—"

"The Boy Scouts of America. A nice piece of change. Medical research is always good. Those people need the money."

"Say, that's not a bad idea. We could find a single researcher, the best, and dump a wad on him, give him some freedom and the equipment he needs." Burlane paused. Then he said, "Randy, this one goes to the National Organization for Women."

"What?"

"That's what I want."

"If the Securities and Exchange Commission ever finds out who you are, they'll have you flagged."

"I assure you once again, Randy, nobody will ever, I repeat, *ever* find out who I am or how I get my information. I chose you because you handle a lot of high rollers and my beneficiaries can blend in."

"Listen, Robin Whoever-you-are. My butt's on the line too, remember. I can't be so stupid as not to know you're trading on inside information."

"You're not taking more than your commission, are you? No tipping your other clients? That was our agreement. You haven't broken it?"

"I'm clean."

"Well, then relax. If you ever should get flagged, you're

still square. I have people who'll fix it like a parking ticket."
Robin snapped his fingers next to the receiver.

"They'll what? Who?"

"Never mind who. People who are very accomplished at
fixing things. They'll do it to protect me."

"That's not good enough, Robin."

"The President. Is that good enough?"

Randy Goetz believed him. He said, "I know you won't
tell me who you are, Robin. But I've got a bet with myself
that you're some kind of tycoon."

"I've got a few bucks, that's so," Burlane acknowledged.

"How much? Come on, shock me."

"Enough to buy anything I want. No problem."

"Jesus!" Goetz said.

"Now then, please do as I ask. Turn the stock over to the
National Organization for Women."

"Who is it you want me to say laid it on 'em?"

"Tell them their sugar daddy is a Mr. Boyd."

"No first name or initial?"

"Boyd'll do," Burlane said.

19

FROM the beginning of Cactus Jack Bonner's long, debilitating illness, Dr. Damon Leonard had charged Flub and Clint everything he thought he could get away with and then some. Leonard assumed it would be comforting to the Bonners to spend unconscionable sums on their father's health—it would show everybody they could do it—and if that wasn't the case, they probably didn't pay any attention to trifles like medical bills. Either way Leonard was the winner. Owing to the size of the Bonner fortune, Leonard felt no remorse about his calculations. Cactus Jack Bonner, who was incapable of having a say in the matter, was one of the most profitable living corpses in the United States.

When Flub and Clint requested a consultation, Leonard's mouth turned dry and his stomach fluttered. What if they were pissed? These were Bonners he was dealing with. He had immediately called a strategy session with Alicia, the receptionist with a mouth that worked on his dong like a taffy machine, and they worked out their strategy for the visit.

Damon Leonard poured himself a double shot of Myers's

rum and took it in a pop. What would he say if they wanted
to move Cactus Jack to another home? Was that what they
had in mind? He'd have to put off buying the new chalet in
Aspen. Who the hell did they think they were anyway? He
was the healer. Leonard couldn't understand bitchers. Alamo
Dreams was the most expensive nursing home in Texas.
What did they want, for chrissake?

Alicia said, "Mr. Flub and Mr. Clint Bonner to see you,
Dr. Leonard." Leonard had told Alicia to mister the Bonners
and doctor himself to remind the Bonners that he was a
professional, a physician. He held life in his hands. Alicia
would leave the volume of her receiver turned up so the
Bonners could hear his reply.

"Good heavens! The Bonners," Leonard said. "I'm run-
ning late. Could you entertain them for a few minutes, Miss
Howard? I still have a patient." His tone said: this is the
house of a healer; bakers and billionaires are all the same to
Damon Leonard. Leonard had taken the Hippocratic oath.
Patients came first. Always.

Leonard poured himself another drink and lit a cigarette.
He didn't have to worry about Alicia blowing her end of the
plan; she was an anal compulsive, systematic and orderly to
the extreme. She wasn't the brightest woman in the world,
but tell her what to do and she did it with almost robotlike
efficiency. He even told her how to appear excited in their
lovemaking sessions, and she responded with enthusiasm,
making little *squeak-geek* sounds that turned him on.

Alicia would now be apologizing for leaving the call box
on high and asking the Bonners if she could get them a cup
of coffee.

Leonard disliked people asking questions about treatment.
Who did they think they were? He knew what was best for
people.

The Bonners would be pawing through the *New Yorker*s
and *U.S. News and World Report*s, looking for a *Forbes* or
Fortune.

"I'm ready to see my visitors now, Miss Howard," he said. He had thought of calling them Flub and Clint but thought better of it. He took a deep breath and waited.

Alicia Howard rapped softly on the door. Leonard stood to welcome the Bonners into his office. They were dressed in black suits and white shirts, looking like huge, coarse penguins. They shook hands as they introduced themselves. Leonard wondered if he should cover their rights with his left as he shook, a gesture of sincerity that worked with women. He decided not to; they might think he was queer.

"Flub. Pleased to meet you, Doc," said the shorter brother.

"Clint." The taller Bonner eyed the medical texts on the floor-to-ceiling shelves that lined three of the walls. The fourth wall was a window that overlooked the International style architecture of downtown Houston. "Must take a lot of reading to keep up, Doc."

Leonard appreciated the opening. He rubbed his temples with his left hand. "Hard on the eyes though, I can tell you." Alicia replaced the books periodically so they wouldn't be dated by yellowing paper: Dr. Damon Leonard did his homework on the latest medical research. Before she stocked a new book she cracked it wide open in five or six places, torturing the covers until the spine gave, then made sure there was at least one fingerprint smudge on the edges. This, following Leonard's instructions, was so that the book might look well read if it were casually pulled from the shelf.

"Won't you sit down, please." Leonard thought the Bonners looked rather like adolescent forty-year-olds. He hoped they couldn't smell the rum on his breath.

Flub Bonner settled onto the red leather sofa and said, "Old Clint here read an article in *Cosmopolitan* that said if you've got kin in a nursing home, you ought to check in once in a while, see how they're doing."

"*Cosmopolitan!* Shit too!" Clint laughed.

"Clint's a tit man. He likes the bra ads," Flub said.

Clint said, "What I saw was an article in *USA Today*."

Flub said, "We was wondering how old Cactus Jack's coming along, Dr. Leonard?"

Ahh, they'd read that bitch's article in *USA Today*. Leonard understood. Their visit, in keeping with annoying, vaguely liberal sentiments, was benign. He was relieved. "The old gentleman is doing just fine. He's getting a well-deserved rest. He's tuckered out after raising a pair like you. He's a fighter, your old man. He's even beginning to show a little emotion, the nurses say."

"And the prognosis for the future?" asked Flub.

"Improvement is a long process, especially at his age. All this takes longer when you get older. But give him time and he'll be sitting up and grabbing at nurses again. He's got a good, strong heart. Solid."

"The old Bonner ticker," Clint said.

"We're monitoring a steady, solid beat. It's a damned good heart." Leonard opened a file on his desk and studied a chart. "Look there. Bump, bump, bump. A good, steady beat."

"And so how many years can we expect, then?" Flub leaned forward on the couch.

Leonard smiled. "Oh, your father has years left. Years. You'd be surprised how long a real fighter can hang in there. Right now he's building. When he begins to clear we can ease him into television. Start him on *General Hospital* and game shows and carefully work him into *Monday Night Football*. Then later maybe you two can bring in a cribbage board or something, help him remember old times."

"Get him laid, huh, Doc! Bring him a jug of Old Crow." Clint pulled a book from the wall and opened it. "Looks like you got pissed off every fifty pages there, Doc. Page fifty, page a hundred, page a hundred and fifty." He pulled another book and opened it. "Same here. Spine's fucked up every fifty pages exactly."

Flub took the book and grinned as the pages flopped open at fifty-page intervals. "Somebody do that to a book of mine and I believe I would show him some secret repositories. Terrible thing to do to a book.''

Leonard's face flushed. He had forgotten to tell Alicia to crack the pages at random. Like a robot, she had cracked them every fifty pages and then had overdone it. The price men had to pay for good sex was amazing. He said, ''Your father is a fine old gentleman. It is a pleasure to see a man with such a will to live. We're doing our part. When he gets these little infections of his, why, we're right on top of them.''

''That's very reassuring,'' Flub said.

''We're on a hot line to the Mayo Clinic and Harvard Medical School. At the slightest hint of trouble we have the world's best physicians in Learjets in seconds. Of course, we have the best heart people in the world right here in Houston.'' Leonard snapped his fingers loudly. ''When your dad goes under, believe me, it'll be in spite of the finest medicine money can buy. Nothing second best for Cactus Jack Bonner.''

Flub got to his feet. ''God, something stinks. Did you pass gas, brother Clint?''

''Smells like a fucking sewer in here, I gotta agree.'' He followed Flub to the door.

Flub said, ''Worse than dog dung. Yuch!'' At the door he said, ''I'm betting you'd fuck a pig for five bucks, Doc. What do you think, Clint?''

Clint said, ''I believe I'd pity the poor damned pig.'' Bonner retrieved a money clip from his jacket and peeled off a five-dollar bill and tossed it on the carpet. He followed Flub through the door and they were gone.

20

FLUB Bonner turned on his Kaypro, slipped in two floppies, called up the menu, typed "B:BULLSHIT.MSS" in front of the cursor, and tapped the return key. The light-green cursor blinked silently, a traffic signal saying start, now, write. Flub said, "The thing is, we have to sound like the old fart. Put ourselves in his boots. Say what he'd say. So we have to think."

"Why would he admit that he has a bastard son? That has to be answered. We're dealing with Cactus Jack now. A lot of men would worry about something like that, but for the life of me, I can't imagine Jack doing this. Let's face it." Clint Bonner sprawled in the leather chair with one long, denim-clad leg flopped over the arm. He thought of himself as a Clint in the manner of Eastwood—a tough-ass Texas billionaire. He lit a thin black cigar—these were as close as he could come to the evil little numbers Yul Brynner smoked in *The Magnificent Seven*—and blew three small perfect rings of sweet smoke.

"Guilty conscience," Flub said. The broad-shouldered Flub

was the steadier of the two brothers, a shrewd competitor. His real name was Norbert, which he hated, but he got his nickname playing Pop Warner football. Once, after he had unaccountably dropped the ball in the open field, he had told Cactus Jack that he had simply flubbed. There was no other explanation. From then on he was Flub Bonner.

"We could accuse him of having a conscience. That'd croak the old fucker." Clint grinned sardonically and re- garded his sweet, black cigar. Clint and Flub enjoyed schem- ing, an inheritance from their father they hadn't fully been able to exercise owing to the provisions of his will.

"I don't see that we have to worry a whole lot. Who in hell'd think we'd pull Jack's plug so we could give away a half-billion bucks? Shit, Clint, we'd have to be off our nut. If we don't fight the provision, who will?" Flub opened the folder that contained Lucien Salvant's autobiography. "Would you just look at the poop on this poor son of a bitch. Pathetic bastard." He sailed the record of Salvant's life across the room to his brother.

Clint leafed through the autobiography. He shook his head. "Jesus, can you imagine? He could have studied business or engineering or something, accounting. He might have gotten somewhere. Made a few bucks. So what does he do? He sits around jawing about James Gould Cozzens and Nelson Al- gren." Clint shook his head.

"Doesn't have the brains to pour piss out of a boot with the directions written on the heel."

"Let's get this done, Flub. It doesn't have to be letter perfect; if we don't bitch, nobody else's gonna. Who's gonna challenge a giveaway? Old Sing Sing Boyd's got it squared with the IRS. Jesus, can you see the faces on those fuckers at Shell and Texaco when we walk off with the Sunyang con- tract. Hoo boy! That's gonna make my fuckin' day."

"Lucky old Jack had the foresight to go public with Bonner Oil. We'll just quietly begin scarfing up the remaining shares over the next couple of weeks. And when the contract is announced, hey boy!''

"We ease into it, the way I see it. What's the SEC gonna get us for? Trading on inside knowledge? Now, just how in hell could we possibly fix the Sunyang deal, Flub? I ask you: how? No way. Hell, we're just a couple of fun-loving Texans, gambling boys." Clint rubbed his crotch, leering. "Besides, they couldn't accuse us of anything without accusing the Chinese of being in collusion with us, and the State Department wouldn't put up with that for a minute."

"Last time we were in there, I swore the old man knew who we were. Did you see him watch us like that? His eyes were moving, I know they were."

"He doesn't know fuck, Flub. Poor son of a bitch. Everything's scrambled up in there. If anything like that happens to me, I want the goddamned plug pulled."

"We shouldn't have let this go on."

"We shouldn't have, but we did." Clint stubbed out his cigar and started digging for another. "We've been chicken-shit is what we've been."

"This way we get Sunyang and give Jack a break." Flub Bonner returned to the keyboard, reading as he typed. " 'I, John Ashby Bonner, being of sound mind and . . .' What is that they always say?"

" 'Health' is it? Say 'good health.' "

"Health doesn't have anything to do with it. You could be in piss-poor health and still think straight. That's all lawyers worry about. '. . . being of sound mind, and thinking of setting things straight with the Lord . . .' "

Clint burst out laughing. "Cactus Jack Bonner? Squaring it with the Lord? We've got to give this veri . . . veri . . . what is that word?"

"Verisimilitude. A professor's word. You should ask our new brother about that one, Clint. Means it looks like it could be true. Believable."

"Jack'd turn in his grave if we put a lot of religious talk in his mouth."

Flub said, "Laugh now. Get it out of your system. The truth is that Christians take that stuff seriously, little brother. They really do. Since they believe it, they don't see any reason why everybody else shouldn't including, I assure you, even Cactus Jack Bonner. Nobody asks real questions when religion's involved. You either believe or you don't. No tweenies. Jack's facing the end, see, and he wants to believe."

"I still don't know, Flub. Jack Bonner?" Clint snubbed out the butt of his little cigar and began unwrapping another one.

"Remember Nixon's old pal Charles Colson? He got out of Allenwood, and the next thing you know he's on the evangelist circuit—born-again Chuck. And John DeLorean. The first thing he did after he dodged the slammer was to grab for Jesus. Everybody believed. No problem. He put all that pious horseshit in a book, and people ran out and bought it."

"It'll be hard to keep from laughing."

"They'll want to believe, Clint. If Jack accepts Jesus at the end, why then he's no different than they are, is he? He's been brought down there with them; everybody's equally off their rocker. They'll want to believe, don't you see? To question the authenticity of the codicil is to question their belief in the power of the gospel. They're very sensitive to that."

"It'll have to be carefully done."

"Yessiree." Flub Bonner erased the "I, John Ashby Bonner" opener and stared at the blinking cursor. "I don't think he'd use all that legal bullshit, would he? 'When I was a young man and feeling my oats . . .' "

" 'Feeling my oats.' That's good!"

"Coming to the good part," Flub said. "Wait. No. 'When I was a young man I always wanted to go to New Orleans for

Mardi Gras.' This'll give him an excuse. He was drunk, see, and got caught up with a bunch of Cajun swampers.''

"Say, 'When I was a young man and feeling my oats, I always wanted to go to Mardi Gras.' That gets the horny part in there and everybody knows Mardi Gras is in New Orleans. He wouldn't be talking about Rio.''

Flub rubbed his hands together. ''Both horny and drunk. Got it. Damn, this is fun! How about, 'When I was a young buck and . . .' ''

"You're making him sound like he was colored."

Flub erased buck and replaced it with ''stud.''

"A born-againer wouldn't call himself a stud."

Flub erased stud and replaced it with ''fellow.''

"No."

Flub put ''buck'' back in.

"You're right. You had it right the first time."

"What else? How old was he in 1946?"

"Forty-four," Clint said. "He's looking back, remember. If you're eighty-four you probably don't think you grew up till you were fifty. He was young and impetuous, see."

"How about, 'When I was an impetuous young wildcatter'?"

Clint said, "That's better yet."

"He's writing this codicil, see, writing for posterity, so he'd want to throw an occasional impressive word in there. Also this gets the oil stuff in there.'' Flub furrowed his brow in concentration.

"Right. We need to get the date in there, and something about wildcatting. And the religion crap if that's the high poke. Here's where we give it to them.'' Grinning, Clint Bonner began undulating his hips obscenely.

"Jack has to show remorse for running around on Mom." Both Clint and Flub knew that as the years wore on, Jack Bonner's loyalty to their mother—who had died of cancer eight years earlier—had become more and more of a fiction. Being a billionaire was like being oiled with an aphrodisiac;

awed groupies hardly out of high school attacked Jack's zipper and belt buckle, pretending they were sucking up the dregs of a six-bit milkshake.

Flub was a quick typist. His fingers danced on the keys: " 'In 1946, when I'd just got back from fighting Japs, I returned to my wildcatting business in Houston. I was an impetuous young man, full of piss and vinegar, and feeling my oats . . .' "

"All fucking right! But full of energy, not piss and vinegar. He's supposed to be mellowing out, remember. And Japanese, he's a Christian now."

" 'To my everlasting regret, I decided to go to Mardi Gras with my running mate, Percy Phipps, from over to Waco way. That's how I met her.' What do you think, Clint? Old Percy's dead. He can't argue. This suggests that Jack started out good but was led astray by Percy, and only now, on his deathbed, does he come to Christ and get squared away."

"I like the 'over to Waco way' bit."

Flub kept writing: " 'Me and Percy screwed 'em up and down the Gulf'; everybody knows that."

"Say they 'had women up and down the Gulf.' "

Flub replaced "screwed 'em" with "had women," and said, "Coming to the mother now. We have to be careful." Flub Bonner studied Lucien Salvant's autobiography. "Is Jack still in love with her? Is that it? Is she dead or alive?"

"Gotta be dead."

"Heroic death?"

"Oh, sure. Add to his guilt." Clint blew a series of tight, neat rings of cigar smoke, his eyes narrowed in thought.

"New Orleans is largely Catholic, right? Suppose he knocked up a good Catholic girl. The old man could have found a legitimate doctor to give her an abortion, even in 1945; he had plenty of bucks. He knocks her up, but she won't get an abortion because of her religion; it would be a terrible sin. Her family sends her to a family in another part of New Orleans where she stays at home for nine months until the baby, a boy, is born in January. The boy is given up for adoption . . .''

". . . A black family . . . a black family takes care of the mother. It's always smart to throw a black in there somewhere. The blacks will be portrayed as being decent and generous. They'll need a reason to want to believe the story.''

"And the mother goes to a convent where she becomes a nun and takes a vow of silence.''

Flub grinned. "Right! She's a regular saint, pissed upon by this rich guy with the big cock. No problem with the feminists there. They'll want to believe it. However, in his last, lucid days, fearing death, Jack turns to the Lord and is repentant. No amount of money will pay for his grievous sin, but he makes a gesture. He gives the kid a half-billion dollars. This is too wonderful not to be true. The newspaper and TV people will want to believe it's true. Are they going to quarrel with the logic? Hell, no. Think of the fun they'll have!''

"Exactly. Who is the nun, they'll want to know? Is she still alive? Where is she cloistered? How does she feel now that her son is inheriting a half-billion dollars?''

Flub laughed. "Hell, Clint, we ought to buy into a couple of those supermarket rags and help them along with some leaked bullshit. When we see the end of the story we could sell short.''

"Jack'd be proud. I'll see what Gottlieb thinks.'' Clint took a notepad from the desk and scribbled a memo to himself.

Both Clint and Flub Bonner were closet racists; they believed Jews were a trifle quicker than themselves, so all their accountants and lawyers were Jewish. They believed the secret to the Bonner fortune was due to the combination of Jewish brains and the Bonners' own Christian knack for laughing a Texas haw-haw laugh and drawing blood at the same time. This ability—in addition to the fortune itself—was their inheritance from Cactus Jack.

Like Howard Hughes, the Bonners were always concerned lest they be on the receiving end of the Texas high poke, and like Hughes they hired Mormons for their guards and drivers. The Mormons were so unaccountably honest and straight that Flub and Clint were given to giggling; at the same time they paid the Mormons well and made sure they got all the milk they could drink. When the Bonners went tiger hunting in India they hired Sikhs. Had it not been for the problem of scarcity—close to the market for nannies—and the inevitable bad PR, the Bonners would have employed eunuchs.

21

IN one of those miracles associated with divine intervention, ghosts, spirits, *fung shui,* or whatever you please,
Cactus Jack Bonner was alert from the moment Flub and
Clint walked in the door. The wonderful circuits worked.
Jack knew who his sons were and—judging from their long
faces and undertaker outfits—why they were there. It was as
though he drifted from day to day in a murk of memories he
did not understand, and the confusion parted suddenly, like
clouds over the Gulf, admitting sanity and clarity.

Jack couldn't see out of his left eye at all, and his right one
was next to useless. But he saw Flub and Clint clear enough,
and was overwhelmed to see them. He would have cried, but
he couldn't coordinate that many emotions at one time. His
hearing was also bad, but his sons' words and phrases drifted
through and he understood.

Flub said, "Jesus, Clint, who'd have thought it would
come to this."

Clint Bonner swallowed and closed the door.

Flub put a briefcase on Jack's dresser and dug a silver

dollar out of his trouser pockets. He flipped the coin high into the air, saying, "You call it, little brother."

"It'll be heads."

Heads it was.

Flub lost. He stared at the coin, transfixed.

Jack, watching this, knew what it was about. He wanted to talk to them, to encourage them. They were doing this themselves, not hiring someone like a couple of pussies. They were being men, damn them, and he was proud of them. He remembered little Flub walking to the plate for his first at bat in the little leagues, remembered Flub taking practice cuts, remembered him swinging from his heels at the first pitch.

Flub, his eyes watering, flopped into a chair.

Jack thought, Do what you have to do, Flub.

"It's gotta be done, Flub," Clint said.

Listen to your brother, Jack thought.

"Why couldn't he have popped off like everybody else? The old son of a bitch earned himself enough money to buy anything he wanted except a ticket out of it all. We shouldn't have let him go on like this." Flub's voice turned soft, regretful. "He can't even watch the fucking Oilers."

Jack wanted to get up and comfort his sons. They were thirty-seven and thirty-nine but still kids to him. He felt proud that they looked like him at their age. Flub in particular looked like his clone. He wanted to hold them.

"I think we lost Cactus Jack a couple of years ago, Flub. This ain't the old son of a bitch who used to cuss us out all the time."

Flub wiped his eyes with his sleeve and opened the briefcase. He started to water up again when he picked up the hypodermic. With tears in his eyes he sat at his father's side. "Poor old fucker," he said. He cradled Jack's cadaverous, nearly hairless skull.

Clint took a chair at his brother's side and gripped Flub around the shoulder. "Get it over with, Flub."

Jack remembered the little Flubber taking his cuts in little league, swinging that bat for all he was worth. He was Jack Bonner's kid, by God, and he stood up there and swung the bat; he didn't Mickey Mouse around hoping to draw a walk.

"Jack, I know you don't understand us, but for whatever it's worth Clint and I thought we should have done this a long time ago. If you can hear us, we loved you, old man."

"You bet," said Clint.

"We're sorry we made you wait, Jack, but listen to this: if we speed your parting up a little, Bonner Oil stands to clear six billion bucks over the next ten years."

"Six billion bucks, Dad. Gonna grease a Chink's palm."

Jack tried to smile. His mouth opened and he made a small sound. He was proud of his sons. Thinking all the time, they were. They made every ace count, every bullet, just as he'd taught them. He was so damned proud.

Clint said, "Look at that, will you? The old fucker's smiling."

Cactus Jack's oldest son, weeping, slid the needle home, and the old man, watching the Flubber swing the bat at six billion bucks, died happy.

When Lucien Salvant returned to Quantrell College, the death of Cactus Jack Bonner was in the national spotlight together with all manner of speculation about his will. At the request of Flub and Clint Bonner, the will was temporarily being held *in camera* by a judge. In announcing the decision, the judge stressed that the reason did not involve a challenge of the will.

No challenge? Well, what was it, then? This guaranteed even more airtime.

The television networks were eager to report the embarrassing details of the Bonner fortune. Were they or were they not richer than the Hunts or the Murchisons? Not having anything concrete, reporters began to speculate. Had one of Jack's many affairs caught up with his sons? Was there in fact some kind of legal challenge being mounted on the fortune?

Salvant regarded the mass media as public theater. In choosing what war, plague, or ribbon-cutting to feature, city editors and television assignment editors were in fact authors of a never-ending script. Artistically, the result was a mélange, rather like a circus presided over by operatic singers, goons, and strippers, a national *Gong Show*. The singers sang illiterate lyrics as loud as they could, while jugglers tumbled over tigers, acrobats dodged elephants, and pretty girls were molested by stuffed gorillas or knocked tumbling by clowns with foam bats.

The Quantrell professors were in a quarrelsome, sour mood. They were locked, they said, in mortal combat with their new president, an outwardly splendid Ivy League model who had unaccountably turned on them, a jerk of the worst order who preferred the company of the industrialists who were governors to that of professors in corduroy jackets. When Salvant had gone on sabbatical leave, the faculty, frustrated over the lack of pay raises, had been divided into implacable factions. Intrigue and gossip had floated like a sulphurous vapor in the faculty dining room. He returned to find a passionate humanist eating celery soup at the side of a rat psychologist with barbecue sauce on his beard.

A friend of Salvant's in the biology department said the faculty was in for a terrible struggle. It was true that the president had been forced to make a series of cutbacks, he said, but that wasn't the only reason people were pissed; it seemed as if everybody had a different complaint. There had been initial skirmishes by official committees. This was followed by the rise of ad hoc committees with their white papers and manifestos. When the Women's Caucus joined forces with the Ad Hoc Stadium Refurbishing Committee, the air had crackled with excitement. Then came more manifestos and white papers. The student editor of the *Quantrell Raider* said he felt like John Reed covering the Bolshevik revolution. He quoted an unnamed history professor as saying the passions were higher at Quantrell because the stakes were lower.

There had followed a pitched battle in which the faculty, feeling a dramatic gesture was in order, foolishly voted no confidence in the president. In the end the bewildered professors, cleaning their spectacles, crying in polysyllabic anguish—some even in foreign languages—had been routed. The colors of noble causes lay trampled in the confusion of riderless horses and horseless riders. Extremely solemn and serious professors—for years the advisors and confidants of deans and presidents—were now ordinary professors like everybody else. There were those who lamented the departure of a civilized dean who would have made a fine president except that he was familiar, and they had gone for the razzle-dazzle and wound up with an asshole.

The president's Ivy League ego was hardly scratched. Followed by his well-tailored toady, he strode defiantly down the halls of Quantrell College, his spine arched like a drawn bow.

The board of governors watched the painful battle through binoculars, well away from the acrid smell of burning careers. The governors were businessmen who judged a man's brains and accomplishments by the thickness of his wallet and so secretly despised the professors for being affected, self-righteous pricks. If professors were so damned smart, then why did they have to drink generic beer and drive old VW vans?

At Quantrell, a faculty line was currency, bullion even, and resigning a tenured slot was like throwing the faculty a luscious bone. Department heads would tumble after it like hounds, toothless old dogs in the lead, howling for what they regarded as their due, females in the rear, baying in anguish at past bones lost, wanting makeup bones. Competition for available spots had nothing to do with servicing students, although students were always cited as the reason. The truth

was that having a larger department was a form of conspicu-
ous consumption. Those professors whose imaginations were
governed by the mirror rather than by books or ideas wanted
more, more, more.

Lucien Salvant retreated to Dickman's Saloon on Paw Paw
Street to celebrate his decision to gamble his future as Sing
Sing Boyd's kept *taipan*. Now all he had to do was hope
Boyd's call came before the fall term began at Quantrell.

22

FLUB and Clint Bonner arranged the Dallas connection to the Lucian Salvant poke through intermediaries, which was how Henry Kissinger dealt with the Chinese to arrange the visit by President Nixon. This was their first solo high poke since Cactus Jack's death and they wanted to show those hand-wringing goddamned lawyers what poking was all about.

Thereupon the Bonners, looking for a little help with their appearance—this was required by the logic of the poke—went shopping in an enclosed Houston shopping mall where the weather was always perfect on a pretend Parisian boulevard, and one could sip cognac by plastic flowers and be served by succulent young women wearing berets and little tiny outfits with black mesh stockings. The Bonners ended up buying a book in which a handsome Hollywood makeup artist, intimate with Streep's nose and Gere's coloring, detailed the secrets of his success.

Early the next morning they lit out for Dallas in Flub's cherry-red Aston Martin. This was so that Flub could blow some carbon out its ass, fuck the Texas State Patrol. The Bonners drank cans of Lone Star beer so they could pretend to be a couple of T. Texas Assholes. The Bonners loved their toys. They were pilots and had their own airplanes and helicopters. They liked to zoom and roar.

In Dallas, Flub and Clint went on a shopping expedition with the book in hand, buying everything the author recommended. Then they went back to the penthouse they kept for their Dallas poking—which was often and plenty—and got down to work.

Flub Bonner poured himself another tumbler of bourbon and branch and tried not to laugh. He adjusted the towel on his shoulders. "Don't get that shit in my eye now. That stuff could blind a person."

"Goddammit, stop moving around, now, and don't be playing with your pecker." Clint Bonner stepped back to admire his handiwork, and took a drag on his mean little stogie. "Look in the mirror."

Flub looked in the mirror and snorted into his drink. "Jesus Christ, get serious, Clint. You made me look like I've got black eyes." He sucked in his little pot belly in indignation.

"Close the damned things and let me swab the muck off. I'll try some of this Deepened Gold here. Maybe that'll do it." Clint showed his brother the diminutive container of makeup. "This gunk costs a couple of bucks. We ought to buy into cosmetics."

"Are you sure they didn't get that out of somebody's pasture?"

"This's gonna turn out to be a big TV thing, so we've gotta look properly haggard." Clint grabbed another cloth and plunged it into soapy water.

"God, can you imagine anyone wearing this stuff on their face? Gloria Steinbrenner's right about that one."

"George Steinbrenner owns the Yankees." Clint readied the soapy cloth.

"Whatever."

"Steinem's her last name."

"This stuff's awful." Flub bunched his face to protect it from the onslaught of Clint's washcloth.

"It's guys like you who've got the rest of us kissing their asses if we want to get laid. All they ask, for chrissake, is for you to keep their gurus straight. I hate to have to do this to you, Flub, but this's gotta be dramatic; there's no other way the public's going to accept this kind of poke from Jack Bonner's kids."

Flub said, "I think we're still pushin' it. Why don't you read that article again before you start smearing that stuff on my face?"

"With anybody else we'd probably be pushing it, I agree." Clint gave his brother a clean towel. "Here, wipe 'em with this and I'll try it again. By the day after tomorrow, we'll have this down pat." He reopened the book. "Who gives a fuck about oil on Cher's forehead?"

"Get your goo out."

"It says here that Ryan O'Neal has 'September Skin.' What does that mean, Flub?" Clint lit another cigar and unscrewed the Deepened Gold. He read the directions with his eyes squinted against the rising smoke.

"Easy does it this time, dammit! You can read what the man says. A little of that stuff goes a long way. All we want's a little natural haggard, not an Academy Award."

"Close your eyes." Clint bent to his task once again, applying the barest hint of color above his brother's eyes. He added shadow with Wild Charcoal and blended the two colors together. "When I took the painting course at Tech, the little fruit professor called this shit raw umber and burnt umber."

Flub, eyes closed, said, "Painting? You?"

"The Delts all said it was Mickey, but the teeny fucker gave me a D. I suppose that's cause I only showed up for two classes. I started a painting of an old shoe. That's it, Flub, take a look.''

Flub Bonner looked at himself in the mirror. Clint had found his touch. "Hey, good work! Looks like I haven't slept in a month.''

Clint turned mock effeminate—Mr. Clint, the makeup man, hinting for a compliment. "You can see the paint, then?''

"Looks great, it really does.''

Clint was pleased with his work. "We'll have to take a break from poking so folks'll know we're for real.''

"The PR folks say six weeks'll do.''

"Then it's back to the poking, brother Flub. Real poking now that we've got them damned lawyers off our backs.''

Clint looked at his watch. "It'll be coming on TV any minute now.'' He slid aside the panel that hid their set and turned it on. "What do you say we finish up with this stuff and have ourselves a big old bourbon before we do it? Loosen us up. What do you say?''

Flub said, "Unregenerate pricks to the last.'' He got up to fetch the whiskey.

"What do you say that on our way back from Beijing we stop by Hong Kong for a couple of days and poke some of that sideways stuff?''

Flub Bonner's belly bobbled as he laughed. "Give 'em a Texas thrill or two. You're on, brother Clint.''

On the television set a woman so beautiful she was boring said, "The will of Texas billionaire Cactus Jack Bonner was made public in Houston today and, as rumored, contained a stunning surprise. Bonner, eighty-four, who died two weeks ago, willed a half-billion dollars to a New Orleans college professor who Bonner says was his illegitimate son.

"In a handwritten codicil dated two years ago, Bonner says Lucien Salvant, shown here receiving the news, was conceived in Lake Charles, Louisiana, and born in New Orleans forty years ago.''

Seeing Lucien Salvant, Flub and Clint burst out laughing,

ignoring the woman who was saying how the judge had suppressed the details of the will until experts could authenticate Bonner's handwriting and the signatures of the witnesses.

"Shit, would you look at him?" Flub Bonner's face was bunched with laughter.

Clint Bonner could not stop laughing either. "My God!"

So this was to be their half brother. Cactus Jack would have loved it. Beautiful!

Lucien Salvant lived in an old hotel that had been converted into apartments almost entirely inhabited by artists, musicians, and assistant professors at Quantrell College. Salvant was the only academic who had stayed after being promoted to associate professor; after the other assistants were promoted they dropped their facade of pride in being broke and began complaining about the Italian restaurant downstairs. Eventually they moved to a safer, more impressive neighborhood.

There were two small theaters in his area of Paw Paw Street; one showed the best old movies, the other foreign films. There were cheap Greek and Indian restaurants, an okay pizza joint, and a good place to have a lingering breakfast—people nibbled butterhorns in the morning and read minimalist short stories. There was a good tavern for a bottle of cold beer or a cheeseburger on a hot afternoon.

One of Lucien Salvant's greatest pleasures was to lounge in a café and read and drink café au lait. This is why he especially liked Europe, where civilized lingering was prized above processing the maximum number of growling stomachs, as was the practice in the United States. Salvant liked to read a newspaper or magazine and consider—between an article on Italian soccer, say, and one on an archeological dig—such things as the quality of light coming through old windows or how life is poured, cup by cup, as coffee from a pot.

In the United States, the best cafés were found in enclaves

near the campuses of large universities. These neighborhoods were frequented by bearded men—accomplished in quantum physics or the translation of obscure texts—who wore blue jeans and veteran tweed jackets, and women who baked bread and wrote poetry or fired ceramics. The people who lived in Salvant's neighborhood didn't mind being surrounded by people who bowled and wore baseball caps that advertised construction equipment and chicken feed. The proximity of bowlers was Bohemia's only defense against invasion by the odious materialists. The yups, who had once proclaimed themselves the moral saviors of the nation, had now turned their energies over to the pursuit of bucks, and their rage was directed at the lack of money being spent on herpes research.

Lucien Salvant was playing cribbage with the bartender at Dickman's Tavern on that fatal afternoon, when he had to go to the john.

When he stepped out of the toilet, his mind still on the game, he found Dickman's stuffed with a crowd of people who all seemed to be shouting at him at once.

Salvant was then blinded by a bank of lights. He squinted and held his arm up to shield his eyes.

Flashbulbs popped and cameras whirred.

People shouted at him:

"Hey, Lou! This way, Lou! How does it feel to inherit a half-billion dollars, Lou? Lucien! Dr. Salvant! What's the first thing you're going to buy? Dr. Salvant! Lou! Lucien! What are you going to buy? Lou, what's the first thing you're going to buy?"

Salvant blinked at the questions, and the blinding light. This blink came at the mention of Lucien and the reporters took it as indicating a preference for his full given name. "Lucien! Did you ever think you'd inherit a half-billion dollars, Lucien? Can you keep your head up please, Lucien? That's it. What are you going to buy first, Lucien? Can you step a little to the right please? A house? A sailboat? An airplane? What did you always dream of owning, Lucien?

Lucien! Lucien! Do you have a girl friend, Lucien? What's her name? Are you engaged to be married, is that it? What kind of women do you like, Lucien?''

Through all this hubbub and shouting of his first name, he somehow heard Dickman's bartender shouting:

"Salvant, for God's sake zip your fly!''

The questions came at him in a tumble, one on top of another: "What are you going to buy, Lucien? What do you want to own? Did you ever dream you'd inherit a half-billion dollars?''

Unzipped pants! He'd been thinking about cribbage combinations. How was he to know that a picture of him standing there with squinted eyes, open mouth, and open fly would appear on the cover of magazines all over the world.

23

TELEVISION reporters seek the currency of the bizarre, which, translated into Nielsens, means higher advertising revenue. Summoned by anonymous tips from the Reverend Bobby Meacham's public relations corps, both broadcast and print journalists were still listening to the details of Lucien Salvant's inheritance on a Dallas all-news radio station when Clint and Flub Bonner pulled up to the world headquarters of the International Gospel of God's Beneficence in an Aston Martin. Those who had seen the scene in the New Orleans saloon were still laughing about how the cameras had ambushed the poor damned professor walking out of the john with his fly unzipped.

As Clint and Flub stepped out of their automobile, there was some confusion and a few questions, but the reporters, in deference to the nearby house of God, were remarkably subdued. Out of the shadows of the dazzling building stepped the Reverend Bobby Meacham, counsel and confidant of presidents and the designated author of a score of ghostwritten best-selling books offering advice and succor to Christians everywhere.

Video cameras waited to capture every moment. Still cameras snapped and clacked. Meacham's media people had considered the quality of light, which pleased the photographers.

Judging from their sorrowful appearances and darkened eyes, the Bonner brothers had been through a dreadful ordeal in the days following their father's death.

Flub and Clint had never shown any interest in religion before. There was not an assignment editor or city editor in Dallas who did not wonder what was up. Old Cactus Jack was dead, and his kids appeared to be his clones. But were they? How would they hold up under pressure after all those years of waiting in the shadow of lawyers? Did they have Jack's guile, or did their mother's genes predominate? Judging from this performance, they were mamma's boys. But were they really Christians? Was that possible, or was it so much more Bonner bullshit?

What kind of poke was this?

The cameras whirred as the Reverend Bobby Meacham, glowing with celebrity and showing his famous smile and incredible white teeth, strode out to meet them, his arms outstretched, laying on his all-purpose southern accent: "Cli-int! Flub! It's so good to see you two rascals again. It's been a long time. How y'all been doin'?" This dropping of the *g* was to please his largely blue-collar following. Meacham divided Clint into two syllables, Cli-int, to satisfy Oklahomans, who were superb givers, among the best in fact. Meacham had never met the Bonners, but because of their fortune had wanted to for years.

"It's been too long, Bobby!" Flub said. "Bobby! Bobby!" He embraced Meacham.

"Praise the Lord, Bobby! Praise Him! Praise Him!" said Clint, hugging Meacham. (Later, Flub would swear at his younger brother for this indiscretion, saying Clint's declaration of faith was too risky at that point. They had too much on the line for Clint to be horsing around with cheap theatrics.)

Meacham stepped back, beaming. "Why, I remember you two when you were just pups. Old Cactus Jack's kids, bless his memory. Gee whiz! By golly, time flies!" The Reverend Meacham, feeling the Power if not yet the Money, put his arms around the strayed sheep.

As the television cameras recorded every detail close up, the anguished Clint Bonner stumbled and was overcome. He sobbed, "Bobby! Bobby!"

The Reverend Bobby Meacham held Clint in a comforting embrace, murmuring encouragement. "I remember you two little tykes aplayin' with your trucks until old Cactus Jack made you skedaddle on account of company. Grown men! How time flies?"

The ordinarily animated Flub looked haunted, anguished. When Clint was able to continue, Flub began sobbing and blubbered, "Thank you, Bobby. Daddy always said we could count on you and he was right."

When they had recovered at last, the distraught Bonners allowed Meacham to guide them inside.

The gathering of television and newspaper reporters grew as the minutes passed. The reporters had fun speculating while they waited, wondering what in heaven the Hunts and Murchisons would think of all this transparent horseshit that they would be required to report with a straight face. An hour later, Flub and Clint Bonner emerged with Meacham; they were smiling and relaxed. After a parting embrace with the Reverend Bobby Meacham, they got into their Aston Martin and drove off.

The Reverend Bobby Meacham then held a solemn press conference. He began the press conference by cautioning the reporters that what had happened in the previous hour was an intensely personal matter. What went on in the International House of God's Beneficence was strictly between a man and his Lord. Meacham had to respect Clint and Flub's privacy.

Meacham then said the Bonners would ordinarily have challenged the codicil to their father's will, but when the experts said, yes, it was executed in their father's handwriting, and that the signatures of the witness and the notary public were authentic as well, then the Bonners began rethinking their lives and their values.

"What kind of men were they?" Meacham asked. "What kind of citizens? What kind of values did they have? What kind of legacy did they want to leave to their descendants? These questions cut to the core of the family of man. Exactly what were they as human beings? What, truly, did they stand for? Were they to be admired or scorned, praised or damned? What was the honorable life?"

Meacham looked at his watch and said, "Between three and four P.M. today, my good and dear old friends, Flub and Clint Bonner answered all those questions and more. After straying from the flock for most of their adult lives they were, in my presence and in communion with the Lord Almighty, reborn unto the bosom of Jesus Christ. They cannot take from their brother, Lucien Salvant, what is rightfully his. This is a matter of personal ethics and of rebirth and glory. We have witnessed a Miracle of Our Lord and Savior Jesus Christ."

After the press conference, the Reverend Meacham said he would grant exclusive interviews to reporters from all the networks and anybody else who asked. This was, he said, "to eliminate speculation and to be fair."

By the time the solemn-faced television reporters had finished the evening news, everybody in the land was talking about Bobby Meacham's extraordinary achievement of converting Clint and Flub Bonner to Christ.

A week later, God's Bountiful Kitchen, Bobby Meacham's program to feed starving children in Africa, received an anonymous donation of $1 million.

Owing to the fact that he served the Lord, the Reverend Bobby Meacham was spared having to pay taxes on the donation. In fact God's Bountiful Kitchen sent $10,000 worth of corn to wheat-eaters in Addis Ababa, a wretched city with a name rivaling Timbuktu and Ulan Bator. If reporters had asked, they would have been told that this sum would have been larger had it not been for administrative overhead and the complicated, expensive cost of doing business in Marxist Ethiopia.

24

THE color photographs that accompanied Pak Tze Fan's listing of available property were professionally done by one Cheung Bai of Macao, who had stapled his card to the lower right-hand corner of the opening page of photos. The photographs, mounted behind clear plastic, showed aerial views of each island plus shots of mooring facilities, if there were any, sources of water, hills, forests, and, in some cases, details of the outlying reef.

To one side of the display table was an easel mounted with photographs of Pak and various celebrity clients—the Filipino pop singer Jaime Alcantara, the Japanese model Tamiko, the Malaysian welterweight champion of the world, Bobby Monoto, and others whom Gene Holt didn't recognize. "Heavens, you're not going to take my picture, I hope!"

Pak laughed. "No, no, that goes without saying. These are public people, celebrities, not somebody like yourself. However, some of them could be your neighbors." Pak turned his attention to a large photo album on the table. "These shots by Mr. Cheung are of the islands that both seem to fit your needs and are fairly easy to negotiate, Mr. Holt. There are drawbacks to them all, as you'll find out.''

"Aren't there always?" Gene Holt was eager to see the pictures. The man without a home would have a place of his own. He was excited. He looked at the photograph of Tamiko, obviously satisfied with her retreat. "I wouldn't mind having a neighbor like that," he said.

"She's lovely, isn't she? Keep in mind that if nothing here satisfies you, my people can keep looking. There are a lot of islands in Southeast Asia, Mr. Holt, and we're pleased to have you as our guest on Fong Wai Chau as long as it takes to find exactly what you want."

Holt turned to the first page, to an aerial shot of a pear-shaped island.

Pak opened *The New York Times Atlas of the World* and pointed to a spot just southwest of New Guinea. In addition to the atlas, he had a number of notebooks, bound in red plastic, that were intended to answer any questions Holt might have. These covered weather, geography, soils, culture, stability of national governments, national laws, availability of forged documents and fake identity packages, and estimates of improvement costs. "This is Fakfak Island in the Ceram Sea. It's about twenty square acres and as you can see has a forest of tropical broadleafs and room for a small airport."

"I was thinking of something a little closer to the action," Holt said. He cleared his throat softly.

Pak went right on about Fakfak. "It's only fourteen hundred miles to Bali. The hippie girls at Kuta Beach are quite amenable, I'm told. One gets them high on marijuana first."

"I was thinking of Hong Kong, and Taipei."

"Nineteen hundred miles to Jakarta, twenty-one hundred to Singapore, twenty-six hundred to Bangkok, sixteen hundred to Manila. The officials at those airports are all bribable. If you had a small jet, a Citation, perhaps."

The distances between Holt's old Caribbean haunts were

closer and his face showed it. But there was no turning back. "I see. And the weather? Soil? Vegetation?" For the kind of bucks they were talking about, Holt wanted to see everything.

Pak Tze Fan consulted a red notebook. "Let's see. Fakfak Island. Hot all year round, from eighty-two to eighty-eight of your degrees Fahrenheit. Relative humidity around seventy-five percent. Rain from April through August, ten inches at both ends and twenty-five in the middle."

"Hot all year round."

Pak rested his notebook momentarily. "I could get you farther north if you'd like, but there are fewer islands there and it's much more difficult to remain anonymous, I have to tell you. Also, the costs go up as you go north. I'm safe here because I have people in the Hong Kong police."

"Fakfak has its charms."

"Chief among them is its own hill, giving you water pressure if you locate your collectors on top, and the possibility of an underground house, keeping you cool all year without air conditioning."

"The wind?"

"Not much in the summer—that's the reverse of your northern hemisphere months—and monsoons from the southeast in the winter. Not enough for a dependable generator. Local warm currents to the southwest. It's safe because it's out of the way and of no economic value to the Indonesians."

Holt turned to the next page of photos, which introduced the next island.

"This is Illana Island in the Sulu Archipelago in the Philippines. I wasn't sure whether or not to include this one. You have ardent Moslems on these islands and they would prefer to be part of Indonesia. But it's so gorgeous I thought I might include it."

"It's lovely." Holt looked wistful. "I'll pass, though. I read a magazine article about some of the problems they've been having down there."

"I think that's just as well. We have much better prospects

in the Philippines, including two superb possibilities in Leyte Gulf.''

Holt turned the page again.

Pak said, ''I don't know whether you're interested in raising your own garden, but the soils vary greatly throughout Southeast Asia. These are tropical soils and so generally suffer from the leaching action of the hot sun and heavy rains. There are some, though, that will respond to fertilizer.'' Pak checked a red notebook. ''For example, you could have raised vegetables on Fakfak.''

''This is fun. Listen, why don't we start with what you regard as the best island first. I'm curious. Never mind the price; let's start from there and work our way down.'' He started flipping forward through the pages of photographs.

''They're arranged alphabetically. If you want the luxury island first, turn to Q—Quintin Island—one of the Leyte Gulf islands as it turns out.''

Holt turned straight to the listing under the Q tab. He spread the notebook and his mouth fell open. ''I want it.''

Pak grinned. ''I bet you do.'' There were four pages of photographs of Quintin Island, and Pak waited patiently while Holt went from one to the next. ''Incidentally, the waterfall comes from a spring higher up on the mountain. The flow can easily accommodate a generator and is steady the year round. You could air condition your house if you wanted.''

''Whoa!''

''The beach there is about two hundred meters long. I should say here that this island is owned by a wealthy Filipino family, which is good—much easier than buying from the government when you have bureaucrats to deal with. The red tape can take months or even years, and the bribes can get very expensive. The best situation is if the owners are willing to give you a ninety-nine-year lease on the land, which this family is. Once you settle in, you'll find the local officials are quite bribable. It is a way of life in the Philippines.''

Holt bit his lower lip as he stared at the pictures. "A natural harbor. I can bet I'm not going to land this one, but tell me about it anyway. Save the bad part for last. You do have some affordable good ones?"

"As you guessed, this one is expensive. But we do have affordable good ones." Pak consulted a notebook, talking as he searched for the right place. "Quintin Island. There would even be a little night life in Tacloban if you want. All you'd need would be a sailboat. The Filipinos are wonderful people, the entertainers of Asia. The women!" Pak closed his eyes.

"What if I wanted to grow some tomatoes or azaleas or something?"

Pak switched notebooks. "The soil in the Philippines varies greatly but is roughly the same as the western sections of the American states of Oregon and Washington, the Appalachian Mountains, Japan, western China, the Guiana Highlands of southern Venezuela, and the east coast of Australia."

"A guy could cut himself a runway in the trees just back of the beach there."

"You get light winds from the northeast in the winter and monsoons from the south in the summer, but Mindanao takes the brunt of those. The hottest months are April and May, with average highs of ninety-two and ninety-one degrees. The humidity is not as bad as some places, running from the low sixties to the mid-seventies."

"Yeah, but because of the waterfalls, when a guy gets tired of the beach he can go kick back in his air-conditioned villa and have a rum and Coke, and watch a game show or a movie scooped up by his TV dish. Would it be possible for a guy's chef to buy decent ingredients in Tacloban?"

"Anything you'd find in most big cities in Asia. But I think I would recommend a Chinese chef."

"How much for the island?"

"It's the class island on the Asian market, and the family knows it. An island a half mile wide and a mile long with a natural harbor, a white sand beach, and a waterfall to run an electrical generator. If you invest a little money, you could have a freshwater swimming pool and a hot tub. All the amenities.''

"Put it in American dollars.''

"Eight million firm.''

Holt's body sagged. "I thought so.''

"As I said, Mr. Holt, we've got some other very nice islands that aren't as pricey. For example, there's a very nice island, Kota Island, available in the Andamans, which belong to India. Kota is only eight hundred air miles southwest of Bangkok and a thousand miles northwest of Singapore. The Indians are a curious people at times, but the British left them with a democratic tradition and a respect for private property. I'd like to say I could bring the price down on Quintin, but in all honesty the chances don't look good. The family has enjoyed it as a retreat for years and won't part with it for anything less.

"For eight million bucks, they can buy a lot of airline tickets for their vacations.''

"At Kota there is a steady light wind in January and harder winds in the July monsoons, but the point is that you could enjoy wind-generated electricity. Most of the islands in Indonesia or the Philippines are subject to long periods of calm.''

"No wind generator.''

"A wind generator isn't worth much in the doldrums.''

Holt sighed. He'd look at Kota, but if everybody there ate curry, he didn't want anything to do with it. The very least he asked was to be in some part of Asia where the food was good. "Well, let's see the other islands, then,'' he said.

Pak said, "Did I tell you I was negotiating the sale of the other available Leyte Gulf island to a Filipina movie actress? She wanted Quintin but couldn't come up with the money. Maybe you'll be neighbors.'' This tidbit, saved for last, was Pak Tze Fan's close.

Gene Holt remembered his first car, a 1951 Chevrolet with hooded headlights then called "Frenched" by young men sporting duck's ass haircuts. He'd never wanted anything more in his life. He felt the same way about Quintin Island. He was not completely dismayed by the price tag. He rarely let the lack of cash bother him. Holt knew that if he put his mind to it, he could get somebody else to pay for his island.

Except for the Fragrance, they were older now, but at one time they had been taken into the secrets of the Chinese Book of the Dead; guided by the Incense Master, they had made the mystical journey to the East, come dawn, where the divine becomes material. They had crossed the mythical mountains, and traveled on the great ship on whose prow stood the goddess Kwan Yin—the Queen of Heaven.

On that trip, they had answered questions about the Eight Immortals. They had traveled to the island of the blessed and had passed under the bridge that was guarded by the Buddhas and the souls of the dead, and then had entered the territory of the brotherhood.

They had mingled among the throngs gathered in the Great Hall, and from there they had gone to the Circle of Heaven and Earth and finally, to a holy city, the City of Willows. They had seen the walls inscribed with verse. They had seen the corpse of the traitorous monk, A' T'sat, sitting cross-legged. This *t'sat,* meaning both death and seven, had ended the earthly part of the initiates.

They had then passed through the West Gate. They had passed the spirit that guarded the fiery mountain and back to the Red Flower Pavilion where they had started. Finally, they had taken the Thirty-six Oaths that bound them to observe all the rules of the Society of the Red Lotus or die. They had learned the secret numbers and the secret signs of rank. They had learned secret triad slang in which "sesame seeds" meant money, and "farting dog" was a cop.

Finally, obeying the commandments and helping their brothers, they had risen to the top of the Red Lotus.

They gathered now at the villa of their leader, Pak Tze Fan, the Mountain Lord, triad number 489:4 plus 8 plus 9 equals 21, and the Chinese character for 21 was the same as the character for Hung, namesake of the old Hung Society. "It's him, the son of a bitch," said the Mountain Lord. "I just bet it's him."

"The farting dogs say they don't know for sure, but I say it's him," said the Second Route Marshal, triad number 438 in which the 4 was set aside, leaving a 3 and the 8, the combined characters of which referred to the Chinese character for the Hung Society. The Second Route Marshal was a small man with thick eyeglasses and thick black hair that gleamed with palmed-on lanolin.

"Never forget that his old man was Hatty Boyd. The British never did believe in free trade, for all their pious announcements," said the White Paper Fan, who was the society's advisor on administration and finance. His secret number, 415, was broken down into 4 times 15 times plus 4 equals 64, the number of hexagrams in the I-Ching. The White Paper Fan flashed gold-capped teeth when he talked and had a wide, square jaw.

"I say we find out for sure," said the Straw Sandal, triad number 432, 4 times 32 equals 128, the number of patriots who practiced martial arts in the original Shaolin Monastery. The original Straw Sandal, it is said, turned into a boat that carried Shaolin monks out of reach of their enemies. This Straw Sandal had a pot belly and wore white slacks and white shoes.

"Whatever it takes," said the Fragrance, triad number 426—that is, 4 plus 26 times 4 equals 108, the number of the legendary heroes of the Sung Dynasty who fought against imperial tyranny. The Fragrance flogged errant 49s with a bamboo rod, and killed those triads who disobeyed the Thirty-six Oaths.

"Should we squeeze his lychees, then?" asked the Second Route Marshal.

The Mountain Lord said, "Squeeze 'em till he's on his tippytoes."

The White Paper Fan said, "If he answers wrong, we spit the pit."

The Mountain Lord looked at the Straw Sandal.

"If he answers wrong, we kill him, I agree," said the Straw Sandal.

"The Fragrance and I will come with something," said the Mountain Lord. He looked out of the window, looked down on his houseguest, Gene Holt, negotiating the entrance to the bay with his mainsail in a broad reach. Pak Tze Fan considered the problem of squeezing Sing Sing Boyd's Eurasian lychees.

25

THE actress Susan Wu—born Wu Mei-ling—was the daughter of Jackson Wu, a British-educated professor of drama at the University of Singapore, and she studied acting under her father's direction. In the spring of her senior year—she had just turned twenty-two—she was cast as Maggie in *Cat on a Hot Tin Roof* and was spotted by a scout for Sing Sing Boyd Productions Ltd., of Hong Kong.

Susan was a good-looking actress. This was mandatory for women in Boyd productions where actresses were either ravished as background to the opening credits so they could become the object of complicated plots of revenge, or they waited in bondage as epic battles were fought on their behalf. Occasionally a Boyd heroine gave birth to the son of some prince or warlord, and spent the movie hiding the child from various assassins bent on doing the little heir in. This gave Boyd's directors a chance to photograph childbirth scenes with much screaming and sweating.

From the beginning, Susan Wu had trouble being the cheerfully dumb women needed for Boyd's scripts. No amount of effort on her part could conceal her amusement at the stupidity of the stories. Thus she was cast as a woman who was tragically doomed, a brooding intellectual who ignored tradition. This independence brought her characters down, movie after movie. Bare tits were okay in Sing Sing Boyd's movies, but Susan's characters never made it to the end, a lesson for younger viewers.

The tormented Susan Wu slashed her wrists in Boyd movies; she jumped off the top of the Building of a Thousand Assholes; she ate poisoned *chow fun*; she threw herself in front of a tram loaded with tourists descending Victoria Peak; she swam in front of a jetfoil headed for Macao. She killed herself in just about every colorful way possible in Hong Kong; plus that, she was murdered in imaginative, action-packed sequences.

When she wasn't memorizing lines or on the set, she stayed at home and read novels in which intelligent heroines met and fell in love with unusual men.

Susan Wu was in her sixth year of playing doomed women when Sing Sing Boyd began looking at foreign markets. Kung fu was becoming quite popular in America, although Americans were told it was impossible for *gweilos* to really understand what it was about. This smug assertion made the Americans wait in line to buy tickets, so the Asian producers seized upon it as a marketing device. They said over and over again: you Americans and Europeans can never understand kung fu; this is an ancient martial art that we have perfected over centuries; it is mystical in its dimensions. You do not understand and cannot understand.

The Japanese had taken the lead in violent movies that aspired to art. The idea was to mix foggy notions of Zen in with brooding violence. The mysticism—which was sort of, maybe, intellectual in its way—justified the violence, which was what people were really interested in anyway. And lately, some American authors had begun to use the formula in best-selling fiction. The market was growing. Sing Sing

Boyd, partly for reasons of the wallet, partly because of ego, decided to try his hand at the form. He too could film men grinding their jaws and sweating.

One thing Boyd needed was a woman to play intelligent heroines in his export films; this would eliminate the possibility of complaints by American feminists. The American feminists were hysterical, he was told; they would raise bloody hell at the usual depiction of women in his movies.

Boyd's directors looked around them and cast Susan Wu as the lead actress in a film called *Chan Rides Low*—to be directed by Sing Sing Boyd himself, and intended to be an Asian "Mad Max" movie: entertaining violence with pretensions of significance. The quintessential Boyd films—the most outlandish, garish, and, some claimed, stupid—were those directed by Boyd himself. Tapes of the latter were highly prized by fans of the genre because of their vulgar excess, the result of Boyd's having given himself a larger budget than his subordinate directors.

In *Chan Rides Low,* Susan played a woman who rises out of a childhood on a junk in Aberdeen Harbor to become an internationally published novelist at movie's end; along the way she is kidnapped by perverts, held captive in the New Territories, and rescued by her brothers in a hair-raising kung fu kick-out.

Chan Rides Low was a movie of uncommon intelligence for Sing Sing Boyd, and when it was finished a geomancer said it had good *fung shui*; Boyd reserved the Asian market for later and sent it directly to the United States, where such movies were sometimes watched by critics and bearded people.

A critic for the *Los Angeles Times* called *Chan Rides Low* "an unusual film." She said Boyd "apparently has watched his Kurosawa, and imaginatively zeros in on the good parts— leaping, kicking, and the crunching of bones." The critic continued, "The intelligent lead actress, Susan Wu—an Asian Etta Terminini—is a rose growing from dreck." Terminini was an Italian actress thought, variously, to have Julie Christie's lips, Sophia Loren's eyes, and Jeanne Moreau's intelligence.

Upon reading the review, Sing Sing Boyd got excited. First, by "unusual film," the critic had obviously meant better than the usual, therefore was saying *Chan Rides Low* was a superior movie.

Boyd noted further that the critic called it a film, not a movie, which meant it was art. By saying that Boyd "apparently has watched his Kurosawa," the critic was saying he had learned his lessons well. Boyd "imaginatively zeros in on the good parts." That is, he had learned the best of Kurosawa. Finally, the *Times* had acknowledged the exciting beauty and grace of kung fu.

But Boyd didn't know what "dreck" meant. He asked his assistant to look it up for him.

The assistant manhandled the unabridged edition of the *Random House Dictionary of the English Language,* and flopped it open. He fingered through the dictionary until he came to the right page and followed the entries down the page with his finger. His fingers stopped. He licked his lips. "It is a slang word, sir."

"Well, what does it mean?"

"It's also spelled d-r-e-k."

"Well?"

"It's of Yiddish origin." The assistant printed the definition on a pad.

"Meaning?"

"Uh, it says, 'excrement; dung.' "

Sing Sing Boyd's response was passed from assistant to assistant until it became legend. In fact it was often cited as the reason Sing Sing had become a wealthy man:

"That means 'shit,' does it not?" Boyd asked.

"Yes, sir, I believe so."

Sing Sing Boyd cleared his throat and said, "I see. Will you please delete 'growing from dreck' and have the entire page of the newspaper reset in identical type and reprinted.

Then send copies to the newspaper and television people in the Asian cities where our movies run.''

Hong Kong newspapers ran stories the next Sunday saying how the ''international film community'' was beginning to take Sing Sing Boyd seriously. The writer quoted ''a source close to Boyd'' as saying there had been talk in Hollywood of nominating *Chan Rides Low* for an Academy Award as best foreign film.

Susan Wu, the Etta Terminini of Asia, became the star of Sing Sing Boyd's stable of actors and actresses.

How any human being could spend that much time deciding on a dress was beyond Kwok Lai Kwon. Kwok didn't understand women. Susan Wu took what seemed like forever thumbing through catalogs and magazines, as the solicitous Hindus hovered, repeating again and again that they could copy anything. Whatever her heart's desire, she could have.

Even from across the street, Kwok could read the Hindus' faces. They didn't have to say anything, really; they had their act down pat. Kwok could fill in the words. They were saying Susan Wu was a nice lady. Class. She had class. And taste. They liked doing business with her. They were tailors, professionals, and they appreciated people with class. She should see some of the crap the tourists bought. They treated their customers right because they wanted them to come back.

Anything at all. They could make anything. Any material. They could get anything. And the price was right. The biggest part of their business was repeat customers who lived in Hong Kong and knew their material and prices.

One Hindu gestured to the window where famous people were pictured trying on jackets. In one window Henry Kissinger, looking sheepish, was being fitted for a jacket. In another picture a grinning Jack Klugman was being measured. They were telling her that if she would let her picture be taken for their window display, they would give her an even bigger break. She was a movie actress and her picture would help them get more business.

Kwok's job was to act occupied and casual at the same time. Occupied at what? That was his problem. There wasn't a café where he could sit and drink tea while Susan made up her mind. He had used up his welcome and his patience staring at carved ivory. Then he pretended to be interested in handbags.

Inside the tailor shop, Susan Wu pointed to a photograph in a magazine and waited while a Hindu pulled a bolt of cloth off a rack on the wall.

The Hindu mashed the cloth for her, twisted it, balled it up with his fist. See? his face said. No wrinkles. Genuine tropical wool. The best in the world. Sure?

How much? Susan's face asked.

The Fragrance was disgusted. His feet were beginning to hurt. How could she spend that much time on one dress? Not only that, but Susan Wu had grown up in Singapore and Hong Kong. She knew the pitch by heart, had to. She'd no doubt bargained with tailors thousands of times. And still she appeared charmed and interested in what they were saying. She had money. Why didn't she just pick out a dress and buy the thing? Why the routine?

Searching for the Big Bargain. How could women do it? Kwok wondered. His feet! Ouch.

He wondered. He had read two newspapers while standing there on the sidewalk. He supposed he could try reading a magazine, but not a book. He would look stupid standing there reading a book. He started walking slowly up and down the sidewalk, hoping that moving would somehow be easier than standing still, feeling the throb, throb, throb of his feet. Two hours. Two hours she had been there, each minute torturing Kwok's feet.

Other than having to watch Susan Wu shop, Kwok was pleased to be back in Hong Kong. San Francisco had been a nightmare for Kwok. It was bizarre. He had read about San Francisco but had regarded it as so much magazine nonsense. After the parade he had arrived shaken for his work. However, in the end his opponents were less dangerous than he had imagined. He was thankful the San Francisco Chinese were really *gweilos* at heart; they didn't know manure about kung fu.

After two and a half terrible hours, Susan Wu left the shop. Kwok, wincing, his feet throbbing with pain, followed her home, riding the same MTR car. He sat on the bench across the street from her apartment building and enjoyed the wonderful relief of being off his feet. His friends told horror stories of tourist husbands and boyfriends who, trancelike, followed their wives and girl friends around the shops in Kowloon for hour upon dreadful hour, their feet swollen, their faces white with pain, eyes glazed with boredom. Chinese women were probably just as bad, but at least the men didn't trail along behind them. Why did *gweilo* men do that? Kwok felt sorry for them.

The Fragrance of the Red Lotus glanced at his watch: 5:30 P.M. His shift was up at 6:00.

At 5:45, Kwok's replacement showed up. Kwok's feet were still aching, so he stayed to chat with the new man for a few minutes. At 5:55, Susan Wu's housemaid, Chung Siu Ping, came down the steps on her way home.

Kwok followed Chung Siu Ping to the MTR where she got on a train bound for her home in the New Territories. Somewhere along the line, he decided, he would have a chat with her. He made a bet with himself that Chung Siu Ping just might like to earn a few extra dollars for some shopping of her own.

26

THE *sam ku* Wong Tsei-Ling had obviously been reading fan magazines, and she had some questions to ask Susan
Wu before she consulted the spirit world to see if Wu Wing-
Ling had any change of heart in her longing for a *taipan*
husband.

"I read where they're calling you the Asian Etta Terminini,"
she said.

Susan said, "I like my privacy."

Wong Tsei-Ling clearly thought that sounded suspicious.
"Is it true that you don't watch your own movies?"

Susan Wu didn't say anything.

Tsei-Ling put the bowl of paper bananas and lychees in the
ceremonial fireplace. She took a match from a matchbook
that advertised "Po Cheung's Pub, Very British Food," and
lit the fruit. She glanced at Susan and said, "We'll give your
sister something to eat first. Maybe that will put her in a
good mood." She looked at her left hand, which was stiffened
from arthritis. She opened and closed it, wincing. "If I find
her, she'll talk through my mouth, as before."

Tsei-Ling closed her eyes. She began smacking her lips as before. She pursed her mouth. The odd sucking noises commenced, followed by the burbling from low in her throat.

The *sam ku* opened her eyes. She said, "Where's my husband?" She glared at Susan.

"I . . . I'm doing my best."

"That's not good enough, is it?"

Susan said, "It's not easy to find a *gweilo* who'll marry a Chinese spirit."

Tsei-Ling started burbling again. She seemed angry. She said, "You're not trying. If you had been trying, you would have found somebody. You're a movie actress. You know lots of rich people."

Susan Wu's mouth hung slack. She stared at the *sam ku* in disbelief. She looked at the peeling paint on the ceiling of the diminutive room. "That's not so."

Tsei-Ling's eyelids fluttered. She said, "Nothing's changed, has it? Be miserable and unhappy, see if I care. The next time I want you to come with a *taipan*. I don't want to talk to you any more. Go away."

Susan fought back the tears.

The *sam ku*'s eyes cleared. She waited for a moment until she was free of her trance. "What did she say?"

The unhappy Susan Wu told her.

Tsei-Ling shook her head and got up to pour them a cup of tea. She opened and closed her left hand, which had begun to ache again, putting her in a bad mood. "In my experience, female spirits are the worst. If they're plain from birth, they're especially jealous of beauty; they can't help it. Your sister, Wing-Ling, is a bad one."

Susan Wu didn't participate in movie colony socializing. Sing Sing Boyd's publicists—one of them called this the Jackie Kennedy syndrome—found that the less people knew about her, the more they wanted to know; thus her fame rose in inverse proportion to the known details of her private life. A baseless hint of her activities gave rise to all manner of exaggerated reports in the weekly sheets that flourished in Hong Kong, owing to its heritage of British journalism.

Susan Wu was enjoying an Australian novel that had twice brought her close to tears when the doorbell rang and her maid, Siu Ping, opened the door to a young man bearing flowers. Susan opened the envelope and read the note:

Dear Ms. Wu,

As you may have read in the *South China Morning Post,* an unusual American, Lucien Salvant, is moving to Hong Kong. This is the man, you may recall—an orphan—who was recently willed a half-billion U.S. dollars by the Texas oilman, Cactus Jack Bonner. Mr. Salvant is arriving next Wednesday, and I have arranged to hold a small dinner welcoming him on Saturday, June 17. He is a potential investor in several of my enterprises, and I would like to make him feel welcome.

Mr. Salvant is a former English professor; you may have read the stories about him, and it occurred to me that he may have seen *Chan Rides Low* and might be thrilled to meet the lovely star, herself a professor's daughter. I know you are a private person and don't like to be displayed at parties for the thrill of movie buffs. I've been told Mr. Salvant is a civilized individualist, rather like yourself, and I thought you might enjoy his company.

This would be a small gathering: myself, my associate Stanley Ho, and your colleague Frank Quetglas. I can send a helicopter if you wish, and we'll welcome Salvant properly with a splendid did Chinese dinner. I have a good supply of scotch on hand; we can have a leisurely brunch on Sunday. You know I respect your privacy, Ms. Wu, so please feel free to say no.

I remain affectionately yours,
Sing Sing Boyd

Boyd's signature was large and flamboyant, two huge *S*'s and a large *B* anchoring dramatic but perfectly illegible loops and tails. It was possible to discern part of the letter *Y* in his surname.

Susan read the note twice. She had despaired of finding anyone to marry her sister. No British expatriate would go along with marrying a spirit. But an American! Americans would do almost anything. Next to an Australian, an American was her best hope and she knew it. She could hardly believe her good *fung shui*. She said, "I've been invited to a small dinner at Sing Sing Boyd's on Saturday."

Siu Ping said, "Really?"

"At his place on Lantau Island."

"Are you going?"

Susan Wu said, "Yes, I think I will. Does me good to get out once in a while."

Ella Nidech, having been prepared for her mission by six hard days of meetings with emissaries from the departments of state and defense, met with Stanley Ho in the Wanchai district just as they had three months earlier. Only this time they walked. As before, the gray sky threatened rain. Ella Nidech—the taller of the two—carried a yellow umbrella and walked with her right hand in the pocket of her handsome Burberry; the tidy Stanley Ho, dressed in a pin-striped blue suit, carried a neat black umbrella.

It had been more than ten years since the Vietnam War, and the faded signs of Hong Kong's sex district looked slightly pathetic over the deteriorating, seedy facades. They walked under a garish canopy of signs advertising "Popeye's"

and "Suzie's," "Caesar's Place" and "Monaco Mama's."
Rust moved in from the edges of the once-garish signs and
the paint peeled like dried mud.

Stanley Ho said, "In China now it is glorious to get rich.
Mr. Boyd's Beijing acquaintances are nothing if not eager for
glory. This month they're offering recordings of the sonar
pings of Soviet vessels entering and leaving the naval facilities at Vladivostok."

"That's interesting. How much would that be?"

Ho glanced at Nidech, but the Company woman betrayed
not a hint of emotion. "We're asking ten thousand a month."

"I would say we're interested in buying, yes, but we don't
have a bottomless purse. We have to do this discreetly."

"We can talk about it, then," Ho said cheerfully. "They
say the prop pitches are rendered with perfect fidelity. They're
very nice recordings."

"Ten thousand a month is far too much for us. My company has given me firm instructions on these matters. I know
what they will or will not pay. It's pointless for me to take
them an agreement that's out of what we Americans would
call 'the ball park.' "

Ho smiled. "There are a lot of American businessmen in
Hong Kong. I understand that expression. Out of the baseball
park. We're offering similarly excellent recordings of traffic
in and out of Haiphong harbor, and P'yongyang harbor."

"We're not interested in any of them at those prices."

"If the price was right, would you be interested?"

"Possibly," Nidech said. It was as Peter Neely had said:
Boyd's Chinese friends would be wanting to get rich, but at
the Russians' expense, not their own. Still, these were pre-
mium secrets. A record of sonar pings matched with satellite
photographs—some of which could follow a submarine running just under the surface—offered wonderful possibilities.

"I see. We can offer you ground-level, high-resolution
photographs of rail traffic between Vladivostok and Khab-
arovsk. As you know, Vladivostok is the Soviet Union's

main navel base facing the Pacific basin." Stanley Ho stopped briefly at a curb, waiting for a stoplight. "I am instructed to remind you that what you know about them is from photographs taken from above. Details of rail traffic seen in profile can be quite revealing. We have nighttime infrared shots, but the details are not clear."

"Is this a one-shot deal? One batch of photographs, or a continuing deal?"

"The Beijing sources are thinking of a continuing relationship. But, they say, as you can see from the quality of the pictures, they could use some better equipment."

"Doesn't that directly aid the Chinese army?"

Ho looked surprised. "What harm is there in telephoto lenses? If they are going to take good pictures, they have to have good equipment."

"I see. Are we talking exclusive photographs here or would we be sharing them with the Chinese army?"

"Why, you'd be sharing them, of course, Miss Lewis. These are army photographers. Are you suggesting an exclusive service?"

"If Mr. Boyd's friends can steal secrets, my company wants to know why can't they contract for specific services?"

Ho said nothing, then, "I can tell Mr. Boyd. There would be extra charges for exclusive secrets, you understand that."

"Also, my company wants to know if it might not be able to suggest secrets they would like filched."

"Requests?"

"Certainly."

"Oh, requests would be extra, I'm sure of that. I'll have to get back to you on that one."

"Well, do you have any samples of your train photography?"

"Yes, but as you'll see, the photographers do need better equipment."

"Assuming my firm finds them acceptable, how much?"

Ho glanced at Flora Lewis, sizing her up. "Five thousand dollars a year in gold."

"What if the Beijing sources were to say yes, they could contract photographers to take other profile shots inside the Soviet Union? There must be plenty of opportunities to get across the border."

"You'd have to pay for the photographers' expenses, certainly."

"We'd have to have an idea of the costs involved before we can say yes or no."

"That goes without saying," Ho said. "You'll find labor in China is very reasonable."

"Would you be willing to make a package deal, photographs along with the Vladivostok soundings?"

"Yes, I'm sure we could come up with something. But I would have to get back to you with the expense figures. Shall we schedule another walk then?"

"Certainly," Nidech said. "Contact me as usual when you have your new figures." She shook Stanley Ho's hand and they parted.

Negotiating the sale of Chinese secrets was a fabulous case, one of those stunners that sometimes surfaced from the Company and was presented as a stunning revelation by newspaper and television reporters who pretended to be shocked and appalled. Cabinet members would be interrogated on Sunday afternoon talk shows.

It occurred to Nidech that she was a natural to write the inevitable best-selling book about the China buy once the truth was leaked, as it eventually would be. This was her baby, hers. She had always thought it would be wonderful to be a buyer for art dealers and antique collectors, fighting a battle of wits with thousands of dollars on the line. She was the one who got to dicker with Stanley Ho. Yes, she, Ella Nidech, with the President and Secretary of Defense McArthur hanging on each report. There couldn't be more than six or eight people including the President who knew about the operation. But she was calling the shots. Nidech thought she hadn't done badly. Haggling with Hindu tailors and Chinese cobblers gave her some of the best training imaginable.

After the China buy was leaked, Nidech could write the book under a pseudonym. She wondered what the author's cut was on a hardcover best seller? Ten percent? Fifteen? A best seller ought to make a bunch in the fall, what with Christmas coming on.

Ella Nidech never dreamed she would have this much luck. After her report to Neely, she decided, she would buy herself a new hat by way of celebration. She would go to a chic little shop in the mall by the Regency Hotel and buy herself a big floppy-brimmed number, something that was sexy and just a little mysterious. Something that was her.

27

THE South China Sea was a milky blue. There was no clear horizon, so the sea became one with the sky and the Cathay Pacific flight seemed to descend in a universe of luminescent, opaque ether. Lucien Salvant was surprised by what looked like a tranquil planet or curious moon floating in the uncommon blue. This turned out to be an island, itself blue at first—although hardly bluer than the sea—then green, then Salvant could see the shape of a village and junks in a small harbor.

Salvant remembered the air, gravid, lying in heavy repose on Paw Paw Street, Rubenesque on a sultry summer's night, carrying a trombone solo and the smell of crawfish étouffé through the opened doors of Dickman's Saloon.

Only then could he discern the fine line that was the point at which sea and sky merged. Then he could see Hong Kong island forward and on the left. He saw barren, unpopulated mountains at first.

Then he saw something perfectly amazing.

He saw tall, white obelisks along the shore that were lined

176

up in neat ranks and files like beehives or gravestones. He understood by the clothing hanging out of their windows that each of these white skyscrapers was in fact an apartment building. He glanced at the map in his lap; he was looking at Aldrich Bay, Quarry Bay, and the model housing project at North Point. As the plane began its approach to the airport on the Kowloon peninsula, and Salvant could see the buildings more clearly, they looked like upside-down wasp's nests, bleached white by the sun, row upon row upon row of them.

Farther ahead, he could see Hong Kong central, the geographic center of the Asian dynamo that ran from Tokyo and Seoul in the northeast through Singapore in the southwest. The Hong Kong stock market was said to handle the third largest dollar volume of any market in the world. Although he had never expected to have any money, Salvant read economic and business stories along with everything else, and these writers—from *Barron's, The Economist,* the *Guardian,* the *Wall Street Journal,* the *Times*—all told him East and Southeast Asia was where the future was. The Europe that had produced Michelangelo and Mozart was to be left behind.

In Hong Kong central, scores of incredible glass and steel towers lay in a haze like cypress in the bayou. A number of them were even covered with something that looked like moss of some kind. The tops of several skyscrapers penetrated the murk, and their tinted widows reflected silver, and gold, and the pale blue sky.

As the plane descended to the field, the Kowloon peninsula was straight ahead. There was an obvious height limitation on the Kowloon side, and here the buildings looked like crew-cut skyscrapers. The razzle-dazzle of the International style was restricted to Hong Kong island.

Salvant took a taxi from the airport to the hotel at the New World Center. The taxi began its journey on Prince Edward Road, which became Ma Tau Wai Road; Salvant wondered if Ma Tau Wai might not contain those wonderful Chinese mushrooms. He discovered there were just five kinds of cars on Hong Kong streets: red taxicabs of plebian brands, and the most expensive models of Rolls-Royces, Mercedes Benzes, BMWs, and Hondas; these were either black, white, or metallic silver. The eccentric exceptions, a defiant little Renault or awkward Volvo, or yellow paint, were nice little surprises.

The New World Center was a vast, sterile mall at the southern tip of the Kowloon peninsula, and Salvant's suite overlooked the splendor of Hong Kong harbor and the inspired, mirrored geometry of the followers of the architect I.M. Pei. The marble and glass of the mall intimidated people who perspired, thus rendering the mall spiritless—a reflection of the corporate imagination that had financed it—and the shops were clearly intended for overpaid businessmen and for travelers whose idea of adventure was to be measured for a suit on the way back from Singapore Slings in the hotel bar.

Salvant had accepted employment as a millionaire without considering all the consequences. For example, was he to give up his privacy? Judging from his experience with newspaper and television people in the United States, he wanted no part of the public theater in which celebrities were eternal players. If Sing Sing Boyd had in mind locking him up in places like the New World Center, a cultural Moonbase Alpha, devoid of ideas not involving some permutation of greed, free of odor and climate, he knew he would surely lose his mind.

He decided to take a walk in Kowloon. He checked his map and decided to walk north on Nathan Street, into the heart of the Kowloon district. Hong Kong didn't appear to be a city of style; the men all wore blue suits and white shirts, and the women neat dresses of little imagination. Nor was it a place of art; a painter trying to set up an easel on Nathan Street would be trampled beneath the soles of thousands of Chinese feet. There was no time and precious little space to tolerate a singer with his hat on the sidewalk.

The literature he had been given at the airport, a service of the Hong Kong Tourist Association, didn't spend a lot of time talking about museums or libraries. One of the pamphlets explained the wonders of a duty-free port, low tax rates, and virtually uncontrolled free enterprise. Another gave shopping tips and recommendations, and listed guidelines for buyers to follow so as not to get ripped off. And finally, Salvant had been given a street map of Kowloon with various recommended shops noted.

He walked up Nathan Road, passing Middle Road and Mody Road, then turned right on Carnarvon Road, and he was square in the center of the reason people went to Hong Kong. The sidewalks were choked with people going to work or from work or shopping or eating or whatever else Salvant couldn't imagine. Salvant had once seen a program on public television that showed blood corpuscles flowing through veins and arteries, millions of them it seemed. That's the way it was with the Kowloon sidewalks; people coursed through the maze of streets.

The telling feature of Hong Kong, though, were the signs that stuck out above the sidewalks and extended above the streets. Salvant couldn't remember seeing anything exactly like them in his travels. If it were true that males provide as females consume, he supposed that a woman might find the signs somehow charming.

The signs advertised camera shops, luggage shops, tailors, brand-name ready-mades, stereo shops, jewelry shops, perfume shops, shops selling copies of Paris originals, eyeglass shops, and restaurants. There was apparently no limit on the size, color, or garishness of these signs. This was competition with no holds barred. Some signs were higher, some lower; some stuck out further. No matter how large a sign, Salvant found it was inevitably made more interesting, if uglier, by signs peering over its top, beneath its bottom, and farther out over the street.

The result of all this frenzied competition was that the streets became tunnels of capitalism, covered by a canopy of garish plastic and blinking and jiggling, crying: cheaper, better, more, faster, sale, sale, sale, cheaper, cheaper, deal, deal, deal, cheaper, cheaper, sale, sale. The signs were so close together—and the canopy so enclosed—that tourists had to adjust their 35mm cameras to let in light among the competing claims. There was more light in a tropical rain forest.

These shops—there were literally thousands of them—honeycombed the ground level for blocks upon blocks. Lucien Salvant had never imagined anything this repetitive and ultimately awful, lacking any redeeming aesthetic.

All in all, Kowloon reminded him of an immense hive, the chief goal of its residents being the pursuit of Hong Kong dollars. Salvant didn't expect to find leisurely cafés and there weren't any. The dazzling towers on Hong Kong island offered no respite from greed or prospect of agreeable companionship.

Salvant was hungry and so went into a small Chinese restaurant, where, it turned out, nobody spoke English. Rather than embarrass himself by leaving, he decided to stick it out. This was Hong Kong and this was where he was to live. All his adult life Salvant had had to study menus, balancing promise and price. Now, being an ostensible millionaire, he decided to hell with it. He'd order what he wanted; price was no object. By various gestures and exhortations he ordered an expensive plate of what he thought would be a steamed fish. He was served awful strips of something, presumably pork and possibly entrails of some kind, in a putrid sauce. It was the worst Chinese food he had ever eaten, vile in fact. He wondered if they might not have done it as a sick trick on a round-eye, stifling laughter in the kitchen. See if he eats it, Ong. This one's for the United States.

Lucien Salvant was sad, and lonely, and anxious, and a little afraid as he walked back to the plush, barren cell that awaited him in the New World Center. He found it difficult to walk leisurely, although that's what he would have preferred. He felt as though people on the sidewalks were speed freaks, walking quickly, carrying him with them, *gweilo* jetsam washed up on the yellow tide.

Salvant hoped his permanent quarters would be more civilized. If he had a place with a wooden floor, then he could kick back and read and maybe write a little if he was in a mood. He liked the comforting feel of warm wood under his bare feet. He would be ill at ease until the magazines began coming from America. The magazines would help him. He would have them delivered by mail from the United States, a trans-Pacific tit.

He walked past the splendid white Kowloon Mosque on Nathan Road, and wondered if Muslims let infidels inside their holy buildings. Although he was himself a nonbeliever, Salvant was curious about the psychology of believing. He had been told the Chinese believed in spirits. He felt believing in spirits was more elemental and understandable than religious dogma, certainly more fun; when he was a child he had believed for a while that demonic little men, some green, some red, lived under his bed. Salvant found it bizarre that a room full of disparate human beings could agree to run their lives by a single set of received truths—much less actually believing in them—and yet at age seventy-five his adopted mother had discovered the pleasures of the Bible.

Salvant bought a bottle of whiskey and went back to his suite of rooms. He knew that any self-respecting millionaire would have ordered the rum on the house phone and so felt self-conscious walking through the lobby with a paper bag in his hand. He poured himself a drink. He took a sip and looked out over the harbor.

Salvant turned on the television set, and the picture settled onto besilked jockeys whipping their mounts to frenzied cheering. Above this furor, an excited commentator shouted in Cantonese. The camera moved in tightly on the straining leader. The commentator was now virtually screaming. The horses were at the wire.

28

STANLEY Ho leaned back in his chair and looked out of
the window at the junks and freighters in Hong Kong harbor.
"This is one of three office buildings Mr. Boyd owns here in
Hong Kong central. This is his flagship, really. He also has
one on Des Veoux and one on Queen's. This one was
designed by the Danish architect Bernard Larsen."

"It's fabulous," Lucien Salvant said. The truth was, he
found it hard to tell one high-rise from the next. One had
blue windows, the next reflected a cantaloupe color, but in
the end they looked the same to him.

"In this matter of our relationship, Lou, I'm not sure what
would be an appropriate analogy. I will be your . . . ahh . . ."

"First sergeant," Salvant said. "City editor. Department
chair."

"Chair?" Ho looked confused.

"Chairmen, we used to call them."

He understood. "Yes, I think that must be it."

"But the Grand High Poo Bah is Sing Sing Boyd."

"Precisely so. We both work for Mr. Boyd. I am in

charge of pursuing investment possibilities, and so you will be helping me out with the information I require."

"I see."

"Our network of contacts in the Hong Kong Chinese business community is extensive and dependable. We have people where we need them. You *gweilos,* if you will pardon my bluntness, are both difficult to understand and clannish." Ho closed his eyes and sighed.

Salvant said, "I thought you Chinese were the ones. Inscrutable and all that."

Stanley Ho retrieved a pack of Camels. "Do you mind?" Taking Salvant's silence as assent, he unwrapped the cigarettes and lit one, drawing deeply, then grinning, letting the smoke drift from his nose. "The problem is that you *gweilos* are so damned loose, talking all the time. It's difficult for us to separate the truth from nonsense . . ."

"From the bullshit. All that talk."

Smoke rolled from Stanley Ho's nose. "I think we should discuss your persona, that is, the kind of rich man you will be."

Salvant leaned forward in his chair; if this was not a Faustian deal he had made with his life, it was uncomfortably close to it.

"You want to know what we have in mind for you; I understand that. As I said, Sing Sing Boyd is a careful man. He would never make a decision like this without knowing something about you. You must understand that we were careful in this matter from the beginning. We just didn't respond to your ad and say, 'Yes, this is our man.' Mr. Boyd fancies himself a good judge of character, but not that good."

"I was wondering about that."

"In a few minutes I'll be coming to how we got to know you. But for now, and based on what we do know about you, Lucien, I will tell you that we want you to be something of an eccentric. A bohemian, I guess, is what we have in mind." Ho snubbed out his cigarette and lit another, grinning as the flame snapped up from his lighter. "Mr. Boyd didn't get where he is by paying more than he has to for anything: a freighter, an oil rig, a high-rise, an automobile. He shops around. Figures out the cheapest way."

Salvant was beginning to get the picture. "Does that mean I can drive a green Ford instead of a silver Rolls-Royce or a Mercedes Benz?"

"That's precisely right. You can own a used car if you want. Your choice. If you prefer to drive it yourself, it will save us the cost of a driver. You came by your money late, after all. Your habits were set before you became rich. It would be ridiculous for you to pretend to be anything but what you are. However, the more you are sealed off in your own world, the less use you are to Mr. Boyd. We need somebody who can circulate. Your half-billion-dollar inheritance will take care of any latent snobbery."

"A bohemian. Well . . ." Salvant didn't know what to say.

"With the edges rounded off so that you're attractive and interesting to the proper social circles. We don't want a hippie or anything like that. You'll have to be motivated by greed as they all are, that's given. There is no capitalist on the planet who doesn't want more, Lucien. This fondness for excess makes the economy move."

"A rising tide floats all boats."

"There are some skills that you'll have to learn. For example, we've arranged a series of seminars by Mr. Boyd's traders on the stock markets of the world. We figure on three or four months on the New York market. We'll spend a few weeks on London and Tokyo as well. You'll have to learn about gold and gems and commodities markets. You won't be making investments yourself, but you'll have to be able to talk with your peers. A good spy has to brief himself on the targets. Mr. Boyd has already arranged the purchase of a nice little sailboat for you. He got a deal on a thirty-five-foot sloop. We've arranged some lessons so you can learn how to handle it. We're taking bids for tennis lessons, and it would be good if you showed some interest in lawn bowling."

"Lawn bowling?"

"We have to be realistic. We understand that." Ho took a drag on his Camel. "You're a bit old for cricket, all that running. But not for polo, we don't think. Polo is a gentleman's game. We have a line on a nice little horse for you."

"Polo? Nice little horse?" Salvant had never been around a horse in his life.

"We also understand you're interested in cooking."

"Well, Cajun cooking."

"We'll import all the spices you need from New Orleans so you can instruct your cook for the parties. Mr. Boyd is of the opinion that the *gweilo* ladies will love the idea of eating Cajun food. We'll begin the sailing and riding and tennis lessons next week. The stock market lessons also."

"You said you would tell me about how you got to know me."

"So I did," Ho said. He punched a button on his intercom and said, "Can you send Mr. Quetglas in, please?"

Lucien Salvant's jaw fell.

Frank Quetglas stepped through the door. "Pardner!"

"Frank!"

They shook hands and embraced.

Quetglas said, "How you been doing, asshole?"

Salvant grinned. "All the time you were . . ."

". . . yeah, man, spying on you. They wanted to know if you were okay for what they had in mind. Mr. Boyd wanted somebody legit. No two-bit hustlers, he said. I felt kind of bad spying on you since we got along so well and all. But hey, it all worked out, didn't it? No more papers to grade, no more department meetings!"

Stanley Ho said, "Mr. Quetglas is an actor in Mr. Sing Sing Boyd's movies. It was his report on your personal tastes that led us to decide on a bookish millionaire, among other things."

"Frank Quetglas? In the movies? What the hell is this?"

"Yeah, man." Frank Quetglas leaped high in the air, did a neat horizontal kick, and landed lightly on his feet. He did it quicker than an all-star asking for a raise.

Lucien Salvant was amazed.

"Just like that, man." Quetglas did it again.

Stanley Ho said, "In addition to his duties on the movie set, Frank will serve as your bodyguard. There will be a considerable saving if Frank and you share a suite. While you will both work directly for me, there will be some periods in which you will carry on unsupervised because I will be out of Hong Kong."

"Kung fu? Are you any good, Frank?"

Quetglas grinned. "Man, I was the real star of *Chan Rides Low* and everybody knows it. Me and Susan Wu, of course. I kicked some real ass in that movie, man."

"Mr. Quetglas has a future. The women are said to be fond of his muscles and smile."

Quetglas said, "Hey, Boyd's Bullet!" He twisted violently and delivered a spinning back-kick at an imaginary target, then leaped high, doing another movie villain in.

Stanley Ho said, "By the way, the two of you have been invited to a small dinner tomorrow night. Mr. Boyd wishes your presence at his Lantau Island estate. This is a welcoming dinner, Lucien. When you get settled into Hong Kong, you'll be receiving tips and suggestions from both Mr. Boyd and myself, and we're anxious to establish a comfortable relationship."

29

FRANK Quetglas paused in his exercises and wiped the sweat from his forehead with a towel. "Now, this one's called 'willow blowing in the wind.'" He stretched his arms and turned the palms out. He leaned and touched the floor with his left and then did the same thing with his right.

"Well, that's wonderful, Frank." Lucien Salvant took another sip of San Miguel. "Touching the floor there. Nimble back. So tell me how you came to be an actor in kung fu movies halfway around the world from Miami, Florida."

"I did study acting. I wasn't lying to you about that. I went to Los Angeles, see, like every other dork, and got just about nowhere. I had a couple of gay guys come onto me, yechh! I didn't want work that bad. Then I see this notice in *Variety* saying how this Hong Kong movie producer was in L.A. auditioning 'athlete-actors' who knew some kung fu. I thought, well, I've got that made; I can do both."

"You showed up and there were a hundred guys there."

"Hundreds. Two or three hundred. Only the L.A. Chinese guys didn't have a chance because Boyd's scouts were looking for *gweilos* to be villains. I did my stuff and got picked. Watch this one, 'mountain falling.' " He pointed his elbow at the ceiling then bent over to touch his toe with it.

"I think I should buy Beck's. After all, I'm a millionaire." Salvant felt good. He was going through a period of euphoria. He was thinking it might not be bad in Hong Kong. Frank Quetglas was a pleasant companion, an enthusiast. Salvant was no longer a young dog, but he was capable of learning new tricks, he was sure of it. "So how are you as a villain?"

"Okay, I guess. Only it gets kind of tiresome having to take a dive in every movie. The stupid *gweilo,* just a half step too slow; that's the angle, see. The Asians get off on it. But a guy has his pride. At first I never got an opportunity to act, not really, except for doltish stereotypes, the dumb round-eye. But then Sing Sing Boyd got the idea of making *Chan Rides Low* for American release, and he needed a couple of good guys on account of Americans and Europeans like to have the Chinese guys take the dives."

"And you got to be a heroic round-eye?"

"Damned right. The only problem is that Boyd's directors won't let me act. Won't even give me an audition. I'm a kung fu guy to them, jumping around and stuff. It's like being hired as a secretary or something—once a secretary always a secretary to the people who hire you. Ask any woman, she'll tell you. Walk in the door as a secretary or a kung fu athlete and you'll walk out the door a secretary or a kung fu athlete. That's the way it works."

"What a grind."

"My time will come. I'll get their attention." Quetglas swabbed off some more sweat. "There's something I have to tell you, Lucien. Sing Sing Boyd kind of likes me, you know, not in a sexual way or anything like that; I think it's because I'm a *gweilo* surrounded by Chinese. His old man was a big-deal Brit, but Boyd has thrived by identifying with the Chinese. He's sort of like my fan and supporter in that way. Anyway, Lucien, he personally asked if I wouldn't fly to Seville to spy on you. He said he guaranteed I wouldn't be harming you. He said all he wanted was for me to find out what kind of guy you are. You know, are you an asshole or something? Are you civilized? I asked him how I was supposed to recognize that, a guy like me." Quetglas laughed. "I didn't go for any of it, and told him so. My old man was Cuban, dammit; I've got my pride. Boyd said ordinarily he wouldn't ask me to spy on anybody, except these were unusual circumstances. He was rushed, he said. In the end, I didn't have any choice. He actually apologized when he asked me."

"I was the one who said yes to Stanley Ho," Salvant said.

"When I found out what I was scoping you out for, I felt a lot better about it." He leaped into a position that resembled a boxer with cracked wrists. "Here we have the seven-star praying mantis stance."

Salvant didn't hold anything against Frank Quetglas. He might have known that Boyd and Ho wouldn't have taken him on without doing some homework. "You've got to hand it to him. He knows how to stretch a buck. He sets me up as the cheapest millionaire on the planet; you get to be a body-guard and a movie villain at the same time."

Quetglas held up his right hand, two fingers extended, like a child's make-believe pistol. "The crane. The fingers are the beak, see. Good for jabbing eyeballs or throats. My elbow is the crane's wing; good for defense." He turned his hand into a tight claw. "Leopard's paw. You get him with the knuckles." He doubled his fist with the knuckle of the forefinger protruding. "All these have symbolic names. This is the phoenix eye fist. You use your thumb to support the knuckle when you sink it home."

"Where's the symbolism?"

"The knuckle is the penetrating eye of the mythical phoe-nix, symbol of power and immortality."

"I think the Chinese are right, Frank. It's impossible for a *gweilo* to learn this stuff."

Quetglas laughed. His physique was wet with sweat. "Hey, I'm bigger than these little *mojoncitos* and I can jump higher. Watch!" Quetglas leaped high, turned horizontal, delivered a hard kick, and landed on his feet. "Those kinds of leaps aren't really kung fu, but they look great on camera and I'm not bad with my lines. You can't use stand-ins all the time."

"You project. Is that what they call it?"

"Yes, that's exactly it. If just once I could get Sing Sing Boyd to let me show my stuff. Just once. Just act, I mean, no spin-kicks. Every year a guy's spin-kicks get a little slower, you know what I mean? I want to be a real actor, dammit. Think of it, Lou, what did they say about Errol Flynn?"

"In like Flynn."

Frank Quetglas grinned. "The Bullet strikes!" Quetglas undulated his hips by way of demonstration. "I can see it now, man. I get the lead role in one of Boyd's export movies and this movie is being shown on Los Angeles TV in the middle of the night, and this producer watches it, all attention because he's popped his cookies with this *mami* but doesn't want to talk to her. So he pretends he just loves these campy, dumb-shit movies, and there I am. Crazier things have happened, Lucien. Look at Debbie Reynolds."

With Quetglas knowing what he did, it was unlikely that Boyd would let him go anywhere, but Salvant said nothing. "The etiquette, Frank. Sing Sing'll expect me to start learning the right way to eat and that kind of thing."

"Starting with what?"

"I don't know. Whatever you think I need to know."

"This is what you call the plum blossom form. See what you can do?" Quetglas went through a series of stylized kicks and punches, talking as he practiced. He said, "If it's

Chinese, it will be a big meal—at least twelve courses, but more likely fifteen. You won't find Sing Sing being modest. The dinner will be served on a round table; that way everybody is equal. Sing Sing will face the door. You'll sit to his left because you're the guest of honor.''

"Good. Good. Keep going.''

"Mr. Boyd's a widower, so there's no wife to enter into it. Sing Sing faces the door so that if some triad kung fu warriors come through the door, he can leap up and order me to defend his guests.'' Quetglas paused in his exertions and grinned.

"Triad?''

"What you've probably heard called a tong society.'' Quetglas rested and mopped his face again with a towel. "When Sing Sing is ready to begin, he'll hold his glass high. He'll hold it in his left hand, like so, and support it with his right. Hold your glass like he holds his.''

Salvant held up an imaginary glass. "Hah!''

"If anybody says *'Yum sing'* during the dinner, that means you're supposed to drain your glass. Repeat after me: *yum sing.*''

"Yum sing.''

"Incidentally, you should top your neighbors' glasses first, then your own. When somebody tops your glass, you thank him by tapping the table lightly with the first two fingers of your right hand.'' Quetglas demonstrated. "Okay, now Sing Sing's servants will bring on the first course. When they bring on the food, everybody will say how wonderful it looks, how good it smells and everything. They'll be enthusiastic and you should be too. Join in. Say, wow, I love the smell of those mushrooms, or whatever.''

"Praise the food.''

"The food will probably be put on a turntable in the center of the table. But you're not ready to start yet . . .'' Quetglas paused to mop more sweat. "Watch Sing Sing. When he picks up his chopsticks, it's time to start. Never lift a dish off the turntable—that's bad manners.''

"Not even to help somebody out?"

"Leave it on the tray. Also, don't reach over someone else's chopsticks. Don't wave your chopsticks or point them at anybody. And do not, I say do not leave your chopsticks in the rice bowl or stick them in the rice. That will remind people of joss sticks that are burned for the spirits at ceremonies for the dead. Also, don't turn over a fish on a plate. That's *mala suerte*. It represents the capsizing of a boat.''

"Don't turn the fish over."

"You'll be expected to eat something from each course, even if it's a few nibbles. Pace yourself. You've got to go the distance. As honored guest, you'll be given some choice morsels on your plate. Eat them with appreciation, but initially refuse seconds even if you want them; you don't want to look like *un puerco*. Never eat the biggest piece of something or the last piece.''

"Don't want to look like a pig."

"Exactly," Quetglas said. "The meal might last for hours, but when it's over it's over. Most Chinese don't linger over brandy or coffee, but Sing Sing does; he got this from his father, who was a British colonial official. Maybe we'll have it in the room where he has his old man's stuff.''

"You've been Mr. Boyd's guest, I take it."

Quetglas grinned. "Oh, yeah. Like I say, I admit to being one of Mr. Boyd's favorites." Quetglas peered from around the corner, his mouth foaming with toothpaste, and growled. "See? Boyd's Bullet." He stepped back in the bathroom, and talked and brushed his teeth at the same time. "If I let my teeth turn yellow, they'll turn me into a character actor. The leading men get the *mejor mujer*.''

"There's a deal!"

"The more porking you get on screen, the more the women want you off screen. Character actors hardly ever get any.

Lucky you drew me to spy on you in Seville, Lou. You'll get laid, believe me.'' Quetglas kept brushing vigorously, then spit the toothpaste into the sink. ''The trick is to be an actor and let stunt men knock themselves out.''

Boyd's Bullet went into his bedroom to dress. He emerged a few minutes later looking splendid in a blue blazer and gray trousers tailored from British tropical wool. He wore white bucks, and a diminutive red carnation was pinned to his lapel. He topped his costume with a stylish Panama. He grinned impishly at first, then laughed, all perfect white teeth. ''What can I say? Good-looking? *GQ,* man! *GQ!*''

Quetglas suddenly leaped high, turned horizontal to the floor, gave a throat-high, vicious kick, and landed lightly on his feet.

''I don't like it when they bind either. A man wants a comfortable pair of slacks,'' Salvant said.

''Not bad, huh? I learned to kick at a place in Miami. I can kill a man if I have to, you know. Just bap! bap!'' Quetglas leaped again, kicked, landed on his feet, and leaped— twisting at the same time—to kick in the opposite direction. He checked his carnation, which had survived intact. ''Anybody fucks with you gets these feet right in the teeth. That's my job.'' Quetglas leaped, uncoiled, and landed light as a dancer. ''Did you see the trick?''

''Trick?''

''My hat didn't come off. That's because my upper body simply turned on its axis. *Sin problema.*'' He tapped his Panama. ''How many millionaires have a movie star bodyguard who can do that? Man, you've got some damned good *fung shui.* The problem is, if there's a face at the other end of a kick, it'll screw up good shoes.''

''Oh, no!''

''You can wash blood off. It's the teeth that do the damage. Cuts the leather.'' Quetglas grinned. He loved the outrageous.

"What do you know about Stanley Ho, Frank?"

Quetglas glanced at his watch. "We'd better go down-stairs. The car will be there. I think you'd better let Mr. Ho tell you about himself."

They were driven to Happy Valley in a black Mercedes limousine. The lights of Hong Kong's skyscrapers rose about them as the taxi went downhill and turned east, joining the red taxis in the confusion of traffic. After a few minutes the driver turned right onto Queen's Road East, which led to Happy Valley.

They rode in silence, each thinking of the deal he had made with Sing Sing Boyd. Salvant looked forward to meet-ing his Mephistopheles. Quetglas was wondering how he might be able to demonstrate his acting skills to Sing Sing Boyd.

Quetglas broke the silence as the Mercedes slowed for a stoplight. "The racetrack is here in Happy Valley, also Hong Kong Stadium, and pitches for cricket and football. There are colonial cemeteries on the west side to our right there. The Chinese say Happy Valley has bad *fung shui*."

"Every racetrack in the world has bad *fung shui*."

The helicopter was yellow with a huge black stripe around its middle so that it resembled a wasp out of Han Solo's nightmares. The pilot, a thick-necked Chinese in a neat blazer, opened the door to the cockpit, hopped down, opened the passenger door, and unfolded an aluminum ladder.

The pilot said something to Ho in Cantonese, then, to Salvant: "We have a clear night tonight, so you should be able to see lights clear into the New Territories."

Lucien Salvant followed the others into the helicopter and they settled in amid a snapping of buckles. The pilot began flipping toggle switches and the cabin lit up, followed by the crackle of communications on the radio. "It'll take about forty minutes," he said, and the blades above the helicopter began moving slowly, gaining speed, gaining speed, until the passengers shuddered. Then they were aloft, away, swinging north over Causeway Bay and Victoria Harbor.

The pilot said, "The skyscrapers on your left, of course, are Hong Kong central. That's Victoria Peak there. On your right is the Kowloon peninsula. That means nine dragons—*gau* is nine and *loong* is dragon. The dragons refer to the hills, although there are only eight of them."

"Eight?" Salvant asked.

The pilot smiled. "The ninth was a visiting emperor. The area near the tip there is Tsim Sha Tsui where most of the visitors stay."

Hong Kong was soon behind them and they were west of the city, over the water, the lights of boats below. They passed over the ferry on its way to Lantau, and several junks far out in the water.

Stanley Ho said, "Lantau is large and quite a nice island, a favorite of Hong Kong residents on holiday. There are several lovely fishing villages and Discovery Bay, a resort area. Mr. Boyd has a villa in an area called Lantau South Country. You've been here, haven't you, Frank?"

Soon they approached the shore, and the pilot curved slightly to follow the coast to the southwest. Ho said, "This is the Chi Ma Wan peninsula we're passing over, Lucien."

A few minutes later they were over a road that followed the coastline, then the pilot suddenly turned inland and followed a narrow valley up the large hill that was the center of this area of Lantau.

"Lantau Peak up ahead," the pilot said.

The helicopter descended until Salvant could see a road below flanked by trees on either side. Then the road led into a forest, and there was a fence, then a compound. As the helicopter hovered above a concrete pad, Salvant saw there was a swimming pool behind a sprawling house whose several wings featured impressive columns and verandas, a combination of Tara and the Alamo, but with a roof of rounded red Chinese tiles.

As they walked toward the house, Salvant noted that Sing Sing Boyd had spared no expense to ensure proper *fung shui* for his villa. The swimming pool was a hexagonal shape so as to function as a *Bhat Gwa* mirror, reflecting bad spirits back into the void.

30

THE swimming pool was nestled in a three- or four-acre garden that was impeccably tended; it was also an arboretum of sorts, for it contained a remarkable collection of exotic tropical trees. Paper lanterns hung from the undersides of the branches, giving the area a dusklike glow. The lanterns must have been recently hung because it had rained earlier in the day.

There were carved wooden tables and chairs under some of the lovelier trees. The lacquered legs and arms were carved in the shape of twisting, snarling dragons with scales that were iridescent even in the dim light.

A tall, elegant gentleman in a white tropical suit emerged from the shadows and strolled to meet them, tapping a carved walking stick against the palm of his left hand. He was smoking; his cigarette glowed as he inhaled.

"Is that him?" Salvant asked as they walked up the winding path of pea-size white gravel.

"That's him," Frank Quetglas said. "Tall dude. Gets that from his father."

From behind them, Stanley Ho said, "Mr. Boyd is six foot three, as you Americans calculate. His father was six foot seven. He is sixty-seven years old, by the way."

Salvant remembered when he had first heard of Sing Sing Boyd. The name had struck him as ridiculous. Sing Sing Who? Then there were his movies, insane things with acrobats kicking one another. Guys like Frank Quetglas, it turned out. Salvant had turned his soul over to this Boyd in exchange for the good life.

It turned out Boyd was singing to himself. Salvant could hear him clearly:

> "You must remember this:
> A kiss is still a kiss,
> A sigh is just a sigh,
> The elemental things apply
> As time goes by . . ."

The smother of sultry air reminded Lucien Salvant of Louisiana.

Stanley Ho said, "Lucien, if he mentions a movie called *Chan Rides Low,* say that you saw it in New Orleans and that you liked it. Did you see it, by any chance?"

"No."

Quetglas said, "Susan Wu rises from the slums to become a novelist. Don't fuck that one up, Lou." Sing Sing Boyd was upon them. Quetglas said, "No beetles and moths tonight, hey, Mr. Boyd!"

Boyd laughed softly and tapped his hand with his walking stick. "Mr. Salvant! Mr. Quetglas!"

Salvant was startled by Boyd's voice, a rich baritone that was surprising coming from such a slender man. It was as though he were imitating Richard Burton. Boyd was surely the most handsome man Salvant had ever seen. He was lean and elegant and poised. He had a long face, his father's evidently, but had his mother's cheekbones and almond-shaped brown eyes. He sported a wonderful empire mustache with full swoop, wonderful because it was beautifully maintained, a salt and pepper that matched his hair. His skin was bronzed from the sun. Salvant thought he was splendid-looking—the best of Suzy Wong and Colonel Schweppes.

Boyd said, "How are you, Stanley? Frank? Pleased to meet you at last, Mr. Salvant. After all the arrangements for your remarkable inheritance. Quite a job! You owe all this to Mr. Ho. He's the one who made it all possible. And how have you been doing, Frank? I think you did a fine job in *Savage Revenge*. You showed some nice leaping ability there. I think you're on your way, Frank, I really do."

Quetglas said, "What happened to the bugs, Mr. Boyd?"

Boyd laughed. "No bugs tonight, Frank. They've established a regular spraying service now, one of the benefits of living on a larger island."

Quetglas said, "Lucien, you should see the beetles around here, real zoomers."

"The spray seems to get everything but the crickets," Boyd said. "That's fine with me, because I kind of like the sound of crickets on a summer evening."

"It's a lovely night," Ho said.

"Yes, isn't it," said Boyd. "Shall we have a gin before we eat? A little Tanqueray. Why not? I say. You'll find, Mr. Salvant, that I have inherited my beard and my love of gin from my father, and my eyes and love of good food from my mother. I do hope you chaps had a good ride over."

"We could see the lights in the New Territories," Ho said. "It was beautiful."

Boyd led the way to a paved island in the grass and they sat at one of the dragon tables. A waiter in a neat white jacket and black trousers came to take their orders. "What do you fancy? Gin? Yes, yes, yes. Good. Four gins, please, Lee. Cold, please. We had a small storm earlier. The dragon put on quite a show."

"The dragon?"

"When the dragon roars, we hear thunder. The dragon brings rain, which the Chinese need for their rice fields, so it's good fortune. I say, have you heard of an actress named Susan Wu?"

"I saw her in a movie called *Chan Rides Low*."

"Ahh, well then . . ."

"I wrote my doctoral dissertation on ambiguity in the American novel . . ." Salvant's voice trailed off suggestively.

"Then you liked the film?" Boyd beamed.

"I thought it was remarkable," Salvant said. He felt a wave of anxiety race across his stomach, then his face.

Boyd was pleased. He waited while Lee served them their gins, neat in what looked like frosted quadruple jiggers. "Susan Wu is a handsome woman," he said in his Richard Burton baritone. "Wouldn't you say she's handsome, Frank?"

"Susan Wu is beautiful, Mr. Boyd, and a nice lady."

"You know, Frank, I worry about her sometimes. She doesn't have any social life to speak of." Boyd took a hit of gin. "She's very clever, Mr. Salvant; her father was a professor like yourself. I've invited her to join us tonight. Surprisingly enough, she accepted." Having finished his little speech, Sing Sing Boyd waved for more gin.

"Susan Wu is coming here?" Quetglas sounded surprised.

Boyd said, "She's an interesting woman, I assure you, Mr. Salvant."

Lucien Salvant caught Frank Quetglas's eye and said, "I think I need to go to the . . . what is that the British call it? The loo?"

"Too polite. The bog," said Boyd.

"I have to go myself," Quetglas said and popped up to show Salvant the way.

Quetglas led the way around the pool to a small building that housed hot tubs, sauna, showers, and toilets. It was a delicate building with a Chinese-style roof of green tiles—so modest and so unimposing as to be invisible in the tranquil garden.

When they were out of earshot Salvant whispered, "Why

didn't you tell me about that movie earlier, asshole? Dammit, man.''

"I fucked up," Quetglas whispered. "How was I supposed to know Susan Wu's gonna be here? She's supposed to be above all this. Some Chinese Etta Terminini she is." He felt bad and looked like a guilty six-year-old.

"Christ!" Salvant stepped into the men's room. "Dammit, Frank, tell me about that movie. Quick! Quick!"

"Let me think. Let me think," Quetglas said. "Let me see, now, *Chan Rides Low*. I'm thinking."

"Less thinking and more talking, Frank."

"Baby girl born in slums. Mother T.B. This isn't going to work, Lou. Father trash picker . . ."

"Keep going."

"Bullshit social commentary. What happens next? Oh, yes, kid traded for wheelbarrow, smart in school, but new family awful. Grows up, nice tits, good ass." Quetglas furrowed his eyebrows, concentrating, trying to remember. "Also smart, independent . . ."

"More, more."

". . . men all want to poke her. Let me think, Lou. A gang of perverts grabs her, and holds her in the New Territories. She's rescued by an old friend and his kung fu buddies. She broods. She meditates. She's an existentialist or something like that. She writes novels. We'd better get back or they're going to think we're playing with each other."

"That's the plot? What's the connection? What's the pervert and the kidnapping have to do with her becoming a writer?"

"Nothing that I could see. Between the fight sequences, Boyd spliced in scenes of his actors and actresses sitting around staring at one another. Pregnant silence. That sort of thing. Sort of Bruce Lee with Much Big Meaning tacked on for theaters that don't sell tickets. This is art, man."

"God!"

"Be cool. Ho and I will keep him off the subject."

"You bastard," Salvant said. "You helped get me hooked into this, you have to start helping me out. Think, for God's sake."

"I'm sorry, man."

When Salvant and Quetglas returned to the table, they found that Susan Wu had arrived.

31

CRICKETS screamed in shrill chorus, a touch of Rogers and Hammerstein, as Lucien Salvant shook Susan Wu's hand. Then Sing Sing Boyd offered Susan his arm, she took it, and the elegant Eurasian led the way inside his villa where they would eat dinner.

Salvant and Frank Quetglas followed Boyd and Susan, their eyes on the twin companions that moved left, right, left, right, under Susan's skirt, their imaginations removing the skirt.

They passed a set of Boyd's dragon-carved outdoor tables and chairs.

"They're fabulous, aren't they?" Quetglas said, not referring to the tables or chairs.

From behind them, Stanley Ho said, "I should say so."

For no reason that he could think of, Lucien Salvant remembered Elaine with the black bangs and brown eyes who had sat to his left-front in Mrs. Lemmon's sixth-grade class, and who had encouraged him to undertake his much-admired relief map of North America. Little Lucien and

Elaine had been given special projects while the slow readers got extra practice.

Boyd looked over his shoulder and said, "In honor of Mr. Salvant, we'll eat in the *gweilo* room tonight. I have a separate room for my Chinese guests." He laughed, delighted at his wickedness in playing to the tastes of both races.

Susan Wu said, "I'm sure Lucien will get all the things Chinese that he can handle."

Boyd seemed pleased that she had called Salvant by his first name. "Actually, we can eat anytime we please. Would you like to see my safari room, Mr. Salvant?"

"Say yes, Lou. Say yes," Quetglas said.

Salvant said, "Whatever's your druthers. How do you feel, Susan?"

"Frank's right, Lucien. You'll probably fancy it. I'm game."

The sweltering warmth of evening made Salvant think of a long-ago swamp in summertime, of a forgotten side road, of unfastening a stubborn bra hook, of sliding his hand over a female hip, of unspeakable loveliness—all this with frogs croaking bass riffs to the trilling of frenzied crickets. Accompanied by these animated and excited amphibian and insect jazzmen, Lucien Salvant had lost his innocence in the bayou.

Now he remembered clearly the surrendering, sharing warmth of his girl friend's body.

They entered Sing Sing Boyd's villa, where servants waited for Boyd's instructions, which he gave in Cantonese, gesturing with his hands as he spoke. The entrance was definitely Chinese, with carved dragons and serpents climbing corners, and snaking their way under the ceiling. On both sides of the entrance hallway there were murals of pale mountains floating in a misty sea so that a visitor was enveloped among islands of the South China Sea. This was Boyd's mother's world.

Boyd slowed for a servant to open a sliding door, and the party stepped into a large room.

Lucien Salvant couldn't conceal his surprise.

"Yes, it's something, isn't it?" Boyd said. "Most of this was my father's, Mr. Salvant. His name was Colonel H.A.T. Boyd, an Arabist; he was an administrator in Calcutta under the British raj, and a colonial official here in Hong Kong. His friends called him Hatty." Boyd had obviously liked his father. "Anyway, here he is with the American explorer Tyler Donald in the Rub' al Khali on the Saudi Arabian peninsula. They were looking for the Lost City of Moo. Mr. Donald had inverted sexual tastes and spent a pleasant week with Ibn Bin Said, Sultan of Oman."

Salvant looked at the framed photograph of Colonel Hatty Boyd, a tall, lean man with his hands on his hips. Colonel Boyd wore an Arab headdress. His cotton trousers and shirt seemed to have pockets everywhere and were filthy with dust and sweat. On his hip there rested an enormous revolver, the butt of which stuck out at a rakish angle.

Boyd said, "This is the same Donald of oil fame. The sultan, who was pleased by Donald's favors, signed over the offshore rights in the Gulf of Oman and the Arabian Sea. Donald didn't know how to type, so the sultan did the honors on my father's portable typewriter. This one, as a matter of fact." Boyd put his hand on an ancient portable typewriter that sat on an antique seaman's chest. The letters had worn off the keys, but the black enamel was still unchipped and handsome in the light.

Salvant paused at a coffee table made of an elephant's foot that had been sawed off and topped with a slab of jade. "And this?"

"A coffee table made from the foot of an elephant Hatty shot on the Serengeti Plain with the American pilot Eddie Rickenbacker. Hatty's boys panicked and ran, but he stopped the bull at twelve yards, they say, calmly firing into the thickest part of its head. You might be interested in this scimitar over here. A Saudi sheik used it to chop off the heads of slaves. Hatty said more than five hundred."

"What's this?" Salvant picked up a polished wooden object.

Boyd flushed slightly, grinning. "That's a dildo used by the women of the Trobriand Islands in certain pagan ceremonies, if you'll excuse me, Susan."

Salvant thought it was a wonderful room. Hatty Boyd had dragged home such oddities as an eighteenth-century Portuguese globe, Afghan spurs, a Hindu mortar and pestle, a Moorish sundial. In the end they sat on camel saddles and drank gin and talked until Sing Sing Boyd, glancing at his watch, suggested that they might want to eat. They agreed and drank more gin while Boyd sent word to the kitchen.

Then Boyd rose to lead the way to the dining room. "I told my chefs to do their best. I do hope you're pleased."

Lucien Salvant, who was beginning to feel the gin, was seated to the left of Sing Sing Boyd, with Susan Wu to Salvant's left; then came Stanley Ho. Frank Quetglas sat on Boyd's right. It was evident that Boyd had looked forward to talking to Frank. While he was charming to his other guests, he showed equal attention to Quetglas. In fact Boyd, a childless widower—his wife Jane, Salvant learned, had died four years earlier—seemed to regard himself as Quetglas's surrogate father.

Sing Sing Boyd smiled and said, "Frank, I don't think I ever got a chance to personally tell you that I thought your eye-gouging sequence was wonderful in *Savage Revenge*. The critics were properly appalled and disgusted. It takes genuine talent to elicit that kind of response, and it fills the theaters. They tell me we had repeat viewers for that bit of action alone."

Quetglas blushed. "Thank you, sir. I . . ." Quetglas wanted to say something more but didn't.

"You musn't be modest, Frank; this is an immodest business. Eye-gouging like that can cause it to become a cult movie among video collectors." Boyd made a *hu*—a tiger's claw—with his hand. He opened his mouth and made a noise with his tongue that was meant to imitate the parting of the bad guy's eyes. Boyd, grinning—his guests laughing—repeated the sound in his Burtonesque timbre several times, clawing at the air with his hand. "You've a talent, son, and that's money in our pocket."

"I'm pleased, sir." Quetglas was red-faced.

"We're talking international distribution, Frank. The Europeans love bizarre violence. Remember how Buñuel and Dali had the eye slit with a razor in *The Andalusian Dog?*"

"How can I forget that, sir."

"The slit eye made that film a classic. American college kids just love to watch it." Boyd leaned toward Salvant and Wu. "I do hope you don't think we're coarse, Mr. Salvant. I think I'm probably of a kind with your American television producers, only more honest."

Leaving Salvant and Susan to themselves, Boyd joined Quetglas and Ho in a discussion of eye-gouging by a fighter using the "come see the great bird" movement.

Salvant knew he had to gamble. He couldn't take a chance on getting caught lying to Boyd. He leaned over and murmured in Susan Wu's ear, "Boyd thinks I saw you in *Chan Rides Low*. I lied. I promise to see it the first chance I get." He said aloud, "I thought *Chan Rides Low* was a marvelous movie, Ms. Wu."

"Call me Susan, please. I'm glad you liked it." She whispered in his ear, "I think I'd pass on seeing it if I were you."

Salvant grinned; he was relieved.

Boyd said, "I'm pleased that you two are getting on. I like to see harmony among people who work for me." Boyd put his hand on Frank Quetglas's shoulder. "I'm especially grateful that you're getting on with Frank here. If you two chaps are to be a team, it's better if you're chums as well.

"Mr. Ho did tell you about Mr. Pak's Society of the Red Lotus, did he not? Barbarians!" Boyd grabbed a shrimp with his chopsticks and popped it in his mouth. "But Frank can handle himself. Can't you, Frank?"

"Yes, sir, Mr. Boyd."

"Did I tell you, Susan, that Frank is living with Mr. Salvant? He's to serve as his bodyguard."

"Well! Boyd's Bullet put to use, eh, Frank?" Susan said.

Boyd said, "If Frank can gouge real eyeballs as well as he can plastic ones, you're completely safe, I assure you, Mr. Salvant."

"He can leap and kick, I give him that," Salvant said.

"It's the Cuban in me, all those black beans and rice." Quetglas looked expansive.

"Mr. Salvant, you might be interested to know that your American *Ms.* magazine did a long feature on Susan." Boyd beamed. He was proud of the accomplishments of his actors and actresses.

"Did you like the article?" Salvant asked Susan.

"I think the writer may have written the article before she talked to me."

Boyd said, "The writer was quite passionate, that's true. We were lucky she liked Susan, so it came out just fine."

"I was careful," Susan said.

"Ms. Wu is an intelligent woman." Boyd topped off their cups with more tea. "Frank, you're hardly eating! Isn't this good food? With all that training, I'd think you'd be a big eater. Those fight scenes must eat up a lot of calories."

"It's fabulous food, Mr. Boyd." Frank Quetglas began refilling his plate. He was both earnest and delighted as he picked from among the wonderful selection of exquisite Chinese dishes; he then set about to please Boyd by devouring thirds, his chopsticks as quick as a parrot's beak.

"I'm pleased that you like it. Last time you were here you ate fourths or fifths as I recall."

"It's delicious," Quetglas said.

If Frank Quetglas found the next bite less tasty than the previous one, he didn't show it. Salvant admired Frank's enthusiasm and pluckiness in doing what had to be done. He thought Quetglas would have made a good corporation executive or politician.

Quetglas leaned behind Boyd and whispered in Salvant's ear, "Doesn't Susan Wu look edible? How'd you like to get it on with her right there on the table with two handfuls of twice-cooked pork and your face in the *chow fun*? *Besame la pinga, señorita!*"

Salvant realized Quetglas was pissed to the gills. He had been doing fine, laughing, joking with Sing Sing Boyd, then suddenly, the booze was upon him. Salvant saw that Boyd had heard every word and was suppressing a grin. He said, "Hey, Frank."

"Egg foo yung clinging to Susan Wu's *culo*. Mmmmm!" Quetglas sat back down.

Salvant said, "I would have thought you got enough to eat, Frank. Fifths! Now you want to sample Susan Wu. I'm impressed."

Quetglas laughed silently. "I guess I did sort of load the old tank." He slapped himself on the belly. "We're in hog heaven, Lucien. When the man fills the trough, we eat. This is the life, man. This is what everybody dreams of. But you want to know the truth? If somebody came along with a plate of black beans and rice, and some fried bananas, and roast pork, and good Cuban bread, I'd eat another meal right now." He was sloshed. He grinned crookedly. The waiter delivered after-dinner cognac.

32

LUCIEN Salvant lay awake for two hours thinking about the inestimable Sing Sing Boyd and the actress Susan Wu before he finally drifted off to sleep at three in the morning. A few weeks earlier he had been Professor Salvant facing the prospect of having to read, edit, and grade rehashes of encyclopedia articles, dreaming of the almost perfect world where he could spend all his time reading whatever he wanted to read and writing whatever he felt like.

Now he saw them again, saw the professors with atrophied laugh muscles, saw his former department chair/man/person. Her very title was the source of an unending, tiresome debate; Salvant felt if people wanted to be called chairs, then call them chairs. Call me Ishmael. Call me a chair. Who cared? Another member of the department did and so the boring quarrel. In his dream, Salvant saw the chair's terrible mouth moving once again. He believed the awful practice of using six-bit words to express nickel and dime ideas was inversely related to intelligence. She believed the reverse. She wielded her mouth like Rambo's M16; dumb and ugly

210

words whizzzzzzed forth on full automatic: computerize, conceptionalize, departmentalize, finalize, prioritize, verbalize, visualize. Department meetings left Salvant weak. Once she raked him point-blank with "normalizing parentalization" and gave him a blinding headache.

Salvant dreamed of being back on the Quantrell faculty. Some of these dreams were good; others were borderline nightmares. In one of the good ones—this took place on the Raiders basketball court, a nostalgic vision—an endless row of young women in low-cut dresses bent over a vinyl-topped table to register for his classes. This was always a pleasant time, the beginning of the term; later on, facing a B instead of the A that was their birthright, many of the students would turn hateful. In one dream, Salvant was at a meeting of the full faculty; he was giggling, along with two psychologist friends; the others, solemn-faced—defending their many turfs and wanting to speak—wagged their hands like eager schoolchildren.

It was still dark at four o'clock, but there was a hint of warmth in the east.

Salvant was square in the wonderful middle of what the shrinks call a "trough," in which most of his mental systems had settled down or shut off. Gone were the surreal memories of his past. Lucien Salvant hurtled through the void of deep sleep as his body regrouped its resources. . . .

The sounds were subliminal at first, a silent yet resonant disturbance in the screeching of the crickets. Then a feather-soft whopping.

Then a terrible whacking. Directly overhead! Helicopter blades lowering machines down from the darkness.

Salvant jumped up with a start, sensing his life was in danger. In an instant he catapulted from mental doldrums into hyperactivity. He scrambled for his Australian jeans and cotton shirt, hands scrambling from zipper to buttons. He had never dressed as quickly in his life yet felt he should be ready for whatever happened.

The lights came on from above so that Sing Sing Boyd's swimming pool and lovely gardens were as bright as daylight.

There was shouting, followed by automatic rifle fire from somewhere on Boyd's compound.

Salvant slipped on his shoes to the *rat-tat-tat-tat* of automatic rifles; as he cinched the last knot of his laces, there came a banging at his door.

"Mr. Salvant! Mr. Salvant!" Sing Sing Boyd's voice boomed with authority.

Salvant opened the door.

"I'm afraid the Red Lotus has arrived in some force, Mr. Salvant. Come with me, please. Quickly if you will." The calm Boyd had Susan Wu at his side. Boyd seemed to have stepped off the set of one of his movies. He was dressed in Kenya convertibles with legs that zipped off if he wanted walking shorts. His splendid safari jacket was resplendent with bellow pockets and zippers. He carried two automatic pistols, one of which he gave to Salvant, along with a box of ammunition.

Salvant, who had never fired a pistol in his life, took it, wondering how it worked.

"Do you know how that thing works?" Susan asked.

"I think you pull this back." He slid the safety. "Then fire."

"That's right," said Boyd. "Reload from the butt. Follow me, please."

They came upon a large window that overlooked the gardens. Boyd shattered it with his foot. Outside, a man with a rifle hesitated, surprised at having located his quarry so easily. Boyd shot him.

As Salvant watched, Boyd calmly shot two more men with his pistol.

Behind them, one of Salvant's guards shouted, "This way, Mr. Boyd!"

Sing Sing Boyd turned to obey, then stopped, as did Salvant and Susan, to watch a striking man in a black martial arts costume leap from a helicopter, inhale quickly, and yell, *"Hai!"*

He did it again, inhaled quickly, sharply; this was done simultaneously between clenched teeth and sinuses—making a *sshhtt!* sound. Then: *"Hai!"* He repeated this, looking about him for heads to pop and hearts to crush. *"Sshhtt! Hai! Sshhtt! Hai!"* He began stamping a foot with each *sshhtt* and each *hai*.

And from Salvant and Susan's left came Frank Quetglas, cursing in Spanish.

"Mr. Boyd!" the guard shouted behind them.

"Sshhtt! Hai!"

Boyd held up his hand to the guard. "Frank! No!"

"Sshhtt! Hai!" Kwok's strange call, with much dramatic stamping of feet, had taken on a malevolent, eerie quality that made goosebumps rise on Salvant's neck.

Quetglas ignored Boyd.

Boyd picked off two Red Lotus men who closed in on Quetglas's flank. "Frank!" he shouted.

Quetglas would have none of it. He was determined to meet the Fragrance of the Red Lotus in foot-to-foot combat.

"Sshhtt! Hai!" Kwok Lai Kwon, looking as friendly as freshly spilled blood, flowed smoothly to his left.

"This isn't the movies, Frank!" Boyd tried to fire his pistol again, but it was empty. He grabbed a Chinese sword from the wall.

A Red Lotus fighter leaped high in front of Boyd. Boyd calmly lopped the man's feet off as the kick was on its way and stood back as his opponent fell to the floor on stumps that squirted blood.

"Sshhtt! Hai!"

Quetglas looked as if he were circling a rattlesnake.

"Frank, lad!" Boyd called.

The Fragrance of the Red Lotus moved in for the kill.

Susan Wu squeezed Salvant's hand.

Boyd's Bullet waited.

"Sshhtt! Hai!" Kwok unleased an incredible kick.

Frank twisted to soften the blow . . .

But took it hard on the ribs.

And straightened . . .

Unsuccessfully blocking a kick flush in the face.

The fight was over—hardly longer than a sumo match or a cockfight. Frank Quetglas lay inert, blood flowing from his mouth and nose.

A crimson bubble formed on his upper lip and held.

Lucien Salvant felt an arm snake around his neck and yank hard.

Earlier, Kwok Lai Kwon and a band of the toughest-looking human beings Gene Holt had ever laid eyes on had set out in helicopters to kidnap a Chinese movie actress. Pak Tze Fan said he was squeezing Sing Sing Boyd's lychees, leaving it up to Holt to figure out what that meant. Holt couldn't remember Susan Wu, but he had watched Sing Sing Boyd productions. He used to scoop Boyd's kung fu movies up in a TV dish at his hideaway in La Paz, before the awful cold got to him. For some reason, he couldn't pick them up in Paramaibo.

Citing the danger involved, Pak Tze Fan had originally planned for Gene Holt to stay temporarily at a Red Lotus hideaway on Lantau Island's Chi Ma Wan peninsula. This, Pak had said, was because of the dangers involved in squeezing Boyd's lychees. Holt would be safe at Chi Ma Wan.

But Holt had pleaded to stay. "Really, what will it hurt? I've snatched people before. I know things can happen."

Not wanting to offend a client who had his heart set on an eight-million-dollar island, Pak agreed.

Now, with the popping of a helicopter growing closer,

Holt was excited. Kwok and his men had left in five helicopters. Had something bad happened? Were the other helicopters downed somewhere? Where did they go? Holt followed Pak out to the brightly lit tennis courts where the helicopter apparently would be landing. He wanted to ask Pak how things were going but thought better of it. Beetles and moths swirled and dived and looped above the brightly lit courts.

Pak saw him and said, "Everything's under control, Mr. Holt. There shouldn't be any danger now."

"And the helicopters? What happened to the others?"

Pak smiled. "They're fine. Everybody's okay."

"Maybe Boyd'll call in James Bond."

"There is no worry, Mr. Holt. When the farting dogs know, we'll know too."

A movie actress. Holt wondered how much Pak was asking. He watched as the helicopter descended into the buggy light. Would the movie actress be tied up? he wondered. That sounded vaguely sexy. He turned his face against the prop wash, using the back of his left hand for protection against bugs sent flying.

Holt and Pak waited for the props to come to a halt, then the door opened and Kwok Lai Kwon stepped out. He waited and a pretty Chinese woman followed. The actress, that must be. Then a European. The European was obviously with the woman. Holt watched them pass through the bugs, escorted by Kwok to their quarters in Pak's villa.

Holt remembered seeing the man before. Where? "Who is the man?" he asked, not expecting an answer.

Pak turned his palms up and shrugged.

"I've seen him somewhere."

Pak turned. "Really?"

Gene Holt was amused. The efficient Kwok had returned with an extra body. Later, in his room, thinking about the man's familiar face, Holt remembered who he was. That was the dumb shit who had inherited 500 million dollars of

Cactus Jack Bonner's money, the guy with his fly open on the covers of magazines.

Holt sat down to consider this one further. The night before, both Roderick Brixton and Hong Kong television had reported the Bonners were spending a few days in town on their way back from having signed the Sunyang oil deal in Beijing.

33

WHEN their turn in line came at last, Ella Nidech deferred to Sing Sing Boyd. She wondered if something had happened to Stanley Ho. Their agreement with Boyd was that Nidech would work through Ho. Now here she was with a rendezvous with Boyd at nine-thirty in the morning. Something had gone wrong.

"It's impossible to get a McChicken sandwich this time of day, isn't it? Or those McNuggets?" Boyd studied the bill of fare on the wall.

"We can get an Egg McMuffin," Nidech said, wondering why on earth he had wanted to meet her in a McDonald's.

"Yes, good stick-to-the-ribs stuff. That would be nice, thank you," Boyd said. "These McDonald's people are so clever—clean, and swift, they are."

Nidech thought, Please don't say "very American."

"Very American," Boyd said. "I like Burger King, too. People never expect to see Sing Sing Boyd in a McDonald's or Burger King, so I can go there and enjoy some privacy. If I go to a good restaurant, people stare."

Nidech ordered and in a few moments the attendant gave them their Egg McMuffins and paper cups of hot tea. He stroked his mustache with the tips of his fingers. "I hope you don't think this presumptuous or panicky on my part to use the emergency number for something like this. One always wants to follow proper form. I've had a very difficult night indeed, Ms. Lewis."

Boyd sounded rather like Richard Burton, Nidech thought. She said, "That's why we give instructions for emergency communications." The Company people who had assembled Boyd's dossier had been singularly impressed by his storied calm. He was always in control, the summary had read.

Boyd took a sip of tea as they headed for an abandoned corner of the McDonald's. "Ms. Lewis, I regret to tell you that the Society of the Red Lotus made a helicopter raid on my Lantau estate shortly before dawn this morning and kidnapped my actress, Susan Wu, and my guest, Lucien Salvant. Pak Tze Fan says not to go to the police or he will kill them both. I don't have to tell you, the Hong Kong police are rife with triads. If I called them, it would be pulling the trigger on two innocent people."

Nidech had heard stories about Pak Tze Fan and the Society of the Red Lotus, but she wondered what they had to do with Chinese secrets or the Company. Surely Boyd didn't expect the Company to bail him out of all his scrapes. "Who is Salvant?" she asked.

"The heir of a Texas oilman. You may have seen pictures of him on the covers of those awful weeklies." He took a bite of his Egg McMuffin sandwich.

Nidech laughed. "The man with the unzipped fly. Pak kidnapped him, too?"

"Ms. Lewis, have you ever heard of the Farmer? These things are always good, aren't they?"

Nidech tried her McMuffin. She sure did know who the Farmer was—or more properly, what he did. As the Company's Hong Kong station chief, she was the designated backup of Farmer's control, Lee Swenson, a Hong Kong officer of MI6. But so far she'd had no need to know the Farmer's identity. The man called Farmer had masterminded an organization of poppy growers to prevent the growth of dealer monopolies. This wasn't a cartel exactly; there remained scattered growers who refused to cooperate with anyone. But with Farmer's assistance, the largest growers did work together, thus guaranteeing their independence; it wasn't lost on them that they were helping the Americans and Europeans keep the trade to manageable size. This was for the suppliers own good and they knew it.

For his diplomatic skills in keeping the growers working together—said to be on a par with OPEC's Sheik Zaki Yamani—Farmer was secretly paid a handsome sum by the Company and MI6. Most of this was American money, but the operation was run by the Brit, Lee Swenson.

Boyd said, "Lee Swenson's in New Zealand on holiday and incommunicado." He waited for Nidech to consider the meaning of what it was he had just told her.

The China buy middleman! Farmer as well? "You?"

"The Red Lotus has been eliminating its competition for the West Coast market. I'm afraid Pak Tze Fan has somehow deduced my identity, and he wishes to do away with cooperation among the growers. Something will have to be done, I'm afraid." Sing Sing Boyd took a bite of his Egg McMuffin and a sip of tea before continuing. "This is far more efficient than trying to rely on the police to control the traffic, Ms. Lewis. People like Pak Tze Fan simply buy the police who are supposed to control the routes. You understand how that works."

Ella Nidech, still shocked by the revelation that the China buy middleman was also the Farmer, said, "I understand methane." The odor of methane lay over Hong Kong with the obstinance of smog blocking out the sun over Los Angeles. She could hardly believe it.

"Methane, Ms. Lewis?"

"Greed," said Nidech.

Boyd colored. "I see. Yes, it's true that with the kind assistance of your company and Mr. Swenson's employers, I simply replaced police greed with agricultural greed."

"And the kidnapping of Susan Wu and Lucien Salvant is an opener to what?"

"Pak has asked for an unlimited supply. I'm afraid it wouldn't do for the Red Lotus to be that large."

"Does Pak know about your relationship to Swenson and my firm?"

"No, he doesn't. And if Swenson were here, he would assist me in retrieving Susan and Lucien. He would provide me with Gurkhas or whatever I need. But he is not." Sing Sing Boyd closed his eyes and sighed. "Lee Swenson is fishing on a lake somewhere in the Southern Alps of New Zealand. Stanley Ho is in the hospital with a fractured skull he suffered in the action. One of my actors, Frank Quetglas, was savagely beaten." Boyd shook his head, his mouth tight. "And I was forced to cut off a chap's feet. How I hate that kind of thing."

"What?"

"These bloody feet were coming right at me. If I hadn't disconnected them from the bloke's legs, they'd have taken my head off."

"And you did this with . . . ?"

"With a scimitar Hatty brought back from Saudi Arabia. I felt like General Gordon at Khartoum." Boyd looked at his wristwatch. "Please don't think I'm denigrating your skills out of casual sexism, Ms. Lewis, but do you think your firm might be able to help me out with some more people? As per Mr. Swenson's standing instructions, in his absence, I am to ask your help. I don't have any other choice, Ms. Lewis. I am in your hands."

34

PETER Neely's wife loved all the color and the food of the Washington parties—some embassies had unlimited entertainment budgets. Also, she liked being able to tell her sister how she had sipped Pimm's Cup with the British ambassador, or told an off-color joke to the governor of California, or got a pea soup recipe from the Vice-President's wife. She did this knowing it twisted her sister's insides like a pair of red-hot pliers.

Neely hated everything about the parties, beginning with the annoying scream of his wife's hair drier. When she dried her hair it was like standing aft of a 747. Neely had taken to throwing the invitations away, until she intervened with his personal secretary. So it was that he was at a party in Chevy Chase when the beeper summoned. The party was attended mainly by Africans with British public school accents and colorful costumes. Neely, who was having to listen to yet another imaginative explanation of Colonel Khadafy's looniness, was grateful for the beep.

The woman on the telephone said, "You have an important call from Ms. Lewis in Hong Kong, Mr. Parson. This has to do with a Chinese contract and a Mr. Randolph.''

The China buy? Situation Randolph? "Give me half an hour, and alert Hastings, please.'' Neely glanced at his watch: 9:30 P.M., Saturday, in Washington; 9:30 A.M., Sunday, in Hong Kong.

They had just arrived, and Neely's wife didn't want to go. "They're saying Henry Kissinger's coming as soon as he can break away from a party at the Belgian embassy.''

Neely knew there was no way Henry Kissinger was going to swap sautéed Belgian morels for candied sweet potatoes. He said, "I can wait for your taxi, or you can stay and order one yourself. I do have to go to the office.''

She went with him, sore. "What is it this time, a Soviet submarine in Chesapeake Bay? Why don't you people grow up?''

Neely said nothing.

"One of your favorites caught with his pee-pee in a Russian's mouth?''

"Please, Maryanne.''

"The entire West German secret service went across, is that it?''

"This all can wait," he said.

"Adolescents." She gave him a look that told him there would be no sex for a month, the final hammer. They waited, silent, stomachs grinding, until her taxi came.

Neely's unscheduled drives to Langley, far from being a curse, had come to be the most pleasant times of his life. He never rushed these drives. There seemed to be nothing short of rockets in a launch mode that would make him hurry. The Mercedes was air-conditioned, so it was always comfortable inside. The oranges and yellows of fall were the most spectacular, but all seasons of the year had their pleasures: the naked grays of winter; the budding of spring; summer's green in the steamy heat. Only in the car was he both free of his wife and as yet ignorant of the details of the next bend in the

Big Muddy. He wondered what on earth could have happened in Hong Kong that would have moved Ella Nidech to invoke Situation Randolph. If she was being hysterical and this wasn't a Randolph crisis, Neely vowed he'd see her behind a Langley desk, woman or not. Randolph was for impending mud only.

The folks on duty had Peter Neely's favorite treats on hand for his midnight visit: coffee and rich chocolate cake. Ara Schott had arrived before him and had read Ella Nidech's report of her conversation with Sing Sing Boyd. Looking thoughtful, saying nothing, he handed it to Neely.

"Good that you were home," Neely said. Eating chocolate cake and sipping coffee, Neely read the report with its revelation that Sing Sing Boyd was also the Farmer! Not even Peter Neely knew that. And the Company's delicate man was at home in Virginia looking forward to *Saturday Night Live*. Neely looked at Schott. "The President?"

"I think so," Schott said.

Neely picked up his phone and dialed a number.

A man answered, "Yes?"

"Who are you?"

"My name is Charles. And yours?"

"Parson."

"Go ahead, Parson."

"I would like to talk to Aristotle, please. We have a Situation Randolph in Hong Kong with regard to our Chinese contract."

"One moment, Parson." After several minutes the man said, "Aristotle says to come on over and will you be coming down Wisconsin?"

"I can go down Wisconsin."

"If you are, Aristotle says can you pick up a couple of dozen chocolate chip cookies at McLander's and a half gallon of cold two-percent milk? If they have the cookies with walnuts, he says, get them. He likes them good and hot. Get the big ones. He'll spring, he says."

Neely smiled. "Walnuts might be hard this time of night. They always go first."

Peter Neely altered the truth only slightly in recounting the details of Ella Nidech's emergency in Hong Kong. Neely did not tell the President about Boyd's status as the Farmer, a complication he and Ara Schott had yet to address. This was a matter of Neely's covering his ass by omission rather than an outright lie and so was easier to justify. Schott stood by, saying nothing, thankful that Neely had to do the talking in this one.

The President bit into one of McLander's big chocolate chip cookies, savoring the flavor, grinning. "Boy, aren't those good? Those foil-lined bags keep 'em hot like that. The chips are still gooey inside. I can't get enough of 'em. My chef's tried to match 'em but can't. No, sir. And we pay him more than they pay the president of the University of Montana. Can you believe that? Supply and demand. Mmmmm. Those nuts!" He took another bite, then said, "You know, this is what we got for kowtowing to the women's libbers. If we'd had a man over there in Hong Kong, he'd probably have had everything taken care of by now. Better not let the First Lady hear that." The President pretended to check over his shoulders for his wife. "I'm not sexist, Neely, but that's the truth and we both know it."

"It had to come, Mr. President. Sooner or later we were going to wind up with a woman out there in the Big Muddy. Sex aside, I think we've got an ace on the job."

"You'd think the President of the United States could find somebody who could bake chocolate chip cookies. They put a man on the moon!"

Neely cleared his throat. "It seems hardly likely that a man in Hong Kong would have done anything differently up to now, Mr. President."

The President grinned jovially. "Why, I didn't know you were a libber, Neely. Isn't this one of those cases where we use our special guy, you know, to clean up a little? Where is he? What's his name? Boy, these cookies are good." The President, chewing, poured himself another glass of milk.

Neely said, "James Burlane, Mr. President."

"Ahh, Verlaing. Hard to forget Verlaing."

"James Burlane," Neely said, louder.

"Can Verlaing do it himself? He's a good one, isn't he? You sent him in for a chat, I remember. He's from an oddball town in Oregon. Our best, you told me. What's our woman's name again?"

Ara Schott said, "Ella Nidech, Mr. President."

"Can she do what she has to do, you know, waste people and everything?"

"She's had the same training as the men," Schott said.

"That's not what I asked."

Neely interrupted to rescue Schott. "The shrinks say she can, but she does need help. Anybody would. To do the job right, we'll have to pull people in from Manila, Jakarta, and up from Sydney."

"Up from Sydney?" The President looked amazed. "Does Verlaing need people from Jakarta? Surely that's a lot of people."

Neely said, "Pak Tze Fan lives on an island that's almost all cliff. This will have to be a coordinated, commando-type raid."

"This amounts to a military action, doesn't it?" the President said. "Against what?"

Peter Neely showed not a hint of impatience at having to repeat the facts of his summary. He said, "A tong organization, Mr. President. The Society of the Red Lotus. If Sing Sing Boyd falls, we lose our Chinese buy."

The President said, "I met this man Boyd once, you know; he seemed like a pleasant fellow. That's when I visited Lee Kwon Yew in Singapore. Boyd's a gin drinker, and an old cricket player. Did you ever understand that game?" The President paused.

Neely said, "You've got your choice, Mr. President."

"I think we should confer with the National Security Council," the President said.

Peter Neely licked his lips. He looked at his wristwatch. "We could call a special meeting, Mr. President, but the media people would be wanting to know why."

The President clenched his teeth. "When's the next regular meeting, Peter?"

"Thursday, Mr. President. That's too late, I'm afraid."

"Jack Verlaing is where?"

"Here in Virginia, Mr. President. We can have him in the air within the hour."

The President said, "I think we should let Verlaing do it. He's the man who did it for us before, isn't he? He's a can-do type, an American through and through."

"He's not Rambo or anything like that, Mr. President. He's not bulletproof."

"Isn't this coffee good? It's from Costa Rica, you know."

Schott said, "I'll contact Burlane immediately, Mr. President."

"You brought him in here when I okayed that arrangement of yours, remember? He offered to work for expenses only if we wanted because he likes his work." The President shook his head in wonderment.

"Our Main Man, Mr. President."

The President beamed. "Yes, that's it! He's our Main Man, isn't he? Otto Graham throwing long. Bob Petit in the clutch." The President squinted his eyes, trying to remember his baseball.

"Reggie Jackson in October!" Neely said.

The President frowned. "I don't know Reggie Jackson. They all seemed to run together after Ralph Kiner retired."

Quickly Neely said, "Bobby Thomson in the ninth."

The President remembered Bobby Thomson. "Yes! Bobby Thomson in the ninth. Jack Verlaing! I don't think he'd combed his hair when he came to see me that day. He looked like Huckleberry Finn.'' The President doubled up his fist and punched the air in support of Jack Verlaing who was going to tidy things up in Hong Kong without everything turning up on the six o'clock news.

The President said, "Do you remember who the Dodger was who threw that pitch? Mr. Schott?"

"I'm afraid I don't know, Mr. President."

Peter Neely furrowed his brow.

"Ralph Branca. There's a lesson there."

Neely wondered what the lesson was. "Yes, Mr. President?"

The President said, "Say, help yourself to some more cookies. They're no good when they get cold."

Neely said, "If I get Burlane in the air by eleven o'clock, he'll arrive in Hong Kong about ten A.M., Tuesday. Plenty of time."

"You know, it's places like McLander's that make this country great. Those people are making a fortune by baking a better chocolate chip cookie."

Peter Neely drove back to Langley and passed word on to Ella Nidech in Hong Kong:

Lewis. Our best man, Marion Morrison, alas the target of your recent complaint, dispatched for Hong Kong 11:30 P.M. our time. ETA 10:20 A.M., Tuesday, your time. Proceed as you think best until he arrives. Morrison will contact your firm upon arrival. You remain in command of China buy. FYI: This assignment on Aristotle's instructions; Morrison remains on probation until Gein report is considered and acted upon. Best. Parson.

35

J AMES Burlane had plenty of time. The clock above the scheduled arrivals and departures said it was quarter to eleven and his flight to Portland en route to Hong Kong left at eleven-thirty. The name and time of the departing flights were entered at the bottom. Each flight worked its way up the board until it departed and its name was removed from the top.

Burlane began at the bottom of the board—wondering if Flight 008 would be leaving on time. He worked through Chicago, New Orleans, Denver, but couldn't find Portland.

Then he saw it at the top of the board. Portland. His mouth froze at the sight of the departure time: 10:47 P.M.

Burlane's jaw dropped.

The man behind the ticket counter said, "Are you going to Portland?"

"Yes."

"They're boarding now. Run. I'll phone ahead and have them hold the plane."

Burlane began sprinting through the crowd at National

Airport, wondering how he had screwed up. He ran to the head of the X-ray line. Just like O. J. Simpson.

When he got to the gate an attendant said, "The man to Portland?"

Burlane said yes. The attendant ripped off the first sheet of his ticket, and he was ushered into the cabin of the plane.

Burlane hoped his close call wasn't an omen of things to come. He buckled himself in, put on his headphones, and searched for the switch of the Walkman in his jacket pocket. He'd heard the attendant's instructions hundreds of times, the hell with that noise.

The cabin attendant said, "Welcome to American International's . . ."

What Burlane needed was sleep so he . . .

"Star Trek flight to Portland . . ."

Flipped the switch: "Hello, big boy." The Company hypnotist—a female for male agents—had a soft, soothing voice. "Are you all kicked back and relaxed? That's good. I want you to feel calm and comfortable. Feel your muscles relax. Doesn't that feel wonderful? I want you to fall into a deep, wonderful sleep so that you will wake up relaxed and refreshed. But if your body senses danger in any way, you will awaken immediately, ready to do whatever is required of you. It will teach you something about your subconscious mind, and the more you use it, and the more you learn, the easier it will be for you to fall asleep without the use of drugs that impair your efficiency . . ."

James Burlane was sound asleep before the attendant demonstrated the oxygen masks that drop down from the compartment above.

Wisps of fog began to flow across the runway as the 727 waited its turn on the runway of National Airport. Finally the Portland flight got its clearance and the plane took off, rising above the national capital, where the fog romped in on puppy-dog feet, and tumbled over the city, slopping dew over diner windows and the toes of cops' polished shoes.

"Sir!" The woman flight attendant hardly touched James Burlane's shoulder. He was wide awake before she could say, "We've arrived in Portland, sir. You've certainly had a nice sleep."

Burlane had used the self-hypnosis tape scores of times, but this was the best yet. Coast to coast and he'd never felt better. He'd use the tape again on the flight from Portland to Hong Kong and wake up ready to go. He looked outside wondering if he'd be able to see Mt. Hood or Mt. St. Helens. He couldn't see either. The fog was so thick Burlane was surprised they'd been allowed to land.

He got in line behind an older couple with a Down East accent and waited for his turn off the airplane.

He peered at the fog outside.

As he stepped through the exit, a female attendant wishing him a good day, he heard the captain say, "Last flight in. That was spooky."

"We'll have fun, even in Portland," his assistant said. "We'll have baked salmon for dinner."

"I'll make book we'll be here for a while."

The interior of the airport had been redecorated since his last time through. Burlane regarded himself as an Oregonian still and liked to go through Portland so he could phone old friends and bullshit a little.

The hallway was decorated with huge, colored photographs of fishermen on lovely rivers and lakes: the Saco River, the Penobscot River, the Allagash River, Lake Sebago, Moosehead Lake, and Lake Chesuncook.

Looking at the photographs and place names, James Burlane was stunned. There was no Rogue River, no Umpqua, or Deschutes. No Columbia. Where was Crater Lake? Where were the obligatory pictures of Multnomah Falls and Haystack on the beach?

What in God's name had he done?

Portland, Maine!

James Burlane was struck dumb. How could he have fucked up like that? How? Portland, Maine! He could hardly believe it. Hours, wasted. And now, a Stephen King fog. He was sure there would be no taking off in that fog. There was no telling how long it would take the fog to burn off.

The man at the ticket counter said, "Might not lift for a few hours, sir. The man on the TV says it's a once-in-fifty-years fog. It's amazing when it closes in like this."

"Boston's closed too, I take it."

The ticket man nodded. "Oh, yes, Boston too. Providence, Hartford, all down the coast. This is a real lulu of a fog. Old Mother Nature. You'd have to take a train to New York to get out of it, but you're looking at five or six hours travel time, and if it started to burn off early, you'd be stuck on the train." The man laughed, trying to sound hearty. "There's always the lounge. You can have yourself a good breakfast with maybe an Irish coffee or two, buy yourself a copy of the Sunday *Globe*. It may be foggy out, but the air is nice and crisp up here. Clean."

Burlane thanked the ticket man. He'd have to tell Neely what happened. If Neely decided to tell the President, then Burlane's days as the Company's delicate man were probably finished. He'd be sent down to a desk job, a veteran of deteriorating skills relegated to telling old war stories in the Langley cafeteria. Burlane sighed and went to the lounge where he bought an airmail edition of Sunday's *New York Times* and ordered himself a double Bloody Mary. Was this what happened to old Hoyt Wilhelm in the end? Did his once dandy knuckler just sail high one day, so bad the catcher didn't even try for it? It was hard for Burlane to accept the showers after all those years of striking them out.

Burlane looked at his watch. He had already lost two hours.

He found a telephone booth and dialed Neely's special number, not knowing exactly where to begin his explanation.

36

LUCIEN Salvant awoke late in the morning to find himself on one side of a king-size bed. On the other side, across an expanse of silken cover, Susan Wu lay watching him. "Good morning, Lucien," she said.

"They drugged us." He sat up. The walls of the bedroom were covered by fabulous Chinese embroideries, murals in fact—a scene from the Yangtze River, rice terraces, lovely mountains, the Great Wall. "Do you feel okay?"

"I'm fine." Susan Wu sat up also.

Salvant got up and tried the door. It was locked.

The door opened and a Chinese man with a wide face and an automatic pistol said, "We have the door barred from the outside. We'll deliver your food. It doesn't make any difference to us if we shoot you now or wait until Wednesday." He closed the door and rebarred it.

Susan Wu went to one of two smaller, vertical windows that flanked the main picture window. The smaller windows opened out to admit the sea air. She poked her head out saying, "Lucien?"

Salvant stuck his head out of the other window that opened. "Whoa!" he said, looking down. They were imprisoned in a villa that had been built at the top of the cliff so that the wall facing the sea continued straight up from the cliff.

The surf funneled directly into an imperfect V-shaped inlet that formed the centerpiece of the vista. To their left, a rock jetty protected one side of the inlet's mouth. Large swells pushed their way through the unprotected half and crashed hard into boulders at the base of the cliff—sending forth spectacular plumes and rooster tails that were whipped skyward by the sea wind that also beat against the cliff and rose in an updraft.

Actually, the cliff was an upside-down triangle—broad at the top and narrow at the bottom. Unfortunately, the window of their imprisoning room was directly above the two-hundred-foot stretch of boulders at the apex. It was an awesome drop straight down from their window—five hundred feet at least.

The brushy sides of the inlet were too steep for buildings but not too steep for a careful hiker; indeed, to Lucien and Susan's left, wooden stairs zigzagged down the eastern slope of the inlet. These stairs, which included a rope safety rail to accommodate sufferers of vertigo, wound down to a thin strip of gravelly beach that ended where larger rocks began, the larger rocks becoming the boulders that received the surf straight on.

Seaward, the beach widened and there was a dock that accommodated three sailboats and two powerboats, and a spare berth. The sailboats were protected by a jetty that stretched halfway across the mouth of the inlet. There was a concrete helicopter pad next to the boathouse, presumably to ferry Pak Tze Fan and his guests to the villa at the top of the cliff.

There was a small island opposite the inlet, a pale gray shape in the distance.

There were no buildings on either ridge of the inlet. Salvant and Wu could hear only the sound of the surf crashing on the boulders far below and the sounds of daytime insects taking over from their nocturnal brethren.

By Hong Kong standards, their room was spacious in the extreme, and lavishly furnished. Their king-size bed was dressed with silk sheets and pillowcases. They had a rattan sofa that was at least eight feet long—Salvant was able to stretch out without touching either end with his head or feet. Salvant and Wu also had two comfortable chairs, and a coffee table on which their captors had left a pile of magazines for them to read. The adjoining bathroom had soap, shampoo, toothbrushes and toothpaste, an electric razor, and towels.

There was no telephone, and they had no radio or television set. The seaward wall of the villa was totally devoid of ledges or architectural frills between windows. "There's nothing to loop onto or hold onto anywhere," Salvant said.

"That'd give me the spooks, leaning out like that."

Salvant ducked his head back inside. "Maybe Boyd'll send commandos up the side of the cliff like Gregory Peck in *The Guns of Navarone*. Human flies and all that."

Susan Wu joined him at the window and gave a timid peek down at the rocks. "Sure, with Sing Sing in the lead dressed in a proper outfit and with a flask of brandy in his hip pocket, and your pal Frank Quetglas at his side."

"Where are we, do you think?"

"We could be anywhere, just off Lantau, maybe, or in the Po Toi group just back of Hong Kong island, or the Ung Kongs, or any number of islands in the New Territories."

"Were we in the air long enough for the New Territories? My sense of geography is worthless, I admit."

"We're probably on one of the smaller islands off Pak Kok or Chi Ma Hang, which are just southwest of Lantau, or one of the islands off Lamma Island."

"At least the wind is cooling. The cliff could be facing the wrong direction. Does the wind blow the same direction all year round?"

"Let me think," Susan said. "It blows from the southwest in the summer, northwest in the winter."

"Then we're facing southwest," Salvant said.

"That's about right, judging from the sun. Which does us no good."

"Which means we could be a hundred yards off Hong Kong island and not know it." Salvant paused. "Or even part of Hong Kong itself, on a peninsula, say. We can't see what's on either side of this bay. Are there small islands like that off the Hong Kong coastline?"

"Two or three that I can think of that face the right direction. We could be on a peninsula on Lantau. There's an island off the southwest tip, I think."

Salvant looked down at the water crashing onto the boulders far below. "God, it's a long way down there."

Susan Wu said, "If it was one of Sing Sing's movies, he'd have us tying sheets together."

"Land on those rocks and we'd be shorts in a washing machine."

"We'd be dead on arrival. It's impossible, I agree."

"I suppose we could overpower them when they deliver us food. You lure them in with your good looks and I knock them out like Boom Boom Mancini. Did they film any kind of daring escape in *Chan Rides Low?*"

"Look, there's someone going down the trail."

"Where?"

"About halfway down, a little more."

They watched as the figures, tiny, barely distinguishable in the distance, worked their way down the trail that zigzagged down the slope. "Women," Salvant said.

"How can you tell at this distance?"

"Their rumps."

Susan Wu was amazed. "At this distance?"

"They're wriggling like fat carp. Maybe they'll sun in the nude, what do you think?" Salvant licked his lips.

Susan looked amused. "I can't imagine you could see much from this distance, could you?"

Salvant squinted his eyes, trying to see the details of the beach. "Fun to imagine, though. They'll be oiling themselves down and everything. All those wonderful parts."

"You think so, huh?"

"They're probably going sailing." Salvant grabbed a Chinese-language magazine from the selection laid out neatly on the coffee table. He couldn't read anything, but the color photographs were gorgeous.

Sing Sing Boyd sat in the chair and squeezed the salesman's hand. They listened to the rainsquall lash against the window while they waited for the nurse to leave. When the door closed, Stanley Ho began to say something. Boyd bent forward to hear. "One more trip on the road, Mr. Boyd."

"The others have always been good, haven't they, Stanley?"

"They were wonderful," Ho murmured.

"You know, I always envied you in a way, Stanley. The privacy of the road. Good at your work. The consummate salesman."

"I was good, wasn't I, Mr. Boyd?"

"You were the very best, Stanley. They don't make salesmen like you anymore. You moved everything: fake Cartier wristwatches, imitation designer jeans."

"Even Chinese secrets, eh, Mr. Boyd?"

"Wasn't that wonderful? Wasn't it? Nobody else could have pulled that off, Stanley. The CIA and the Bonner brothers, and Lucien Salvant. You sold them all. Nobody but you. Nobody. I mean that.''

"Thank you, Mr. Boyd. But we both know it was you, sir, a gentleman. Our buyers always knew they were dealing with a gentleman. Whenever I made a sale it had Sing Sing Boyd's name on it.''

Sing Sing Boyd flushed at the praise and squeezed Ho's hand. "This terrible business is all my fault, you know. I should have been more careful. I was having a good time and wasn't thinking. I should have hired more guards.''

Stanley Ho was having difficulty breathing. "Not your fault, Mr. Boyd,'' he said.

Sing Sing Boyd knew Ho was dying. "You never married and had a family, but I bet you knew some wonderful people. Did you ever fall in love when you were on the road, Stanley? I bet you did, out there riding Cathay Pacific with your salesman's smile and polished oxfords. Tell me about it.''

"Her name was Tila. She lived in Kota Kinabalu in Sabah. I was there buying coconut milk for our swap with the Japanese two years ago. We got a deal. You remember, Mr. Boyd. You said, 'Good heavens, Stanley, whatever are we going to do with that much squid?' Remember?''

"I remember, Stanley.'' Tears in his eyes, Sing Sing Boyd embraced his old comrade as he faced new territory.

The salesman's eyes cleared in his last minute. "You're the one who taught me how to close, Mr. Boyd. I owe everything to you. Find out what it is that people think they want and sell them that, you said. Treat them right. Make them feel special. This is good for everybody, eh, Mr. Boyd? They get what they want. I make a few bucks. You make a few bucks. Everybody's happy. Folks see one of your kung fu movies and they go away laughing and kicking at imaginary villains in the shadows. I want to tell you it's been wonderful on the road, Mr. Boyd. I look forward to each trip.''

*   *   *

Lucien Salvant pointed at the photograph in the magazine. "What's this article about?"

Susan Wu studied the Chinese characters. "It's about a man named Yi Lin who set a world record for . . . the English word would be 'para-sailing,' I think . . . by jumping off the peak of . . . let's see, it would be about twenty-five thousand U.S. feet . . . Mt. Gongga Shan in Sichuan province."

"Really? Gongga Shan. What a perfect name for a mountain. What else does it say?"

"He was raised in Tibet. Do you want to know about his family and everything?"

"Come on. I want to know if it says anything about his parachute or whatever it's called."

"The English would be something like 'para-wing,' I think. It says Yi's rectangular para-wing is more of a glider than a parachute. His was made of Chinese silk rather than nylon, which is what the Europeans use. The lightweight silk was easier for him to carry to the top of Mt. Gongga Shan. It says these rectangular parachutes unfold like an accordion. Mr. Yi, who is an expert parachutist, went from twenty-five to forty kilometers an hour coming down but landed standing up. He is to give a demonstration of his skills at the Paris Air Show."

Lucien Salvant turned up the covers on the king-size bed. "The sheets aren't fitted. Somebody had to tuck those corners in there."

Susan looked at the man in the photograph. She looked at Salvant, then back at the photograph.

"We'd need needles and thread," Salvant said.

"We've got needles." Grinning, she dug into her handbag and came out with a small plastic box. "One each, sewing kit. You always need a sewing kit on a movie set, Lucien. That and a Swiss Army knife."

"They left your Swiss Army knife?"

"No, but I have four needles of various sizes. And some white, brown, and black thread."

Salvant went into the bathroom and came back with the extra set of sheets. "That makes two apiece and they're just huge—look at them."

Susan went to the window, looking down and to her right. "There are two powerboats down there."

"We still don't have any silk thread." Salvant flopped the extra set of sheets on the bed.

Susan went into the bathroom and wrestled the chrome-plated hood that covered the roll of toilet paper from the wall. She held one side of the fixture in front of Salvant's face. "Can you see yourself in there?"

"Sure. I like looking at myself in toilet paper holders."

Susan ignored him. She ripped out some magazine pages and wrapped them around the shiny hood, tucking corners into slits she made with her thumbnail. In the end, she left a hexagon on each of the three exposed sides. She adjusted the paper to make the hexagons a little neater and looked pleased.

Salvant watched all this with interest, saying nothing.

Susan sat the object in the middle of the coffee table and aimed the middle of the three hexagons at the window.

Salvant hesitated, wondering if he could ignore whatever the thing was, thinking he might already know. He looked at his beautiful companion, coughed softly, and said, "What's that?"

"It scares away bad spirts and it will give us good *fung shui*."

Susan stooped and tilted the sofa onto its back legs and looked at the underside. "Twine. Yards of it."

"For the harness, yes, it could be done, a simple loop under our armpits. We still need silk thread."

Lucien Salvant was still thinking about *fung shui* when

he suddenly looked up at the embroidered murals on the wall. He stood and felt the Yangtze River with his fingers.

Susan Wu saw immediately what he meant; all they had to do was unravel the mysteries of the Yangtze and they'd have all the silk thread they could use.

37

ELLA Nidech got off at Admiralty and hiked the elevated sidewalks along the harbor to the ferry terminals to Macao. An hour later she was settled into her seat in the first-class cabin that was designed to imitate the inside of an airliner. The engine began a low whine that rose in pitch and intensity.

Behind her, clouds backed up against Mt. Nicholson, Mt. Cameron, Mt. Cough, and Victoria Peak, so that the sleek obelisks of Hong Kong rose through murk; the reflecting windows of the penthouses were splendid in the sun.

The late afternoon sun peeked through a break in the clouds somewhere above the western end of the New Territories so that Hong Kong harbor, reflecting the light, looked like a mirror upon which rested splendid junks and freighters waiting their turn at the docks.

The whining rose higher still. Gargling was added to the whining as though on cue—say, baritones and basses in the sixteenth bar. The jetfoil began backing out at the sound of the gargling. When the bow was pointed west, toward Ma-

242

cao, the gargling turned to a rumble that gained in speed and intensity. The captain began winding up the fanjet in earnest, the *rrrrrrrRRRRRRRR* changing into a relaxing *mmmmmmmmmm* as the craft rose on its foils and gained momentum. In minutes, the jetfoil was skimming inches above the water with hardly more vibration than an airliner in good wind. Ella Nidech thought the jetfoil was rather like a sea duck flying low over the fabulous, silvery water. She would be in Macao in forty-five minutes.

Even from a distance, Nidech knew Macao would not be crawling with the same brand of Chinese yuppies as Hong Kong. But then Macao was administered by the Portuguese. Nidech admired the Portuguese for the fact that they were the opposite of the reserved, efficient Brits. Macao had about it an air of Graham Greene or Somerset Maugham, of indolent, steamy days where both Portuguese and Chinese, rather than worrying about time, felt it was something to be considered along with a good story, or various philosophies of satisfying sex or life well lived. This contemplation—with an open collar and over a cold beer or opium pipe—was inevitably held under the cooling wash of a civilized if inefficient overhead fan.

Back in Hong Kong, she felt, money was the aphrodisiac; men used neckties to prevent blood from penetrating the regions above their shoulders; they made their calculations to the driving, devouring hum of air conditioners, ears going *bum-bump, bum-bump* from lack of blood.

When the jetfoil docked, the Hong Kong Chinese aboard leaped up and pushed toward the entrance. It was standard practice in Hong Kong for people to rush from one entrance or doorway to the next. To Nidech's way of thinking they were the most determined and committed hurriers she'd ever seen, outdoing New Yorkers and residents of Tokyo. Once on the sidewalk, she knew, they would sprint to the crowd in front of the customs officers. Once through that holdup, they would run to the line that had formed at the taxi stand. Their lines and gatherings were never loose and informal; they were tense, packed, competitive.

Nidech herself joined the line, resigned to the repressed pleasure of Chinese men pressed up against her *gweilo* figure—to them, a surfeit of womanflesh. When her turn came, she tried to get some Chinese to share the ride with her, but she knew from experience it was pointless. They looked at her as if she were crazy.

Ride with a *gweilo*?

The taxi turned onto a street that paralleled the shore of a promontory. Macao was on a peninsula at the western side of the entrance to Zhujang Kou, an inlet that led to the delta of the Xi River. There lay Canton, the capital city of China's Guandong province, which was scheduled to become a "special administrative" district when Hong Kong reverted in 1997.

The understanding with the Hong Kong capitalists was that the Guandong province would be a capitalist cancer allowed to exist apart from the rest of China—perhaps even minting its own money—until political truths had time to be redefined by Beijing.

Nidech's taxi bore to the right, and on her left was a causeway of recent vintage that led to an island a half mile offshore. Straight ahead was Macao itself, which Nidech appreciated because it remained locked in the grip of colonial torpor, its rhythms given to pleasures of the senses. Hong Kong architecture, she felt, was both adolescent in its taste and anal compulsive in the severity of its lines.

Nidech didn't go to central Macao, because on the open front of the rounded promontory stood the wonderful Hotel Lisboa—painted yellow ochre with white trim—whose architect had given himself over to the inefficient celebration of circles. The main entrance was supported by two columns and contained a series of huge, swooping, clamlike curves Nidech thought looked rather like the flamboyant pudenda in Judy Chicago paintings.

This was the welcoming maw of Macao's most popular casino. Nidech passed under the pussy-curves into the first circular room, which had counters where postcards and stamps were sold and entrances passed into various other round rooms.

Nidech made her way to the main circle of the casino, where Chinese gamblers pressed in around blackjack, baccarat and fan-tan tables. Smaller circles around this contained more gaming tables and banks of "hungry tigers"—slot machines that accepted Hong Kong dollars. This facilitated the passing of coins from the pockets of the gamblers to the proprietors of the casino without the intervening fuss of currency exchange.

The entrance to the main circle was decorated with a large carving, in buxom relief, of eleven mermaids; Nidech was uncertain whether these ladies were present for luck, or whether they were standing by in case of a typhoon, in which case gamblers were to be warned by a red sign on the wall: *Sinal de Tufão*. The sculptor had been reluctant to chisel too much wood from the mermaid's unreal bosoms.

The casino at the Hotel Lisboa was not the province of the wealthy as at Monte Carlo or other playgrounds of the rich. It was the people's casino. Bankers mingled with bank clerks. There were no lounge shows or Las Vegas diversions; alcohol, in fact, was prohibited in the gaming areas. The players, fearful of bad *fung shui,* didn't want to startle the spirits; they placed their bets in a silence broken only by the clicking of fan-tan tiles and an isolated murmur. They collected their winnings and accepted their losses seemingly without a hint of emotion.

She eased her way into the crowd of gamblers, looking for the fuss that must be attendant to the presence of Pak Tze Fan, and sure enough, there he was, looking elegant.

What was extraordinary about the scene was the space given him. The elegant Pak radiated power and authority; both fearing and respecting Pak, the gamblers allowed him to appropriate an enormous space so that he and his guest might have a private chat if they wished. They were regarded with awe and wonder; they might have been two bejeweled daggers.

Macao blackjack was played with six decks, with the gambler with the highest bet calling the hits, rather than the player with the cards. The most curious thing about it, which evidently amused the *gweilos,* was the ritual of the Revealing of the Cards. A player did not casually flip the cards up, a seven and a nine, say, if that is what they had drawn.

Things were far more dramatic in Macao than in Las Vegas. In Macao a player left the first card flat on the table, then took it by the corners with his or her thumbs. Then the player bent over the table, his eyes inches from the card, then . . .

. . . slowly, rubbing it with his thumbs . . .

. . . slowly, rubbing it with his thumbs . . .

Doing what? Ella wondered. Changing the card's *fung shui*? Exorcising bad spirits?

. . . until he bent the top edge of the card and peered at the number, studying it, while the rest of the players waited, eager to see what it was.

Then at last, dramatically, a player turned back the card, quickly, sharply, setting a crease along the card, revealing its identity for everyone present.

This absurd process was repeated for the second card and any thereafter.

Ella Nidech eased her way into the crowd that had gathered around Pak. She felt like an icebreaker plowing her way through the gamblers; the crowd closed in at her wake.

She was halfway to her objective when a hand strayed too far onto the inside of her thigh and remained there. There was no room for her to knock the hand away. She located the owner of the hand and glared at him. "Remove your hand."

The hand stayed.

"Do you speak English? Remove your hand or I'll break your face."

The man removed his hand, and she continued plowing ahead.

Nidech got to within one body from the edge of the gamblers who, on the pretext of waiting for a spot at the blackjack table, were enjoying the heady thrill of watching Pak Tze Fan, bad *fung shui* incarnate. Pak and his guest were watched over by a muscular man in a black martial arts outfit. He guarded with fierce eyes and was, in fact, one of the most savage-looking men Nidech had ever seen.

Pak's guest was a short, stocky man with kinky red hair. He was cheery-looking, a nonstop grinner. Ella Nidech knew who that man was. It seemed as if the Company had everybody looking for him: the Blowfish, Gene Holt.

But she couldn't hear what they were saying.

38

THEY might have been celebrity holders of American Express for all the attention they received. In the casino at the Hotel Lisboa, they were merely two more middle-aged American men, businessmen perhaps, bent on collecting stories of what it was like to gamble in a casino in Macao. An account of the Lisboa would be a good lead-in to stories of what it was like to gamble in Monte Carlo or Rio. These accounts crumbled the will of those less wealthy and less traveled, and assured a low poke with whatever good-looking woman might be listening.

As bucks begat ego, ego begat presence, but Ella Nidech knew them from their connection to the China buy: Flub and Clint Bonner.

Ella Nidech sensed that she was onto something good. She fell in behind them at a judicious distance. Were they here because of Pak Tze Fan and Gene Holt?

She followed them through the casino. Yes. A coup for Nidech:

Flub and Clint Bonner were here to see Pak and Holt.

Nidech was amazed. After much shaking of hands, the four men apparently began to talk business. That is, Gene Holt did the talking. Holt talked. Flub and Clint Bonner listened. Pak Tze Fan watched. Holt was an animated, earnest talker. He punctuated his pitch with short bursts of laughter. His stumpy legs bounced his athletic frame like stout springs. He waggled his finger in the air to help make a point. He put the palm of his left hand in front of Flub Bonner's face and tapped it furiously with the forefinger of his right hand, making his pitch all the while. What was he doing? He might have been selling them a house, or a new car, or a machine that peels vegetables or makes yogurt.

Holt was selling the Bonners something. What?

Nidech eased through the crowd as she had earlier, only this time she got closer.

The *gweilos* were soft-voiced southerners who communicated as much with their expressive faces and their bodies as by what they said. It didn't take Ella Nidech's inside knowledge to know they were rich, arrogant, and given to posing as boorish but saloon-smart, don't-fuck-with-me kind of cowboys.

Flub Bonner asked a question.

Holt laughed heartily and replied, waving both of his short arms.

The taller brother asked a question, and Holt laughed even louder.

Once Holt asked a question of the stoic Pak, and the latter murmured an answer, his face impassive, his eyes on the Bonners, assessing their reactions.

Holt continued talking, his arms gesturing. Once he slipped alongside Clint Bonner and clapped heartily on the small of Clint's back. He was animated. He was happy. He was optimistic. He was the most trustworthy man in the world. He was a tipster. A good old boy. This was a sure thing, a fabulous deal, his face said. How could anybody not trust Gene Holt?

The Bonners were loose and polite at first. Then Holt said something that literally caused Clint Bonner to almost choke on his little black cigar. Flub looked momentarily discombobulated, then hitched his britches just a tad, biting his lower lip.

Holt kept talking. Nidech listened as best she could, memorizing every expression and shard of conversation, seeing it as she would write it in her report.

Holt: "Mr. Bonner." Unintel, unintel, "ien Sal . . ." unintel, unintel, ". . . is inheritance?"

F. Bonner: (Hitches britches) Unintel, unintel, "my brother and me."

C. Bonner: Unintel.

F. Bonner: Unintel. (Laughter)

Holt: Unintel, ". . . ouldn't have spent," unintel.

F. Bonner: (Shakes his head) Unintel.

Holt: Unintel.

Bonners: (Clint chokes on cigar smoke.) "Huh?"

F. Bonner: (Open-mouthed) "You what?"

Holt: Unintel, ". . . erfect alibi."

F. Bonner: (Pale. Looks at brother, back at Holt): Unintel, "uch."

Holt: Unintel, ". . . en percent."

C. Bonner: Unintel, "appens then?"

Holt: Unintel, "ant see any," unintel, unintel.

F. Bonner: Unintel.

Holt: Unintel, "sily done," unintel, unintel, "o problem."

C. Bonner: (Loudly) "We thought those things was sideways in China. You mean to say they're straight up and down?" (Laughs)

Holt: (Laughs) Unintel, ". . . olks see us tonight why," unintel, unintel, ". . . we're in the cle . . ." unintel, "just having a helluva time, old buddies from way ba . . ."

Nidech thought it was remarkable that Holt had been able to be so optimistic during his palaver when it was obvious that things weren't going as planned. Holt beamed as though the brothers were agreeing to everything he'd said when in fact they seemed increasingly mortified. He then spoke to Pak, who was more restrained in his enthusiasm. Holt and Pak then turned to leave, trailed at some distance by the Bonners. Ella was able to hear a snatch of their conversation.

F. Bonner: ". . . pportunistic little prick."

C. Bonner: "What the fuck we do now, big brother?"

Nidech headed for the women's rest room so she could reconstruct everything while it was fresh in her mind . . .

. . . when she was confronted by the man whose hand had strayed earlier. Although no one else had apparently witnessed the incident, he had felt himself embarrassed and was infuriated, and there he was, wanting some kind of jackass satisfaction.

"You!" he said in English.

Ella Nidech smiled graciously. "Oh, how are you?" She put her hand on his shoulder in what appeared to be a friendly gesture. She dug one thumb then another into his carotid arteries and squeezed, hard.

The man was taken by surprise. Should he hit this woman here in the casino, his face asked? Before he could decide, he wilted, unconscious, and Nidech continued on to the ladies' room. She had work to do. She went down the pages of her notebook and penciled in some *F*s and *C*s to identify the two Bonners, and an *H* for Holt. She wanted as many details as possible for her report to Peter Neely.

Five hours later Sing Sing Boyd listened to Ella Nidech's recounting of her night in Macao with a shake of the head, and poured them both another cup of coffee. "Clint and Flub Bonner. What do you think of that, Ms. Lewis?"

"I think Gene Holt was offering to murder Lucien Salvant for a fee of some kind, but I can't be sure."

"And the Bonners?"

"I think the Bonners turned him down."

"I certainly hope so." Boyd started to say something else,

then stopped. Then he said, "You Americans are the most extraordinary people, do you know that, Ms. Lewis? I have arranged for your government to buy secrets directly from Chinese bureaucrats—at some risk to my people. That's why it's expensive. But your employers must surely know it's both a cheaper and more efficient way of complementing your satellite photographs than maintaining spy networks. A nation famous for taking risks, and nurturing the spirit of free enterprise." Boyd shook his head sadly. "Why do they dither so?"

Ella Nidech shrugged her shoulders.

"Where else will you find a middleman like me? Beijing secrets? Where?"

"I'm afraid I don't understand either, Mr. Boyd."

He said, "I told Frank he couldn't come, but he insisted."

Frank Quetglas's lips, still swollen, were only slightly less purple than the night before. "This is like trying to talk through fuckin' sausages, if you'll excuse my language, Mr. Boyd, Ms. Lewis. I'm gonna kick ass, man."

Ella Nidech said, "Far more efficient to stitch them with this, Frank." She retrieved a machine pistol from her handbag and popped a silencer into place.

"What a remarkable instrument. May I examine it, please?" Boyd weighed the pistol in his hand and grinned. "Wouldn't it be fun to have Pak Tze Fan in the sights of this beauty? You Americans have the best of everything, eh?"

"Just let me at the Fragrance." Quetglas made a phoenix eye fist—one knuckle stuck out to gouge eyes. He made noises with his tongue to imitate the surrendering of Kwok's eyes.

Nidech said, "You're going to have to practice your blocking, Frank; only use rolling blocks. Don't take Kwok's blows straight on or he'll snap your arm."

"I did use a roll. Otherwise I'd be dead by now." Quetglas's pathetic lips were nearly incapable of movement. He felt the ridge of his broken nose with his fingertip. "Ouch! Damn!"

Sing Sing Boyd spread a map of the British colony on the table. He indicated the island with his finger. "Fong Wai Chau is here. It is uninhabited except for a shelf of land—a swale actually—located above a cliff at the end of an inlet. The south wall of the main villa rises straight up from the face of the cliff. It wasn't built by Pak, incidentally. He recently bought it from a *taipan* who made his fortune in ready-made blouses and designer jeans."

"And the flanks?"

"The rest of the island is sheer cliff rising straight from the ocean."

Nidech said, "The first thing to do is photograph it this afternoon to see what we're up against."

"One of my sailboats, the *Lady Jane,* is berthed just three islands over from Fong Wai Chau. It's a twenty-eight-foot sloop, nicely rigged."

"Is there anyplace around there we can put in for the night?"

Boyd pointed to a tiny island opposite Pak's inlet. "On this island here—Lung Chau—is the village of Po To Kok, and the Hotel Nevil Blevins. One can almost see the lights of Pak's villa from the Nevil Blevins's dining room. The Americans must have a lot of faith in you to give you all this responsibility, Ms. Lewis. I'd have thought they would have sent you some help."

She said, "They tell me I'll be getting help."

Frank Quetglas, wincing slightly as he spoke, said, "You're talking fuck-ups sending yo-yos."

Boyd said, "Frank, Frank. I shouldn't be so harsh on my countrymen if I were you."

"But it's the truth, man," Quetglas said.

Sing Sing Boyd said, "I should think we'd need more weapons than your pistol to mount an operation of this magnitude, Ms. Lewis. Pak's guards are well armed, and they'll be on the alert."

"We'll make a list of whatever we'll need: more of these

pistols, proper knives, explosives, antitank rockets to blow holes in walls. Whatever we need, I can get, believe me.''

''I'd say all of that if possible. I'm only guessing, but I think our only chance is from the front. Someone will have to swim ashore and ambush the guards.''

''And the others bring the gear ashore in a launch.''

''Unless we can spot a break in the cliffs. We should be pushing off as soon as possible, Ms. Lewis. But where on earth can we get that kind of gear in a couple of hours?''

''I know a place.''

Boyd was pleased. ''You Americans are go-getters.''

Ella Nidech penciled in an extra set of everything for the Company's Mr. Can-Do, James Burlane. What the hell had happened to James Burlane?

39

ELLA Nidech had grown up in Rowayton, Connecticut, and had spent a lot of time sailing on the Long Island Sound. She had never seen a more impressive sailor than Sing Sing Boyd, who seemed as nimble as a man half his age. While Ella took the helm, Boyd barked orders at Frank Quetglas, who pushed his bruised and aching body at a punishing pace, yelling "Aye, aye" through lips still swollen from the beating he had taken from Kwok Lai Kwon.

Quetglas labored under the handicap of having eight broken ribs trying to heal and of being seasick at the same time. He winced each time the boat plunged into a swell, cursing only when the combination of nausea and pain was too much. The Cuban felt more like an awkward shotput at large on the deck, at the mercy of the *Lady Jane*'s pitching and swaying.

"*Dios mio! Dios mio!*" he cried, his eyes turning. He was in torment. He crossed himself fervently, mumbling the names of Catholic saints: "*San Lazaro, Santa Barbara! Ayudame!*"

"Coming about!" Boyd yelled.

Quetglas, flinching, ducked to make way for the boom.

When the *Lady Jane* was away on the new tack, Sing Sing Boyd, followed by the tortured Quetglas, slipped in out of the wind.

"A little to port, please, Ms. Lewis! Keep plenty of wind in the sails. We've got a bit of a run here without having to come about," Boyd said. "I wanted us to have a nice long tack here while we talk it over. You see it there, Ms. Lewis? Dead ahead."

Ella Nidech couldn't see the island at first. Then she thought she saw it as a ghost, a suggestion that resolved itself into a pale blue profile of a steep-sided, apparently uninhabited island. A far smaller island sat, moonlike, just off a promontory that was the port side of the profile. Whereas Fong Wai Chau looked like a barren pinnacle jutting straight from the water, the smaller one had a narrow shoreline. As the *Lady Jane* drew closer to the larger island, Ella saw that it was devoid of trees, but green, covered with low brush.

Boyd said, "The larger island is Fong Wai Chau. The smaller island is Lung Chau. How are your ribs, Frank?"

Frank's swollen lips started to move, then stopped in a terrible moment his companions recognized as a wave of nausea; they stepped back, quickly but courteously. Frank held it down, a moment of triumph. He grinned weakly. His eyes watered.

"Stout lad, Frank! Steady as she goes, Ms. Lewis."

Quetglas gagged and scrambled up top, holding his mouth with his hand.

Boyd continued as though nothing had happened. "The truth is, the island's a fortress more than anything else, Ms. Lewis. As you'll see, Pak's compound sits atop a cliff at the base of a small bay. The villa sits atop a cliff about a hundred and thirty meters high. The only real soil on the island is on the five-acre shelf and the two flanks of the bay, which is about three hundred meters from its mouth to the base of the cliff."

"And the rest of the island?"

"The rest of Fong Wai Chau is rock that rises straight out of the water. The smaller island, Lung Chau, has a good natural harbor on its lee side and Po To Kok, a little fishing village; that's where we'll be staying and that's where we'll pick up our powerboat."

"And the hotel is there."

"Right. The Hotel Nevil Blevins is very popular with local sailors enjoying the good wind in the area. Most of the villages in these islands are very Chinese, but the Nevil Blevins is resolutely British colonial; Chinese yachtsmen love it. They can have exotic ale and pasties if they want, or pork pies."

"So there are other sailboats on the water. How close can we get to Pak's enclave?"

"Pak's chaps have strung a series of lighted buoys about a kilometer out from the mouth of his private bay. Inside those buoys thou shalt not sail."

Frank Quetglas returned from up top, wiping his mouth with the sleeve of his jacket. He looked ghastly, and his jaw trembled slightly.

Boyd said, "I say, do you think you ought to lie down, Frank?"

Quetglas shook his head. "You're looking at a Cuban, man."

"The afternoon light is fine," Nidech said. "I say we pass by and take the best shots we can. Will the wind stay pretty much the same?"

"I think we can count on it. There are enough boats on the water for us to blend in."

"Then I think we should circle the smaller island, and take it on a broad reach from the southwest. We want things as calm as we can."

The camera and the 1800-millimeter lens had been developed for the Company by a German camera firm. Ordinarily the photographer would have required a tripod and solid base for a shot from that distance, but the Germans—knowing the camera would be used in unusual circumstances—had risen, Japanese-like, to meet the challenge. They had come up with a beaut.

Because of the difficulty in focusing the lens on details needed to plan a raid on the compound, Ella Nidech knew she had to remain as steady as she could. The camera came equipped with a clamp in case there wasn't room for a tripod, but that was impossible in this case.

Nidech decided to take advantage of the best light and begin with Pak's personal residence at the top of the cliff. Those were the most important details. Then she would back off, beginning with the jetty, bay, and boathouse, then photograph the trail, and finally the steep slopes on either side of the inlet, and the stairs that zigzagged up from the boathouse.

With her eye at the camera, her right arm straining under the weight of the enormous lens, her legs wide, braced, rump stuck out, knees bending to the roll of the deck, her left arm, brandishing the shutter cable that she operated with her thumb, was extended in the manner of Karl Wallenda. She knew it was going to be a long, long day.

Nidech began to photograph the enclave, frame by carefully selected frame. She reloaded from a container that snapped in place rather like an ammunition clip. When one roll was empty, Nidech hit a button that ejected the exposed film and a new roll automatically popped into place.

It was Quetglas's job to catch the ejected film in a small bag.

When they had finished the first run, Nidech began feeling the strain on the arm that held the camera.

At the end of the second run, Nidech's arm was trembling, and she could feel her thighs working overtime.

Her blouse was wet with sweat at the end of the third run. Sweat slid into her eyes and burned as she concentrated on the details of her shots. This would have been Burlane's turn if he'd shown up.

Nidech shot the fourth run on reserves she hadn't known existed.

She was inert from fatigue as Sing Sing Boyd headed the *Lady Jane* toward Po To Kok. She considered the relationship of Lung Chau to Fong Wai Chau and got up from the bunk, taking a deep breath. "I think we should take a close pass around this island. There's still enough light."

Boyd looked shocked. "Are you sure you're up to it?"

Nidech popped more film into place. She said, "I don't think it takes Admiral Nelson to see how close Lung Chau is to Pak's inlet."

The last pass of the *Lady Jane,* the trip around Lung Chau, was the longest run of all. *Click-clack. Click-clack. Click-clack.* Ella Nidech, numb with exhaustion, shot the shoreline of Lung Chau, which had an inhabitable shoreline.

When it was over, Nidech sank back on a berth in the boat's small cabin and closed her eyes. In the cabin and out of the wind, she was hot. She felt a trickle of sweat slide from her underarm. Her blouse stuck to her ribs. She said, "I take it they have hot water at the Hotel Nevil Blevins or whatever it's called," she said. "God!" Where the hell was James Burlane?

"Plenty of hot water," Boyd said. "We'll get you a good bottle of gin."

Frank Quetglas moaned his sympathy through his split, pathetic lips.

Pak Tze Fan took a swipe at the bugs that had collected around him. He leaned over the rock wall to enjoy the wind that kept the insects off him.

The cameraman to Pak's left worked steady, *clack-clack, clack-clack.* The camera was mounted on a neat aluminum tripod. The telescope was on an aluminum tripod also. Aside from the bugs, Pak Tze Fan was in good humor, grinning as he watched the distant sailboat. Pak held on to his yachtman's cap with his left hand.

Gene Holt needed no hat. The wind wasn't going to do much to his hair. He laughed in staccato outbursts at the pending adventure of squeezing Sing Sing Boyd's lychees. He looked like a tight-muscled, merry bulldog.

The third man, Kwok Lai Kwon, had his hair cut so short the wind didn't bother him either. He stood to the rear, which was his place as Pak's bodyguard.

"It's him, all right," Pak said, following the sailboat carefully with the telescope. "Sing Sing Boyd himself. He's not half as good a sailor as everybody thinks he is. Never was. Would you like to see, Mr. Holt? Sing Sing Boyd's the tall fellow there in the white trousers."

Holt took a turn at the telescope, adjusting the focus.

Pak took another turn. He looked at Kwok. "Boyd's Bullet, Mr. Kwok."

Kwok blinked in disbelief. "How could that be? I caved his face in."

"I don't know the woman. But that's Frank Quetglas, all right. Would you care for a turn?"

Kwok Lai Kwon looked through the telescope. "Quetglas! All I did was knock him out. How in the . . ."

Gene Holt said, "Then it's working as you said. Boyd has to try to get them back himself."

"All we have to do is be patient. Reward comes to those who wait. Mr. Kwok here will get his chance." Pak batted at a bug that hovered above his head. "Dreadful bugs."

Holt swatted at one also.

"I'll have to have them sprayed again. One disadvantage of living on a private island is you can't contract for regular spraying. Would you like Mr. Kwok to give us a little demonstration of kung fu?"

"Sure!" Holt said. He tried to spear a bug with his right hand.

The three men left the photographer to continue tracking the boat while they went around to the swimming pool and landscaped terraces behind the villa perched on the cliff.

Pak's layout was every bit as splendid as Sing Sing Boyd's estate on Lantau Island.

There was no wind away from the face of the cliff, and the heat settled in. Pak and Holt sat at a table under the shade of a locust tree. The air was humid and insects went *zit-zit! zit-zit! zzzz! zzzz! zit-zit!*

"I think the sprayers did a better job over here. The bugs aren't so bad," Pak said. "You'll hear Mr. Kwok before you see him. He goes through a routine before combat, a series of quick, deep inhalations followed by intimidating cries. Kwok always gets his man. Always."

"Except for What's-his-name Quetglas, Boyd's Bullet."

Pak smiled. "Frank Quetglas was lucky."

They soon heard Kwok inhaling viciously through his sinuses, followed by his cry. *"Sssnnhhhttt! Hai! Sssnnhhhttt! Hai! Sssnnnhhhttt! Hai!"*

"Quite lucky, Mr. Holt, and quite embarrassing to Kwok. One can hear his anger."

The Fragrance of the Red Lotus, the memory of Frank Quetglas fresh in his mind, began his demonstration by ripping an incredible tear in a heavy canvas sparring bag held by four men. This blow, with Kwok's right foot, was so vicious that even his assistants were shocked.

Holt was stunned. "Jesus H. Christ!" he said.

"As I say, he was embarrassed," Pak said. He grinned as the Fragrance of the Red Lotus turned to smashing huge bricks and prime four-by-fours.

40

ELLA Nidech took a long hot bath; she wallowed, luxuriating in the soothing hot water, pulling on the handle with the red *H* when the temperature cooled. The *H* control was on the right rather than on the left and opened clockwise and closed counterclockwise. The result was that Nidech took a blast of scalding water on her foot; she hoped this was not an omen of disaster.

As part of her determination always to be physically ready for the demands of her job—and to fight the good fight against developing a fat butt—Nidech ordinarily swam thirty laps a day in a swimming pool that by the end loomed as large as Lake Michigan. She spent another hour struggling with terrible machines endorsed by Arnold Schwarzenegger. While her delts and pecs didn't bulge, they were trim. The woman at the gym, who had developed an incipient Sylvester Stallone neck, said Nidech had a body like Jane Fonda's.

But Nidech's Jane Fonda torso had been ravaged by the contortions required to keep that insane camera steady through four awful runs past Pak's snug harbor. That goddamned

Burlane had, for some unimaginable reason, left her in the lurch at crunch time. Although she couldn't imagine there would be a masseuse available on Long Chau—even in the Nevil Blevins—she called the desk to make sure.

The man at the desk said, "Our masseur is said to be the best in Po To Kok, madame. I'm sure you'll be pleased."

Ten minutes later Nidech opened her door to allow a young Chinese man to roll in a folding table.

He said, "I am Mr. Chen, madame."

"I'm exhausted, Mr. Chen. I would like a thorough massage. I need the knots worked out." She turned onto her stomach on the table.

Mr. Chen blinked twice—he'd never seen a finer *gweilo* figure than this woman—such a handsome rear end—and set to work. He had strong hands and knew how to knead a muscle.

"That's it. Go for it." Nidech thought Mr. Chen must surely be the best masseur in the South China Sea.

After a roast beef dinner in the Nevil Blevins's Victorian dining room, Nidech set up the Company's portable darkhouse in her bathroom. All things considered, she thought the photographs had turned out well. She had the inlet and its docking facilities covered from several angles as well as the board sidewalk leading to the top and close-ups of all the windows in Pak's villa that faced the inlet. There were three soldiers assigned guard duty in the small dockhouse.

Pak surely must be expecting trouble, she thought. Why only three guards?

Then she turned her attention to the photographs she had taken of the windows that faced the sea. Her efforts were rewarded:

Lucien Salvant and Susan Wu were being held captive in one of the rooms. But they weren't just sitting around waiting for the end to come. They were involved in some kind of activity that required a lot of bending and staring at the floor. What were they doing?

Then she shot close-ups of the rest of the dock area, the board stairs, and the edge of the low stone wall at the top of the cliff on both sides of the villa. One of these brought forth a soft "shit!" She saw, clearly, Pak Tze Fan and Blowfish, and next to them a photographer with a telephoto lens.

She went on to the photographs of the remainder of the Fong Wai Chau shoreline and the shoreline of Lung Chau. These told her nothing interesting until she got to a shot of the back side of Lung Chau. Behind a small, thin grove of trees, she saw what appeared to be the profiles of helicopters. Could that be? She searched through the negatives until she found the right frame, which she blew up. The results were washed out and grainy, but she was able to trace outlines of one, two, three, four, then five helicopters.

There was no agriculture on Lung Chau, certainly not enough to warrant helicopters for spraying. Also, there was plenty of open space around Po To Kok. Why hadn't the pilots set down there?

Nidech made prints of the critical photographs and hung them up to dry. Then she got out her tiny Masuno, a combination cassette player, radio, and alarm clock. This was a wonderful package for a traveler, light and built to take knocks, good work for a firm that did not exist. The Masuno contained a transmitter in its innards that allowed Ella Nidech to transmit a coded message to the U.S. embassy in Hong Kong, which would be reencoded and sent to Peter Neely:

Parson: Blowfish dancing with the Bandit on Fong Wai Chau. Photo evidence. Situation Randolph. Five unknown hornets on Lung Chau. The Bandit's, I think. Suspect trap for the Chief Thief. Mud begins at 0100 with me as Steve McQueen in flippers. I've left charts for Morrison in care of Bee-Vee associates who remain on duty. Very deep mud. Randolph remains. Need Morrison now. Repeat: Need him now. Immediate response, please. Lewis.

When she had finished, Nidech was mad enough to spit. Dammit, she needed some help. She had a right to complain. She imagined Neely and Schott reading that message and shaking their heads—the China buy was on the line, and who did they have in the field? A hysterical woman. Nidech retrieved a flask from her valise and poured herself a hard shot of bourbon. Now she was going to be a frogperson. Jesus! It was reading *Ms.* magazine that had gotten her into this fix, she knew. She vowed that if she survived the Big Muddy she'd write Gloria Steinem telling her what she could do with her goddamned magazine.

The message came back fifteen minutes later:

Lewis: Unfortunately, Marion Morrison was held up. He has been informed of your situation. He is on his way. Should be arriving in Hong Kong later tonight, your time. He will stop by your local office for provisions and your instructions. Proceed with your plans. You remain in command. Hastings and I have utmost confidence. Our fingers are crossed. Aristotle has been appraised, says that's the spirit, just get wood on the ball. Parson.

This was truly unreal. Hastings was Ara Schott. Aristotle was the President, who apparently regarded himself as a third-base coach. Nidech slipped the crucial photographs into an envelope and went down the hall to see Sing Sing Boyd. Frank Quetglas, on Boyd's orders, had gone to bed.

Boyd spread the photographs out on a coffee table.

"The other man is Gene Holt," Nidech said.

"Gene Holt? Really?" Boyd put the magnifying glass over the shot with Holt in it. "He looks simian."

Nidech took a look. "He is simian."

"What do you make of the helicopters? Five of them."

Boyd said, "A regular convoy. There's no reason for them to be there that I can see."

"No, there isn't."

"Do we proceed, then, Ms. Lewis?"

Nidech said, "I'm under orders to go ahead."

"Are they sending you help?"

"There's someone on the way." She gestured with her left hand, indicating the gods in general and James Burlane in particular.

"They told you that yesterday."

"They sure did."

"They must have extraordinary confidence in your abilities."

"Maybe they think I'm hysterical."

"If this man of theirs is wonderful, why hasn't he gotten here to give you some help?" Boyd scowled and returned to the photographs. "They've got wires running up to the main compound; there's electricity and telephone at the boathouse." Boyd traced the walkway up the slope with his finger. "No problem with using the walkway that I can see."

"There has to be an electrical generator somewhere; in the building on the right, do you think? And the best for the last." She spread some more photos on the table.

"Salvant and Susan. Well done!"

"They're doing something, aren't they?"

"They appear to be," Boyd said. "They're working with something spread out on the floor. You must be exhausted, Ms. Lewis. Maybe we should get a few hours' sleep."

"I don't feel too bad. I had a hot bath and a nice massage from Mr. Chen. I thought he was very good."

"Mr. Chen? I had a young lady."

"Was she good?"

Boyd said, "I thought she was quite talented. She gave me a good massage, too."

Before she went to bed, Nidech sent another message to Bee-Vee for Burlane on his arrival:

Marion Morrison: I am at the Hotel Nevil Blevins in Po To Kok on Lung Chau opposite the Bandit's estate on Fong Wai

Chau. My associates have the proper charts but no need to know what they're for. I am accompanied by the Chief Thief and a damaged Raul. Deadline for imprisoned subjects remains noon, Wednesday. Possible trap for the Chief Thief, aka the Farmer. Have confirmed subjects' location in villa. Underwater advance my responsibility. Will depart two miles offshore at 0100 hours Wednesday, Hong Kong time. Face three guards at a dockhouse, and steep wooden stairs on the eastern flank of the inlet. Force above is unknown, but have located five, I say again five, hornets on the back side of Lung Chau. No reason for their being there. The Bandit charming the Blowfish, repeat: Blowfish on Fong Wai Chau. Can you fly a helicopter? My associates will get you whatever you need. Very, very big mud here, Morrison. Can you do anything right? Please move your butt, man. Lewis.

Nidech slipped into bed, glad that she'd included the last two sentences. Burlane deserved it. She hoped she survived the mud if for no other reason than to tell the son of a bitch what she thought of him. Never before had she wanted to literally take a man by the throat and shake him around a bit. And all of Neely's bullshit about her being in command. What good was being in command going to do her when she was dead? She had a chance for a few hours' sleep and she needed every minute of it. She couldn't afford to lie there pissed off at Burlane. Although Norman Mailer had not begun *The Naked and the Dead* with the frogmen who had no doubt preceded the marines, she remembered the opening line. It was the night before the island landing:

"Nobody could sleep."

Those were the bad old days. Times had changed. Ella Nidech set the alarm on her Masumo and punched the button that started the cassette.

A Company hypnotist, a man with a calm, reassuring

voice—the stuff of fathers and gentle lovers—said: "Hello, little girl. Are you all kicked back and relaxed? That's good. I want you to feel calm and comfortable. Feel your muscles relax. Doesn't that feel wonderful? . . ."

41

THE seaward windows were open to catch the cooling ocean breeze; Lucien Salvant and Susan Wu could hear laughter and the murmur of voices at the party above them. The only voice they could hear clearly was Pak's loud American guest. Once, above the giggling and squealing of women, he shouted, "You're goddamned right!" Another time he yelled, "Tootie to toot!" And then later, " 'Balls!' cried the queen!"

"If I had two I'd be King," Salvant said quickly.

"If I had two I'd be King!" the guest shouted to more laughing and squealing.

Susan said, "He's very clever."

Pak had assembled a band for his guest's pleasure, and a jazz singer with a voice like Karen Carpenter's held forth, accompanied by a pianist, bassist, and drummer. Salvant nudged his neatly folded para-sail with his foot. "The parachutes look splendid at least. Do you suppose Yi Lin felt like this?"

"Yi Lin knew what he was doing. Lucien, remember

when you discovered the Yi Lin article? I told you all about
fung shui, and geomancers, and people who can see spirits
and talk to them. *Sam kus.* Remember that?''

"I like it better than predestination."

Susan Wu told Lucien Salvant about the curse that had
been relayed from her sister through the old woman in Kowloon. "Lucien, that's why I agreed to go to Sing Sing's
dinner. Ordinarily I avoid those kinds of things. I was after
you to marry my sister. You can laugh if you want to, but I
believe. I can't help it."

"I'm not laughing and I'm not your brother-in-law yet, am
I?"

"No, not yet."

"Well, then, I feel a little chilly. How about you?" Salvant
didn't wait for the obvious answer. The heir and the star of
Chan Rides Low wrapped themselves into a comforting ball
on the rattan couch.

Flub and Clint Bonner pitied the pathetic men who were
forced to trail their wives through the mind-numbing shops in
Kowloon. And they pitied the businessmen who had to ask
the hotel help to please send up a call girl. Being a billionaire
was like being smeared with Spanish fly from head to foot.
When word got out that Clint and Flub were in a hotel
showing off their cowboy boots and boorish manners, beautiful, intelligent women—apologizing for also being nympho-
maniacs—began offering themselves up for whatever services the Texans demanded.

Since their reputation preceded them in magazines edited
for women who dreamed of wealthy and powerful men, their
fortune was no less an aphrodisiac in Hong Kong than
in other cities they had visited. In keeping with their
long-standing practice of encouraging cultural, economic,
and other forms of intercourse, Clint and Flub had taken
on two Chinese models for the night. The sexual poke was

called the low, which the Bonners bestowed upon the models in that sweetest and most desirable of nature's many orifices.

Incredibly, each model confided to her Bonner for the night that she had always wanted to go to America. Each model said she just loved Americans, they were so open and enthusiastic. The British were tight-lipped prigs (the same models told wealthy Brits that Americans were obnoxious loudmouths). And each young woman threw herself into the low poke with enthusiasm, shuddering with pretend orgasms that suggested she was being impaled by an electric cattle prod. This celebration of the hornier gods was a repeat of a performance given on Friday night by Australian airline attendants and on Saturday by stunning Filipina entertainers.

Suddenly the doorbell of the Bonners' Hong Kong penthouse began ringing. This was impossible unless the management had somehow gone mad, or someone had overcome the guards at the doors and at the elevator.

"What the fuck is this?" Flub Bonner sat up in his bed. He got out of bed and grabbed a silk bathrobe.

Clint arrived in the living room seconds after Flub. "Christ, Flub, it's two o'clock in the fucking morning."

"Uncle Sam calling," said a voice behind them.

They turned, startled. There on the couch sat a tall disheveled blond man who looked as if he'd slept in his clothes for a week. He had a long nose that was turned slightly to one side. He was casual. He held a lethal-looking machine pistol in his hand. He used the pistol to wave the models back to their respective bedrooms.

"Could you ladies please stay away until we're finished or you're called upon to do something? On second thought"—he got up and strolled over to the paralyzed women—"do you like massages?" He massaged one on her shoulder and her knees buckled. Then he did the second. The two young women lay sprawled like nightied China dolls. Burlane said,

"They'll wake up in a few minutes. You two guys've been having some fun, eh? Sit, please."

The Bonners sat.

"I assure you that you're perfectly safe. I'm not here to hurt you, although I can if I want." With that he held up his pistol. It made a fluttering sound as he traced a design in the air. A neat MM appeared on the opposite wall in a beautifully formed cursive. "My name is Marion Morrison," he said.

Flub Bonner was wide-eyed.

The pistol fluttered and the wood splintered in a neat loop around Flub's toes.

"Whoa!" Flub yanked his foot back. "Mr. Morrison," he added quickly.

Burlane popped another curved clip into the side of his exotic-looking machine pistol. "We're isolated up here, remember? Banging on walls or shouting won't help. And your phone won't work." Burlane looked at his wristwatch. "I recently read a file on you two that is maintained by historians in the company I work for. If you or your lawyers should ever ask for it, you'll be told it doesn't exist. The file says you both know how to fly a helicopter. Is that true?"

"We've got a couple of Spoelberchs at our Houston place," Flub said. He looked at his brother. "What the hell is this all about?"

"Are you any good?" Burlane asked.

"We can make the girls squeal," Clint said.

"You know how to fly a Doherty?"

"One of those ugly Irish jobs?"

Burlane glared at him. "Good looks don't count for warm poop in my business, Tex. You've gotta be faster than fan blades if you want to make sunrise."

"Yes, sir, Dohertys are quick. I can fly one. No sweat."

Burlane gestured with his pistol. "Mr. Morrison."

"Mr. Morrison, sir."

Burlane said, "I'm in something of a hurry here, so I'll try to get straight to business. If you don't listen very carefully to what I have to say, it could cost you your Sunyang oil contract. From what I read, that's a lot of money."

Flub Bonner said, "Come on, now, Mr. Morrison."

"Hey! Listen! Last night you talked to Gene Holt in a Macao casino. I just bet that stumpy little fucker offered to get rid of Lucien Salvant for a small fee, didn't he? If Salvant were croaked, he said, you'd get your half-billion bucks back. You look shocked. You wonder how I know? Holt says he'll do the evil deed when you're back in the United States; that way, you're in the clear. One fee if you get your money back, a smaller one if you don't—was that the pitch? Did I miss anything there? Yes, I did: Gene Holt doesn't know Lucien Salvant's inheritance was a bribe for the Sunyang oil contract."

"The little prick!" Clint said.

"In a few hours Gene Holt's gonna cut your schlong off. Did he tell you that he and Pak Tze Fan kidnapped Lucien Salvant and one of Sing Sing Boyd's actresses on Saturday night? No? He didn't tell you?"

Clint looked incensed. "He had Salvant all along? The high pokin' little bastard! Telling us how much planning and cost it would take to make Salvant's death look accidental."

"The son of a bitch," Flub said.

Burlane leaned forward, looking at the Bonners with a determined face. "Holt and Pak and a whole bunch of armed Chinese triads are out there on an island right now waiting for Sing Sing Boyd to play commando, which he is about to do in a few minutes in an effort to retrieve his actress."

Flub Bonner flushed. "Why, that little bastard!"

"If anything happens to Boyd, you lose Sunyang, guaranteed. I don't have time for the details, but boiled down, it's that simple.'' The delicate man glanced at his wristwatch and grinned sardonically. ''In a few minutes I have to hustle on out to a warehouse of a toy company so we can pick up a few things. I'll get quickly to the point: gentlemen, I come to you bearing greetings . . .''

42

LISTENING to the slapping of waves on the hull of
the powerboat, Ella Nidech poured herself a cup of coffee
out of Sing Sing Boyd's thermos. She took a sip and began
stripping off her clothes. Then she sat, bare as Gypsy Rose
Lee, contemplative, and finished the coffee before she began
the struggle of putting on the wet suit. She could hardly
believe she'd been called upon to do all this by herself while
those monumental assholes back in Virginia cracked their
knuckles at the suspense.

And the President! Telling her he was going to be cheering
her on, for God's sake! Is that what President Carter had
done when those poor bastards put down in the Iranian desert
pretending they were as good as Israeli soldiers?

What would anybody be doing with five helicopters on
Lung Chau?

Nidech put on a one-piece wet suit and strapped a diver's
knife onto her ankle and an underwater watch to her wrist.
She tightened the regulator connection to her aluminum eighty.
She checked the vestlike buoyancy compensator she would

275

wear around her torso, making sure the power-inflating button was where she could get at it if she wanted. A console snapped to the BC's backpack contained a depth gauge, bottom timer, pressure gauge, temperature needle, and compass. Her underwater boots doubled as running shoes. She made sure her feet were comfortable in the graphite fins.

Then she went through her checklist of those items she would take with her in the plastic mesh underwater bag.

A French FR F1 sniper's rifle with an infrared scope, and an Israeli Mini-Uzi, both in waterproof containers. Ammunition in waterproof containers. A combination dive light/flashlight. Six hand grenades in a waterproof pouch that Nidech could strap over her shoulder.

She glanced at her wristwatch: 0040. She gathered up the heavy bag and headed for the rear of the boat where Boyd and Frank Quetglas waited by the apparatus they had used to lower the resin-bodied diving vehicle into the water. The Noble, twenty inches long, looked rather like a bomb that was both rounded and rectangular. There was a light in front and a prop and fins on the back. The fins were connected at the tips by a large circle with handgrips and controls on either side.

This bomb-shaped tractor would tow Nidech and her heavy load two miles to the inlet in Fong Wai Chau and the territory of the Society of the Red Lotus. If the Noble wasn't the best underwater vehicle on the market, it was certainly the most expensive. It had a *ker-chunk*-Mercedes-door-slamming look about it: high-tech dependable.

The Noble, hanging from the cable, waited in the water.

"Steve McQueen time," she said to Boyd.

"Erroll Flynn time, Ms. Lewis. Much more stylish, pink tights and all that." Boyd gave Nidech a hug.

Quetglas said, "No! No! Zorro! Zorro!" Quetglas unsheathed an imaginary sword and slashed a big *F* in the air—big swish, little swish, little swish. "She makes the sign of the *F!*'' He hugged her as tightly as he could without his knees buckling from the pain of his broken ribs.

Saying no more, Nidech slipped on her flippers and went over the side, swimming around to the Noble's control handles. She received the bag of weapons and snapped it into place on her console. "I won't get full speed with all this stuff," she said, and started up the Noble. She reached up and unsnapped the diving vehicle from the cable.

"Good luck, Ms. Lewis," Boyd said.

"You're one hell of a lady," Quetglas said.

Nidech checked her watch: 0100. Then the depth gauge. "One twenty-one feet," she said. She checked her bearings with the compass. She turned on her air. She waved at Boyd and Quetglas, then put both hands on the controls. She twisted one wrist slightly, and was off—at just shy of three miles an hour—through the black void that was the South China Sea at night.

The powerboat well behind her, Nidech felt as alone as she had ever been. She was possibly about to die; it was the details of the moment—the wet suit, the prop wash under her stomach—that made her think of the existentialists she had studied in college. Images and memories tumbled one after another in an evocative mélange that made no sense and yet was everything.

For example, although she had no children and would be having none, Nidech thought of pregnancy.

Pregnancy was one experience that was female—never fully appreciated by men. Childbirth was woman territory and Nidech had never been a member of the sorority.

She checked her watch: 0120. Standing at ninety feet.

Nidech thought of a young mother she had seen in the States at a grocery store checkout counter. Nidech had caught her admiring her son and daughter. The mother, who was unaware she was being watched, smiled to herself, pleased. Ella Nidech, Ph.D., on her way to kill people on a cold war beach, had been envious, even when the mother produced food stamps to pay for her bill.

Men had war. Those who had known war—real war, shooting at people and being shot at—were a special fraternity.

Nidech thought the prop wash running over her breasts and down her stomach was in its way caressing. Sensual even. Her last lover. She grinned around her mouthpiece, feeling the pressure of the moving water against her face.

She remembered being six years old and playing a game called, simply, house. In this game, a house was made of pretend walls that were in fact stones lined up neatly and resembling an architect's floor plan. Players assumed roles of mother, father, and other adults. The players held pretend conversations of adults discussing Sears Roebuck, deciding whether or not to put 10-40 or 30-weight in the car, or how they could both do without a snotty aunt. It had taken several years before little Ella learned that 10-40 was motor oil.

At 0140, Nidech was running at fifty-eight feet.

In her mind's eye, she could see the pretend houses of her childhood, the bathrooms, the hallways, bedrooms, living rooms, and kitchens, where agates lined up neatly against the rock wall were pretend pots and pans. She remembered how she had swept the pretend rooms clean with pretend brooms and how furious she got when some callous boy walked through the walls as if they weren't even there.

The Company hot dog, James Burlane, Mr. Can-Do, had fucked up. If she had previously waffled about the wisdom of writing the letter of complaint to Rollo Hinkley, Nidech was now certain she was correct—if, perhaps, for the wrong reason. The Mighty Burlane had struck out in the clutch.

She reminded herself that she was in a man's game and had to think like a man. Burlane had screwed up, but that didn't make any difference now. She had to do her best. She had a job to do.

She checked her compass and brought the Noble slightly to

port. At 0200, she was ten feet deep with twenty-one feet to spare.

She remembered her first serious boyfriend, Billy Geneen, and the night he had finally, at last, worked up the nerve to slide his hand onto her breast. They were parked in the woods on a warm summer night in Billy's Volkswagen bug. They wrapped their arms and legs around one another, like squid in a cigar box, and Billy, foreshadowing his moves by quickened breathing, set about to experience raw breast for the first time.

Billy Geneen had lingered hesitantly on the borders, playing with the buttons of her blouse, running his fingers along the collar, "accidentally" brushing the forbidden territory. She had wanted his hand on her tit, dammit, and he obviously wanted it there as well, but Geneen, however eager for the wonderful initiation, seemed uncertain as to what to do next.

She had thought, Do something, asshole. You're male, aren't you? Use your imagination. Yes, there. No, no, you damned fool. In the end, she'd almost stuck it in his mouth. Then the idiot had suddenly grabbed it and began kneading it with a frenzy. Ouch!

Was that what was wrong with Burlane? Was he another Billy Geneen, an eagle scout type, always prepared, making sure everything was correct before venturing ahead? Had he survived by being extra careful? Would he arrive with Swiss Army knife, shaving kit, balled socks, and galoshes clipped to his belt like flea-market baubles?

The water turned shallow, only eighteen feet, and Nidech brought the Noble to the surface to have a look around. She should have surfaced sooner. She was maybe a hundred feet from the huge boulders at the edge of the island and already could feel the push of the surf behind her. The boulders ahead were jagged, flat-sided things that rose straight out of the water. She didn't want to enter the inlet for fear that Pak had the entrance covered with a warning device of some kind. Better to spot some simpatico-looking boulders and do her best. The monsters ahead were anything but simpatico.

The jetty protecting the moorage had been dredged from the inlet. While it was made of the same jagged rock as the boulders, it was of manageable size. Far less formidable than nature's own.

Nidech banked the Noble to the left to parallel the shore-line. The machine responded nicely, then conked out and started sinking. She thumbed the starting button and glanced at her depth gauge.

It was suddenly sixty feet deep!

She held on to the vehicle as it sank deeper, thumbing the stupid starting button, not knowing what else to do. It wasn't as if she could lift the hood or kick the tires. All she could do was thumb a button, thinking, Damn you, you brand-name son of a bitch! Start!

At last the Noble kicked on. Nidech was joyful. That gleaming red high-tech gadget was going to do the job after all—as advertised. Nippon's submarine. Yes! You do in fact get what you pay for, she thought.

She glanced at the depth gauge. Eighty feet. What?

She broke the surface at the base of a jagged outcropping of rock.

She was caught in the tide. She aimed seaward and turned the accelerator full-speed with her wrist. The machine didn't respond. Exactly how this had happened to her, she wasn't sure. All she knew was that her stomach rolled with the surf and the Noble wasn't making any progress.

In fact it might be just the deal if she were diving for grouper or conch.

Nidech felt herself being swept backward. Was this the way this whole thing was to end, at the mercy of a machine that had looked so damned efficient? She twisted the acceler-ator as hard as she could, as though forcing it would some-how make the Noble perform beyond its capabilities. Then the machine stopped, strangely becalmed at the base of the rock wall. She was in a trough. A big one was on its way.

She started unsnapping her gear from the Noble.

Aw, shit!

The Noble crashed sideways into an outcropping with a jar that shuddered the control handles.

She abandoned the vehicle and headed seaward, dragging the webbed bag of weapons and ammunition behind her. She drove her thighs, pushed hard, pushed them until they were callous to pain. Everything depended on her kick, and Ella Nidech kicked as if she were driving for the gold in the Olympic games, pushed her Jane Fonda body as hard as it would go.

She felt like a silk slip inadvertently thrown in with greasy coveralls, ripped this way and that by the hard cycle, suffering bleach, hot water, and the teeth of open zippers.

Is this it, then? she wondered. Was this to be the end of the woman who would be a spy? She remembered a book from her childhood, *The Little Engine that Could*. The lines from that book now tumbled through her mind, and became a rhythmic chant to the driving of her thighs:

I think I can.

I think I can.

I think I can.

She bashed against the cliff, her head slamming hard against the rock. She momentarily lost the grip on her mouthpiece and swallowed a hard shot of saltwater but held on to her gear. Trying not to vomit, Ella Nidech kicked even harder if that was humanly possible, aiming for the bottom, hoping the water was more tranquil there.

43

BURLANE sent his sleek black McDougal up at a forty-five-degree angle, followed on each flank by the Bonners in their larger Dohertys. "Up ahead is what my firm now calls the Big Muddy. When I began, it was called vits, for V.T.S., very tough shit. If we live, we'll all want hot showers afterward, and later on, when you're flaccid old men, you'll remember the mud in amazing detail." Burlane checked his instruments.

"We'll ambush them from high above—that is, I'll jump them, coming straight down. They're expecting a pigeon shoot with Lewis and Boyd; their eyes'll be on the ground. When they attack, you retreat and stay just out of range. They won't want to go too far away from the island." He rested a hand on the butt of the American 7.62mm M60D machine gun mounted in the left door. A matching M60D was mounted in the right door.

"Spread 'em out," Flub said.

"That's precisely right. I'll burn them for whatever I can get on the ambush, then retreat to attack the one you have

282

isolated, Flub. You go a mile west and hang loose. Clint, you do the opposite; you go east. That way I'll know where to run you down. Zoom and swoosh. Keep 'em busy. You'll be surprised how quick those Dohertys are. Take advantage of your speed. If you see me coming, try to take him low so I can come down on him. I know you're itching to try out your machine guns, but this is the way it's going to be. Got that, Flub?''

"Yes, sir, Mr. Morrison."

"I'll run them down one at a time. Which one of you is the better pilot?"

There was a silence. Then Flub Bonner said, "I believe Clint is a little more nuts than I am."

"Then I'll try for yours first," Burlane said. "Speed and coordination are everything. We have to keep them spread so I can make my kills without people on my back. We remain calm and patient. We'll get them because we're faster than they are and they're not expecting us. I might even get a deuce on the bushwack. Once we control the air, we can go on downstairs and help Flora Lewis and Sing Sing Boyd."

Flub said, "Then it's time for the Texas high poke."

"Ain't no son of a bitch who's better at the poke than my brother Flub and me," Clint said.

"Goddammit, isn't this wonderful! Adventure! Malcolm Forbes is a pussy compared to us, Clint. A pussy."

James Burlane looked out through the open door of his McDougal. "Okay, gentlemen, let's go through it now. Basic training. Communication is everything."

"On the job training," Flub said.

"When we join battle, you will speak only when spoken to or when you have something to report. Is that understood, Flub?"

Flub Bonner had been scolded. He was the humble schoolboy. He said, "Yes, sir, Mr. Morrison."

"Clint?"

"Yes, sir, Mr. Morrison."

"Our lives depend on us working as a unit. Now, when I jump them, I want you both hovering high and acting as my spotter. If one of them tries to get behind or above me, I want to know about it. If one of them goes for you before I'm finished, protect yourself. Take it up to nosebleeds if you have to. After the jump, I'll holler go! And you see if you can draw one to you. Is that understood, Flub?"

"Yes, sir."

"Clint?"

"Yes, sir."

"Maintain your relative positions on the jump. You above, calling the action. Up, down, left, right. We move as one. Now then, we'll practice a little. Pay attention. Hard noon, watch it!" Burlane goosed the accelerator with his left wrist and the McDougal shot straight upward. "Hey! Hey! I said be alert! Come on up. If I head your way, back off and maintain your position. If you're not paying attention, I might run the fuck over you." Burlane said, "Quick ten, Flub," and veered in Flub Bonner's direction, yelling, "Flub! Flub! Flub!"

Flub's response was not quick.

"Watch now, Flub. Be alert. I'm apt to run over your ass."

"I'm onto it now, you bet, Mr. Morrison. I'm watching."

"Diving for five."

The McDougal and two Dohertys dropped down and to the right.

"Atta way!" said Burlane. "I'll have to keep my eye on the targets, so I can't be giving you warning when I make a move. You have to watch me, and them."

"I'm convinced," Flub said.

Clint said, "I'm scared shitless is what I am."

"That's exactly what I mean."

"Are we gonna get vets' benefits?" Flub asked.

"Cheap loans and stuff, sure we will, Flub. Extra points on the civil service exam."

*　　*　　*

Ella Nidech crawled up on the rocky jetty and thought if she was ever to become religious, this was the time. She lay on her back for a moment to appreciate the stars and the warm air blowing off the water. So what if she was a trifle too handsome in her keister and thighs; they had powered her out of that horror. She had made it! She was alive! She felt the side of her bruised face with her fingertips. She was lucky she hadn't been knocked out.

Nidech carried the weapons bag well clear of the water, then slipped out of her aluminum eighty and diving vest. She unpacked her weapons and gear. She crisscrossed her shoulders with bandoliers of ammunition and hand grenades, then—picking her way carefully on the wet rocks—moved along the outside of the jetty toward shore. She carried the silenced Mini-Uzi in her right hand and the French sniper's rifle strapped to her back.

She worked her way over the sharp, barnacle-encrusted rocks with the surf crunching hard at her heels. The waves swelled and grew in the darkness; the early-morning wind was picking up speed. The night had cooled to the mid-seventies, and if the wind was not balmy, it was close.

Three sailboats and two powerboats were berthed to the right of the jetty. Pak's servants cleaned the guests' catch on a small table at the jetty-end of the narrow wharf.

In the photographs she had taken from the *Lady Jane,* the jetty had obscured the bottom half of the guardshack. There could have been more guards that were invisible to the camera.

Nidech got her silenced Uzi ready for action.

She heard the guards before she saw them. They were listening to popular music. She could hear the song even, the singer Madonna telling would-be suitors how it was that she was a material girl. Nidech eased along the seaward side until she could see the guardshack clearly. There were three guards, two of them were inside drinking tea at a table that

contained a ghetto blaster and a pile of magazines. The tea
drinkers were talking to a third guard, who leaned against
the side of the shack's open door.

Nidech could hear herself breathe as she watched the
guards. They couldn't be accused of Germanic discipline and
attention to duty. One of them changed the cassette in the
ghetto blaster, and they all three laughed as the cash registers
began jingling in Pink Floyd's "Dark Side of the Moon."

"Money!" sang one of the singers.

With a kidnapped heir and actress in the villa, Nidech had
somehow imagined that the guards would be a little more
rigorous.

She unstrapped the rifle from her bag and unsnapped the
hinged lens caps.

She used the rifle's infrared scope to trace the stairs up the
side of the steep bluff. There were no breaks that she could
see, but the stairs looked old and well used. Then she
followed the silhouette of the low rock wall at the top of the
cliff, then the villa itself. She wasn't able to see much more
than shadowy forms from that distance and wasn't able to
make out the details of the interior.

Should she get closer and shoot the guards when she could
see the whites of their eyes, or should she be safe and take
them from the top of the jetty? The closer she got, the less
chance she would muff the kill and let one of them warn the
villa.

"Money!"

She took the Uzi and moved back along the jetty until she
was to the rear of the guards' vision, then she crawled on her
stomach over the top, momentarily exposed.

She eased around the side of the guardshack, staying in the
shadows and out of the guards' sight.

Nidech took a deep breath, licked her lips with her
tongue.

"Money!" sang Pink Floyd.

Ella Nidech stepped into the light and wasted Pak's guards

with a neat sweep of her silenced Uzi. This was at nearly point-blank range and their eyes were wide with surprise as their bodies crumbled, blood squirting.

Nidech's instructors at the Squirrelhouse had said that when the time came, she would do what she had to do. With the exception of the weapon's wire butt jumping hard against her shoulder, it struck her as being remarkably like sucking spiders with the wand of a high-powered Hoover.

In anticipation of an untimely headache, Gene Holt repaired to his bedroom where he dumped three aspirin from a plastic bottle, then shrugged his shoulders and added three more. Dammit, he didn't want to have a hangover when the fun really began. Pak Tze Fan said Sing Sing Boyd's lychees had been squeezed but that he had not winced. It was now time to spit Boyd's pit, which Holt took to mean the worst for the movie man.

Holt stepped over two naked women who slept intertwined, covered against the cooling marine air by various blouses, skirts, and petticoats. He looked at the curve of a naked hip and smiled. He'd butt-fucked that one an hour earlier. Packed her fudge. What a night.

They had started the evening with all the Chinese food they could possibly eat: marvelously prepared chicken feet; eggplant with a sauce that was of the gods; roast duck with sweet, piquant skin; elegant roast pork with a hint of ginger. And more. And more. And yet even more! Pak had been a gracious host all the while, explaining the history of the dishes, and how they were prepared.

Then—for his client's entertainment rather than his own— Pak had brought on the women.

But the real fun, the spitting of the pit, was coming up. Holt joined Pak Tze Fan at the window and picked up one of several pairs of infrared binoculars Pak had bought for the theater. "No action yet?" he asked Pak.

"There will be. The three of them left in their powerboat

almost three hours ago. They stopped two miles out. That was a quarter to two.''

Pak glanced at his watch. "Almost an hour and a half ago. They'll want to strike before it gets light."

"They did what, send someone forward in scuba gear?" Holt thought this was as much fun as watching a chicken fight.

"That's what I would do," Pak said.

"Who would they send? Boyd, at his age?" Holt was impressed with the ruthless efficiency of the trap Pak had laid for Boyd. Pak had left nothing to chance.

"I'm betting the actor, Frank Quetglas. He's from Miami. In the travel ads one sees young people with white teeth carrying aluminum eighties on the beach. That's Miami, isn't it?"

"Or Hawaii," Holt said.

"Mr. Kwok says Mr. Quetglas's kung fu is movie kung fu. Pretend kung fu."

Holt liked to inflict damage on other people but avoided physical danger himself. He didn't like the idea of underestimating the opposition. "Quetglas survived Kwok's attack on Saturday, didn't he?"

Pak focused his infrared binoculars at the boathouse. "Frank Quetglas was lucky then. We'll take his pit tonight, and the woman's."

"And the two captives?"

"Those too," Pak said. "This is a matter of discipline. Lessons must be learned."

44

THERE are no tables for fortune's tides, nor charts for fortune's rocks. As for the wind, watch the clouds and the birds, big boy; lick your finger and hope. Every sailor sets out alone, ties his own knots, and runs his own sheets. Floating on the anxious ebb of fortune's tide, Sing Sing Boyd and Frank Quetglas stared at the ghostly form of Fong Wai Chau, wondering if they were to die that day.

Quetglas turned his wrist up and stared at his fingernails. He said, *"El viento!"*

"It's not too bad, Frank. It'll be at our backs at least."

The wind had picked up not long after Ella Nidech had disappeared into the water like a sleek black fish. At first the powerboat rose and fell softly to slow sighs of the South China Sea. A half hour after Nidech had gone, the wind picked up and the boat began to rock gently.

"Do you think she can do it okay?" Quetglas asked.

Boyd smiled. "I'm not sure I understand."

"You know, Mr. Boyd. She being a woman and all. She has to waste those guys."

"I can't imagine the Americans would send somebody on a job like this if he wasn't up to it."

" 'She' wasn't up to it."

Boyd said, "She'll do just fine."

"And what if something happens?"

"Something could happen to a man. If something happens, we do it ourselves."

"That's what I thought," Quetglas said. He poured himself another cup of coffee. They were well into their second thermos.

"I fought with Mountbatten in Burma in the Second World War. I was a twenty-two-year-old lieutenant and one of Mountbatten's aides for a while. My father saw to the commission. I think the British thought that because my mother was Chinese, I was somehow privy to the Asian mind. Even Mountbatten paid careful attention to my opinions." Boyd grinned. "I remember waiting like this. When the time comes, you'll find you'll have an amazing ability to do what you have to do. Of course, Pak's people will have the same ability. Everything will happen more quickly yet more slowly than you had imagined. It will almost seem that you're outside of yourself looking in. That's how I remember it. Burma was a long time ago."

On their receiver, Ella Nidech said, "Come on ahead, gentlemen, the water's fine."

Boyd punched a button and said, "Yes, ma'am. We're on our way." He eased the throttle and turned the bow away from the wind and toward the island. To Quetglas he said, "Remember, now, Ms. Lewis is in command. She'll be quicker on her feet than either one of us and she's had training in the weapons."

"Mr. Boyd, I'm gonna get Kwok Lai Kwon tonight."

"An Uzi's far more effective than the side of your foot."

Quetglas looked offended that Boyd should think he was stupid. "Hey, I'm from Miami, man. Of course, shoot him. I'm gonna nail *él maricón.*" Quetglas held his Uzi up and made noises meant to be an imitation of his weapon on full automatic, emptying the slugs into the pretend figure of Kwok Lai Kwon.

Pak Tze Fan answered the phone and said, "Yes?" He waited, listening. "I see." He listened some more. "I agree. Make sure everybody's alert. He hung up the phone and said to Gene Holt, "It's begun. I'm told that the guards didn't make their check-in call."

"That was a wonderful sucker move, leaving them out there exposed and relaxed like that, no warning about anything. Takes hair to do that."

"They've lived the good life for months now. Nothing to do down there but drink tea and tell lies about the women they've had. By now the movie actor will have called Boyd and the woman."

"Boyd's on his way, then."

"He could have responded to the squeeze. He was given a choice. Now we spit the pit." The phone rang again and Pak answered, saying nothing. He hung up and said, "Confirmed. Boyd's boat just began to move."

"Time for the helicopters?" Holt looked down on the boathouse again with his infrared binoculars. All he could see were red ghosts. He thought people were bullshitting themselves if they thought these things worked worth a fuck. He could make out the profiles of the boats and the boathouse, but not a lot of detail. He traced the rail of the rickety stairs that went up the hillside. He said, "This is fun and all, but I think I'd like a quiet little island in the suburbs."

Frank Quetglas checked the snaps and buckles of the ammunition packs he would be carrying. A pain streaked through his ribs every time he took a breath, but Quetglas ignored it. In spite of his ribs, he had youth on his side. He was both stronger and quicker than Sing Sing Boyd. He said, "I can see it off to starboard, Mr. Boyd. See it there?"

"Got it, Frank. Thank you." Boyd adjusted his course and throttled down. "Be alert now. Check your gear."

It was an overcast night, but it was even gloomier in the shadow of Fong Wai Chau. Neither Boyd nor Quetglas spoke as Boyd guided the boat slowly into the inlet, the end of the jetty to their right. The wind was at their bow and the boat seemed to rise higher and sink lower as they got closer to the opening. Then gloomy sides of the inlet rose both port and starboard. They were inside the entrance. Boyd guided them to starboard, behind the protecting jetty. The water flattened. Boyd eased the boat slowly toward the moorage, its engine barely idling, the exhaust a mellow throbbing. As they got closer, they saw the details of the sailboats and powerboats.

"There are two empty berths on the left there, Mr. Boyd."

"I see them, Frank, good lad. Be ready with the rope." Boyd chose a berth and cut the engine, letting the boat glide the final yards.

Quetglas kneeled, rope in his right hand, his left hand out to break the impact of the boat against the rubber tires that served as bumpers for the hulls of Pak's boats. The boat hit with a slight rebound, and Quetglas hopped ashore with the rope and was surprised to find Ella Nidech standing there waiting.

Carrying his Uzi and his share of the ammunition, Boyd followed Quetglas ashore. "Good morning, Ms. Lewis."

Nidech said, "We've got a long climb on those stairs, and if all the steps are in as bad shape as those on the bottom, it's going to be a real thrill. Pak either sacrificed those three men to lay a trap or he thinks he's safe enough. Shall I send word to Lucien and Susan?"

"I think so," Boyd said, and he followed Nidech down the catwalk to a dockside equipment trunk.

Nidech unsnapped the lens caps of the infrared scope and leaned the barrel of her sniper's rifle against the edge of the trunk. She found her target window but couldn't see if there was anyone behind it or not. She took a deep breath, let it out slowly, found the bull's-eye pause in which she was still, and squeezed the trigger, and when the scope came to rest again, she saw that the glass was shattered. "Got it." She hoped that Lucien Salvant and Susan Wu hadn't been standing at the window. She started for the stairs, her feet going *crunch, crunch* in the gravel, wondering if she had forgotten anything on her grocery list. Boyd and Quetglas were carrying enough ammunition for a full-blown assault. So far she seemed to have time on her side. She said, "If we come under fire, remember to flatten out. The curve of the hill will give us some protection."

"Some climb with no stairs," Quetglas said.

Ella Nidech began climbing the stairs. They were about forty feet up when she heard the sound of helicopter blades. "Back to the boat! Back, back!" As she turned, the rotten stair under her right foot gave way, and she almost tumbled over the edge. Those would be the helicopters from Lung Chau. She saw their running lights, then real lights came on, impossible blue-white lamps on the bottoms of the choppers. The water under each of the five helicopters lit up like high noon. The incredible lights moved swiftly over the entrance to the inlet and made straight for the boat harbor. They'd been had. She said, "Up the stairs, quickly! Watch for rotten boards!"

She turned, taking three steps at a time. Behind and below her, the helicopters hovered over the moorage. She heard the buzz of machine guns and knew without looking that their powerboat was now sunk. Of course there would be no spark plugs in Pak's powerboats.

That's when the lights came on from above them, shining down and across from the cliff, shining directly down from the brow of the hill.

Behind her, Frank Quetglas said, *"Dios mio!"*

Nidech kneeled and watched the helicopters, five of them. The copters fanned out, preventing any retreat to the jetty and the water on the other side. "We have to get to the top of the hill before they get us with the helicopters. I'm going for the lights. If the choppers come, do your best with your Uzis." She ditched her Uzi, extra ammunition, and hand grenades and continued alone up the stairs with the sniper rifle until the huge lenses of eight searchlights loomed above, making her squint. The upper third of the slope was as bright as day. She snapped a filter onto the scope and found the light on her far right, dimmed to the glow of a cool moon by the filter. She took it out and quickly found the second. She took it out as well.

The operators of the remaining lights doused theirs.

Nidech retreated down the stairs, her eyes on the copters that hovered just out of range, blocking their escape by sea. Their searchlights were as suns out of science fiction.

Frank Quetglas said, "*Madre de Dios! Santa Maria!* What the hell is this?"

"Dunkirk," Sing Sing Boyd said in his resonant baritone.

45

IT was only after Lucien Salvant and Susan Wu had sewn their rectangular para-wings together—two king-size silk bed sheets, each with crude channels that narrowed toward the rear to slow down the air—that they began to have second thoughts about the whole idea. Would they or wouldn't they work?

Susan was on her hands and knees, separating the folds on hers. "They're big, and strong, and we've got channels just like those in the picture."

The twine harness was crude but could withstand a hard yank and could hold Salvant's weight. Whether a man's weight hanging from a shower rod meant anything, neither one of them had any idea. All they wanted to do was crashland into the brush on the side of the hill without breaking too many bones.

"Maybe we should wait it out," Salvant said. "Maybe Sing Sing Boyd will come through."

Susan Wu stepped to the window and checked her wrist-watch. "It's going to get light soon. One way or the other we'll have to make up our minds. If we could get our hands on one of Pak's powerboats with any darkness at all left, we could make it to that island out there.''

Susan turned and the window imploded into the room.

They both stood for a moment, stunned.

"Are you okay?" Salvant asked.

Susan was shaken. "I'm fine."

"A high-powered rifle." Salvant pointed at the ceiling.

"Sing Sing Boyd telling us he's on his way."

Salvant looked out of the window. "The boat dock, I'll bet."

Susan Wu joined him. She held out her hand, feeling the wind that was deflected up the face of the cliff. "Plenty of wind if we have to jump."

"I think our best bet is to stay put now. Boyd's people know where we are."

"But if Pak comes, we jump." Susan leaned against Lucien Salvant.

"I agree. If Pak comes, we jump. Shhhh! What's that?"

"Helicopters, I think."

Lucien Salvant and Susan Wu saw the running lights of Pak Tze Fan's helicopters in the distance, coming from Lung Chau. At the very least they had regarded their para-sail project as a way of keeping occupied for two days. Now they were thankful they had done it. They had given themselves an option in the unfolding drama. They started tying on their makeshift harnesses just in case.

James Burlane began his breathing exercises, inhaling deeply and exhaling slowly, telling his body that it was time, requesting his subconscious mind to come up with the proper image to prepare him for battle. Then he remembered duck hunting on the Umatilla River, saw the mist running off the water, saw the hill with the sagebrush on the far side of the river. Yes, this was what he wanted.

He saw the ducks coming, high but in range. He remembered swinging his twelve-gauge in front of one and pulling the trigger. Saw the mallard fold, and tumble to the river, and land with a soft splash in the current. Felt Gutly's haunches tighten as the big Chesapeake Bay headed for the water. The gunpowder had smelled curiously sweet in the cold air.

He readied his weapons, a Bee-Vee-made American M60 machine gun mounted on each door and firing tracers so Burlane could see what he was doing.

Below him he saw a blaze of lights.

He said, "I believe it's time, gentlemen. Stay alert, now." He slipped the sound mufflers over his ears so the machine wouldn't destroy his enjoyment of a whorehouse piano. He set the stick straight up, twisted the pitch lever, and plummeted straight down in his sleek McDougal, a single wasp where John Ford had had thundering hooves and a bugle in the lead.

It was like ground-sluicing coots. He took them in a rhythm.

Burlane stitched the first in a jarring roar of the M60, brass casings rattling on the floor, recoil bucking against his hand, slugs looping yellow in the night. His target burst into a ball of orange and dropped.

He switched guns for the hornet on his left. Stitched again. Hammering roar. Looping slugs. Downed chopper.

"Holy shit!" Flub Bonner exclaimed.

"Get the fuck out of here!" Burlane shouted, keeping a third chopper in the corner of his eye. He saw the obedient Flub taking off like a striped-assed ape in his Doherty.

Burlane goosed the McDougal and it shot straight up. The other machine was slower. They looked at him, still surprised, a pilot and a gunner. Burlane stitched: three down. Shooting Pak's choppers on the jump was about as sporting as shooting a drunk in the back of the head; by the time the pilot and gunners figured out there was a stranger among them, they were dead. Still, firing yellow tracers had a certain color and festive splendor about it, and the eager James Burlane set out to stitch Pak Tze Fan's remaining two helicopters. It occurred to the delicate man that Karl Marx was right: a person has to feel good about his job to get any joy out of it.

In Pak's villa, there came a pounding on the door, which Lucien Salvant and Susan Wu had locked from the inside. "Open up!" a man yelled.

"What do we do?" Susan Wu asked.

The man in the hall put his shoulder to the door.

"We join our friends on the hill," Salvant said.

"I agree. Me first." She kissed Salvant briefly and squeezed his hand. Without fuss, she jumped. She had decided to do it that way, like diving into cold water. If she thought about it too much, she wouldn't do it, she knew.

It was okay: her para-sail held. She was aloft and headed out over the chasm.

Salvant jumped. His held too.

"Yes, Lucien!" she yelled, thrilled that her para-sail was working, pulling on the twine with her left hand, which pushed her to the left. She was aloft in the darkness, going in the right direction. She was maybe going a little fast, yes, but she wasn't falling. She could see the steep hillside in the darkness, looming, getting closer, closer.

"Just like Yi Lin!" Salvant yelled up at her, thankful that there was a good updraft to help them. He was heavier than she was and was somewhere below her, to her rear, and traveling faster.

On the slope, Ella Nidech was so overcome by the surgical ambush of the black helicopter that she was literally moved to tears and knew for a fact that any human being would have been equally as grateful, male or female. She wiped her eyes with the back of her arm. The Company's Main Man had arrived just one button from disaster. James Burlane, yes!

Down the hill from her, Frank Quetglas yelled, "*Sí! Sí! Sí!*

Look at him shoot, would you? Look at him shoot! It's like the Fourth of July. What a gunner!''

Higher on the hill and closer to the villa, Ella Nidech heard a woman call a name in a stage whisper.

"Are you okay?" a man called back. That much Nidech heard clearly. The man was farther down the hill than the woman. Would the triads use women soldiers? Nidech didn't think so. She wondered if that might not be Susan Wu.

Nidech didn't have to be a graduate of West Point to know she had to secure her real estate. "Frank, I want you down that hill and make sure nobody comes out of those downed choppers alive. Mr. Boyd, up here, please."

"Yes, ma'am," the two men replied almost as one.

In a few moments Sing Sing Boyd was at her side. "In the nick of time, eh, Ms. Lewis? You Americans have a way, I'll grant you that."

"We've got voices out there on the side of this hill. I'll be back in a few minutes. I want you to stay here and shoot anybody who tries to come down this walkway." Ella Nidech started crawling over the brush on the steep hill, Uzi in hand. She heard the chatter of an Uzi at the base of the hill as Frank Quetglas wasted a survivor of one of Burlane's downed choppers.

She saw two piles of red silk, one straight in front of her and one higher on the hill.

She felt a presence . . .

And turned, stopping her trigger finger a heartbeat away from wasting Lucien Salvant and Susan Wu, who were lying on their stomachs holding hands, their eyes riveted on her weapon. Nidech glanced back at the piles of silk. "You jumped?" she said in astonishment.

"They were caving the door in," Salvant said.

Nidech appreciated every break she could get. She said, "Follow me. Quickly. Quickly." She led the retreat back to the board sidewalk. By the time they got back, James Burlane had returned in his McDougal, together with the two larger

Dohertys. The choppers settled in, protected from gunfire above by the curve of the hill.

Sing Sing Boyd, Uzi in hand, embraced his actress, saying to Nidech, "Ms. Lewis, you work miracles. However in heaven did you find them?" Before Nidech could answer, they heard the sound of someone coming up the boards and were joined by a tall, blond man with a nose that was slightly off, and Frank Quetglas.

"Marion Morrison," Burlane said. He shook hands, eyeing the villa at the same time. He too was impressed that Nidech had Salvant and Susan Wu in hand. "Well done," he said. "My two recruits are in their choppers ready to go. If anybody tries to escape from up top, they'll take them down."

"They won't be going anywhere. You took out all five of their machines," Boyd said.

Ella Nidech sighed with relief. "Well, then, shall we quietly withdraw?"

Burlane said, "Is Gene Holt still up top?"

"As far as I know."

"Then I'm for continuing."

Boyd said, "I agree, Mr. Morrison. I think Pak Tze Fan needs a little lesson on whom he picks fights with."

"I want Kwok," said Quetglas.

"You're still in command, Ms. Lewis," Burlane added quickly.

Nidech took a deep breath. Audie Murphy they wanted, Audie Murphy they'd get. She said, "Okay, I want you, Lucien, and you, Susan, to get on down to the boathouse and stay there. You, Mr. Boyd, I want guarding this walkway. You, Frank, I want to circle to the left on this hill and let them know where you are. An occasional burst of fire will do. But protect yourself; stay below the brow of the hill. I'll circle up the hill to the right and get an angle on them with my sniper's rifle. Is that understood? You, Morrison, I want in your chopper, waiting. Give me half an hour to get into position, then start your engine. That'll hold their attention for a moment, and I'll see what I can do with my French piece here.''

"Nice!" Burlane said.

"If they retreat inside the villa, we'll burn it and waste them when they run from the smoke, but none of you is to risk his life. I'll say it again—none of you." She looked at Frank Quetglas. "And that includes you trying to take on Kwok Lai Kwon. That's stupid.''

Quetglas opened his mouth to protest.

Nidech ignored him. "When we get them backed into the villa, you put down and join me, Morrison. Tell your people down there to go aloft and take over when you put down. If everything goes okay, we'll assemble at the top of these stairs. Questions?" There were none, so Nidech began the task of circling right up the steep hill carrying both the Uzi and the French sniper's rifle. She had about a hundred yards of brushy, forty-five-degree slope to negotiate, and it was tough going. About five minutes into the climb, she heard the first burst of fire from Quetglas, who had worked his way toward the head of the inlet. She heard return fire from the low rock wall above.

Nidech heard another burst of gunfire, then another and another from Frank Quetglas, who had changed positions each time. Nidech didn't know how he was moving that fast with broken ribs. She wished he wasn't so enthusiastic. If he overdid it, he'd run out of ammunition.

Finally Nidech reached the summit, and looking down the rock wall toward the villa on her left, she saw six triads peering down the slope, trying to locate Quetglas.

Nidech carefully surveyed the scene. To the right of the villa, beyond some perimeter lights and at the edge of a putting green, there was a helicopter. The windows of the villa were open but the shades were drawn. Inside, she knew, Pak Tze Fan and Gene Holt were calculating the risk of trying to fly out in a single helicopter when Boyd's demon pilot had already shot down their fleet of five.

She sighted in on the first of her targets and waited.

She heard the *pop, pop, whuf, whuf* of Burlane's helicopter.

She took the first, then the second triad *snap! snap!* before the third realized what had happened. She folded him, then the fourth, whose attention had been directed toward the sound of the helicopter starting.

The fifth ran.

Ella Nidech took him square on the spine between his shoulder blades, and he pitched forward, twitching, sliding on gravel.

Unfortunately for the sixth man, he had tried to open a door to the villa, and so he too got his spine shattered, the force of the bullet twisting him to one side where he lay jumping in death throes.

Nidech slung the sniper's rifle on her back and began loping, head down, toward the villa. She ran along the narrow lip just outside the low wall, using the wall for protection. She stopped where the stairs began their zigzagging descent, and waited while Burlane circled the compound warily, on the fringes first, up high, then lower and closer in. He drew some gunfire from the villa itself and retreated. The grounds were clear. Burlane put down just beyond a tennis court that remained brilliantly lit in what had been a defensive measure.

She watched as Burlane, Uzi in hand, circled the villa, heading in her direction in the predawn darkness. In a few minutes she, Burlane, and Boyd were assembled at the top of the stairs. Burlane's companion helicopters circled high above the compound.

From below, Quetglas called, "I'm coming! I'm coming!" He had ended up far down the hill and had a long way to climb.

Burlane said, "How many?"

"Six," she said.

"Nice!"

Boyd, still panting from the arduous climb up the stairs, said, "Do you suppose there's anybody else in there but them?"

"I . . . there." Burlane, followed by Nidech and Boyd, began sprinting toward the rear of the villa. From behind the villa, three figures were running toward the helicopter at the edge of the putting green.

As Pak Tze Fan passed beneath the perimeter lights, Boyd yelled "Mine!" and dropped to his knee firing his Uzi. He fairly cut the Mountain Lord in half. "Thank you," Boyd said.

The helicopter was running.

Gene Holt, outlined by the cabin light, grabbed the edge of the helicopter's open door and started to scramble aboard. For the briefest of moments, Holt had both his hands and feet inside the helicopter so that his rump stuck straight out . . .

. . . which is where James Burlane bored a Holland, emptying the Uzi in one awful, sustained burst. Holt's hollowed corpse was literally blown into the helicopter's cabin. The helicopter rose swiftly.

And from above, Clint and Flub Bonner descended in their Dohertys, guns blazing, which they'd been itching to do all along, and Pak's helicopter crunched back to earth, making a terrible divot in the green. Its blades whirled slowly to a stop. The battle of Fong Wai Chau was over amid the screaming of "Hee-haw!" and "Yah-hoo! Poke 'em! Poke 'em!" from the hovering Dohertys.

The delicate man strolled nonchalantly to the downed helicopter. He reached in the open door, glanced at the dead pilot, and pulled out what was left of Gene Holt's corpse, careful not to get anything on his shoes. "Well, he got what he wanted. He made it," Burlane said.

"What's that?" Nidech said, turning her face from the sight.

"He's the biggest asshole on the planet. Nobody's arguing."

Sing Sing Boyd said, "Where's Frank?"

"At the tennis court," Nidech said, pointing.

The three of them began running for the brightly lit court, Boyd yelling, "No, Frank!"

Frank Quetglas was squared off against Kwok Lai Kwon. Boyd's Bullet and the Fragrance of the Red Lotus were about to go at one another in foot-to-foot combat.

46

Fortune's bug it is that
flutters wildly to the light,
on a sultry summer night,
on the South China Sea.

So went the poem by the Chinese master, Ng Hua.

The nocturnal bugs of Fong Wai Chau sure loved the light. They seemed to have arrived almost instantly, frantic, as many as there were stars in the sky. They zoomed, and hopped, zany with happiness at the wonderful light above the tennis courts. There were tiny, shiny beetles with little skinny wings. There were huge, fuzzy moths plowing through the humid air on wings that seemed as big as Chinese fans. All the bugs were having a good time. The most muscle-bound moths seemed vivacious if not downright manic. Flying ants did the tango with mosquitoes. The insects hopped and looped and swirled on that inviting stage of light. Their happy little bodies said, Yes! Yes! Fabulous lights over here, everybody! Come on over. Party time! Hot damn! There were so many

bugs and they were so energetic, so excited, that they re-
bounded off one another, joyous insect bump-dancers.

Into this light, and into the partying, boogieing bugs,
stepped the Fragrance of the Red Lotus, bearing with him
fung shui that had seen him through forty-six known kung fu
kills.

Kwok Lai Kwon began his fabled *sshhtt! hai!* routine.

From the other side of the courtyard, Frank Quetglas
stepped forth to accept the challenge, pain shooting through
his broken ribs. *"Besame los juevos, pendejo!"* he yelled at
Kwok. A bug whacked *splat!* against his temple.

Kwok was in no hurry. He knew he was menacing enough
to begin with. The effectiveness of his routine was that it
came in steps that he had learned to pace. His opponents
were rendered paralyzed waiting for the next escalation.

First Kwok inhaled. This was deep and slow before combat, then shallow and quick, turning downright vicious at the
moment of truth.

Then he shouted *"Hai!"*—a terrible echo to the *sshhtt!*
The *hai*s, soft and chantlike at first, got louder and more
feral as the hyperventilation became more menacing.

Then he began stamping his feet. Softly, in keeping with
the drama of the routine. Then louder.

Until the fatal *"Hai!"* triggered a kick, and Kwok felt the
satisfying feel of the arch of his foot against a folding
cranium or sternum.

Kwok didn't like to mix it up before delivering the fatal
blow. There was always the chance that an opponent might
get a blow in. Kwok didn't like pain. He abhorred bruises.

Better to build the drama. Make them wait.

Kwok advanced through the swirling bugs like Satan through
a sandstorm, the *sshhtt*s and *hai*s as yet violins and cellos to
the coming drama. The tympani and brass lay just ahead.

"La madre que te parió fue una puta!" This literally
meant "the woman who gave birth to you fucked up" and
would have earned Frank a broken face back in Miami.

"Sshhtt! Hai!" Kwok's face was flushed. He had worked himself into a fury. Bugs swirled and whirled around his head.

Frank Quetglas had never learned how to swear properly in English. Spanish was more comfortable. *"Metete la lengua en el culo!"* he said.

"Sshhtt! Hai!"

"That means stick your tongue in your asshole."

"Sshhtt! Hai!" Kwok showed a flicker of emotion. He had killed lots of men, but never a mouthy Cuban. All of his other opponents had treated the occasion of being killed with the dignity it deserved. Kwok would show Quetglas whose tongue got stuck where. He raised his foot high and slammed it to the ground.

"Mamame la pinga!" Frank tapped his crotch with his right forefinger and made sucking sounds with his mouth. His meaning was clear.

Kwok's rhythm was interrupted. Then he went: *"Sshhtt! Hai!"*

Ng Hua's bug was a stout-bodied moth, zooming to a rock tune. The moth dove low, looped up, showing off, going for max speed, aiming for lights.

"Rajate una paja!" Quetglas, still circling to his left, looked the annoyed Kwok straight in the eye and pretended to masturbate.

"SSHHTT! HAI!" Kwok's dark eyes blazed. He slammed his foot to the ground.

Fortune's bug circled.

"Me cago en tu madre!" Quetglas smiled, kept moving to his left, kept his eye on the Fragrance as their dance moved to conclusion. "That means I shit on your mother."

"SSHHTT! HAI!"

The moth dove . . .

"Maricón!" Quetglas went kiss, kiss with his lips and let his left wrist go limp.

. . . and zoomed straight up, heading for the stars . . .

"SSSHHHTTT!"

. . . went *smack!* straight into Kwok's right nostril. The moth, frenzied in that moist chamber, frantic, wanting freedom, twisted and vibrated in panic:

ZZZZZZZZZZZZZZZZZZZZ!

No *hai* followed. A heartbeat of danger.

Kwok snorted, grabbed for his nose, digging . . .

. . . and was killed by his own forefinger embedded, stilettolike, in the farthest reaches of his cerebrum.

Frank Quetglas—remembering that his mother had admonished him never to pick his nose in public or while riding his tricycle—leaped for joy. He landed awkwardly, wincing at the pain in his ribs and in the broken arch of his left foot. The metatarsus of his foot had yielded from the blow—delivered squarely on the back of Kwok Lai Kwon's hand.

The breathless Sing Sing Boyd, who had arrived just in time to witness the fatal blow, said, "Are you okay, Frank?"

Boyd's Bullet was jubilant. Saved by a bug! What luck! *"Un bicho! Un bicho! Gracias, Señor Bicho! Gracias! Sí Sí! Qué suerte!"* he yelled. Then, calming down but trembling with emotion, Quetglas accepted a simultaneous embrace by Ella Nidech and Sing Sing Boyd, saying, sheepishly, "I fucked up and ran out of ammunition down there making all that noise."

James Burlane made it a foursome, drawing Nidech's little squad to him with his long arms. He too felt glad to be alive.

47

JAMES Burlane was distinctly amused at Ella Nidech's reaction. "You looked shocked? Why?"

"Why?" Ella Nidech was incredulous. "What are you talking about?" She looked at Sing Sing Boyd slumped to one side in his seat. "A candy man!"

"It's perfectly logical. We all should have known. Boyd'll be okay. When he wakes up he'll just think he dozed off. He's an older man and it's been a long day. He'll suspect nothing, believe me. One sip of that coffee and that's it. Bingo! Into the stupor, out with the truth, off to sleep." Burlane snapped his fingers.

"That was amazing." Nidech was truly impressed. "How did you know what questions to ask? You went straight to the truth. Straight to it. I've never seen anything like that. Who figured this out? You and Neely and Schott? Who? Did you people know this all along?"

"I have a nose for methane."

"Oh, my God."

"No, no. I know my methane. I can smell it in the pores

of an automobile or on a pair of shoes. For example, if I'm not mistaken, you have just a hint of it, which is normal, certainly not enough to take over your personality. As far as I know, Neely and Schott don't have any idea.''

Nidech checked Boyd again. "How long have we had that stuff you gave him?"

"The drug?" Burlane thought about that. "This is June. Let's see. Eight months. Wonderful little capsules, don't you think? One capsule to a thermos. Well, there you have it."

"I still don't believe it. He answered your questions like a schoolboy."

"When he starts to stir, you're going to have to pretend you're asleep so he won't think it's unusual that he dozed off. When he wakes up, I'll offer him a cup of undrugged coffee."

"What do we do?"

"About what?"

"About that story he told us under the influence of the drug."

Burlane tapped a rudder pedal to alter his course. "We do nothing."

"Nothing! What are you talking about?"

"We do nothing. We say nothing." Burlane glanced back at the sleeping Sing Sing Boyd. "What do you think would happen if we told Ara Schott about it?"

"He'd tell Neely."

"Of course he would. He's an eagle scout. And Neely? Who would Neely tell? Right. The President. And who would the President tell? Right. Mrs. President. And who would the First Lady tell? Correct. Her hairdresser. This kind of secret is impossible to keep. In a week it'd be on the front of the *National Enquirer*."

"What if Neely and Schott figure it out on their own?"

"They won't. Well, Schott might, but it's unlikely. Neely, never."

"I guess I wondered if I'd ever get involved in something like this."

"When I was a kid growing up in Umatilla, Oregon, I had a foster sister for a while who was part Nez Perce, and we had ourselves a blood-brother/sister ceremony like we saw Jeff Chandler do in the movies. The gravity of that moment has always impressed me, and I bet she remembers it too. I propose that we decide right now what we're going to do about this. I say we agree to let Sing Sing Boyd's secret stay with him—as though I had never drugged him."

"I agree."

"A regular handshake won't do. Give me your thumb. Thumbs up." He caught the palm of her hand, hooked his thumb around hers, and gripped her hand solidly. "On my honor, I swear it."

"On my honor, I swear it."

"Well, that's done." Burlane turned to check on Boyd again. "He'll be waking up in a few minutes, then we'll let him down at his villa. I bet he's plumb tuckered. That's a lot of work for a man his age."

"God, did you see how he cut old Pak in half?"

"Wasted him slicker than a whistle."

Sing Sing Boyd began to stir, and Ella Nidech slumped down in her seat, pretending to be asleep.

Boyd shook his head. "Heavens, I must have dozed off."

"So did our commando friend." Burlane nodded toward Nidech.

"She did amazing work. Is there any way she can get recognition from your people for what she did? She took charge like a bloody man. I haven't seen soldiering like that since Burma. She was bloody cool as hell, she was."

"I guarantee that the right people will hear every detail."

"Handsome woman, and quite a scrapper," Boyd said.

"Very clever, too. Would you like some fresh coffee, Mr. Boyd?"

"Yes, that would be nice. My cup seems to have cooled off."

"Your estate should be coming up soon, Mr. Boyd. My friends in the other helicopters should have Lucien and Susan and Frank back to Hong Kong by now. If this map's right, that must be your place there on the right, up that road."

Boyd looked down. "It is indeed. I want to thank you, Mr. Morrison, for your wonderful flying skills and marksmanship. You saved all our lives."

"I hesitate to say better late than never." Burlane glanced at the form of Ella Nidech pretending to be asleep. "Ms. Lewis?" He touched her shoulder gently.

Nidech sat up, yawning and stretching. She gave Burlane a sly grin in the dim light of the helicopter cockpit. She was proud of Boyd's compliments. "Where are we?"

"Lantau," Burlane said. He started the descent toward Sing Sing Boyd's villa.

They began the ride back to Hong Kong in silence, listening to the leisurely chopping of the McDougal's blades. James Burlane didn't appear to be in any hurry. He didn't know what to say and so said nothing. Ella Nidech apparently felt the same way. The business of Boyd's secret was taken care of; it would never be mentioned again. The other problem, between colleagues and sexes, remained.

Finally, Burlane, glancing at Nidech, wondering what she looked like without a wet suit on, said, "Good work pranging those triads up there. Six of them. That's quick shooting. Sweet." Burlane made a kissing sound.

"Thank you. That's nine dead people including the three setups. A wonderful evening's work."

"I apologize for my late arrival. I . . . I was held up." Burlane tapped the rudder pedal.

"Why, or should I say how, were you held up? Under the circumstances, I think you owe me."

Burlane sighed, and told her what happened at National Airport and in Portland, Maine; there had been chores in his life that he had enjoyed more.

"The tape knocked you out before the attendant came to the Maine part of her routine." Nidech looked numb. Because of that screw-up and the fog in Maine, she'd almost sunk in the Big Muddy at Fong Wai Chau.

"It could have cost you. I know, I know."

"Tell me, did they let you see Gein's report before it was sent to Rollo Hinkley?" Nidech looked amused.

"I saw it."

"I see. What did it say?"

"You asked for a fair report and you got it. Gein said I was an asshole and had fucked up. He included photographs of the stitch marks on the street and on the side of the building, and there was sworn Q. and A. from you. Gein made no recommendations of his own, just organized the facts, which was his job. He attached my statement saying it was a nonsexist act because I would have done the same thing to a male colleague. Neely and Schott attached a plea for temporary suspension, saying I was the best man they had. I assure you, Rollo Hinkley got the straight story." He dug into his jacket pocket and retrieved a fat envelope that he handed to her.

"What's this?"

"A copy of Gein's report." Burlane said nothing while she read it. She finished and looked up, surprised and amazed. "It's all here."

Burlane said nothing, then, "Everything that had to do with you is there."

"But not everything else?"

"Not anything else. Good pictures, though, don't you think? Tell me, do you think one of the long dogs would have submitted a fairer or more accurate report than Edward Gein? On this one charge, that is."

Nidech looked at the report. "Gein didn't nail you with spikes like he said."

"He was lying about that, the bastard. Would you like him sent up on charges?"

Nidech grinned. "No. In fact I wish I hadn't written the letter now."

"No, no. You were pissed. I understand that."

"No word yet from Hinkley?"

"Nope."

"The black hair and colored contacts were good, but I think you looked too anal compulsive as Gein. I don't like men who are too neat-neat. Do Neely and Schott always let you pick your pseudonyms?"

Burlane laughed. "I have a good time."

"And Edward Gein is . . . ?"

"He was a man convicted of murdering people and eating them. This was back in the fifties. He had them hung up in his garage like pork bellies, as I recall."

"A cannibal? Do you eat people—is that it?"

Burlane leered at her, licking his lips. "Sometimes." He let his glance travel down her wet suit.

"Oh, shit!" Nidech looked disgusted.

"And Marion Morrison is—"

"Yes, yes, I know, John Wayne's real name. You do this around Neely and Schott?" To Nidech, Neely and Schott were powerful, distant gods.

"Sure," Burlane said. "And Aristotle too. He's a real card." They could see Hong Kong coming up in the warming morning. Burlane wished he could make the trip with Ella Nidech last longer. He eased up on the throttle.

"That was some nice shooting, dropping down on those hornets like that. Thank you, Marion."

"No sweat, ambushes are fun," Burlane said. He felt her hand on his thigh. She gave a little squeeze. "I . . . is this some kind of sexual harassment, Ms. Lewis?"

"I was thinking maybe you might want to come up to my

place for an after-combat drink.'' Nidech squeezed his thigh a little harder. "If you treat me right, I could make it worth your while.''

"Please, Ms. Lewis!'' Burlane made a pathetic, pretend effort to rid his thigh of her hand. He turned Vivien Leigh in *A Streetcar Named Desire,* his voice a helpless southern drawl. "Please, please, Ms. Lewis, I do put myself in the hands of strangers.''

"I could always write Senator Hinkley a letter saying please not to be harsh on you.'' She squeezed again.

Burlane shifted in his seat so that Ella Nidech might do whatever she wanted with her hand.

Nidech leaned against his shoulder. She said, "Marion, will you tell me what you would ordinarily have done instead of our bargain earlier?''

"Ordinarily you'd be dead right now. That's if I had insisted on completely professional work. I get a little sloppy now and then, same as everybody else.''

"That's what I thought.'''

"If you ever break your word about the candy man, I'll have to kill you,'' he said.

"You break yours and I'll show you what stitching's all about.''

Burlane asked Hong Kong Airport for permission to put down. The delicate man, killer of eleven but unable to take the twelfth as logic dictated, had a hankering for a tender woman, killer of nine, and they most certainly needed rest.

48

THE *sam ku*, Wong Tsei-Ling, opened the door and there stood Susan Wu in a splendid white dress; she was beaming, joyful, and had a gentleman admirer. Her boyfriend had his arm around her waist and had a smile that was all teeth. Tsei-Ling had seen his face somewhere before.

Behind them, she saw, was a man with some plastic shopping bags resting on his left forearm, a *gweilo* woman, a tall man with a slightly crooked nose, and a Eurasian holding a bouquet of red roses. She immediately recognized the last as Sing Sing Boyd. All the men wore tuxedos, with red rosebuds pinned on their lapels. They looked neat and handsome, except that the tall *gweilo* man hadn't done a very good job with his tie. The *gweilo* woman wore a sexy, soft pink dress that clung to her body.

Susan Wu introduced her boyfriend: "Wong Tsei-Ling, I'd like you to meet my fiancé, Frank Quetglas." She held out an engagement ring for the *sam ku* to see.

"Me and Susan are gonna get married," Quetglas said. He gave Susan a special squeeze around the waist.

In her slow English, Tsei-Ling said, "I'm pleased to meet you, Mr. Quetglas. I've seen you in the movies, I believe." She had given Susan Wu an impossible curse. How had this happened?

Susan said, "I would also like to introduce Mr. Lucien Salvant, who has agreed to marry my sister, Wing-Ling."

"Pleased to meet you," Salvant said.

Tsei-Ling was momentarily at a loss for words.

Susan Wu opened her handbag and withdrew a large wad of newspaper clippings that she unfolded and handed to the *sam ku*. The clippings, from Chinese-language newspapers, told how Cactus Jack Bonner's lucky heir had decided to live in Hong Kong. One clipping featured the photograph taken of Salvant when he learned the news in Dickman's Saloon.

"You said that when I found Wing-Ling a proper husband, you would perform the wedding."

"I . . ." Tsei-Ling's lips made an inadvertent sucking sound, a little *sssk!*

"And this is Miss Flora Lewis . . ."

Tsei-Ling shook hands with Ella Nidech, thinking her clinging pink outfit too sexy for a wedding. *Gweilo* women were a bit show-offy for Tsei-Ling's taste.

". . . Mr. Marion Morrison, and you probably recognize Mr. Sing Sing Boyd." Messrs. Burlane and Boyd each shook hands with the *sam ku*.

Tsei-Ling, not liking the idea of Susan Wu having found a boyfriend but looking forward to being on television, said, "Won't you come in?" She knew the television people would be coming because Sing Sing Boyd would want the publicity for his actor and actress.

Salvant said, "I thought to bring a little New Orleans tradition along—the tuxes and flowers and so on. I hope my bride won't mind." He dug into one of his bags and came up with a bridal bouquet. He winked at Susan Wu, who gave the blushing Quetglas a big, lingering kiss on the mouth.

"Who'll throw the bouquet for the bride?" Quetglas asked, grinning at Susan Wu.

"I'll ask the bride," Tsei-Ling said. "I'll have to call her up. She has to approve of both the groom and the arrangements. Do you have a suitable dowry? Wing-Ling thinks she has suffered terribly and deserves a good dowry."

"I've seen to that," Salvant said. "I went to a special shop." He dug into a shopping bag and began withdrawing miniature furniture and other items needed to stock a new household. He had chairs, couches, and beds, as well as pots and pans, plates and bowls; all of these were made of paper, and few were larger than a matchbox or jewelry box. He had a paper refrigerator, a paper freezer, a paper television set, a paper video recorder, a paper stereo system with tiny little knobs, a paper hot tub, a paper microwave, a paper something that looked like a popcorn popper, a paper personal computer, a paper Porsche, a paper airplane, and a paper sloop. There was a paper poodle and a paper pony. There was a splendid paper villa, and two paper beach homes, one presumably for Bali, where the groom and his spirit bride could smoke pot and screw strange people, and the other for Georgetown on Penang Island. All this plus a bundle of happy money of extraordinary denominations.

All this was to be burned in Wong Tsei-Ling's special little fireplace so that it might be enjoyed by the bride in the spirit world.

Wong Tsei-Ling and the members of the wedding party stared at the largesse, each impressed in his or her own way.

The tall blond man said, "Does the refrigerator have an ice-cube maker?"

Salvant said, "Yes, it does, and the stove has a self-cleaning oven."

"I like the kind where you pull the handle and the ice cubes pop out, *pup, pup, pup!* You spend a hard day at work, then have to sit in that traffic an hour and a half, why there's a certain pleasure in pulling on that handle."

Wong Tsei-Ling knew the shop where Salvant had purchased the miniatures. The paper figures were expensive at that shop; the dowry must have cost him several thousand Hong Kong dollars. For a second, Wong Tsei-Ling regretted that the groom-to-be hadn't waited for the television photographers before he unpacked the dowry. Then she realized that the burning figures would make even better footage.

"I'd like Frank Quetglas to be my best man," Salvant said.

Wong Tsei-Ling began stacking Wing-Ling's dowry in the firebox, starting with the villa, cabins, and automobiles, working up to the kitchenware. She wondered if her ceremonial fireplace could safely handle that much paper. She packed each item neatly, so it would get oxygen and burn quickly, without a lot of smoke.

Behind her, Susan Wu said, "We knew you wouldn't want a big fuss made, so we made all our arrangements in confidence. I didn't think Wing-Ling would want anything splashy."

Quetglas said, "Don't want anything splashy? Look at you, peaches. Outshining the bride. This is the bride's moment, remember." He kissed his intended. "Mmmmm, you're beautiful," he said.

"A wedding's more fun without a bunch of cameramen poking lenses in your face," Susan said.

No television? The *sam ku*'s face hardened. Wong Tsei-Ling knew who was to blame: Sing Sing Boyd. Boyd was both half *gweilo* and part of the money crowd that had scorned her services since she'd forced the *taipan* to construct the Building of a Thousand Assholes. *Sam ku*s were said to lose their power if they operated out of greed, so there was little she could do in that case. That wasn't so in this one.

An irritated Wong Tsei-Ling began working up to her trance so that the lovely bride might be able to join the wedding.

Lucien Salvant had seen some pretty weird stuff in some of the Mardi Gras parades in New Orleans—everything from a man walking around with his genitals encased in a plastic grapefruit to a woman sitting on a veranda showing her private parts to a cheering crowd. In Mardi Gras—where the celebrants were inevitably altered by alcohol, psilocybin mushrooms, speed, cocaine, or pot—anything was possible. This unfolding rite of matrimony topped anything he had ever seen at crazy time in February.

The members of the wedding party stood transfixed, although Salvant noted that Quetglas still had his hand on Susan Wu's butt. He wondered if Quetglas might not be overdoing his part.

The *sam ku* began descending into the spirit world in pursuit of the bride-to-be, Wu Wing-Ling. Wong Tsei-Ling pursed her ancient lips and began making a high-pitched motorboat sound, taking slow swaths from left to right, right to left. Spittle flew. The members of the wedding party stepped back. Then, to their unspoken relief, she stopped sputtering and opened her mouth wide—exposing her throat and the insides of her dentures; she began making a rhythmic "ah, ah, ah" chant in the manner of Indians doing a war dance in old Hollywood movies. When that evened out to a guttural bee-buzzing sound, she fell silent.

Descending, descending, deeper and deeper into a trance, she stared through them with glazed eyes.

At last Wong Tsei-Ling said, "Wing Ling is in me." She stared. She was now Wing-Ling. Wong Tsei-Ling and Wu Wing-Ling were one. "I will speak as Wing-Ling."

The wedding party waited.

Salvant glanced at Susan Wu, who bit her lower lip.

"I'm not sure I like this man's looks." Wing-Ling sized up the prospective groom.

The wedding party waited, its members attempting to mask a range of emotions.

Wing-Ling took her time. "I don't want you," she snarled at Salvant. "I want a different husband. I want you." She pointed at Frank Quetglas, looking through him with glazed eyes.

Quetglas laughed nervously. He drew Susan Wu close and she buried her face in the hollow of his neck.

"I don't like this man at all." She looked at Salvant with disgust. "I don't want money. I was just saying that. I want a movie actor."

The scheme was working. Salvant wanted to turn around and congratulate the imperturbable Marion Morrison, the author of the idea, and Boyd, who had been pleased to direct rehearsals of its execution.

Susan Wu paled. "What?" She projected disbelief.

"I want to marry Frank Quetglas. If I can't, then your curse will continue. You may think you love him now, but wait and see."

Lucien Salvant thought Sing Sing Boyd's actors weren't bad. Susan Wu had a radiant I'm-in-love look about her, and Quetglas was perfect as the horny, pawing lover. The rest of them had only to keep their mouths shut.

Susan Wu alone played the scene for the benefit of her spiteful sister, Wu Wing-Ling. The others kept their eyes on a spiteful old woman.

"Oh, no!" Quetglas cried. *"Dios mio! Por favor, ayudame!"*

Susan Wu burst into uncontrollable sobbing. "No! No!" Her voice was pitiable. Her body shook with spasms of grief.

Quetglas held her tightly, murmuring, "It's gonna be okay, honey. I'll never leave you. Never."

"I want you for a husband," Wing-Ling said.

"I'm not going to marry your sister."

The *sam ku*'s voice rose. "Yes! Yes! I want you. Only you, Frank Quetglas."

Susan Wu wept.

"Oh, honey. I'm not going to leave you, honey." Quetglas turned around, his face awash with tears, and pleaded, "Oh, Mr. Boyd! Mr. Boyd! What am I gonna do? Mr. Boyd!" Quetglas's back was now to the *sam ku*. Crying, his face twisted with grief, he winked at Salvant.

Then Salvant realized that Frank Quetglas wasn't playing this one entirely for Wong Tsei-Ling. He was playing to Sing Sing Boyd. He was showing his stuff. This was his chance to show Boyd he was an actor, not a stunt man, and he was giving it everything he had. Salvant thought, Yes, go for it, Frank. Do it. Flash your style.

"I love her, Mr. Boyd. What am I going to do? *Dios! Dios! Ayudame!*" Quetglas pleaded to the movie man and to the gods. Susan Wu was his love of loves. Oh, the heartbreak.

Salvant thought Frank Quetglas was outdoing Susan Wu. This was more fun than the soaps. He glanced at Sing Sing Boyd. Boyd, too, understood what the audacious Quetglas was doing, and was impressed by the craft he saw.

With the instincts of a star, Susan moved to recover the scene: she began hiccuping in the middle of crying, a neat dramatic tic that caught everybody's attention. It wasn't that she begrudged Quetglas the attention, but rather, in the manner of jamming musicians, he had challenged her and she had accepted. Salvant thought of the dueling banjos scene in the movie *Deliverance*.

"I love you, Frank," she sobbed, and her small body began shaking, her nerves shattered by despair. "I can't live without you, Frank!"

"Mi amor! Mi amor!" Quetglas cried with as much broken heart as he could muster.

Wing-Ling said, "You'll find another man, Susan. If you thought this so-called groom was good enough for me, why don't you marry him yourself?" She gestured disdainfully at Salvant.

Salvant didn't like this kind of talk. "Hey, wait a minute," he said. He felt Morrison's toe nudge him on the back of the leg; Sing Sing Boyd had said to let the actors do the talking. They were experienced at improvising, he had said; it was part of their training.

Frank Quetglas swore in Spanish. He mopped his eyes with the sleeve of his tuxedo, and closed the sale. "Okay, look. What if I marry her sister? Right now, what if I marry her? Is it possible that I could buy my way out later on? I'm willing to pay her to divorce me. Name it. How much? A thousand American dollars? Two thousand?" Frank Quetglas was a desperate man, so desperate that he was willing to bribe a *sam ku*.

Wing-Ling considered the offer. "I want a marriage that is forever, but I understand that things can go wrong."

"Does that mean yes?"

"Not necessarily."

Susan Wu said, "As long as Wing-Ling thinks we might be in love, there's no way she'll let you go."

Quetglas said to Wing-Ling, "It's possible if I'm willing to pay enough, isn't it?"

Wong Tsei-ling/Wu Wing-Ling said nothing.

Marion Morrison's ploy had worked! Salvant felt jubilant.

Quetglas said, "I'll marry her, then. I'll marry her so Susan can have a break. We'll let the future take care of itself. If I really love her, I can be man enough to give her her freedom. We can wait, darling. It'll all work out. I swear it to you. I swear."

"Frank! Frank! Oh, Frank!"

Thus, with much weeping—what Quetglas later called "real Lee Strasberg stuff"—Frank Quetglas and Susan Wu began their remarkable scene of grievous parting.

It was a wedding Ella Nidech would never forget. First there was Lucien Salvant, the man who had come to be wed only to be scorned by a spirit. Salvant stood, shoulders stooped, a pariah. Then there was Susan Wu, weeping in the comforting arms of Sing Sing Boyd. James Burlane, whose idea this all was and who had written a loose script leading up to the offer of a bribe, watched the drama unfold with authorial pride. Then there was Nidech herself in the clingy dress she had worn to tantalize Burlane. Burlane couldn't take his eyes off her and she knew it.

Wing-Ling let Wong Tsei-Ling take over momentarily to give the wedding ceremony in Cantonese, giving instructions to both the groom and his spirit bride. This struck Nidech as the sort of transformation that would have appealed to Peter Sellers. Wong Tsei-Ling was the bride, then the marrying official, then the bride again. She did this with childlike aplomb, as though it were the most logical and rational act in the world.

Frank Quetglas, his eyes reddened from weeping, mumbled, "I will" at the places indicated by the *sam ku*. He thus agreed, with the countenance of a whipped dog, to uphold marital responsibilities of which he remained ignorant.

In Cantonese, Wong Tsei-Ling pronounced the couple man and wife. In English, the bride said, "I'd like my bouquet, please." She reached for the flowers.

Susan was now crying out of happiness at being free, although the *sam ku* did not know that. Boyd gave the *sam ku* the flowers, and they turned to watch the outwardly pathetic Susan Wu receive the bridal bouquet. According to tradition of round-eye weddings, whoever caught the bouquet would be the next to marry.

Ella Nidech was moved by the sweetness of the moment. It was so romantic. Susan Wu and Lucien Salvant had flown to freedom together on homemade para-sails and came out of the ordeal holding hands. Nidech had witnessed the first spark of romance, and so they were a special couple to her. Nidech got goosebumps first, then started crying, not caring whether Burlane saw or not. It was like being part of a sentimental movie, and Company representative or not, Nidech loved to cry at movies.

She was crying and watching Susan Wu, wanting to hug her after she caught the bridal bouquet. This is why Nidech wasn't paying any attention to Tsei-Ling/Wing-Ling.

The surprised Nidech saw it coming only at the last second . . .

The bridal bouquet!

Coming her way . . .

Roses!

She wanted them . . .

. . . no, she didn't.

She dived.

As did Burlane, laughing, pushing her from the flowers. The delicate man, looking horrified, got tangled up with the bouquet and juggled it for a heartbeat before the roses flopped harmlessly to the floor.

Nidech sat up on the floor, looking disconsolate. "If I'd been smart, I'd have caught them." The vice-president for research and development of the Bee-Vee Toy Corporation was momentarily overcome by dismay and regret.

Burlane said, "No, you did exactly the right thing."

Sing Sing Boyd helped Ella Nidech off the floor. He said, "Believe me, a woman with your skills is very rare, indeed, Ms. Lewis. There are plenty of women who will be pleased to do the other."

49

DENG Shaoqi didn't like the practice of government limousines bullying their way through the streets. His drivers had standing instructions always to arrive early so Deng could float through the streets as though they were canals and enjoy looking at the people. This ride was perhaps the best he had ever taken. Deng closed his eyes and contemplated his walk in the garden after *xui-xi*.

The limousine slowed before a tangle of bicycles. Deng thought about meeting his mother's brother, his Uncle Chen Li, in Shanghai—this amid the confusion of terrible choices, of dying and separation in the final days of the revolution. It was by then clear that Mao Zedong and the Red Army had overcome Generalissimo Chiang Kai-shek, and wealthy Chinese everywhere were fleeing the country with their capital.

Deng was then fifty years old and like his younger brother a follower of Mao, believing that the only hope for improving the life of the Chinese peasant was through discipline and a socialist economy. But Deng Shaoqi was also Chinese and an oldest son; the aging, childless Chen had always favored him. When Deng was called by Chen, he went, never mind that Chen had grown wealthy cooperating with British opium traders. Chen was Deng's uncle, and he wanted to talk to Deng even as soldiers were on their way to confiscate his fortune. The eldest son obeyed.

Now Deng was an old man, and he remembered, as old men do; in this case it was easy because his conversation with Chen Li had lasted only a few minutes and over the years he had thought about it so often that hardly any detail was lost:

Chen Li's eyes were rheumy. His hand trembled slightly as he sipped tea. "We don't have a lot of time, nephew," he said.

"No we don't, uncle."

"I'm not going to Taiwan."

"No?" Deng Shaoqi was surprised.

"I don't want to die on an island. This is my home."

"Yes, uncle."

"It will never work, what your Mao Zedong wants."

Deng said nothing.

"So many girls in my family!" Chen sighed. "It comes down to this, Shaoqi: you're the oldest surviving male in my father's family, so you're my heir." Chen bunched his lips until they turned white. "A communist! I hope they shoot me." He closed his eyes and opened them again. He sighed again and gave Deng Shaoqi an envelope. "This contains instructions for retrieving my fortune, which I have converted into gold bullion. As my heir, the gold is yours, nephew."

"Uncle, that gold belongs to the people now."

"It belongs to you and your heirs. You're still Chinese, Shaoqi. No matter what you might tell yourself, you're my nephew and an oldest son first, and a communist second." Chen poured himself some tea. "Obey it or suffer bad fung shui. Don't interrupt me; I don't have a lot of time. You'll smuggle this gold to Hong Kong; the communists aren't

strong enough to challenge the British just yet. Find some-
body there to serve as your proxy until this communist fool-
ishness passes; someday you'll be able to bring it back and
invest it in China."

   "I can't do this, uncle."

   "You're not to tell Xiaoping. The ability to understand
simple logic runs in Deng blood, but whether your brother
will ever take advantage of it remains to be seen."

   "I can't, uncle . . ."

   Chen ignored his nephew. "Find somebody with connec-
tions to the British so you can have your money moved to
Singapore if you have to."

   "Uncle—"

   Chen cut him off with a hard look. "I want you to manage
the money yourself, not someone else. You make the deci-
sions. You'll be glad you have it one day, believe me."

   "I—"

   "Your comrades will be coming soon. You keep this to
yourself. Go now. I mean it, now. Go. Get out of here."
Chen Li had stated his desire. He was finished.

Remembering that, Deng Shaoqi smiled. His Uncle Chen
Li would be proud. In 1950 Deng smuggled $10 million
worth of gold to Hong Kong and found himself a partner,
Sing Sing Boyd, a thirty-five-year-old Eurasian who was
eager to get into the movie business. Boyd agreed to serve as
surrogate owner of the dragon portfolio, as the two men
called it. Boyd's father was the Arabist scholar H.A.T.
Boyd, a fact that guaranteed that he would be able to move
the portfolio if the Maoist government attempted to seize the
British colony.

Deng Shaoqi, a self-effacing, minor communist official—he
was the chairman of the committee in charge of maintaining
the houses on his block—was by occupation the keeper of a
Beijing candy store. However, owing to the influence of his
little brother, he had a fine home not far from Deng Xiaoping's

own compound on Bright Mountain Street. While Deng Xiaoping rose in power within the party, Deng Shaoqi measured out candy for the parents of excited children.

Almost from the beginning, with Sing Sing Boyd's first awful productions, Deng and Boyd communicated through messages concealed in metal film canisters. Boyd's kung fu movies turned out to be very popular in China, and Deng—through unnamed Hong Kong sources—managed to obtain the latest films to share with his comrades. Being able to get kung fu movies was one of the perks of being Deng Xiaoping's older brother. This odd form of communication continued even through the worst of the Red Guard hysteria.

The way Deng Shaoqi managed the dragon portfolio was simple. Boyd hired the best accountants, stockbrokers, and lawyers he could find; he sent their research findings and advice to Deng via film canister. After considering the options, Deng issued his decisions by return canister. Boyd sent Deng Mandarin translations of *Forbes* magazine, *Fortune, Barron's,* and the Asian *Wall Street Journal,* plus Japanese and European financial magazines and newsletters so that Deng could keep abreast of the international financial world.

Coincident with Deng Shaoqi's recognition of his own startling skill as a financier—as measured by the growing size of the investment portfolio—came the realization that his younger brother was absolutely right: a pure Marxist economy was no economy at all. It simply did not work.

So it was that Deng Shaoqi had set out to aid his little brother through a subterfuge known only to himself and Boyd. He became an agent of one: a capitalist mole determined to overthrow the regime of Mao Zedong and restore private initiative to the Chinese economy. He did not regard himself as a capitalist; he did not identify with the Nationalist Chinese. Like his famous brother, he simply believed that what worked should come first, *before* ideology, not the other way around.

The remarkable ups and downs of Deng Xiaoping's politi

cal career—twice imprisoned, a third time purged, to rise yet again—were popularly attributed to his intelligence and commitment to economic reform, but in truth they were brought about by the long-rumored massive bribes from sources mysterious even to Deng. In fact the bribe money came from the dragon portfolio.

After Deng Xiaoping's final triumph in 1977, his older brother realized that in order to gain support for their ideas, he had to do something dramatic. He had to make capitalism personal for the comrades. He'd been having a good time being a closet financier; he wanted to show them how much fun the market was and give them a stake in its rewards. To that end, he began dealing Deng Xiaoping's trusted intimates in on investments "proposed by my Hong Kong acquaintance, Sing Sing Boyd," but which were, in fact, Deng Shaoqi's schemes.

"Boyd" suggested that the comrades invest their money in poppy fields. "Boyd" figured out how to protect their investment with a cooperative and get the Americans to pay for it.

"Boyd" advised them how to invest their money on the international stock markets. When "Boyd" sent word to the comrades that substantial sums of money could be earned by selling carefully selected Chinese secrets to the Americans, comrades began looking around for secrets whose disclosure would primarily injure the Russians, not themselves.

The returns on these investments were wonderful, and the joyous communist officials agreed to even further reforms in the economy. In time, Uncle Chen Li's prophecy came true; Deng Shaoqi was able to reinvest his fortune back in China as he saw profitable opportunities. In fact Beijing was urging foreign capital to invest in China.

Following his uncle's instructions to the letter, Deng insisted on planning each investment from his portfolio down to the last detail. Boyd was the faithful aide-de-camp, seeing to it that Deng's wishes were carried out—and taking credit for

Deng's financial genius. Still communicating by film canister, they had developed, Boyd said, "a Charlie McCarthy—Edgar Bergen relationship," a reference that puzzled Deng.

One thing that Boyd did do on his own was to attack Fong Wai Chau with Ella Nidech. Deng was horrified when he found out and said so in no uncertain terms. What if something had happened to Boyd? Like his brother, Deng was much given to practical solutions. The practical solution would have been to let Pak kill the actress and Salvant, then figure out a way to have the Chinese secret service discipline the Red Lotus. Boyd could have found a relative to inherit Salvant's fortune and they'd still have their *gweilo* spy. Deng secretly blamed the error on Boyd's sentimental round-eye blood.

Deng Shaoqi didn't get too angry. Everything had worked out and their secret was intact, which was what counted. As his little brother so frequently quoted, "Who cares whether the cat is white or black so long as it catches the mice?"

Deng Shaoqi's limousine slowed. Up ahead, a tall, handsome man unfolded from another automobile. This was the elegant movie producer, Sing Sing Boyd, arrived in secret from Hong Kong.

The two men, now old and trusted friends bound by a secret that had made them virtual brothers, had in fact met just once, almost forty years earlier in a New Territories farmhouse. Trying to drown the pain of conscience, Deng Shaoqi had smoked opium on the train from Shanghai to Canton en route to Hong Kong. The rich, guilty communist-cum-capitalist had smoked opium with young Boyd as they negotiated the terms under which Boyd became the surrogate owner of the dragon portfolio.

Boyd waited while Deng's driver helped the old man out. He bowed deeply and shook his employer's hand. "I'm very honored to meet you, Comrade Deng."

The master capitalist gripped Sing Sing Boyd's arm in

gratitude for all the younger man had done. Comrade Deng Shaoqi grinned. "It's been fun, hasn't it, Mr. Boyd?"

Boyd smiled. "Being able to make movies has to be one of the greatest pleasures any man ever had."

"I thought *Chan Rides Low* was very good. You know, I'm not too old to imagine myself playing hide-the-eggroll with Susan Wu."

"She's lovely, isn't she?"

"I liked that young round-eye actor. What's his name?" This was a gesture to his friend's British blood.

"Frank Quetglas."

"He has a fine spinning back-kick."

"You know, I think Mr. Quetglas may have some acting talent as well." Both men had vowed to go to the grave with their conspiracy kept secret; Boyd, gripped by the emotion of the moment, murmured, "Maybe one day we can fix it so you can try a spinning back-kick on T. Boone Pickens. We've got plenty of capital."

Deng beamed, acknowledging the compliment of the suggestion; he was pleased to be put in the league of the storied American corporate-takeover artist. "I think I might like that very much."

Loyalty to family had prevailed, which was the Chinese way. Without anybody being the wiser, Deng Shaoqi—faithful to the wishes of his departed Uncle Chen Li—had used his inheritance to literally purchase China from the Maoists who had come close to destroying the country. It had been a long and complicated buyout.

Sing Sing Boyd paused, uncertain as to whether it was proper for him to precede or follow Deng Shaoqi though the door.

To Deng there was no question as to protocol. He went first so that his shill, the honored guest, might come last and be properly congratulated. For the unprecedented takeover to go forward as planned, the dragon portfolio had to remain the secret of secrets.

Deng Shaoqi gave his charimatic younger brother a deep bow. Deng Xiaoping had been credited with being the savior of modern China. He was said to be leading China into the future. Well, into the present at least. He had become the latest of revered Chinese leaders that extended from the Ming emperors to Mao Zedong. Deng Xiaoping had been *Time* magazine's Man of the Year. He had even been interviewed on television by Barbara Walters, and had come across looking thoughtful and sincere, practical—a man the West could do business with. The candy man was pleased with the results of his investment portfolio.

Deng Shaoqi stepped aside to admit the Hong Kong movie man, Sing Sing Boyd.

50

SING Sing Boyd was led into a chamber that would have
dazzled Tutankhamen. The red, bejeweled roof was supported by the backs of two fabulous dragons—facing opposite directions in the manner of yin and yang. The ivory
doors at either end of the room were supported by twisting
dragon tails and scarlet dragon tongues. The scales of the
dragons resembled nothing so much as polished gold coins.
The dragons breathed rubies; their eyes blazed emeralds.

The waiting party officials, following the lead of Deng
Xiaoping, broke into enthusiastic, prolonged applause for
their financial mentor. The man from Hong Kong did his best
to hold back the round-eye emotion he had inherited from
Hatty Boyd.

Boyd was introduced to Deng Xiaoping himself while
Deng Shaoqi looked on, pleased that his Hong Kong friend
should be so honored. The comrades, having recently learned
certain customs from European and American businessmen,
were drinking cocktails and eating exotic tidbits with colored
toothpicks—each tipped with a tiny Chinese flag.

Hatty Boyd had taught his son that the American practice of pouring whiskey over chunks of ice or mixing it with dreadful soft drinks was barbarous. But judging from the assortment of odd-looking cocktails, the Americans had been in town to do a little business. Portable bars had been set up under the bellies of the golden dragons, and at these bars enthusiastic Chinese bartenders in Mao jackets ruined expensive whiskey and gin with colorful syrups and squirts from small, mysterious bottles.

The assembled comrades were served these concoctions by waitresses dressed in clinging, pajamalike outfits. A waitress with an admirable bosom asked Boyd if he would like ''a cocktail.''

The question was asked in Mandarin. Boyd blinked and ordered a proper scotch, that is, neat, in the Mandarin he had learned from his mother. Boyd was appalled at the idea of cocktails and displayed tits. When the Chinese market was opened completely, would American cocktails and boorish manners take over? And those ghastly hard A's! The American President sounded like he was from bloody Liverpool.

Under the loin of each dragon there were tables heaped with exotic hors d'oeuvres—miniature egg rolls, escargots reeking of garlic, Greek olives, wisps of fried squid—from which poked the beflagged toothpicks.

Comrade Deng Xiaoping led Boyd on a round of introductions to the assembled party officials. Boyd, struggling to remember names, wondered if the chaps might not be hitting the booze a little hard. Boyd noticed that drinks with rum and fruit juice were especially popular; the bartenders made impressive if not downright uncivilized Bangkok Bangers and Singapore Slings—151 proof rum, easy on the juice.

Boyd had wondered if the opportunity to meet him personally might not have been the principal if unspoken reason for this extraordinary occasion. Now he knew. Of course it was!

Deng Shaoqi was an old man and in frail health; the comrades would never have discussed it out loud, he knew, but whatever their rationalization, the real reason for the honor was that they worried they would lose contact with Boyd when Deng Shaoqi died. They wanted to be remembered and included in future investment opportunities. This was their one chance to meet Boyd personally—all at once, so no one comrade could command an advantage.

There were twenty-seven party officials in all. Each official repeated his name two or three times so that Sing Sing Boyd could not possibly forget it. Each one slipped a business card into Boyd's hand just to make sure. One comrade, containing too many American cocktails to allow for modesty, repeated his name five times, holding eye contact to make sure Boyd remembered.

To show everybody that he understood the necessity of maintaining communication, Boyd repeated each name and title at least once. He made a point of studying each business card before he slipped it into his wallet. Each man—and woman, actually, there were two women—impressed upon Boyd how grateful he or she was to be working with such an intelligent, farsighted businessman as Boyd. Each comrade was willing to accept risk, no problem. Without risk there was no progress, Boyd was told. Risk was what made the world go round; that was understood.

It was Boyd's task to maintain a convincing and reassuring level of interest through the introduction of twenty-seven communist officials who were behaving as though they were auditioning for one of his movies. He approached his task with the same bemused but courteous persona he used to direct a crude fuck scene or episode of stupid violence. If he was disgusted or repelled, if his attention wavered or his mind drifted, he gave no evidence of it.

Deng Shaoqi did not appear offended that such urgent preparations were being made in expectation of his demise.

On the contrary, he listened to the introductions and repetition of names with a grand smile. Childless himself, he had willed his fortune to Sing Sing Boyd, who, quite properly, was at last getting to meet the cooperating flock in Beijing. The candy man waved for a second, then a third Bangkok Banger. He drank with gusto.

Deng Xiaoping said, "I'm pleased that you're getting a chance to meet everybody, Mr. Boyd." He eyed his older brother. "I see that my brother is having a good time. He's always taken great joy in other people's accomplishments, an admirable trait, don't you think, Mr. Boyd? By the way, we're going to have a private screening of *Chan Rides Low* after the ceremony. This is by popular request."

"Really? That would be wonderful! I'm very flattered." Boyd was amazed at the enthusiasm the comrades were showing for the amenities of the developed world.

"Some of us were wondering how you filmed those splendid fighting sequences, Mr. Boyd. Mmmm, and your lovely Susan Wu. Tell me, do you spend a lot of time around actresses? I bet you do. By the way, we're to have Coca-Cola and popcorn for the movie." Deng's aide touched him on the shoulder and murmured in his ear. Deng Xiaoping said, "I'm told it's time now, Mr. Boyd."

The older Deng had admired Susan Wu as well. Boyd caught Deng Shaoqi's eye. "Ahh, a Bangkok Banger," he said. "Is it good?" he asked, not meaning the drink.

Deng understood. "It's wonderful. Congratulations again, Sing Sing." Deng and Boyd shook the handshake of partners.

Boyd turned and took a deep breath to calm his nerves. He thought of Hatty Boyd and his mother, of Stanley Ho, and Flora Lewis, and Frank Quetglas, and the strange American, Marion Morrison. He remembered the satisfaction of eliminating Pak Tze Fan with the Uzi bucking hard against his shoulder. He hoped passionately, fervently, that everything would work out for the Chinese, and that one billion people might some day have a more comfortable life.

Sing Sing Boyd was to be the first recipient of the Order of Deng, for extraordinary and meritorious contributions to the people's socialist enterprise.

A Note on the Candy Man

To the author's knowledge, Comrade Deng Xiaoping does not have an older brother named Deng Shaoqi.